HOUSE OF GLASS

a novel

Pramoedya Ananta Toer

Translated and with an
Introduction by Max Lane

PENGUIN BOOKS

PENGUIN BOOKS

Published by the Penguin Group

Penguin Group (USA) Inc., 375 Hudson Street, New York, New York 10014, U.S.A.

Penguin Group (Canada), 10 Alcorn Avenue, Toronto,

Ontario, Canada M4V 3B2 (a division of Pearson Penguin Canada Inc.)

Penguin Books Ltd, 80 Strand, London WC2R 0RL, England

Penguin Ireland, 25 St Stephen's Green, Dublin 2, Ireland (a division of Penguin Books Ltd)

Penguin Group (Australia), 250 Camberwell Road, Camberwell,

Victoria 3124, Australia (a division of Pearson Australia Group Pty Ltd)

Penguin Books India Pvt Ltd, 11 Community Centre,

Panchsheel Park, New Delhi – 110 017, India

Penguin Group (NZ), cnr Airborne and Rosedale Roads,

Albany, Auckland, New Zealand (a division of Pearson New Zealand Ltd)

Penguin Books (South Africa) (Pty) Ltd, 24 Sturdee Avenue,

Rosebank, Johannesburg 2196, South Africa

Penguin Books Ltd, Registered Offices: 80 Strand, London WC2R 0RL, England

First published in Australia by Penguin Books Australia Ltd 1992
First published in the United States of America by
William Morrow and Company, Inc. 1996
Reprinted by arrangement with William Morrow and Company, Inc.
Published in Penguin Books (U.S.A.) 1997

11 13 15 17 19 20 18 16 14 12

Originally published in Indonesian by Hasta Mitra Publishing House, Jakarta, 1988.

THE LIBRARY OF CONGRESS HAS CATALOGUED THE MORROW EDITION AS FOLLOWS:
Toer, Pramoedya Ananta, 1925–
[Rumah kaca. English]
House of glass: a novel/Pramoedya Ananta Toer: translated and introduced by
Max Lane.—1st ed.
p. cm.
Originally published: Australia: Penguin, 1992.
ISBN 0-688-14594-9 (hc.)
ISBN 0 14 02.5679 2 (pbk.)
I. Title.
PL5089.T8R8613 1996
899'.22132—dc20 95–46294

Printed in the United States of America
Set in Bembo

Deposuit Potentes de Sede et Exaltavit Humiles.

(He has brought down the mighty from their thrones
and raised up the lowly.)

TRANSLATOR'S NOTE

This is a novel set in a time prior to the establishment of an official national language and when the choice of language was intimately tied up with social status and power. I have thus tried to preserve as much as possible of the different usages, including honorifics, of the original. These are usually Malay, Javanese, and Dutch terms. These are italicized the first time they appear. If explanations or translations are required, they can be found in the Glossary at the back of this book. The Glossary also includes some English terms and acronyms that may not be familiar to the English-speaking reader.

This is the fourth translator's note I have written for this series. During the course of translating and revising and refining the translations, a process which I am sure will continue into the future, a large number of people have helped. I must take the opportunity of this final translator's note to thank all of them, especially Kerry and Caroline Groves, the late R.F.X. Brissenden, Blanche d'Alpuget, Jackie Yowell, and Elizabeth Flann. A special mention must be made of the late Dr. Geoff Blunden, who put considerable effort into editing the manuscript of *This Earth of Mankind*.

I must also express deep gratitude to Pramoedya Ananta Toer, Hasyim Rahman, and Yusuf Isak, who together provided permission, support, and most important of all, inspiration to finish this project. Indeed, I thank all my friends in Indonesia for the inspiration that they have given.

Finally I thank Anna Nurfia and Melanie Purwitasari, who have been tolerant of my absences, both physical and mental, while I have been working on this project.

INTRODUCTION

*H*ouse of Glass is the fourth volume of Pramoedya Ananta Toer's novels inspired by the life of one of the pioneers of the Indonesian national awakening and of Indonesian journalism, Tirto Adi Suryo. These novels, along with other manuscripts, were written in the last period of his fourteen years of imprisonment under barbaric conditions on the prison island of Buru in Eastern Indonesia. Pramoedya, along with thousands of others, was imprisoned in Jakarta jails and the Buru Island concentration camps without ever being tried and sentenced. Many, including Pramoedya, were beaten or suffered torture. Many died during their imprisonment.

Pramoedya obtained writing materials and the opportunity to write only in the last few years of his time at Buru. Prior to this he had narrated to his fellow prisoners the story of Minke, Annelies, Nyai Ontosoroh, Robert Suurhof, and the other characters of *This Earth of Mankind, Child of All Nations, Footsteps,* and *House of Glass.* He had to rely on his memory of the historical research he had undertaken in the early 1960s to be able to capture the detail and color of the Netherlands Indies of the early twentieth century.

House of Glass is not only the final volume of the tetralogy. It is also the finale. The story begins with the event that ended the third volume—

the arrest of Minke. His newspaper has been banned after his young
assistants published a biting editorial attacking the governor-general of
the Netherlands Indies. The policeman, Pangemanann, takes Minke
away while Princess Kasiruta, Minke's wife, is visiting her father in a
village nearby.

Those who have followed the saga of Minke might have been afraid
that the story would now be at an end. For Pramoedya, however, Minke's absence provides the opportunity to reveal who has been the real
protagonist of these four novels. It is true that we, as readers, have been
taught a great deal through observing the actions and following the
thoughts of Minke. We have watched him develop from a naive and
somewhat self-centered teenager to a mature and experienced man of
politics, yet still complex and subject to human foibles. A man of vision,
he saw, before any other, the nature of Indonesia's future as an amalgam
of peoples united behind revolutionary political goals—before the word
"Indonesia" had even been invented.

Minke was at the center of the maelstrom created by the unleashing
of a whole range of social forces as the awakening of the Indonesian
consciousness met a seemingly irresistible force—colonialism. And this
awakening was not the product of some mystical or metaphysical process.
It was brought about by changes in the material world: Java being turned
into a sugar plantation crisscrossed by railways; rivalry and war between
colonial powers; the spread of the printing press and formal schooling;
the upheavals caused by other Asian peoples' struggles for liberation; the
telegraph, the automobile, the steamship, the camera. The impact of all
these changes on the consciousness of the natives of the Indonesian archipelago found its most concentrated form in the new personalities it
created. And in Minke's development, Pramoedya has been able to ex-
emplify the path of these changes. Minke did not simply mature from a
teenager to an adult. His development exemplified the formation of a
kind of personality that had never before existed in Javanese or Sumatran
or Timorese or Celebes society. He represented a new form of social
being.

It could be said that he was a new kind of personality for the Indies
only, of a kind that was not new in Europe. He was a pioneer of the
Indonesian bourgeoisie. "Liberty, fraternity, equality," the slogan of the
greatest bourgeois revolution, was the slogan that inspired him. He was
a businessman, an entrepreneur, a publisher who struggled to bring the
best of bourgeois values to his society. But as with other Asian revolu-
tionaries of the period, his confrontation with colonialism also placed
him on the side of the impoverished and oppressed masses of ordinary

people. The bourgeois dedicated to the people is a rare but persisting phenomenon in Asian society, even today.

The impact of these changes, and their contradictions, are focused and concentrated in the character of Minke. Other characters, such as the concubine and successful businesswoman Nyai Ontosoroh, the Dutch journalist Ter Haar, the Chinese revolutionary Ang San Mei, the peasant rebels of Java and Minke's radical helpers, such as Mas Marko, only partially reflect the impact of those developments. Minke is the cutting edge.

Yet *House of Glass* shows that he is not the real protagonist. And the way in which Pramoedya reveals who the real protagonist is also reveals for all to see his great abilities both as a historian and as a novelist.

The reader who has already glanced at the first few pages of this novel, or who may now be tempted to do so, will perhaps think that the protagonist I am talking about is the policeman Pangemanann who, in Minke's absence, takes over the task of narration. It is his notes that make up *House of Glass*. It is his consciousness that we now dip into, that is revealed to us as it reels under the consequences of the tasks he has been set.

But I do not mean Pangemanann. Pangemanann is merely a guide to help us understand the nature of the real protagonist. And he is the best of guides. Dedicated to the destruction of this protagonist, and a serious and intelligent man, he lives up fully to that well-known motto— know thine enemy!

And who or what is Pangemanann's enemy? It would be arrogant for me to try to set out here in a few pages what is so wonderfully told over the next few hundred. Moreover, it would take away from the reader too much of the surprise and challenge that lie ahead.

However, I have made one assertion that I should explain, that *House of Glass*, perhaps more than any of the volumes, and certainly as the seal on the tetralogy as a whole, makes very clear what is the essence of the greatness of these four novels. Somewhat like a Hindu god, the protagonist of these novels appears in several forms. Perhaps the highest form—which many readers will already have discerned from the earlier novels—is history, the inexorable march of history itself. This is what Pangemanann has set himself against.

To explain the reasons, the dynamics, the causes, the forces at work in pushing history forward without dehumanizing or depersonalizing it is Pramoedya's great achievement. These are not novels set against the background of historical events, in which the uninformed can become informed about those events while enjoying a good story, as is the case

with many historical novels. History is not the background to these stories, it is the protagonist. The most powerful historical energies are reflected in the character of Minke, in one form or another. He is history's
child at a turning point in his society's history. Pramoedya has shown us
how a revolutionary is born.

But Pramoedya also knows that history does not have only one
child, that we are all the products of the world we live in as it is transformed, being made and remade by us all. In *House of Glass*, Minke leaves
us for a while, but history does not stop despite all of colonialism's best
efforts. So now we meet many more of history's children, men and
women, all borne upon the same newly unleashed energies, but all trying
to bend those energies in a direction of their own.

Commentators have talked about the epic quality of Pramoedya's
works, how they are like sagas with their kaleidoscope of characters and
sweeping panoramas. Some have compared him to the great nineteenth-
century social realists, perhaps Dickens, perhaps Dostoyevsky. I think
there is truth in this, but also something else. Pramoedya is a novelist
writing historical realist novels with the advantage of the twentieth century's scientific approach to the study of history. He is fully aware of
how human consciousness invents and reinvents its own histories—
something wonderfully evoked by Pangemanann's curiosity about Minke's novels, *This Earth of Mankind, Child of All Nations,* and *Footsteps.* As
a fighter in the revolutionary movement for liberation against the Dutch
and for the completion of the revolution after Independence, he has been
an active participant in the twentieth century's most important new social
phenomenon—the conscious attempt by the masses of humankind to
mold their own future; the shape of their future society. I think it is not
an exaggeration to claim that the combination of Pramoedya's great sto-
rytelling abilities, that so inspired and encouraged his fellow prisoners
during the many years in Buru Island prison camp, and his insight into
the dynamics of history makes him a revolutionary in literary terms. More
than a great writer of historical fiction, he is a great writer of history in
fiction.

But this is not the time or place for me to attempt what Pangemanann was fated to attempt as regards the novels of Minke. There are
many full literary critiques waiting to be written where the revolutionary
character of Pramoedya's work, including all its contradictions, will be
discussed.

In the meantime, I wish you, the reader, all the best as you set out
on the final chapter of this particular journey. I would ask you also to
remember the plight of Pramoedya himself—under town arrest, unable

to publish either books or articles, his rights as a citizen denied. All his books remain banned in Indonesia. The same applies to his publishers, Yusuf Isak and Hasyim Rahman, also victims of long-term imprisonment without trial, also banned from publishing or writing.

And what of the younger generation of men and women who want to read and be inspired by works such as these? Bambang Subono, Bambang Isti Nugroho, and Bonar Tigor Naipospos were only recently released after serving more than six years each of sentences in prison of up to eight years for possessing and circulating Pramoedya's novels—these novels you have been reading.

—MAX LANE

HOUSE OF GLASS

1

1912. This was the year that brought the greatest burdens for Governor-General Idenburg. His predecessor, van Heutsz, had in fact prepared the way for Idenburg. He had succeeded in breaking the back of all armed resistance against the Dutch in the Indies. Then came his replacement, descending on the Indies like a prince from the heavens, relaxed and as if without a care in the world. He had a big heart and his brain was full of a million plans for humanitarian improvement. Then, after just three years in Batavia, just when he should be showing the angelic face of the Netherlands to all, the times changed and carried him in a direction of their own. The epoch of van Heutsz, of the triumphant cheers of victory, of the tormented wailing of defeat, disappeared like a thief scuttling off to find his own grave.

Now His Excellency the governor-general was anxious. Humanitarianism—that ethical duty to which he was sworn—was now confronted by the needs of the times. The times were choosing their own direction, buffeting his humanitarian face like a stalking whirlwind. It was hard, hard for Idenburg, and, of course, hard too for me who received new and special tasks.

During 1911, the previous year, we began to feel in the Indies the lapping at our shores of waves brought forth by the storm that was raging to our north. The Ching Dynasty in China was overthrown. A child of the masses, a doctor as it happened, ascended the stage to become president and leader of the heavenly kingdom of China—Sun Yat-sen. The eyes of the world were on this first president of China as all the world waited to see what he would do. It was six years ago now that he had shaken the world, his first blows echoing around the globe. He succeeded in something that nobody believed could be done—he brought under control the international terror network known as the Tong societies. This was a network of terror gangs that operated in almost every port town in the world, including the Indies—and especially in Surabaya.

It was said that the Tong gangs were originally exiles who fled China when the great peasant rebellion that spread from south China right through to the north was finally crushed by the emperor's armies. The Taiping rebellion failed. Its organization was broken up and its leaders fled to all parts of the world, building a network of terror outside the country of their ancestors, and holding tight in their grip the lives of the overseas Chinese.

Sun Yat-sen met and conferred with their leaders. He was successful. They accepted his leadership and promised to help in the struggle to make certain the victory of Chinese nationalism.

But it was not only this that was disturbing the sleep of His Excellency. No, not only this! As a way to add to their funds, the Tong were smuggling Burmese opium. The Opium Selling Service and the Police Patrols were always meeting trouble. The Service was selling opium to addicts at a lower price, but it was a lower-quality drug, and there was no credit allowed, as there was in Hong Kong. *Ei, ei*—where else would Burmese opium and nationalism become intertwined if not in the Indies! It could only happen in the Indies. By junk and every other type of boat, the opium emerged from the South China Sea to find its way along the rivers of the great islands of the Indies, and the smaller islands, too, like Bangka and Belitung. In West Borneo the intertwined virus of northern nationalism and Burmese opium had also wormed its way into the society of the Dayal people. And in Java they found a new method of smuggling—along all the rivers, big and small, up the edge of the *Vorstenlanden*, the officially recognized princedoms in Central Java; then they traveled by land. They were distributing opium to all the small towns of Java. Idenburg did not know what to do.

The success of the Chinese revolution and the unity of the Chinese people under Sun Yat-sen also shook the Indies. It was as if a fresh wind had blown out the fire of terror and division that had previously disturbed the Chinese community. Chinese nationalism in the Indies grew stronger and stronger and climaxed when the Republic was declared in 1911.

In *Betawi*, the Indies-born Chinese, the educated youth, full of nationalist fervor, published the paper *Sin Po*. Governor-General Idenburg could do nothing to dam up this torrent of Asian nationalism. He had no authority to ban the paper, not even by using his Extraordinary Powers. Issues relating to China and its citizens were the affair of the Ministry for Foreign Affairs in s'Gravenhage, in Holland. The Indies was just a colony.

Idenburg was able to take only a small initiative, an attempt to dam the torrent—but it was a long-term plan. He established the HCS, the *Hollandsch Chineesche Schul*, a Dutch-language school for Chinese children at the same level as the ELS Dutch-language primary schools for Europeans. He hoped that these schools would eventually create a core of people in the Chinese community who would look to Europe instead of China. It was true, however, that he could pass on most of these problems to the Dutch Cabinet. But there was one area that was his responsibility alone and that he could not avoid dealing with. This was the effect of the Chinese revolution on the educated Natives of the Indies!

There was one educated Native man, who was not just being influenced by the Chinese Revolution but was its great admirer. He was a *raden mas*, a former student of the STOVIA medical school for Natives. He had established an organization using non-European methods and seemed to want to follow the example of the Nationalist Chinese. He was very much interested in using that weapon of the weak against the strong—the boycott. He dreamed of uniting the Native peoples of the Indies, both in the Indies and overseas in other parts of Asia and in Africa, just as Sun Yat-sen had done for the Chinese. He dreamed of an Indies nationalism that the peoples of the Indies themselves would understand. It was possible to gather all this from reading the editorials in his paper *Medan*, even though he rarely mentioned China or the Chinese.

With the formation of the *Sarekat Dagang Islam (SDI)*, and with his teachings about the boycott, he had planted time bombs in almost every town in Java. And Idenburg had begun to imagine the day when those time bombs would explode and set Java aflame, if nothing was done to stop him.

This heavy task was entrusted to me and thrust upon my back—me, Jacques Pangemanann.

The official view was that the government was caught between the rising up of the Native and Chinese bourgeoisie, both becoming a force sharper than the point of a spear, or an arrow or a bullet. It was the governor-general's desire to channel both these movements, from outside and within, along the gentlest possible path. Eliminate them altogether? Impossible. Nationalism was but a natural product of the modern era itself. There was a special officer appointed to deal with the Chinese nationalists. It was my task to handle the Natives.

My work was of a special kind, not known to the general public. Among the forty-eight million people of the Indies, it was not even certain that there were ten and a half that knew of my work. So it was indeed an interesting experience. And worth recording. Who knows but that one day such notes may be of use?

I will set down first of all some notes about what was happening in education. After all, it is education that causes one's eyes to see, causes one to hear, and to evaluate the things that are occurring far away, outside your own country, so that you reflect upon your own situation, and discover how far it is you have advanced and just where you are situated in the state of things.

The ELS schools had become the object of anger among the second layer of rulers, the Native officials I mean, because they were not allowed the opportunity to send their children to these European institutions. I myself could understand their anger. For their children there were only the special schools for the *Inlanders*, the Natives.

In each regency, under the control of a Dutch assistant resident, assisted by a Native *bupati*, the government established only one public primary school, which had two curricula—Grade 1 and Grade 2. In Grade 1 students received a little instruction in Dutch. In Grade 2 there was no Dutch instruction at all. The buildings had wooden frames and the walls were made from bamboo. In a few places, the walls would be covered with plaster, so that from afar they looked like stone walls. In the villages there were also village schools that taught a three-year course. They taught a little reading in the local language and some basic numeracy. It was only students from the Grade 1 courses who would know a little Dutch, who would learn a little of the outside world. The others would be more or less blind to that outside world.

But the children who graduated from the ELS, the European children and the children of the Natives at the pinnacle of Native society, could, with their Dutch, immediately come to terms with Europe and all things related to Europe. As a graduate of ELS myself, I had understood ever since primary school just how great was the gap between us and the students in the Grade 1 and Grade 2 public schools, let alone those in the village schools. It felt as if it would always be impossible to cross that gap.

One school divided into two streams, in each regency. And to serve how many thousand children? At least ten thousand. Yet, according to government regulations, wherever there were forty European children the government was obliged to establish an ELS school. The building must meet health regulations for European children, and the children must wear European clothes and shoes and speak in Dutch. This last was particularly emphasized because there were quite a few European children in the Indies, including some of Dutch descent, who did not speak Dutch. The fees were ten times what it cost to send a child to a Native primary school. So, of course, there were many middle and lower ranking Native officials who grumbled about this—but only grumbled. They did not even dare to put their grumblings down on paper as an official complaint. And the Indies bureaucracy took no heed of grumblings. Indeed, even official letters of complaint often did not arrive at their destination. They would be thrown into the wastepaper basket by officials who felt they had been bypassed.

ELS students who did not get official jobs could become a source of trouble for the government. They knew some geography, which was not taught at the schools for Natives. They knew about the world and the world's peoples, and about what products the different nations of the world produced. They knew what was the same and what was different between the peoples. They were a product of Europe. They rose far above their fellow countrymen, and could, of course, become the eyes of their people. And if their mouths could speak well, they could become the voices for their people, and at the very least, spokespeople for themselves.

The HCS schools were established in an attempt to divide the Chinese. They had earlier been divided by the Tong. Now they were to be divided by the new orientation to Europe, and by loyalty to the Netherlands Indies. But something different happened. The new generation of educated Natives did not just grumble to themselves like the generation before them. They announced their dissatisfactions in newspapers and magazines, in whatever languages they were capable of using. Their concerns became public, and became public knowledge too, and were no longer just their own private problems. The newspapers and magazines had given birth to a democratic spirit, in spite of the government's wishes. Of course, the government could just remain quiet about it all and pretend it didn't know what was happening, but in reality the government in its silence felt that all that was being written and discussed in these newspapers and magazines was also endangering its authority. The face of the Indies was changing as more and more printshops were established and with all these Natives who could read and write. And in all this, there was one person whose share was not at all small—in fact, he had the leading share in it all. Yes, him! That's the one. Minke!

A graduate of the ELS, but no government job? That's him! A Native who was the eyes and mouth of his people? Him again! So it wasn't too surprising to find that the special case that had been given to me to handle was the case of Minke himself. Like his teacher to the north, Sun Yat-sen, he too was a medical student, except that he did not graduate. A graduate or not, in the eyes of the government he was somebody who had all sorts of potential—potential to give rise to big problems in the future. But the situation that he faced, perhaps without realizing it, was pushing him in more and more dangerous directions.

When I was given this task, I was struck dumb. I had been hoping that someone else would be given the job. But my boss, Chief Commissioner Donald Nicolson, an Englishman, said to me: "We are giving you this task based on your own report, Mr. Pangemanann. No one else understands the ins and outs of this case like you do. This is not a criminal matter, not a case of arresting some burglar. This is a special problem, and it has been you yourself who has pointed the way forward in handling it."

A special problem, he said—a problem that had taken me out of the work I loved so much, police work, and transferred me to this other arena, where it was your brains they squeezed instead of your muscles. For the last five years, my work had consisted of reading the newspapers and magazines of the Indies, interviewing people, studying documents, and preparing various reports. And now I was reaping the harvest—this new task before me. This time I let it show very clearly how unhappy I was.

"But you have advanced very quickly in these last few years. You are the only one who can handle it, Mr. Pangemanann. Only a sensitive hand can deal with a sensitive problem."

These events all took place last year in the Betawi Police Headquarters, at the beginning of 1911. They shook my soul. What was it that I was supposed to do to him? He was not a criminal, nor was he a rebel. He was just an educated Native who very much loved his people and his country, the Indies, who was trying to advance his people, who was trying to see justice done for his people on this earth of the Indies, for all peoples on this earth of mankind. What he was doing was totally right and I not only agreed with what he was doing but was one among many of his sincere and genuine admirers.

There had never been any report of his involvement in criminal activity. I don't know about anything that the police never found out about. And where was there any person who had not carried out some bad deed at some time or another? Big or small? Known only to themselves? Nobody knew this better than the police—there was no such thing as a totally innocent person on this earth. Everyone had done something wrong, made some mistake, done some evil. Including the police themselves. People were arrested by the police because their evil could be proved, because there were witnesses. Where there was no proof and no witnesses, then their deeds would remain their secret, perhaps until death.

He was basically a good man, not evil. Clearly he was no criminal. That he had a weakness for pretty women need not be discussed here. In any case, that is a basic characteristic of real manhood. I don't need to discuss here the hypocrisy of the *priyayi*, those members of the Javanese aristocracy who became minor officials working for the Dutch, and of others who go about parading their piety. Anyway, I had often watched this man. He didn't know me and, for the time being, did not need to know me.

He always wore Javanese clothes—a *destar* on his head, a white vest-shirt, with a gold watch-chain hanging from his top pocket, widely pleated batik sarong and leather slippers. When he walked he did not swing both arms. As far as I knew, his right hand always held the bottom corner of his sarong. He had smooth creamy skin like the *langsat* fruit and a well-kept mustache, very thick and black and twirled up sharply at each end.

This man walked along confidently, with the authority of somebody with a strong and solid body. Perhaps he had once played some heavy sport. He was about 1.65 meters tall, not much less than that at all. He gave the appearance of someone who would have his own opinions about things. But his writings were not like that. They read as if written by a person who was restless, uncertain, always groping about, and somewhat confused, drowning in a sea of hodgepodge European ideas, all of which he learned in fragments. For a Native, he could be considered handsome, manly, and attractive, especially to women.

Neither his hands nor his mouth were frugal in their use of words, so that even the Natives, who liked to sit and chat, avoided him. And according to my assessment, his general knowledge was quite limited, if measured by European criteria. But in the life of the Natives, it could be said that he was the ignition point for the developments to come. Never in the last hundred years had there been a Native who, as a result of his personality, his good intentions, and his knowledge and understanding, had been able to unite thousands of Natives without reference to a *raja*, prophet, saint, *wayang* hero or a devil.

He had thousands of followers from among the Moslems, and especially from among the Moslems of the independent classes. He himself was from the priyayi, so it was easy to guess how deep was his Islam. For him Islam was what was available to unify the Indies. And he used it cleverly. And with as many followers as that he had the right to consider himself as the possible third Asian president, after Aguinaldo in the Philippines and Sun Yat-sen in China. Perhaps my guess was not too far wrong. He was very confident of his own strength. He was the kind of person who knew he was striding off toward greatness. He truly believed in the picture he had of himself. People would forgive, forget, and close their eyes to his weaknesses. He strode firmly and without hesitation in the direction of greatness.

He never quoted from the verses of the Quran. He was actually a liberal, someone who had thrown off the vestiges of feudalism but retained his title only for the purposes of helping him in his work. He was more successful as a trader in words than in money. He found it easier to mix with Europeans than with his own followers. He had been able to lead them without interfering in their religious affairs.

I personally truly honored this outstanding man. He had achieved far, far, far more than I had been able to in my much longer life. Silently I honored him.

As a servant of the state, and on instructions from my superiors, I had written a paper analyzing, assessing, and putting forward what the different outcomes might be of all his attacks on the government. Now they had given me the task of carrying out my own suggestions and recommendations. This meant that I would now have to spy on and take actions against this man whom I respected and honored so much. I would be spying on him and moving against him from very close up. My admiration and respect for him would be from afar.

To refuse an order would be considered an act of rebellion. Even if I carried out my task only halfheartedly I would still feel that I had violated my own feelings towards him.

Yes, I now found myself in a difficult situation. *Zihhh—zihhh!*

Perhaps I was getting weaker as I grew older, or perhaps because in these last ten years I had grown used to violating my own conscience, perhaps, perhaps—no, I could say for certain—the truth was that when it came to sticking with my own opinions I was losing my backbone, my principles, like a crawling worm, just like the criminals I used to arrest ten years ago.

Don't think I carried out these duties happily. But of course I carried them out in accordance with the recommendations in my report.

First, the activities of Minke were not illegal. There were no laws that could be used to stop his activities, neither colonial laws nor any laws from Holland. But every activity that tended to lead toward the accumulation of power was a danger to the government. At the very least, the coming into being of powerful political groups would diminish the government's authority. Such groups would try to pressure the government to do what they wanted, which would ultimately lead to their opposing the government. Every concentration of power would lead to some form of disturbance for the government. And it would be only when the government began to feel that its authority was being defied that it would be able to act against such groups.

But the Indies was not Europe, just an occupied colony. There was no House of Representatives here that could contain the power groups that existed. The government based its power here on the strength of its armed forces and the loyalty of the Native officials who served it. Its foundations were not as strong as those of the European democracies. Every wound against authority encouraged further moves toward the growth of power groups. And all of this had an effect on the natives of other colonies.

Second, the activities of this raden mas were to be expected of any Native in whatever colony, especially where they had begun to be exposed to European knowledge. His actions were in fact simply the logical and proper result of his new knowledge and understanding. He was the bearer of reform and change in the life of the Natives, a reflection of the spirit of European knowledge and understanding. The fruit of European education and learning in all the colonies would always be the same—trouble for the governments concerned.

As the colonized people grew in understanding, so too must the governments of such colonies because the process of advancement could not be stopped. Whenever a colonial government tried to stop this development, all that would happen is that the people would find their own way around this obstacle, with or without the government. It was foolish and stupid not to pay heed to the laws of progress, even though the government might not be sufficiently equipped to do so.

But I don't think I need explain all this here in these notes. The thing was that something startling had happened, something I now had to confront. Minke and his SDI had moved more quickly and grown much bigger than anyone had predicted. The concentration of power in his movement now hung like the sword of Damocles. Such a situation could not be handled effectively within the law.

"Not be handled effectively within the law," I had written. And so it was that I found myself speaking with an *Indo* in a Chinese restaurant. The meeting had been arranged by the commissioner. He introduced me to the Eurasian.

"Suurhof," the Eurasian introduced himself in a rather arrogant voice.

I immediately understood what the commissioner wanted me to do. It seemed that my report had been read by members of the *Algemeene Landbouw Syndicaat*, the association of plantation owners. If not, I don't think I would have ever found myself face-to-face with this Suurhof, head of the private henchmen of the association. So I had fallen as low as this?

"You will be able to work well together with Mr. Suurhof," said the commissioner, as he left the restaurant. This person was being made available to me—this scum—so that I could deal with my target outside the law. Who among the Betawi police did not know of Suurhof? A paid henchman whose task was to terrorize lower-level local officials and powerless village people, and who sold false evidence whenever needed—all in defense of the interest of the European business houses. A recidivist who spent his time going in and out of jail. And now I had to work with him! This was how low I had fallen! Must I accept all this? All with the approval of the authorities up there in heaven? But why was it I who had to carry this out? It was an insult to the intellectual work I had done.

"What is it that I must hear from you?" asked Suurhof, still in an arrogant tone of voice.

"I don't know what the commissioner has told you."

"He didn't tell me anything, *Meneer* Pangemanann. I am here to get my orders." He looked piercingly at me in an attempt to assert his authority over me, another Eurasian.

My blood boiled that a rotten bandit like this dared speak so rudely to an official, trying to pressure me to give him his orders. It truly offended my priyayiness.

The restaurant was at its busiest. I was wearing civilian clothes. He was dressed in a plantation worker's uniform. He wore a hat the same color as his uniform—khaki. I wore white with a woven bamboo hat. Neither of us took off our hats.

He kept tapping his glass on the table top as if he was trying to force me to speak. The tapping grated on my nerves.

"It seems *Tuan* is not ready yet."

"Not ready for what? I don't know what you mean."

"Have I been summoned here for nothing?"

"What kind of work are you hoping for?" I asked.

He laughed bitingly. Perhaps people saw my face go the dark red of fury. His left tooth shone like a pearl. The furrows in his face, which had been sunburned once too often, had become rigid lines. Suddenly he stopped his grinning and nodded twice.

It seemed it was indeed his custom to try to startle people and surprise them with sudden changes of mood.

"Very well. Tuan does not want to speak yet." He stood up, tipped his hat a little and prepared to leave. He dawdled for a while at the restaurant door. He quickly pulled out the front of his shirt to cool down his body. Then, as if he had just remembered something, he turned around and came back to the table.

"You haven't changed your mind yet, Tuan?" he whispered, bending down and peering into my face.

His attitude was insulting, as if I were the criminal and he was the policeman.

I shook my head.

He sat down again. Now he spoke quietly: "I know we can work together, Tuan Pangemanann. I will visit whatever address you give me and everything will proceed smoothly, just like the Betawi-Surabaya express. You agree, heh?"

"I don't know what you're talking about," I said, and made to get up to go.

"Don't be in such a hurry, Tuan. We have time, don't we?"

"A pity, but I have other work to attend to. Good morning," I said as I stood and went to pay for my share. He too paid his bill. He followed me out of the restaurant, tagging on behind me, more loyal than my lapdog. It made me feel better to see him following on behind me in such a humiliating manner.

Walking along like this in civvies, out of uniform, made me feel like an ordinary person out for a pleasant stroll—if only Suurhof wasn't there too. Having him following me like this made me feel as if there were some piece of dirt stuck to my clothes that made everybody look at me.

When we reached the bridge across the Ciliwung I pretended to glance back, just to witness for myself how he needed me. He smiled, and signified that he was still there. I stopped, leaned on the railings, and watched the flow of the river.

Soon he was beside me again, mimicking my actions.

"You still haven't spoken," he said amicably. "I am sure we can work together, Tuan. I swear it."

"No!" I answered briefly.

"I'm sorry, but you shouldn't say that, Tuan."

"There is no reason why I should work with you."

"Very well, I await your orders."

"You know who I am?"

"Of course, Tuan. Everyone knows Chief Inspector Pangemanann. People say that you *are* the Betawi Police!"

"Zihhh!" I hissed, and an all too familiar face flashed before my mind's eye—Si Pitung, the bandit, who had brought me to these undreamed of heights in the police force.

"Why *zihhh*, Tuan? Robert Suurhof is not a dog!" protested this rotten bandit.

I was glad he was angry. I had offended him.

"Perhaps some other time," I said.

"Impossible," he challenged me again. "Do you think that the Algemeene Landbouw Syndicaat is not as powerful as the police?"

"Go and sell your fake letters, con man," I said. "No one needs you here."

This gangster had become practiced in sudden changes in attitude. Or perhaps it was just a part of his personality.

"I'm sorry, Tuan Pangemanann. I have been putting things wrongly. It is I who wish to help the police."

"No. You are not needed. Nobody needs your help. The police are quite capable of handling things. You're just looking to get in good with the police. You think that way everyone will forget who and what you really are. Yes?"

"That's true, too," he said, conceding. "Now, what is it that Tuan wants me to do? I wasn't summoned here by the commissioner for nothing."

"Do you think you are on the same level as the commissioner, and I am just your underling or something?"

"Yes, I have not behaved correctly, Tuan."

I remained silent for quite a while, just to check if he really had thrown off his arrogance. I was right, he had become just like a lapdog, wagging its tail while waiting for its master to throw it some scraps. I think that was how he would always be whenever he faced a person he could not intimidate. It made me sick.

"Very well. Because it is what the commissioner has ordered, and not because it is my own wish, wait for me at Buitenzorg station at five o'clock. Bring only the minimum number of men."

"Good, Tuan. There will be three of us, besides myself."

"Go now! Don't bother me anymore."

I didn't hear any good-bye from him. I was gazing down into the waters of the Ciliwung. Two sampans were passing each other, each carrying a *kwintal* or so of cargo, packed in sacks. Who knows what it was? Hopefully, it wasn't opium. The oarsmen seemed to be sure of themselves and the safety of their sampans and cargo. They sang in Sundanese in a villager's accent and I could not understand a word.

The next day, at Buitenzorg station, he was there waiting. He stood there on the platform, hands on his hips, like a governor-general ready to inspect some department of state. I am sure he never dared behave so arrogantly before developing his current friendship with the police. I hid myself behind other people on the platform so I could get a chance to observe him. But his sharp eyes soon discovered me.

I walked on out through the ticket gate, pretending not to see him. And he followed me from about five meters behind. Carrying my briefcase, I stopped under a palm tree at the edge of the station gardens. He quickly caught up with me, nodded, and said good afternoon.

"You know the risks involved with this work?" I whispered.

"There's nothing risky here, Tuan."

"Who said there are no risks? You are acting outside the law. The risk is that if anything happens to you, if you're wounded or even killed, the law will give you no protection. The law will pretend that it knows nothing about what happened. Understand?"

He laughed contemptuously. "There will be no risk, Tuan," he said, giving his guarantee.

"You don't understand me, do you? Don't you ever listen to anything that people tell you? Listen well, because this is a promise. If anything happens to you or any of your men, the law will do nothing about it. Understand? Do I have to repeat it to you again?"

"I understand, Tuan."

"No regrets?"

"What is there to regret when we only have one life?"

"Whether you have four or five lives is no concern to me, that's your affair. Listen. Will you regret doing this later?"

"No, Tuan," he answered respectfully.

"Where are your men?"

"Waiting on that corner over there, Tuan."

"Good. Now listen to me again. I don't want any comments from you. I am going to visit somebody in his house. When I come out, it will be your turn to pay him a visit. You don't need to know who it is I am visiting. You will have to make sure he does not get a chance to leave his house after I have visited him. Understand?"

"I understand, Tuan. It's quite clear."

"All you have to do is frighten him."

"Just frighten him?" protested Suurhof. "Just frighten him? Suurhof is only to frighten him?" he laughed contemptuously again, while pointing to his chest.

"In that case, you can go. Damn it! I'll do this work myself."

"I didn't mean it like that, Tuan. I thought we were going to have to fight somebody."

"Fight with whom? With some Native who is unable and too frightened to defend himself? That's the kind of work you're used to, isn't it?"

"But they fought back, and in a number of places we always finished the fight properly."

"Fighting is not always needed in this work."

"Very well, Tuan. I hear what you say."

"Very good. So just make sure you only give him a fright. So that he stops his activities. So that he disbands his group. That's all. Understand?"

"And if he's not frightened?"

"That's your problem, stupid. What schooling did you get?"

"HBS, Tuan."

"Why are you so stupid then? It seems that the higher your schooling, the more stupid you get."

"Fortunately, I only got as far as HBS, Tuan."

"Indies or Netherlands HBS?"

"Indies, Tuan."

"*Zihhh*. If you're really an HBS graduate, then I won't have to show you the way to the address. You should be able to find it yourself. So here's the address. You can make your own way there. Remember, just frighten him. I will wait at the entrance to the Botanical Gardens."

He laughed as soon as he saw the address, nodded to me, and left. The three others, all Eurasians, quickly followed after him. One of them was thin and shriveled, perhaps an opium addict. I walked along slowly, following.

They were clearly heading for the right house. He knew the man who lived there well. Suurhof's gang, *De Knijpers*, had often attacked the SDI, even wounding and killing some SDI people. I wanted to see what would happen when these two men confronted each other, face-to-face, challenge awaiting answer, and all happening to close to the governor-general's palace.

I had spent a whole evening deciding how to use De Knijpers, sometimes known as TAI, *Totaal Anti Inlanders*. The commissioner had given me this gang to use as I liked. And now I was going to use them against a man I respected and honored with all my heart. He must not be injured in any way. In any case, the palace guards will take action should Suurhof and his gang overstep my orders.

I saw the man's friends Mr. and Mrs. Frischboten leave the house with Native escorts. Suurhof's gang walked slowly toward the target house. The family in the house said their good-byes to the Frischbotens. And the carriage bearing their guests and another with their escorts set off to who-knows-where. It looked as though they were heading for the station.

I followed Suurhof and his men. I knew that all they were going to do was frighten him. The family would not be hurt in any way. But how would they react to their attackers? That was the important thing.

Suurhof and his friends were entering the front yard. I had also approached very close to the front yard but I stayed outside. They approached the house. I walked past the front gate and found a place from which I could watch what would happen.

The sun was slowly setting. I stopped under a tree. I didn't even notice what kind of tree it was. I took out a cigarette, lit a match, then: *Bang!* There was the sound of a gunshot, obviously from a revolver. Again and then again.

How dare he! Suurhof had gone too far. I saw in my mind's eye the body of that man I admired and respected so much sprawled out on the ground, covered in blood.

I saw Suurhof and his friends leave the house, running head over heels. They ran off leaving behind their weapon and what it had spewed forth. Suurhof headed for the entrance to the Botanical Gardens. He passed me without even realizing I was there. There were no more sounds of shooting.

Then a group of palace guards came hurrying out, not in formation. As if they had already known where to go, they headed straight for the house where the incident had occurred.

There was no sign of Suurhof. One of his men, the shriveled-up Eurasian, came panting past me. When he saw the guards heading in his direction, he slowed down and began walking normally. He took out a handkerchief from his faded blue trousers, stopped on the edge of the road, and wiped his face and neck.

I found Suurhof leaning up against the gate at the entrance to the Botanical Gardens. He obviously wasn't used to running. His face was dark red, and he was short of breath.

I went up to him and whispered: "You overstepped your orders. You shot him."

He fell in step with me as I walked on, and answered in a whisper: "No, Tuan. I swear I did not shoot him."

"Liar! Cheat! Criminal!" I swore at him in a whisper.

"I swear, Tuan. We were the ones that were fired upon."

I stopped in my tracks. I looked him in the face, and asked unbelievingly: "It was he who fired? Him? Minke?"

"Not him, Tuan. His wife!"

Now it was my turn to have the sudden change in mood. From anger to amusement, and I couldn't stop myself from bursting out laughing.

"You're making fun of us," he protested.

"*Wah!* Hotshot fighters falling over each other, frightened of a woman." I continued walking. "What an accursed bunch of fools!"

"It's not so easy to deal with a weapon like that, Tuan."

"They say you are a Dutch citizen."

"That's right, Tuan."

"They say you have lived in the Netherlands."

"Yes, Tuan."

"You never had any dealings with the militia there?"

"I was arrested by the police and sent back to the Indies, Tuan," he answered and there was pride in his voice. He followed on close behind me.

"Fighters, four of them, all running head over heels, falling over each other . . . huh! Only because of a woman! So shameful. Just give up being humans. You're all cursed!"

He did not protest.

I began to walk faster and he increased his pace, following on like a pet dog tagging behind its master. When I turned around, we stood facing each other. His figure had lost all its manliness. His mustache, beard, and sideburns no longer gave the impression of a fighter. He was more and more disgusting to me. A man without principles, without honor, no ideals. He got his enjoyment from oppressing and terrorizing the powerless. And faced with a woman with a revolver, he went to water, like a bowl of green-pea porridge.

"What must I do now, Tuan Pangemanann?"

"Nothing. There's nothing else for you to do. You're not worth a cent. Go!"

He still followed me, like a diseased, sore-covered dog, revolting to everyone.

"Must I use my gun to get rid of you?" I growled.

"I will go to see the commissioner."

"Who gives a damn!" Only then did I finally rid myself of that disgusting filthy scum.

It turned out that he managed to see the commissioner before I did. The commissioner warned me that I was being too hard with him.

"You don't need to be so hard," he said as he stroked his mustache, as big as a fist, corn-red mixed with gray.

"He could destroy all my work."

"There is no one else."

"I can succeed better without him. You have forced upon me a 'third leg.' "

"But this is what you yourself recommended. Frighten him with the most vicious thug we can find, you said. The gods above have agreed to all this."

I returned to his house, Minke's house, a few weeks later, but this time without Suurhof's gang. I alighted from my carriage and walked into the front yard where I found husband and wife sitting outside in the garden. After we introduced each other, the wife, who had scattered the TAI gang, stood and left the two of us.

So this was he, Minke, up close. He seemed anxious. Every now and then his eyes communicated with a man who was sitting on a bench across the way. He had reason to be worried after the visit of Suurhof and his gang. The people of West Java had all heard rumors that among the De Knijpers, alias TAI, there was a man from Menado. He knew that I was a Menadonese; at least I had a Menadonese name. He was suspicious.

I had prepared what I wanted to speak to him about. The main subject was the story *The Tale of Siti Aini* by Haji Moeloek, which in recent days was on everybody's lips in Java. It was a good story by Indies standards for Natives or Eurasians.

I began by declaring my admiration for him, an admiration that came sincerely from my heart. It was all praise. Such praise made him even more vigilant. He was difficult to get close to, I thought. I began to talk about Haji Moeloek's story. But he didn't seem to be paying any attention or not much attention, to what I was saying. Still suspicious, he remained vigilant throughout.

It is always difficult to talk with somebody who is suspicious. Their perceptions are always colored by their suspicions. And he did indeed have grounds for being suspicious.

I had to quickly change the topic of discussion, and offered him a manuscript by a relative of mine, entitled *Si Pitung*. I had owned the manuscript for a long time. I had gone through and corrected it in accordance with what was in the police archives. But the author never appeared again. I had checked and corrected and read that manuscript so often, it almost felt as if I had written it myself. The author was also a Pangemanan, but with only one *n*. He was a Protestant, not Catholic like my family. My wife did not enjoy his visits at all, and so he soon stopped coming around.

Minke accepted my offer very politely, a politeness obviously put on for my benefit. I felt it was going to be very difficult to have a genuine conversation with him. And, yes, I had to admit I wasn't being genuine with him anyway. It seemed I was not very clever at putting on an act at being two-faced. In that, I was like him. I had only one face, one heart—

the face and heart of a *priyayi*, of course. Yes, he too faced the world without hypocrisy, but as a human being.

Caught in a dead end in my conversation with this man, whom I admired and respected so much, the real contents of my heart spilled forth from my mouth. I talked about *De Knijpers*. In a mixture of sincerity and playacting I expressed my concern about the recent incident that he had experienced. The look in his eyes grew more piercing. Totally losing control of the conversation, I started talking about TAI, and then about De Zweep. At that moment, I felt truly ashamed of myself.

He commented only briefly, but it cut me to the quick: "Very interesting!"

He had effectively asserted his authority over me. There was no point in trying to prolong a conversation like this. It would only throw me into more confusion, so I stood and, bowing, excused myself.

Back at the Hotel Enkhuizen, I contemplated the results of my work. The conclusion I came to was very simple. Like Suurhof, I had also run off head-over-heels. Except that there were no witnesses, praise be to God. I could deny everything if I ever needed to save face. Perhaps others could do this work better than I. If my superiors found out what had happened, they would laugh at me just as I had done with Suurhof. If being honest would bring that kind of laughter, then there was truly no need for that kind of honesty. This time I would just say that there was nobody home. My good name would not be sullied and my prestige not stained. Ah, I didn't need to report anything.

And I made another resolution. I had to help this good-hearted man who had only good intentions for the Natives, his people. By God, I would help him! He as a human being, and I too as a human being, by God! Give me strength. He must succeed. The situation was on his side. The Natives needed an organization to meet the challenges of these times. I must side with that which was taking things forward, with the forward march of history. This was my conscience speaking now. Pure. There were no personal interests mixed up in any of this.

In Betawi my boss just nodded as he listened to my chatter. Then he made a truly stinging comment: "Writing a report, it seems, is much easier than putting it into practice."

"You can always try to write such a report yourself, Meneer," I answered somewhat viciously, and I knew that his words were targeted at me not so much as a commissioner seconded to work for him but as a Eurasian who held a position above his station.

"Well, if I had also spent several years at the Sorbonne . . ." he repeated his old sarcasm, "then you needn't worry about that, Meneer Pan-gemanann."

"Even without the Sorbonne, I could prepare such a report, Meneer. I wasn't appointed a commissioner for nothing. And you know that I was not promoted to commissioner because of some paper. And anyway, do you think organizing this kind of work is easier than leading troops?"

"Europeans evaluate people according to the results of their work, Meneer."

"Exactly. That is indeed the glue of modern European civilization. That is also why we are now sitting facing each other like this. We both know what it is that we are carrying out. But why are you trying so hard to belittle it? Perhaps this is a remnant of the old Netherlands culture. I hope you are satisfied."

I saluted and left the room.

I knew that he would not take away my promotion or withdraw my task. I had prepared my paper not on his orders but on the orders of the *Algemeene Secretariat.* He was just an intermediary. There was no power that could obstruct the will of that pinnacle of authority. So in the end this all meant that I had to return to my task of controlling the activities of the man I admired most among all men. I would have to do this using actions, methods, and people outside the law. It was I who would have to do this. I, a police official; a servant and an officer of the law.

I had fallen so very low, though in my heart I refused to admit this fact. It still felt as if I had my honor, like the scholarship student I was fifteen years ago, or the police inspector of ten years ago. But the reality was different. Mud now stuck to my fingers, brain, and heart. It was not the fertile mud to be found on the farmers' hands. It was colonial mud of use only to carpetbaggers and businessmen—mud that, in fact, made filthy the clothes of a priyayi.

It was true that I had been given this task based upon my own report and recommendations. And it was the first time too that the editor of *Medan* had been made the object of such a rotten operation. Colonial power itself never knew the meaning of selflessness and honesty. Justice and law? And the guardians of the law! Even more rotten. What I had written in my report was nothing more than the logical extension of all the rottenness of colonial power and its lust to remain in control of the Indies for another thousand years.

You must understand, however, that De Knijpers was operating before I was pulled in to handle the SDI. At that time the police were not involved at all. Suurhof's gang had been hired by the plantation owners to terrorize their workers, to keep them timid and afraid. That was the beginning of it all. Then people began to think that there were wider benefits to be gained and the gang's activities spread to the towns. They became the heroes of colonial society because of their seeming success in smashing up the SDI. They did indeed carry out many actions, often exciting and quite dramatic. It was only afterward that colonial society began to realize that these attacks by De Knijpers were strengthening the resolve, unity, and resistance of the SDI membership. The government was forced to bring its activities to an end by reprimanding the Algemeene Landbouw Syndicaat. The government's actions were definitely not a result of anybody's working paper, but were the result of a face-to-face conversation between Meneer W—and myself in his office at police headquarters.

If the De Knijpers did not stop its activities, I said, there was a good chance that the nature of the clashes would start to change. It would no longer be a question of the SDI versus De Knijpers, but of Islam versus Christianity. Once this happened, the government would find itself in new difficulties. Perhaps this would not be a major problem, but it would be there for the long term. I reminded him that Machiavelli was the example that colonial regimes followed, in the Indies and around the world. No one ever actually mentioned his name, and there were no statues to honor him, yet it was he who had been defied.

And yes, it happened. De Knijpers was reined in. In its disappointment, the gang dissolved itself simply by changing its name to TAI. But the government was not satisfied and disbanded it altogether. As a consolation to Suurhof, he was promised protection and was allowed to keep a few men, no more than ten. These remnants took the name *De Zweep* and were given to me, against my will, to help me in my task. Yes, I was now the head of a gang of thugs. Who says I had not fallen as low as anyone could fall? Curse them all!

The situation turned out to be worse than I thought. It appeared that Minke had decided to answer my visit and my discussion of De Knijpers, TAI, and De Zweep by beginning an offensive against the *Sugar Syndicate*. There was a massive exchange of letters between the Netherlands and Betawi, between the sugar mills of Java and the Netherlands, that lasted forty-eight hours. Stacked on top of each other, the pile of papers was as thick as a dictionary. I came in for more insults from my boss. I took it out on my subordinate. He no doubt went home and took it out on his wife, who in turn took it out on the children, and the children took it out on the servant. Only then did it all stop, because a servant is at the end of the line in life. In the evening, at the end of a day of slaving away, she will go into her quarters, often forgetting even to eat dinner. She will surrender her tears and her supplications to Allah, reminding Him of her right to some little corner of heaven and the punishment of hell for all employers. But tomorrow she will go out and serve her master again—working as usual again, insulted as usual again. Leave her master? Never! Just like me. I will never leave the service, no matter how many insults rain down upon me.

I truly felt that the editor of *Medan* was challenging me directly, and that it was a direct challenge also to my position and my pension. I mobilized De Zweep. I ordered Suurhof to send an anonymous threatening letter to Minke. Then I myself made the pioneering visit to his office in Bandung.

The only purpose of my visit was to check if it was going to be possible to keep him under control. No. He was indeed planning to challenge the Sugar Syndicate. If this man was paralyzed, would then his influence and his organization also be paralyzed? His political capital was no more than his daring thinking and his courage to act. Fortunately, not everybody was like him. And more than that, he was prepared to risk the consequences of his own actions.

I left his office. I signaled Suurhof to carry out his task. What else could I do? As time went on, Minke's writing in *Medan* were causing me more and more difficulties. I was not prepared to face the shame of the failure of being unable to control him. He must submit to my will. What is the meaning of just one individual, Minke? As an individual, he is no more important than I. I too have my own importance.

Medan itself printed a report of Suurhof's attack. Mr. H. Frischboten, in his usual vigorous manner, brought the case to court. They could not avoid this. His resolute struggle meant the matter was dealt with by the *White Court*. And once again this accursed bandit called Suurhof for the umpteenth time got me into trouble. The Betawi Police had to contact the prosecutor's office and once again the insults thundered forth around me, as if they would never stop, like a huge explosion of dynamite. Gaping mouths all around spewed forth their gall, mouths decorated with mustaches and those without. The mouths of Pure Europeans. All Protestants. All my superiors.

Of course, I defended myself. Suurhof had not acted according to plan. He had overstepped his orders. Then they blew their bad breath all over me once again. There were those who smelled of alcohol, others of lime juice; there were even those who smelled of petai beans—and they were all my superiors. They were so clever at finding fault. And I was only a Native who was occupying a position above my station. Scholarship and a degree meant nothing in the Indies. Here, once you became just another instrument of the powers above, the higher you went your mouth got bigger and your ears disappeared; the lower you went your ears got bigger and your mouth disappeared. Those whose education was inadequate tended to be the most sadistic and the ones who most enjoyed making others feel their authority.

They had no desire to hear excuses. So Suurhof became the rubbish bin of my misfortune. Watch out, you bastard! You will have to pay for every injury to my pride. I will not let you get off without paying. You're lucky you're being protected by the authorities. In the court you were able to prove you had been a journalist for the *Preangerbode* for the last few years. All proved by a predated letter of appointment, of course. Frischboten was unable to counter such proof as that.

And me, Suurhof? From me, nothing can protect your skull now.

On arriving at my house, I found several unopened letters from my children in the Netherlands.

"I am sure they're all doing well at school, Jacques?" my wife got in her question first.

"Of course, darling. Why wouldn't they be doing well? You taught them all yourself, didn't you?" I humored her so that she would not guess at how I was feeling. "Read them yourself."

"You usually read them for all of us."

"Very well. But let me rest a little first," I said as I walked into my room, changed clothes, and lay down.

"Have you eaten out?"

"Yes, darling. I'm sorry," I answered, even though hunger was worming away in my intestines. But I had lost all my appetite.

And as usual Paulette felt the need to check for herself the truth or otherwise of what I said. She was the woman of the house and she would not allow anyone else to interfere with the feeding of her husband, from the moment the cooking got under way until the table was cleared. Usually, while pretending to do this and that, she would try to smell my breath. Once she was sure there was no smell of alcohol, she would embrace me and kiss me just like when we were newlyweds, but her hands would be checking out my stomach.

"You haven't eaten at all. Don't let all my work be for nothing."

Here at home, I could not escape from this excessive love; I had no choice but to get up and sit at the dinner table.

"You don't like my cooking anymore. Or would you prefer Native food? Let's go to a restaurant. Would you like that?"

I shook my head and began to eat. She too began to eat but all the time watching me spoon the food in and swallow it down.

"Is there trouble, Jacques? You don't seem very happy."

Her excessive attention to my needs further killed my appetite. "You can eat alone tonight, darling. I have a headache," I said, making excuses.

I went to the front and sat down in the rocking chair. And I knew for sure that my wife would stop eating and come out and busy me with her demands for attention.

But I was wrong. She continued her dinner, and remained out in the back until evening. Sitting by myself—I didn't know where the younger children were—the problem of Suurhof was pushed aside by the same thoughts that always came to me during these moments in our marriage. Had I married a Native woman, I would never have had to worry about any of this nonsense. A Native women would just serve her husband because that was her one and only duty in life. I would not have to worry about what she was thinking, and I could enjoy the unlimited freedom of my kingdom as a man.

It was five o'clock in the evening before she came out and reprimanded me: "Have a bath, Jacques. What is it that you're worrying about? Leave your problems at work at the office. Here at home you belong to your wife and children, isn't that right?"

"Forgive me, darling," and I stood up and went off to the bathroom just so that I wouldn't have to speak to anyone.

The cool and refreshing water revived me. Yes, my God, how compassionate you are to revive my spirits like this. Back in my room I put on office clothes again, and kissed my wife good-bye.

"You promised you would read the letters to us."

"You can read them the letters, darling."

"But they're not addressed to me." We even have to organize the reading of letters according to an official division of labor, I thought. It's driving me crazy. "Very well, darling. I'll make sure I'm back before the children go to bed."

Back at headquarters I reported to Donald Nicolson that everything had gone smoothly in the Suurhof case and that the police had in no way been embarrassed. It was true that Suurhof and his men had in the end been given a jail sentence but there were no embarrassing implications for the police. It was a pity, but when I sat before the chief commissioner, the words did not come out as firmly as I had planned.

"Nah, Meneer Pangemanann"—he pulled on his lips, thick and stiff—"once more you discover that it is much easier to write a report than put its recommendations into practice."

Anger and the fear that I was losing my good reputation left me unable to answer.

"And the idea was Meneer's own. A pity."

"Do you wish to send me back to police work?" I dared him to demote me.

"That time will come," he answered. "Your job now is to make sure that the Suurhof case causes no more problems. It was your own recommendation that we take action outside the law."

"It's a pity that Suurhof was no better than a diseased, sore-ridden cat in a sack."

"Do you want to find someone better than him, a bandit with some brains?" He truly knew my weakness. And that hurt. "Please put forward another name," he said.

Well, it looked as if Suurhof was going to be my problem until he was sacked or reached retirement age. And, no matter what, I would get my pension. I would not retire even one day early. Once again I swallowed defeat. I swallowed and swallowed. If my stomach were to become too paunchy because of all this swallowing, I just hoped that there was some mechanism that would expel it all. If not, I could explode into little pieces.

"And you see from that"—and he pointed to the wall where there was a graph upon which there were no explanatory notes—"the SDI has still not troughed."

"Perhaps Meneer is waiting for me to say that I can't go on with this work anymore?"

"I am the one who can decide that, not Meneer," said the chief commissioner. "You should examine it yourself." He pointed again to the graph.

I went over to look at the damned thing on the wall. There was a new line drawn in pencil, drawn somewhat hesitantly, that indicated that every time Suurhof took action against Minke, there was a big leap in the membership of the SDI.

"A challenge," the chief commissioner commented.

"It's only a provisional line anyway. It's still in pencil," I protested.

"You can take that fountain pen. There is some Chinese ink where it's usually kept," he replied.

I took down the graph board and put it on the table. I filled the fountain pen with ink, and took a ruler ready to draw over the pencil line with ink. I wanted to find out whether he was playing around with me or not.

"Go on, put the line in. No need to hesitate," he said.

So the SDI membership had increased. I drew the line in ink. I put the graph back up on the wall.

"Another 'time bomb.' That's what you call it, don't you?"

"You're not wrong, Meneer," I answered. "There is much work to do."

"It's not a question of being finished or not finished. I think you are becoming less and less confident in your own report, Meneer."

"The intellectual work of Commissioner Pangemanann remains intact, Chief Commissioner. There is not one word that I would take back. But the technical implementation of these ideas is not my specialty. This is not just a matter of catching a thief. An architect is not necessarily also a good builder."

"So who would be a good builder, then?" he cornered me.

"That's your affair."

"But you have been appointed to be the builder too. And you have never indicated that you are not prepared to carry out these duties. Not even now."

"You could replace me with someone else."

"Yes, I could. But it seems that you do not realize, Meneer Pangemanann, that your report is not for the general public. Only a very few people in the Indies and in the world have read and studied it. I was one of those who have had the privilege. You will never know, and indeed do not need to know, who else has read it. Your work of scholarship, as you like to call it, will never receive the honor of being kept in the State archives. Once everyone finished reading it, it became dust and smoke, in the safekeeping only of the devils of the night."

His words struck right at the weakest point in my soul. They hurt, they made me feel sick.

"Don't be angry," the chief commissioner spoke gently. "This is the first time the Indies police has ever had to carry out work like this. All our superiors fully agree with your report. They don't just agree with it. They value it greatly! You do not need to be discouraged. You are considered to be the only official who has the knowledge, familiarity, understanding, and the ideas to handle these new developments in the Indies. It is only Meneer who can come to the right conclusions and make the right recommendations. Before you now is laid out a great career, bright and glorious. . . . Yes, it is the only one, and it is for Meneer."

I went home in high spirits. I felt as if my chest would explode with pride. On the other hand, I also felt very, very ashamed. How was it possible that someone who was almost half a century old could feel so proud just because of praise like that, which could even be groundless? One moment it was shame; then I was startled when, for a moment, the image of Si Pitung flashed before me. That fighter from Cibinong sneered and flung his insults: Without me, Tuan Pangemanann, Tuan would never have been

promoted; yes, you would never become governor-general, but chief commissioner is just one step away.

    Zihhh, get away, you, Pitung! I crossed myself, then began to examine
my own soul. Why was I experiencing these sudden changes in mood? Was
I going mad? Why was I letting hopes and reality confront each other like
this inside me? Would I have to face that choice? My principles or my
career? Morality or position? I knew for sure that I needed both. But I also
knew that I could have only one, not both. That was what the problem
had been all along. Not only in the life I had been living but also in my
soul. And I knew for sure that this was a problem that only I could solve.
And I, I wanted to have them both.

    While lost in thought like this, I read André and Henri's letters to the
rest of the family and their mother. It was nice. It always made us happy
to read their letters—they provided a reflection of an orderly European
civilization. Any bitterness I was feeling in myself disappeared as I read out
to everybody all the happy reports in the letters. All the stories were happy,
though it is well known that everybody faces their own troubles. Even the
baby in the womb. But this was still better than telling only stories of trouble
and difficulties and keeping all the happy things to oneself, don't you think?

    Their mother was happy, their brothers and sisters were happy. Every-
one knew that the children in Holland were working their guts out in their
studies; studies that might never be of any use to them in their life or in
their seeking a livelihood. At the most, their degrees would be just an
ornamentation to their name.

    After I finished reading the letters, my wife quickly repeated a prayer
of thanks. We all just added an amen. It was done to keep everybody happy.
And the work that was gnawing at my heart still remained for me to deal
with—a responsibility that was aging me quickly. But what surprised me
most of all was that the machine of civilization kept on working, and always
seemed to stay young.

    That evening I hardened my resolve to free myself of Suurhof. How?
Any means were permissible if the end was just to get rid of a lowlife who
only caused everyone trouble. The power machine often carried out this
sort of thing and, anyway, what was the meaning of a Suurhof?

    May my efforts be blessed. . . .

2

Robert Suurhof's stay in jail did not at all lessen my troubles. Donald Nicolson never let up harassing me with his new data—the SDI's membership was still growing. He was trying to trap me into taking even harsher measures against the editor of *Medan*.

With Suurhof a very loose cannon, and by putting more pressure on me, perhaps the commissioner thought that I could be cornered into ordering Suurhof to take even more brutal action against Minke. If we were not unlucky, then we would all be safe. But if Suurhof was caught and once again dragged before the law, where he squealed that I had given the orders, then it would be I who was the marble that rolled down the drain. My livelihood would vanish, my good name would be destroyed.

No matter what they said, there were no Pure Europeans who were happy to see a Native like me hold the position of commissioner, let alone chief commissioner. And there were very many traps to bring about my downfall. And I knew the colonial ways off by heart, and by instinct as well. To stab a fellow worker in the back and get him demoted was one way of crawling to the top.

A trap or not, an attempt to corner me or not, my job was not only to stop the growth of the SDI but to push it back as well—if possible, to get rid of it altogether. Meanwhile, the only high-caliber thugs available were the likes of Suurhof. There wasn't one who wasn't chalk-brained. Usually a policeman would be grateful to know that the criminals were more stupid than he. Look, what kind of work was this? And, yes, it was I who was going to carry it out.

Without Suurhof, I could do nothing.

"Very well," said Nicolson, "we'll wait for Suurhof to get out."

The time that cheap hoodlum spent without his freedom was a happy time with everything being in abeyance for me. But meanwhile the commissioner ordered me to prepare a report on what would have to be done if our efforts outside the law did not succeed. Ah, there was no limit to what we could do outside the law. A brainless donkey could work that out. No need for all these reports and studies.

For the purposes of preparing this new report, I needed to meet with Meneer L—at the State archives. I needed to hear his analysis of the peoples of the Indies.

"The Natives' way of thinking has not yet been changed by modern ideas," he explained. "They live in the same mental world as five centuries ago. Their way of dealing with the world has not changed. Natives who have absorbed some elements of modernity are not like anyone else—such a person is half European in a Native body. Like Meneer himself. You have to approach and deal with such people in the European way. There is no need to deal with them in any other way. Meneer's questions are related to your work, yes?"

"No, I'm just interested, that's all," I answered.

He laughed incredulously.

"Could you explain to me a little about the form and the character of these Native organizations?" I asked.

"Oh, that?" He glanced sideways at me, then answered promptly. "Their form and character have not changed, Meneer. Perhaps their methods have changed. But the rest, the same, Meneer, the same."

"And what is it that is the same?"

"They have no organizations like we have in Europe or the West. Their associations arose because of the lower classes' awe of those above or because of the charisma of their superiors."

"But these new developments don't seem to be like that because there is no question of superiors and subordinates."

"You have proof of this?" he asked, not really believing me.

The look in his eyes seemed to be demanding I take intellectual responsibility for what I had said. Hesitantly, I began to speak about the SDI. He listened carefully to every word.

"How does it compare to *Boedi Oetomo*?" he asked suddenly.

I talked about the Boedi Oetomo, and added, "Several of the nobility who joined Boedi Oetomo denied that they were doing so to assert their authority or charisma."

"Do you know for sure that they did not join simply to advance their own interests or their group's interests? And with the aim of manipulating the organization? This kind of development has always occurred throughout the history of humankind's organizing, I think."

"The history of humankind's organizing?" I asked, quizzing him further.

"Yes, it's the same everywhere," he answered firmly.

"Do you really believe what you're saying, Meneer?"

He gave some examples. He explained about how certain people rose to the top among the Papuan tribes, and among the Minangkabau in Koto Gadang, about the intrigues in implementing customary law. His words launched forth unchecked from his lips, and I studied this much younger official with respect.

"Has Meneer studied the history of Diponegoro? People also followed him because of his charisma. Half a million people were prepared to die for him. And what kind of organization did his courageous followers have? Like all such organizations. As soon as the object of their awe, the center of charisma, disappeared, either because of age, or because some disaster befell them, it all vanished into nothingness. Their organizations are different from criminal organizations, of course. Criminal organizations are built upon terror, and become dynamic also because of terror."

I was able to understand the essence of his lecture. In dealing with Minke, the editor of Medan, some disaster had to be planned for him. Once our raden mas was no longer with us, his organization would also vanish, because organizations in the European sense did not yet exist in the Indies. And this was exactly as I had thought all along. The only problem now was to work out what kind of accident should be organized for Minke, and how drastic it should be. SDI was clearly not a criminal organization. The criminal organization was the one run by Suurhof. And there was that much bigger criminal organization run by His Excellency the governor-general, namely, the Netherlands Indies government, and I was a petty criminal among its ranks.

I did not try to protect myself and my name from my own intellectual conclusions. But I did want to protect the secret of my membership in this gang, and also the pension that I would receive in ten, or even only seven, years. And so what was my value compared to such a person as Minke? But what I did know for sure was that my wife and children must always be able to tell and write wonderful letters and stories to make me feel good, and I must be able to do the same for them. And we would silently swallow our own bitterness, unheard by any other creatures except ourselves.

How simple was life really. It was only the twists and turns in life, and their negotiation, that were complex. Millions of ants are squashed to death under the feet of human beings. Thousands of millions of insects die every second at the hands of farmers in their fields. These souls die and those who survive multiply their numbers again very, very rapidly. People also die in the fields of war, just like ants and insects. And those that survive also multiply themselves with no less rapidity. Why do we have to be sentimental about death? Only because we have been pumped full of all these fairy stories about devils, angels, heaven and hell? They are all just people's opinions, and that's all they will ever be. Millions of people have disappeared from the face of the earth. Even the ruins of their civilizations have disappeared because of great natural disasters. Who is going to be sentimental? Instead, people give thanks that they themselves were not victims.

And I? If I wasn't clever in negotiating the rapids, then I would be annihilated and eaten up by all the colonial big shots, who, like sharks, need a constant flow of victims. Why shouldn't I become a shark like all the powerful colonialists? There is no need for indulging in these petty sentiments. All those humanitarian values are of use only to those who understand and need them. The great humanist values sound beautiful when they are spoken by the great teachers of the world, and beautiful too when heard by those students with talent, but tedious to the stupid ones. Happy are the stupid students, because they are given justification to do whatever they want.

By twilight my plans were fully worked out. To the devil with all this petty sentimentality. I must be more pragmatic. Why do we have to condemn the use of terror? The colonial world is a world of terror. For two centuries now, perhaps longer, people have debated about the purposes of the law. One side says that the law is there to safeguard the rights of the people. The other side says the law is there to control the people. And for scores of other purposes as well. And what is the law really about? The law is an instrument that can be used when appropriate and when it is appropriate to your needs.

For the sake of my career, I must get rid of this Minke, the editor of *Medan*. And for the sake of my good name, I must also get rid of Suurhof.

I don't know how many times Nicolson had urged me to tell him of my plans. Now I could answer in a confident and proud voice: "You need not worry, Meneer Chief Commissioner."

He did not ask me to look again at the graph. I could see from where

I was sitting that there was no new entry. The police had not received any new reports.

"But you have not told me what your plan is, Meneer."

"As the implementation of our policy on this matter has been put in my hands, let me worry about it all."

He smiled. I knew he was happy. He had turned me into a wretched criminal. I left the Betawi Police Headquarters feeling empty—conscious that I was a colonial official, I was a bandit, I was a terrorist.

Suurhof was now free. He was going to report to me in Kwitang, at the house of Rientje de Roo, a young prostitute whose beauty had stirred the hearts of all Betawi's young peacocks. She was an expensive prostitute. Only bandits, corruptors, speculators, and high officials could afford to become her clients. It was Suurhof who suggested this meeting place.

She lived in a small flat attached to another house in a quiet part of Kwitang. Rientje de Roo invited me in straightaway. It seemed the rather small *pendopo* was deliberately unfurnished. Inside, the parlor was full of furniture that was not needed by a prostitute at all. It was all to signal to her customers that her tariffs were high.

"Meneer Pangemanann," she greeted me sweetly, displaying all her allure for me to savor. Without any kind of preliminaries, she sat herself on my lap. What I had been taught long ago made me feel sick to see this kind of behavior by this kind of woman.

And she protested: "This is not what you desire, Meneer?"

A guffawing voice inside me laughed at me. You have quite happily turned to banditry, why do you reject this then? Hypocrite! Haven't you already cast off all your principles for your career? Yes, and for the sake of my career also I would not be brought down by someone like Suurhof, who is using this pile of beautiful flesh to make me into his slave. Pangemanann was not as low as Suurhof.

Rientje de Roo got up and sat across from me, quickly covering up her disappointment with a myriad of smiles.

"Just let me admire your beauty, Rien," I said, humoring her.

The sun was almost gone and there was a quiet, relaxed atmosphere about the place. Through the curtains I saw a group of people pass by.

"You'd like something dry to drink, of course," she suggested. "It's humid today."

"No, no," I turned her down. I knew that this was all arranged by Suurhof so he could get me in his grasp.

"What about your customers, Rien? Is Robert Suurhof your favorite?"

She got up and came close to me, showing off her body in its light brown silk evening gown. She sat down on the arm of my chair. I could feel the aroma of her perfume beginning to anesthetize my brain. So sweetly, she brought her face close to mine and whispered: "I have never had a favorite. Perhaps if one day I have one, he will be a police commissioner."

"Did Suurhof suggest you say that?"

Seeing that I was becoming friendly again, she sat down on my lap once more and I could not refuse. There was something I wanted to find out about Suurhof. I caressed her, and it turned out that the silk was not as smooth as her skin. She grew more sweet and endearing, this child who was perhaps the same age as my young daughter. "Where is Suurhof?" I asked.

"Didn't you see me lock the front door? That means there will be no guests."

"This is the time we agreed to meet. He should be here!"

"He will come when the time is right, Meneer. No one will disturb us here. Relax, enjoy yourself. Your work will wait for you. This will perk you up."

It was no doubt Robert Suurhof who had stuffed these words into her mouth. This girl had never worked in her life and wouldn't have a clue about how to make conversation about work.

"And your work would never be finished either," I said.

She answered by pinching my cheek.

"When did you first meet Suurhof?" I asked.

"I can't remember, Meneer."

"I am a policeman, Rientje. You must answer me."

She started again, in her kind of nuzzling up way. She stood, and pulled me up against her.

"When did you meet Suurhof?" I asked again.

She stopped her carrying on. I saw nervousness in her eyes, but in the end she answered: "About a month before he was jailed in Bandung."

"Where did you meet him?" I asked, pressing her.

"People don't usually ask things like this here, Meneer."

"Suurhof has told you my name and rank?"

She bit her lip.

"You must answer all my questions. We have never met but you know I am a policeman! Answer me!" I said resolutely.

"Yes, Meneer, maybe . . ."

"No maybes, Rientje. Don't be afraid. All I want you to do is answer me. That's all. Nothing else." I grabbed her hand and sat her down where she had been sitting earlier. She looked pale.

"Just sit here quietly."

I caressed her hair for a moment. Then I suddenly darted over and opened the door to the back room. All I could see was a pair of blue-trousered legs hurriedly leaving via the back door. Someone had been eavesdropping on our conversation. I did not need to chase after him. I had little doubt that it would be none other than Robert Suurhof himself.

I went back to Rientje de Roo, and quickly repeated my question; "Where, Rientje?"

She answered by sobbing.

"Why are you crying?"

I put to use my knowledge of the ways of these criminals and the game they hunted, pretty girls like her. "You aren't here of your own free will, are you?" I asked again.

She stood up then and buried her face in my chest.

"Why won't you answer? Afraid? Robert Suurhof ran out the back door just now. He was wearing blue trousers."

She nodded, but couldn't speak.

"Suurhof has forced you to do this kind of work?"

She nodded, but couldn't speak because of her sobbing.

"You are tormented living like this?"

Once more she nodded.

In her embrace, and with her head nestled up against my chest, it felt once more as if she were my youngest daughter. It was easy to understand. She was a normal girl, with all the hopes of a normal girl, who had been torn away from her family by this criminal Suurhof, to be made into just another accoutrement of his power.

"Do you want to go back to your family?"

"They will not take me back, Meneer," she answered at last.

Just at that moment there was a knock on the door. I opened it: Suurhof stood before me. This time he wore no mustache or beard, but a white silk shirt and gray trousers with black stripes.

Just a moment before, I had been like any other normal person, among his family and society, educated and with his principles. But it was just for a moment. Facing Suurhof again, I changed. I was just another member of Suurhof's gang.

"Forgive me for being a little late, Meneer Pangemanann." He smiled widely and held out his hand. But my eyes studied his trousers that were not blue and his face that no longer featured a mustache or beard.

"Don't you recognize me, Meneer?" he said, laughing. Neither his beard, mustache nor side whiskers had left a trace upon his skin. It was smooth and shining—he had only just shaved.

"Please sit down, gentlemen." Rientje de Roo suddenly became her earlier merry self again.

Suurhof and I sat down. Rientje de Roo went out to the back room. Suurhof stood, went over to the corner, and put some music on the phonograph. He sat down nearby so that he could attend to it when necessary.

As music from *La Traviata* wafted around the room, so too laughter echoed inside me. The three of us were the worst play actors in the world.

"We're not here to admire that new phonograph," I chided him. "No doubt one of the many presents you have given Rientje."

Suurhof laughed. "There is no need for us to hurry, Meneer. We can take things easy." Suddenly he stood up, went out back, and dragged Rientje out just so he could say to her: "Heh, my sweet, you don't seem to be looking after our guest."

"You knew the front door was locked, but you came anyway," was her riposte.

"Yes, yes, it's my fault. I turned up one hour too early. Meneer, have you seen Rientje's room? Come on, don't worry, have a look!"

As if she had just received orders, Rientje de Roo once again sat herself down on my lap. Nuzzling up sweetly, she caressed my face.

"We can talk tonight. I will come back later at a more suitable time," Suurhof said to me.

He turned off the phonograph and, with a stylish flourish, strode out of the parlor through the front door.

"Would you like to see my room?" asked Rientje.

"I have to leave now, Rientje."

"Please don't go, Meneer. Robert will be very angry with me. Please, come." She stood and tried to lead me off.

"No, Rientje. You remind me of my young daughter."

"Then just sit here and talk to me. We can talk about whatever you like."

And then I saw in my mind's eye my wife being guided here by Suurhof, and so he would thus be able to get me in his grip.

"No, Rientje. I must go now. Perhaps I will have a chance some other time."

I left behind some money, at her rates, and departed without saying good bye.

I had just taken a few steps down the street when Suurhof was behind me: "Why are you leaving so quickly?"

"It's not the time for that, you damned bastard! Are you a bit smarter now or still as stupid as before?"

"Meneer will have to decide."

We stopped on the footpath, far from any streetlights. There were just one or two people passing by, and they didn't seem to be bothered with us. I took the initiative and sat down on a low concrete fence outside some building, under a kamboja tree.

"Are you ready to carry out my orders?"

"Anytime, Meneer."

I ordered him to be in Bandung at a certain time and place and to follow me from far away. He and his men were to wear clothes whose color I would decide later. I told him that my target was Minke. I would try to meet with and talk to him. After he and I separated, Suurhof and his men were to attack and kill Minke, but without using any guns or other weapons, sharp or blunt. They had to do it with their bare hands.

"And be careful, Suurhof, there must be no second court case. You and your men will get my bullets in you if you muck things up. You've caused me enough trouble already, with that second failure of yours."

"We will be more careful, Meneer."

Later at home something happened that made me change all my plans. A conversation with Paulette, my wife, changed my resolve.

We had just finished eating. The children had gone into their rooms to study. We sat outside on the veranda. My wife had just finished telling me about what had been happening at home and then she turned to another subject.

"They say, Jacques, many women say, wives I mean, that it is better that the husband dies before the wife. If the husband is left behind, then the children will not be looked after properly, no matter how clever the husband. But if the husband dies first, then the children will always be looked after even if they have to live in poverty."

"Ah, that's just idle talk," I answered. "The reality is that every day there are husbands and wives who die. And their children go on living just the same, even if no parents die."

"The children lose something, which they will not get from anywhere else or from anyone. Your thoughts are evil tonight, Jacques."

"I'm sorry, darling, but that's the reality. Most of humankind dies because of some calamity, not because of old age . . . " and at that very moment I realized I was actually planning for such a calamity to befall another human being. On a date, and at a time, perhaps at the precise minute that I would determine, he would die because of my will and my orders. For the sake of my position. And for the sake of the undisturbed sleep of His Excellency the governor-general, for the sake of His Excellency's angelic image.

"Jacques!" Paulette was stung. "What's wrong with you? Your thoughts are so frightening today. I think you must be overtired, darling. A few days ago, too, you really frightened me. Like just now. You said the death of a high official makes all his subordinates happy. Then you went silent rigid like wood. The look on your face was really terrifying."

"And you rejected what I said. You said that if the person who died was a good man, then he would be farewelled with respect and sadness. Those left behind don't always feel like that. The dead are dead, that's all."

"Jacques, Jacques, why do you have to bring all these dark thoughts home. Get rid of them before you get home!"

It had made me realize just what I was doing. She was right.

"You didn't have these terrible thoughts before, Jacques. You know that's why I was happy for you to bring me to the Indies. Lately you haven't been nice at all."

"Yes, perhaps I am too tired."

"I don't think that's the reason. It's not only because you're tired. Perhaps you would really prefer me to die first?"

Her question put me on the spot. My thoughts had been so full of viciousness lately. I almost responded: "Or perhaps you want me to die first?"

"It is not we who decide, Jacques. Whoever leaves first will leave behind the other saddened. Why must we discuss something over which we have no control?"

As the time to go to bed approached, the question of death increasingly disturbed my thoughts. Wherever I looked, I could see him slumping to the ground, I don't know where. And the Princess of Kasiruta, that respected woman, would be crying out for the husband she so much admired. Sprawled out on the ground he would be just like any other mortal. The woman held her husband in great esteem, and always encouraged him to take a strong stand. Perhaps they were suspicious of the recent calm they had experienced, coming as it did after the Princess had chased away Suurhof's gang with gunshots. It would be easy now to find ways to speed up Minke's and his family's destruction. But the shooting incident did reveal just how greatly that woman admired and honored her husband. And she wasn't wrong. A person like Minke was indeed worthy of being held in such great esteem, and not just by his own wife, but also by his fellow countrymen. He had begun to change the face of the Indies, he had called forth new forces, even to the extent that the governor-general himself was worried. Not everyone could do such a thing. And it was clear I could never do it. I did not even have the slightest ability to do such a thing. In accordance with what my intellect told me, I myself also sincerely honored him and respected him.

So, why should his fate be to fall victim to a gang of thugs? It was true too that his death would surely bring forth new leaders in his place, so could my plans for him be intellectually justified? Wouldn't it burden me for the rest of my life? Would there be accusations from my intellect as well as my conscience?

Minke must be removed some way besides murder. I needed another week to work out a new plan. No, no, I would not change my plans, because Suurhof knew what they were. But I would add another plan on top of that one. And this new idea truly stemmed from my own chaos. My resolve had been shaken once more and I had gone to jelly.

I sent Princess Kasiruta an anonymous letter just after her husband left Buitenzorg for Bandung. Her courage, her loyalty to her husband, must be able to save him from the actions of Robert Suurhof and his gang. And in that way Minke would not need to die. That fierce woman would kill Suurhof and his men without hesitation. She would be prepared to do anything to save her husband. With just a little provocation, she would take action without ever thinking of the later consequences. If Suurhof escaped the Princess and Minke was killed anyway, then I would think it had been God's will.

I completely understood that my plan and now these changes all stemmed from my own vacillating state of mind, the hesitation that flowed from wanting to safeguard my own position, to continue to enjoy myself in the name of position, career, and family. But on the other hand, I found it all hard to justify intellectually. And so it was that all this was turning me into a bandit, ignorant and without principles. How costly it was to enjoy such self-gratification and security. Other people had to be sold and sacrificed. I think everyone who thinks for themselves understands all about this question of personal gain. And I am not the only one who has been caught up in such matters.

On the day it was all to happen, I saw the Princess arrive at the place that I had told her about in my letter. She soon saw the people wearing the color of clothes that I had also mentioned. She calmly followed them, hiding her face behind a black umbrella. Police spies had informed me of where Minke was. I followed this man's every confident stride until he entered a street stall, and then I followed him inside.

Minke seemed suspicious. He was very vigilant and obviously wanted to get away from me as quickly as possible. He needed to move from where he was seated so he could better observe whatever I might do. As soon as he heard gunshots, he forgot about me altogether, and vanished from view.

Suurhof and his friends were all sprawled on the ground. And that is just what I imagined would happen. But there was a knife that had got one of Suurhof's men. I hadn't predicted this at all. And the police were also unable to find out who had stabbed him.

And to Donald Nicolson I spat these words: "The man you gave me was useless, no better than a village thug. He was shot. How could he have let that happen? Perhaps because he always reckoned there was no one better than him."

"And his prey got away again," he lamented.

It did give me some satisfaction to hear his laments. And it gave me even more satisfaction to know that I had got away with perhaps the first ever lie to him.

Minke's household was investigated. The investigations were concerned with the shooting of Suurhof, and Princess was the suspect. But she could prove her alibi—that she was home all that day. Piah, her servant, confirmed her alibi, as did several of their watchmen. An examination of her husband Minke's revolver did not discover any signs of use. The number of bullets accorded with the last report.

Suurhof did not die, though he would never be able to use his left arm again. His case would remain a mystery. And although the case was being pursued by the police, they would never make a public investigation. Frischboten would be able to expose their incompetence if they did. The chief commissioner and I were both of the same mind, although we never came to a spoken agreement. It would be best if Suurhof died. It would be best if he were escorted to hell while he was laid up in the hospital.

There were no reprimands from those above. We all hoped that this would wipe the case from everyone's memory. Suurhof would have to suffer the consequences of his outlaw actions. If he tried to drag my name into it, then perhaps I would have to get rid of him while he was in the hospital.

Meanwhile the graph with no explanatory note showed no new entries. My commander expressed the view that we could not continue these illegal actions. The police did not have enough experience and it was very difficult to find trustworthy men who were also clever enough to see it through. It seemed I was the only member of the police force who had been involved in this accursed work. And at any moment this work could turn upon me too. There were many ways indeed that I could be ruined.

I would not be ruined and, of course, did not want to be ruined by my colleagues. I would carry out my duties as best I could. I had a few more years during which I could rise even higher, obtain greater honors, a more substantial reputation, more money, for the sake of—what?

Perhaps Nicolson would be able to convince the government that a course of action outside the law could not or could not yet be carried out. I did not know what happened up there among those high above.

Then something happened that I never expected. I received orders to carry out the verdict of the Batavia prosecutor's office upon Minke, the editor of *Medan*—he was to be exiled to Ambon. My hand shook when I received these orders. I would have to confront face-to-face the man I was to ruin.

He retained his greatness. While I had lost all my principles, and turned into another person. I did not even recognize this new person as myself. He was a great man, he had started great work for his people. I was an insect without form, wrapped in a uniform with epaulets. What kind of life was this? But for the sake of position, and many other for-the-sake-ofs, I left for Buitenzorg. I took a platoon of police from the local station, and arrested him.

Minke remained calm as if nothing was happening. He didn't want to take anything with him. All he took was his papers. And Piah—*ya*, my God, that village girl, what a great heart she had! It seems it is not true that it is only in European history that we find people with great hearts. She was a mountain, I was a pebble! I was European educated, I had sat in the lecture halls of the world's greatest university, and yet I could not achieve the greatness of a domestic servant called Piah. She was capable of taking a stand. And I? What did I amount to—with my glamorous uniform and my heavy revolver hanging at my hip?

I was unable to hide the true character of my soul during the trip to Betawi with Minke. He remained mute the whole journey. He never stopped speaking, but without a voice, just through the look in his eyes and the changes in the look on his face. Every one and all of his unspoken words said one thing and one thing only. What kind of human being are you, Pangemanann, candidate chief commissioner?

I was ordered to share a cabin with him during the journey to Ambon. I had to stick with him wherever he went. I could not sleep during the day, and I had to wake up before him every morning. For five days he refused to say a word to me, no matter how nice a face I put on for him. I knew that I had lost all value in his eyes and in his heart. And yes, it was true, I had lost all value even for myself. Only a false arrogance enveloped my body. Without my uniform, without my gun, without signs of rank, without my position, it was clear that I was more contemptible than Piah. Yes, I admit this, with all the honesty in my heart.

It was a fact also that Minke was not the only person who had been exiled from Java to Ambon. Just a little while before, a prince had been exiled there also—a prince who had been brought up and educated in Europe, who grew up to be an adventurer, a fighter and creator of all kind of disturbances. He was the Prince Van Son. Minke was also an adventurer, but an adventurer in history. Prince Van Son was a different kind of adventurer, a street-gutter adventurer. They would meet in exile, an odd couple, perhaps bound to be in conflict, thrown together in one place. He was being treated as if he were a criminal. And I? It was I who was the criminal, who had planned his murder, so that all the determinations of the government, the governor-general and colonial authority could be implemented without disturbance. How rotten is life's drama!

And what wasn't rotten in colonial life? All the big fish ganged up together to be the wielders of power. All the little fish rotted, scattered about and spoiling the sea with their rottenness.

Look now, the assistant resident of Maluku in his white uniform is here to receive this disappointed exile and to tell me that my duties in regard to him are now finished.

I watched another official take over my duties, witnessed by the assistant resident. Laughing, he asked for my signature on his orders. Then he said to the new exile: "Welcome to my area, Meneer. I hope you will enjoy your stay in Ambon, Meneer," as if he were an invited guest.

Minke just nodded, not saying a word. He who had been so generous with his words in his newspaper was now being very sparing. This man who was used to people listening to him now had to listen to all the rules that colonial authority had decided to enforce upon him. This man whose writings were always read now had to read all the regulations that had been designed to restrict his freedom.

I went with them to escort him to his home in Benteng Street in Ambon town. Before returning to Betawi, I tried once more to say a few words to him, words that came straight from my heart. His lips and ears were closed to me. Someone as contemptible as I did not deserve to receive his attention. He kept his greatness even in defeat. His greatness was not in the slightest demeaned. Someone who was so resolute in the face of the loss of his freedom would surely be resolute in the loss of everything else that remained.

And I? It seems there was no other way for me—I would remain in my contemptible state. Yes, my God, isn't it amazing how position can change a person's soul like this . . . ?

It is said that as you approach half a century you begin to achieve full maturity and confidence in yourself. Your attitude toward life starts to stabilize, and your experiences of life have become rich. But not with me. As

I approached the half-century mark, I had grown weak and unprincipled instead. And worse still, I knew exactly the reasons and did not dare fight back.

This accursed situation began in a no less accursed event. It occurred about ten years ago, when I was forty. I was healthy, strong, played heavy sport every day, was simple, was humble, and held the highest rank in the police force of any Native—police inspector class 1. I believed in goodness and charity and I was prepared to dedicate my life to them, as a human being and as a policeman.

I knew that all my friends were envious of my good fortune as an official, as a husband and as a human being. Their envy of my rank was declared through slander and false reports. This made me very cautious in everything I did. I made sure I did not give anyone the opportunity to pull me down. I carried out every task I was given with great diligence. I believed in and carried out my work based on the teachings I brought with me from home, from school, from my environment, from my religion. That was the morality that I completely believed in. To wipe evil from the face of the earth, no matter how small, that was truly doing good.

My commander at that time, Commissioner Van Dam tot Dam, who was so proud of being a pure Dutchman, free of the taint of either English or Jewish blood, called me in and gave me an unusual task, to eliminate the remnants of the Si Pitung gang, a band of outlaws active around Cibinong, Cibarusa, and Cileungsi, all in the Betawi and Buitenzorg area.

I had moved from criminal investigation work behind a desk out into the field.

At that time, domestic security had been handed over to the police. The army was not involved anymore, except if they were requested. The big and small wars that were taking place outside Java were what brought a permanent police force into being. And I was among those who joined it from the very beginning.

And so it was that I left for the field with a force of almost sixty men from the Betawi and Buitenzorg police.

In the area where Si Pitung's men reigned, there was no more law or government. There was only terror, fear, murder, kidnapping, and violence. I roamed this no-man's-land fighting small battles with quick, hard, and merciless moves. The English, Chinese, and Dutch landlords and their families had fled from the area to Betawi or Buitenzorg.

I was able to break the resistance of the gang wherever I found them. They used sawed-off rifles, so that they were able to carry them without being noticed. They had also been able to defeat the plantation police from all the local plantations. This was something that made our work more difficult. Usually the landlords' plantation police were able to help us, although I knew that they were no better than terror gangs working to protect the landlords' interests.

Whenever we wanted to enter a village, a few shots in the air would empty the streets. Everyone would run off and hide. It was only the gang members who would not hide inside a house. They would seek cover behind clumps of bamboo. Once we understood this, it was easy to work out a way to defeat them. Every time we got rid of a member of the gang, I would praise the Heavenly Father, and give thanks that I had the opportunity to carry out His will. And then I would pray that my children would follow in the footsteps of their father.

Three hundred prisoners were proof of my success. It was true, though, that it was almost impossible to get much information out of them. While squatting, they just rocked back and forth or spat, inviting my men to crack them over the head with their rifles. I was not able to get much information at all, but the region around Cibinong, Citeureup, Cibarusa, and Cileungsi was secured. So although I was unable to obtain any meaningful information, there was no way that people could deny my success. I had broken the gang and secured the region with sixty men in two months.

It was easy to identify the leaders despite their silence. Whoever was not afraid of a threatening bayonet was certain to be one of their leaders, one of the village fighters who were often led by men who were considered invulnerable and who believed themselves to be invulnerable. Among the three hundred prisoners, there were eight invulnerables. Once these men had been taken away from the others, the remainder would begin to lose their courage and would begin to answer our questions. They were a mixture of Malays and Sundanese, with most of them from the latter group.

Each of the invulnerables had so many wives each, legal or otherwise. And it was these wives who eventually became the source of the best information. One of them was called Nyi Juju. When she was brought before me, I was startled into a reverie for a moment. She was big-bodied and neither her skin nor the shape of her face was that of a Native. She was obviously a first-generation Eurasian. The interrogation took place in a police post in Cibarusa.

"Juju, who are your parents?" I asked in Malay.

"Karta bin Dusun, Tuan, sir."

Karta bin Dusun could not be summoned. He had died in one of our raids. He was just an ordinary Native, like his wife Nyi Romlah.

I interrogated Nyi Romlah in another room. "Is it true that Juju is your daughter?" I asked.

"It's true, Tuan, sir."

"Is Nyi Juju your daughter with Karta or someone else?"

Romlah went pale for a moment. She started to behave strangely. I slammed the table with my cane; she shuddered. "Tell me everything. Anyone who gives me false information will be caned," I threatened her.

Romlah fainted, afraid to tell me the truth. She was afraid of me and of other forces that I did not yet understand. I went back into the room where Juju was waiting.

"Yes, you are the daughter of Romlah. But Karta bin Dusun is not your father. Your father was a Dutchman, wasn't he?" I asked gently.

"How would I know, Tuan? People say I am the daughter of Tuan Piton."

I knew that she meant Pinkerton, a relative of one of the Tanah Abang landowners, an Englishman, and a jockey who had won several horse races in Betawi.

Immediately Romlah regained consciousness after being splashed with water, I shouted at her: "Juju is your daughter with Tuan Piton, yes?" She was too afraid to answer.

"Don't be afraid of Piton. Answer me."

"It is true, Tuan. But it was against my will, Tuan."

"Good. Who else suffered the same as you at the hands of Piton?" I saw her pull the skin of her lips because of her fear. "Don't be afraid. Just tell me."

"Many, Tuan. Very many."

"How could it be so many?"

"The landlord's bodyguards fetched me and the others from our homes, and took us to Tuan Piton's house."

"Didn't your husband say anything?"

"Everyone was afraid, Tuan."

"Why didn't you report it to the village head or the police?"

"We were afraid, Tuan. And anyway, they would probably just be angry with us. That's what usually happens, Tuan."

"Did this happen to your daughter Juju, too? She was taken from your house by the Kelang criminal?"

"The same, Tuan, but she wasn't brought home."

I went back to Juju in the other room.

"Were you taken by Kelang as his wife with your agreement?"

"I was taken from my mother, Tuan."

"Be careful if you are lying."

"No, Tuan, I am not lying."

Twenty-one women, the wives of the gang leaders, all gave similar answers. Eleven of them had been properly married. It was clear that all these women were chosen for their beauty. Perhaps because of people like Pinkerton, Cibarusa had many attractive Eurasian girls, who were seldom known to the outside world. And they were bound then to fall victim to the Europeans on the plantations, their henchmen, or the outlaw gangs.

The interrogation of these women revealed that the Europeans and their henchmen had robbed people of their worldly goods, their honor, had extracted excessive taxes, beaten people up and murdered people. And none of this had been investigated by the authorities. These women's stories made my heart shrivel up. This gang that had grown under the protection of the charisma of Si Pitung turned out to be fighting against the arbitrary oppression by the local European and Chinese landowners and their agents.

The police should have taken action against these foreign landowners and their agents before Si Pitung's resistance emerged.

The reality was that I was a policeman who had smashed the attempts of village people to fight back against oppression.

I returned to Betawi with a brilliant victory over village people whose only desire was for a decent life. My success brought a heady sense of triumph for a field policeman. But it also brought a new awareness of the white politics that exploited the local people, and I went home a knotted spirit, not knowing what was right. In the meantime, fourteen people had died during the operations I led.

I prepared a comprehensive report, with the hope that I could transfer the responsibility and pangs of conscience to those in authority who had given me this task. But the forty-page report didn't give me any satisfaction either. My soul cried out for everything to return to what it had been before. I wanted once again to be someone with a clear conscience who always did God's will.

There was no reaction, no response. Except that Commissioner Van Dam tot Dam spoke to me in passing. He said that everyone was praising me for the success of my operation, that they were very happy with my report, and that even Europeans could rarely do what I had done. But the responsibility for the annihilation of that rebellion against oppression continued to burden my mind and soul. I felt that I had sinned.

To try to forget this burden, I attempted to study all the papers that had been written about Si Pitung. I couldn't get any rounded picture from these. All they talked about were his acts of violence against rich people. He was depicted as a vicious man, acting without reason, a barbarian who attacked villages with his big band of men, killing, stealing, burning, and torturing the tax collectors as if they were his personal enemies. He eliminated all those working for the government, no matter what their race. Then the remnants of his gang rose again and did the same. They rebelled for the same reason. And not one of them could explain why they were rebelling. They were unable to explain how they felt.

I began to see Pitung's face everywhere. There was a sparse beard and mustache, and smooth skin the color of the langsat fruit. He wasn't tall, more of a stocky build. According to the reports I read, he always wore white robes when he attacked, and a turban, and to his left and right he was escorted by two aides, carrying a betel-leaf box and his weapon. That picture left a strong impression on me and would not go away. It started to follow me as if it were my own shadow.

I knew that my nerves were under a great strain.

During the ceremony appointing me adjutant commissioner I was almost unable to stop myself from trying to shoo that image of Pitung away with my hands. I could feel his sparse mustache brushing up against my neck, as if he was there whispering, mocking me: Death for us, promotion for you, heh, Tuan Pangemanann?

I was now the adjutant commissioner. There were thousands of Europeans and Eurasians, let alone Natives, who would never savor a rank as high as this. Now even the Harmoni Club was open to me. My character was swept away by this rank and by the law that also made me equal to a Dutchman. With or without my uniform, the Harmoni management would have to let me enter, even though I would still suffer their angry glances. I was now officially a member of the club and they who caused me to be born on this earth would never have guessed that I would reach a rank that was allowed only to Europeans.

I knew for sure that Si Pitung never strode up the stairs into the Harmoni Club, though I knew he used to operate nearby when he was young, around the Harmoni Bridge and the land owned by the landlord Alaydrus. But almost every time I came to the club, there he was, standing on the corner, in his robes and turban, raising his hand and greeting me: "Greetings, Tuan Pangemanann, are you well today?" I was the only one who could see him. . . .

Ziihhh, I hissed, chasing away the image of that devil. And only then would he disappear. I never told my wife about this nervous problem I had developed. And it was not possible for me to go to a psychiatrist. There was not a single one in the Indies.

So my promotion to adjutant commissioner was accompanied by my new habit of hissing *Ziihhh* to get rid of my vision of Si Pitung. On top of this, every time I received a visit from one of the landowners who wanted to thank me, I suffered an attack of high blood pressure, often becoming extremely irritated. They all tried to thank me in their own way, rarely coming with empty hands. They always brought something, either for my wife or for the children. They were thanking me because now they could continue to oppress the Natives again without disturbance.

Then there was another explosion of unrest in the hamlets of Lemah Abang and Tambun. This was another people's rebellion against the power of the English and Chinese landowners. Then there was trouble on the Pemanukan en Tjiasem Landen plantation, a private estate in Pemanukan and Ciasem. All the rebellions took the same form as Si Pitung's. Each time a rebellion occurred it was I who was given the task of getting together a combined force of police and suppressing the revolt. The nature of my work changed from routine police work to something that was virtually military work. I used the same methods as those I used against the remnants of Si Pitung's gang.

Another one of history's ironies—Governor-General Daendels had built up defenses right around Java in order to keep the English army out of the Indies, and out of Java in particular. And so the military road between Anyer and Banyuwangi was built. Finding his administration facing bankruptcy, he sold government land to a number of private owners. But the English still invaded. And so the Indies had a new governor-general, namely Thomas Raffles. He too fell into the gully of insufficient finances. He followed in the footsteps of Daendels and sold more land to wealthy Englishmen and Chinese. Private estates became strung out across the north coast of Java. And almost one century later Adjutant Commissioner Pangemanann had to solve the unrest that was the heritage of these two men.

Neither of them would ever know Pangemanann with two *n*s. They would never know how he had to bow down, with his tortured conscience, becoming, against his will, a man without principles. He had become a kind of servant cleaning up their mess. The ethical face of Europe must not be sullied, and so it was that I was obliged and was permitted to use even the dirtiest methods.

I knew with certainty that I was being manipulated by supernatural phantoms of almost one hundred years ago, by supernatural spirits that I could not feel, whom I could only get to know from files on nice white sheets of paper and from the filth that was their legacy to colonial life, the life of my own times.

To whom could I take my grievances? In my era the power that is always victorious is colonial power. Everything that is not a part of colonial authority is its enemy. I myself was an instrument of colonialism. The great teachers beautifully taught about the enlightenment of the world that would be brought by the Renaissance, the *Aufklärung*, about the awakening of humanism, about the overthrow of one class by another that was begun with the French Revolution when the feudal class was removed by the bourgeoisie. They called on people to side with the progressive march of history. And meanwhile, I was sinking into the disgusting colonial mud.

And before I had a chance to put some order into my confused and topsy-turvy psyche, another disturbance occurred in the English private estate in Curuk. The leader was Bang Komeng. Once again they sent me. With a small unit of Betawi police, I suppressed these rebels, my will overwhelmed by the turmoil in my conscience. They were only a very small group, much smaller than the remnants of Si Pitung's men. Within just three days I had cleaned up two areas. All that was left to do was make some arrests in Balaraja, Cengkareng, Tanggerang, Banten, and Serang.

My successes meant that I was greeted with flattery whenever I arrived at the Harmoni Club, even after their amazement at hearing me hiss *ziiihh*. They just gossiped among themselves that this strange habit of mine was a result of my having killed too many people with the usual Asian viciousness and Inlander's barbarism. And it is indeed probable that had I been a European I would have ordered other people to carry out such work. But I was a Native who was caught up in a European position, who built a fortress around myself through service and dedication so that I would not lose all I had because of the colonial intrigues that could easily descend to depths of contemptibility yet unknown to humanity.

My superiors and their superiors did not just respect my success in the field. They were even more impressed with my written reports that used a combination of interrogation and interview, social research and historical background. I was able to explain the mentality of the people who lived in the estates and how it manifested itself in their actions.

In just seven years I made great leaps upward. I was made a commissioner and no longer had to carry out field assignments or handle criminal cases. It was my wife who, of course, was the happiest of all. Her husband no longer had to risk his life in the field and now received a salary equal to that of European officials. And to a certain extent, I too was grateful that I would no longer be given the task of annihilating these outlaws. At the very least, I thought, I would have a chance to repair my image of myself. Once again I could be an educated man, who hated evil and loved good.

A month after sitting at my new desk, I received an order from Van Dam tot Dam to make an analysis of the different kinds of groups causing disturbances, categorizing them according to their different attitudes toward the government. I won't burden you here with that paper. What it did mean from then on, however, was that I now dealt with Chief Commissioner De Beer.

One afternoon he invited me to come along with him to that famous club. *Ziihhh*, and the image of Si Pitung evaporated, chased away from those very long steps in front of the building. Inside we did not find anyone playing billiards, darts, or cards, or even sitting gossiping to each other. They were all sitting around a European. All I could see was the bald top of his head and a few strands of yellow hair that formed side-whiskers.

Without having to see the rest of him, anyone could tell it was Meneer K—, an intellectual and lawyer who was much respected by all the leading colonial figures. He was considered the most brilliant of colonial theorists. His name was often headlined in the press. He had never written anything himself. Perhaps he didn't know how. People could not look him in the eyes, while his voice made them crane forward to listen. He was always at the center of the attention of the colony's elite. People waited upon his every word. He spent more time in Europe than in the Indies. It was reported that the last three governor-generals all needed to hear his advice and his views.

The electric chandelier hanging above, with its fifteen or so bulbs all glaring, made his head reflect light in waves in rhythm with the movements of his head. A wicked caricaturist might not be able to contain his wickedness and would have to draw this rather uncommon sight.

It seemed it had been a long time since the Harmoni Club had held a poetry reading or lecture or a concert. Cultural life was very barren in the Indies. And so the hearts of the people in the Indies were also barren. And of course there was no opera, no ballet. Even small ensemble concerts were usually available only when there was a group traveling from Europe to Australia.

Meneer De Beer and I said good afternoon, drew up chairs, and sat down.

It was pouring rain outside. The atmosphere in the club became murky and cold. It wasn't as pleasant as it usually was. A cold wind swept inside along with a soft mist. And none of the guests was wearing warm clothes. There were no stories of scandals, which were the traditional fare at the club. There were just the same old stories of intrigue, but with changing players.

It had been stormy all day. It continued on into the night. I could see the carriages in the distance looking for places to shelter their horses out of the rain. The only way to get home was to order a taxi over the telephone. But taxis were very expensive in the evening. And it had become a Dutch tradition that to squander money was a sin.

However, the discussion began to get interesting. Meneer Lawyer K— answered every question openly. He spoke in a deep voice like a growling bear. Then I heard those words that I would never forget all my life.

"You must all pay more attention, gentlemen. If not . . . we could have a second Philippines here in this pearl of a colony of ours. We could be kicked out. Another one of the Western countries will come in, perhaps America, perhaps Germany, or perhaps even England. Or perhaps none of them."

"What do you mean by a second Philippines?" one of the others asked.

"A second Philippines! It's very sad indeed to think that you gentlemen do not understand the case of the Philippines. It seems that none of you pays any attention to colonial developments outside the Indies. That is very bad, gentlemen. Colonial affairs in Asia are all interconnected, like links in a chain."

Everyone was silent, not trying to break through the wall of silence from Meneer K—. And this distinguished gentleman did not say another word until the rain eased.

It had become an almost religious belief in the colony that the Dutch would control these islands until the day of judgment. The French and English had been able to dislodge the Dutch in the past. But the fact that the Dutch retrieved the colony later only served to reinforce the belief.

Even when the rain had turned to drizzle, Meneer K— remained silent. Indeed, it was he who was first to stand, nod his bald head, say good night, and then lead the way out. The others followed his example. De Beer too. And I as well.

As soon as I reached the second tier down the very long steps of the Harmoni Club, that accursed vision of Pitung spoke to me again: "Going home, Tuan Pangemanann? Is there important work for you to do, Tuan?"

I tried to challenge him.

But he spoke again. "Ayoh, I'll join you."

Startled, I hurriedly sprayed my hiss of *Ziihhh*. It was very embarrassing to see everyone turn and look at me. I suppressed my awkwardness and hurried off in the other direction. I had forgotten all about De Beer.

All the way home through the drizzle, cold and mud, I could not escape either Meneer K—'s words or the vision of Pitung. Why were the distinguished intellectuals and Pitung's vision following on each other inside me like a pair of Manila ducks? Why even after half a dozen years was my conscience still disturbing me through these visions of Pitung? Did I still have a conscience and did I still long for it to be clear? And what would the Indies be like without the Dutch? Everything would be turned upside down in this colonial world—people, ideas, and also I myself. Nothing would be spared. And the Pitungs, in who knows how many hundreds or thousands, would be running about seeking their revenge.

The filthy street mud started to soak into my socks. I knew that it was not healthy, mud mixed with the waste of all Betawi.

It was now normal for me to arrive home late so my wife was not surprised.

"So cold like this and damp and wet, darling," she cried in French, so full of love, after she opened the door. She kissed me lovingly, as if she had been without her husband and missing him for ten years. Then she went on in French, because that was our family's language of intimacy: "Come on, get your shoes and socks off quickly. Didn't you wear galoshes?"

I took off my shoes outside the door. The servant would clean them tomorrow. My wife would be furious if I wore such dirty shoes into the house. I entered the house barefoot, no shoes, no socks. She began to pour some hot water from a thermos into a washbasin, which she put under the chair where I sat. I did everything she asked. I sat down in the chair after I changed clothes, and soaked my feet in the basin. But my thoughts were harking back to the words of Meneer K—. Was what he said true? He held such an important position in the colonial world today, so what he said must be correct. I could be wrong. But such an important colonial figure could not be wrong. The genius of such people was the guarantee of the Dutchman's eternal hold over these islands.

These words of Meneer K—, which had set my mind in motion, had implications for my work. The Indies could become a second Philippines, he said. We could be kicked out!

If I was not mistaken, Meneer K— was reminding us of how the educated Filipinos revolted against the Spanish colonizers, inviting the Americans to enter the Philippines, where they now sat as the new colonizers. The Dutch did not want to experience the same fate as the Spanish.

His words were like a torch for me. Beware, Pangemanann, of the educated Natives of the Indies. They too could do what the educated natives of the Philippines did—invite in another colonial power to help them because of their own lack of experience.

Pitung resumed his disruption of my thoughts, even more intensely than before. He too had rebelled in his own way. He was not an educated person, he was not capable of explaining his reasoning and his desires. He ran amok like a wild buffalo. Ah, it was so easy to defeat you, Pitung.

Ziihhh.

"What is it, Jacques?"

"Nothing, it's just cold, that's all."

"Will I get some whiskey?"

"A very good idea, thank you."

She moved smoothly across the room to the drinks cabinet and brought me back a tumbler of whiskey. I grabbed the tumbler and gulped it all down.

"No, one is enough. Come on, off to bed now. It's almost morning."

I stepped out of the washbasin full of hot water.

"No, the children are all right. They're big enough to look after themselves," and she turned off the lights.

Under the sheets, Madame Pangemanann embraced me and asked: "Why are you always saying *ziihhh*? It scares me."

"You ask the strangest things, my darling. Good night."

Soon afterward, she fell asleep.

And still Meneer K——'s words vexed my consciousness. The educated Natives!

They would become the eternal enemies of the power of the Netherlands Indies! Colonialism was jealous of the educated Natives! It was no coincidence that the government made education as difficult as possible for the Natives to obtain. Knowledge and learning could take simple and primitive people to a world where their ambitions could no longer be measured only in meters. So it was logical, wasn't it, that every educated Native was indoctrinated to be loyal to the government? It was no wonder they were so spoiled, with good wages, good status, and all sorts of no less unworthy honors.

Meneer K——'s warning had another meaning. This situation would not last forever. Sooner or later there would emerge an educated Native with strange ideals. He, or they, would not be like Pitung who knew only what he experienced in his own life. Pitung had no broader vision and so could do nothing else but evil. And evil in the end brought him new enemies. But what about educated Pitungs who refused to become the paid workers of the government, who wielded the same weapons as the government, who did not need do evil to earn a living? And who would it be that would rise before me as the first educated Pitung—a modern Pitung?

Ziihhh! Ziihhh! It was the old Pitung whom I saw once again, in flowing white robes, guarded on either side by one of his men, one carrying his betel box, the other his rifle.

I felt my wife hug my neck. She whispered: "Jacques. You frighten me with all your *ziihhh, ziihhh*. You must go to the doctor tomorrow. You're exhausted. Sleep. Do you want me to fetch some sleeping medicine?"

"Yes, we'll go to the doctor tomorrow."

"You're so cold and your body is bathed in sweat, Jacques."

She did not know that there was something gnashing and eating away at me inside. . . .

My education did not condone hypocrisy. I believed in goodness, as I had been taught when I was small. I always thought that I had found my place in life as an officer of the law. My conscience started accusing me only after the affair with the Pitung gang. I had thought this over several times. It was Pitung who was the cause of it all. I could not lie to my inner self. Pitung was not an evil person. It was his social and economic situation that forced him into crime. He remained a man who fought back against the power of the white and yellow landlords, who were given protection by the government over and above the Natives. And now came Meneer K— bearing omens that the next challenge I would have to face was the educated Natives.

"You'll have time to think about things tomorrow, Jacques," my wife chided me in a sleepy voice.

"Yes, there'll be time tomorrow."

And my wife did not sleep again that morning. She lay awake keeping her husband company, as he fought with his restless heart. She was an amazing woman. She always wanted to be with her husband, whether in good times or bad. And it was because of her love and her faithfulness that I was sinking further and further into this work that went so much against my conscience. I wanted to give her the best I could. I had to, it was a moral duty. I had wrenched her away from her country and her family just outside Lyons, in France. She was pretty and young, a peasant girl who knew nothing of the world. We met, we were both still very young, and we fell in love. We married in an old village church, witnessed by her parents, who did not agree with the marriage. She had accompanied me to foreign countries—first the Netherlands, then to the Indies. She had given me four children. Two were continuing their education in the Netherlands.

The other two were still with us. One was called Marquis, but we shortened it to Mark, and the other Desirée, which means "she who is longed for." We called her Dede.

Our life was beautiful. We were happy. Such happiness could not be bought with money. And the two children who were studying in the Netherlands, one in HBS and the other in the geology faculty, promised an even more beautiful future. It was worth paying out the seventy-five guilders a month for them. Mark and Dede were also good children, obedient and clever. And it was all because of their mother who loved them and cared for them.

But the reality of life was different. Times changed. The times forced me to change. To pay for all this happiness I had to forget all the beautiful teachings I believed in, and all the values I held. Since I was small, I was happy when people said I was a good child who knew how to perform a good deed. One time I felt so happy when I heard an old man, a neighbor, say these words: "How happy must his parents be, to have such a good boy, so kind, who behaves so nicely."

It was such praise that guided me through life. Yes, perhaps my parents were happy to have a child like me. It is a pity I never knew them; I was an orphan, adopted by my father's younger brother, Frederick Pangemanan. Just as I was about to finish ELS in Menado, I was taken as the foster child of Meneer De Cagnie, a Frenchman, an apothecary. This couple liked me very much. They had no children. And so it happened that I was taken home by them to Lyons, where they owned an apothecary shop and small medicine factory.

My life was as straight as a piece of wire pulled taut, without twists and turns. It was only since my battle with Pitung's men that the wire had never been straight again. And now it was not just bent, but tangled. And I could not see how I could unravel the tangle. Every day I felt my throat in the tighter and tighter grip of an outside power, namely, position.

The next day I went with Paulette to the doctor, who gave me one week's sick leave. And it was impossible for me to cope with having nothing to do for a week. The words of Meneer K— kept shoving me along toward the new work that I knew I would have to face soon. I would have to destroy people of the caliber of Bonifacio and Rizal of the Philippines.

The national consciousness of the educated Native was not yet as developed as in the Philippines. Even so, I would now have to be on the lookout, like looking for a needle in a pile of paddy stalks. The needle must be found, even the paddy stalks had to be destroyed. All this even though it was a small piece of pure steel, without the rust of evil, except for that speck of idealism, that history of love of people and country, that seed of patriotism and nationalism whose final flowering could not yet be clearly seen. And you must be careful that you are not pricked by that needle yourself. For the government, and I as its instrument, must, however, look upon any such idealism as criminal. But why does my conscience keep needling me? Neither civilized humanity nor my own soul could deny that this idealism was their right, something to be exalted, representing values that raised high the dignity of humankind. And I and my family depended on my work, which was to destroy all this. I had become a paid destroyer. Now in my middle age, I did not have the strength to say no.

As time went on I became more and more convinced that my superiors had deliberately put me in this unhappy position. And there was nowhere I could take my grievances, not even to a priest.

My promotion, as a Native, from inspector to adjutant commissioner and then commissioner, made my colleagues not only unhappy but also

...ous. As a prisoner among all these Protestants, I felt isolated. My new ...k made it very difficult for me to mix with them. Relations got worse and worse. I became a peacock among jungle chickens. Wherever I went and wherever I was, they were always watching me closely, ready to note my every mistake. So I was forced to live as vigilantly and carefully as I could.

After the Aceh War there did seem to be an improvement in the way Catholics were treated inside the Netherlands Indies army. They had begun to demand equal treatment with Protestants. In war, death and injury do not distinguish between Catholics and Protestants. They succeeded in their demands. Catholics were no longer discriminated against in the matter of promotions. There were signs that it had been decided that Catholics would get a quota of promotions in the army and that there would be a quota for Protestants in the navy. But in the police force I was still a peacock among jungle chickens. There was no system of quotas as in the other services. Here in the police force, I was not just a peacock, but also a guinea pig, a Catholic and a Native who had been given equal status as a European.

And so it was that the police had become both my life and my prison. I was a policeman and, at the same time, the prisoner of the police. It was as if I no longer had a will of my own, as if I had become blind to all the teachings about what was right, no longer faithful to what I was taught by Monsieur De Cagnie and his wife, by Uncle and Aunt Pangemanan.

I had read many books in Europe and I had gained much knowledge about the liberation of men from oppression—spiritual and physical, economic and political. So I fully understood that colonial rule over any part of the world was evil. I was disgusted by the work I had been doing ever since I was promoted to adjutant commissioner. I felt as if I had been robbed of all my dignity in order that I could feed my family.

All that I had been imagining and had been afraid of became reality. On my first day back at work, Meneer De Beer greeted me with the words: "Meneer Pangemanann, you look very well now. There is some new work awaiting you."

"Another special assignment?"

"Correct, Meneer."

The instructions I received were exactly as I imagined after I heard Meneer K— speak at the Harmoni Club. My new assignment was to study the writings of the Natives that were being published in the newspapers and magazines. Analyze them. Interview the authors. Compare them. And make some conclusions about their caliber, the direction of their thinking, and their attitude toward the government of the Netherlands Indies.

The police had never done this kind of work before. And the first person to receive the honor of carrying out such an assignment was me—Commissioner Pangemanann. From that day I became a painter who would show to the government the true colors of these writers. My work was not done for the sake of furthering knowledge, but so that the government might forever perpetuate its rule.

According to the colonial Europeans, everything that is done by the white race for the colonized people is superior to that which the Native rulers had previously done for them. Everything that is done to the colonized people is motivated by the whites' sacred duty to civilize them. How great was this sacred duty! At one moment it was the banner under which any and all actions could be justified. The next moment, it became an opiate putting their consciences to sleep. And what about me? I, whose soul had already been penetrated by humanism, either through the church or otherwise, could not accept this, yet here I was being dragged into carrying out such things as an instrument of colonial power.

There was only one way for me to protect myself now—to be two-faced and to consciously entertain different emotions at once. After growing used to cultivating so many different and opposing feelings and appearances, my soul also grew strong enough to create a new Pangemanann. But I always longed for the old Pangemanann, who was honest, who was simple, who believed in the goodness of humankind. And no one knew better than I that sometimes you could not keep it up, living such a divided and splintered spiritual life as this, without giving in to battles within yourself, fighting back and forward, destroying your different selves, each part of you humiliating the other. All this mixed together to make a great, tumultuous battlefield. But both sides must win! They must! One is called principles, the other livelihood.

Madame Paulette Pangemanann and children, André, Henri, Mark, and Dede—perhaps you see me as a husband, a father, and an official who is strong, reliable, and successful. Yes, I hope you will always see me in that light. A husband and father who loved you, and an official who could always be trusted to do his duty. But I will not have been fair to you if one day, when I am gone, you lose this respect and sense of pride because of my playacting.

This must not happen. So I have decided to write all this so you will know, my wife, so you will all know exactly who was this person Pangemanann. He was not as good as you all think. Perhaps he was in fact the opposite, totally the opposite. And you, my children, do not copy your father's example, a slave of his livelihood who lost all his principles. You all know that in European civilization a person without principles is the most contemptible of all people, human scum. Do not follow my example.

Look upon your father as a personality who was destroyed completely, a defeated person, a slave. Be instead a person pure of heart, principled, with integrity. These are the ideals of European civilization. Be people who are free of pretensions and ambition. Be civilized people. Forgive your father for being incapable of providing you with the kind of example, the best of examples, as was his wish.

You must never speak well of me in front of your own children. This would go against all that is good and honorable, even though my failure as a human being was because of my dedication to your interests. Look upon me as a representative of a defeated generation of Natives, defeated by colonial force and power.

I began this project at the age of fifty. I think that being half a century old means that I am now able to evaluate all that has passed, which I have experienced and witnessed. It is right and proper that educated people, when they reach such an age, look back and make a judgment on what they have done, the good and the evil, the right and the wrong.

It would not be right to leave this world silently, pretending to be good and pure before my own wife and children! I want my children to succeed, to be far better than I, to be better people, to do more good, and to be wiser. My first evaluation of my life during the last half century is clear—from when I was little up until I became a police inspector, I walked along a path that was in accord with God's will. From the time I became an adjutant commissioner until now, when I am full commissioner, there is no doubt that I have been walking in mud. As time goes on I walk farther and farther into this field of mud, and farther and farther away from God's path.

It is you, my children, who must judge me. You will know everything about me and about the whole of the Indies, the country where I was born and worked as a servant of the government for the sake of a living and the pleasures of life. Perhaps it would be more honest if I said it was the place where I became coated in mud.

Isn't it all clear? Whether as an inspector or as commissioner, my work has been nothing other than to monitor closely my own people for the sake of the security and perpetuity of the government. All Natives, especially the modern Pitungs who so disturbed the peace and serenity of the government—yes, I have and will continue to put all of them into a house of glass which I will place on my desk. I will be able to see everything. That is my assignment—to watch every movement that takes place in that house of glass. That is also what the governor-general wants. The Indies must not change. It must be maintained as it is forever. So if I am able to preserve this writing of mine and it comes into your hands, I would like you to give these notes of mine the title *House of Glass*.

3

Then one day I received new orders. These were also in accord with the work program that I myself had prepared and that had been approved by my boss. So at nine o'clock the next morning I arrived at the State archives building with a letter of introduction from the General Secretariat of the governor-general.

I myself had no idea why my letter of introduction came from the Algemeene Secretariat, headquartered in Buitenzorg, and not from the police office in Betawi. It was a puzzle to me just why such a high office had involved itself in my work, though it did mean that all the archives officials jumped from their chairs to look after me. The Algemeene Secretariat was just one step away from His Excellency the governor-general. A few people held the view that power had moved out of his hands when the Indies Council was established. The reality was different. The *Raad van Indie* or Indies Council was nothing more than an advisory council to the governor-general. The Algemeene Secretariat continued the work of implementing the government's policies.

As soon as he saw the letter of introduction, the relevant official came rushing out of his office and greeted me. He stared at me skeptically. How could I have obtained such a letter? After all, such a letter amounted to nothing less than a direct commission from the Algemeene Secretariat. He quickly changed his attitude and said politely: "Ah, Meneer Pangemanann. What is it that I can supply you with, Meneer?"

He was a Pure-Blood Dutchman, young, an archivist not well known to the public, called Meneer L—. He liked to wear a lorgnette with a thin gold chain. He wore a white cotton shirt with a buttoned-up collar. He also wore white cotton trousers. He had blond hair, parted in the middle. He wore black shoes and was quite tall and solid.

"At this stage, Meneer," I said, after introducing myself, "I want to study whatever documents you have about the Philippines."

"Ah, an important question," he said, responding. "Hardly anybody is paying it any attention here. But, Meneer, I will need several days to gather all the material together. Are you after any documents in particular?"

"Everything there is."

"Everything? Yes, well, that will be easier. Our archives are not as well organized as in America, Meneer. If you had wanted specific documents it would have been quite difficult. Could you come back, in, say, three days' time?"

I returned exactly three days later. The front grounds that stretched a long way in from the street, the green lawns on either side of the pathway up to the main building, and the red-painted main building itself, all reminded me of the palaces of the landed nobility in the French countryside. It was said that three governors-general had used this building as their palace. I am not sure who they were—De Eerens maybe, or Van Hogendorp or Rochussen. I didn't know for sure. The path leading to the main entrance was also flanked by two rows of pine trees. I had heard that they were planted after the building was no longer used as the palace.

Meneer L— met me in the pendopo, which had, in its day, been used for receptions. And people had danced to the music of the waltz there too. But now it was silent. There was just a guard, who also received any guests, and Meneer L—.

I was taken straight inside, into a big room that was even quieter, where the air was damp and it was cooler.

"Ah, here is your table, Meneer." He left me and returned a few moments later with an attendant carrying a pile of papers. "All that you need should be among these, Meneer. If you need anything, then just tell Meneer De Man here," nodding toward the attendant: "Meneer De Man, this is Meneer Pangemanann. Please look after him properly. Good luck with your work, Meneer Pangemanann."

"But, Meneer L—," I interrupted his departure, "must I read everything here? Can't I borrow them?"

"No, Meneer. These documents must not leave this building. I'm sorry. You will have to study them all here."

He nodded, excusing himself, and disappeared into another room.

And I was not allowed to touch the almost twenty-centimeter-tall pile of documents until I signed the receipt of loan that De Man put in front of me. After I had signed it and he had put the receipt away, he removed himself to the corner of the room. I felt as if I were under the observation of some petty clerk.

His ever-vigilant eyes, guarding that not a single sheet of paper disappeared into my pocket, made the atmosphere in that still and silent room increasingly distracting. The great high ceilings and all the furniture from the days of the Company, the large windows as big as doors, with the wind blowing freely in and out, with nobody there except De Man and me, all reminded me of a mausoleum. I myself began to feel a part of the mausoleum, as old as all of its furniture.

The indistinct echoes of the traffic from the main road outside made their way into the room and bounced around from wall to wall, sounding like the never-ending rumbling of the earth underneath. While the papers that lay before me represented a past full of secrets, the building itself represented the ghosts of the past. The hairs on the back of my neck stood on end.

De Man sat motionless in the corner. It was only his eyes that never rested from watching me and the pile of papers before me.

I would never have come here if I hadn't been instructed to do so.

The papers, following the practice now of who knows how many archivists, were divided into groups according to issues: crime, immigration, the instructions of the various governors-general . . . but there was no separate section on the Philippines, let alone about Bonifacio or Rizal. There was one document, an instruction from Governor-General Sloet van de Boele, that really startled me. It was not the original, just a copy. It ordered the government's boats patrolling the Indies waters to watch out for American pirates who worked out of a small Philippines island. These pirates were kidnapping young men from the North Celebes coast to be sold as laborers to the mines of South America. They were replacing the Chinese labor that the pirates could no longer get from the Chinese coast. The order was dated 1864, when my older brother, whom I never met, was still alive.

I was reminded of the old peoples' stories of white pirates who captured the fishermen out in the sea. The fishermen never returned to their villages. Nobody knew where they were taken. From that time on, every fisherman would set off in his boat as soon as he saw a big ship approaching.

But I had never imagined that those pirates might be Americans. And if, say, those Menadonese did not die during the trip like so many Negroes did during the previous century, and did not die from the hard labor in the mines, then they probably multiplied their numbers with the local people. And they would no longer be recognized as Menadonese but Chinese.

The revolts of my own people in North Celebes, the Menadonese, against the Spanish were not of interest to me, not at this time anyway. I was after more recent information about the revolts of the native Filipinos themselves. Most of the documents were written in the old spelling. Some were written in Spanish so that I had to work through them very slowly. There were no notes to indicate where the Spanish-language documents came from. This did not make my work any easier.

Five hours later I asked De Man if he could get me a drink. He did not move from his chair where he kept watch on the papers before me, but called another attendant. And it was this other man who brought me my glass of warm milk.

"Meneer De Man." I summoned him, and he came over to me. "It's very difficult to work like this. Perhaps I could hire a scribe to make copies of the documents I need?"

"Unfortunately, that is not possible, Meneer."

"In that case, please take these documents back. I will come again tomorrow."

"You don't seem well, Meneer."

He was right. Enveloped in this very disagreeable atmosphere, I was beginning to feel dizzy.

He began to check the papers against the list of material I had borrowed. There was no change in the number of papers.

"You may return tomorrow, Meneer."

I left that cemetery of the past with a sense of relief. As I climbed up into my carriage, I couldn't help glancing back. The reddish-colored building did indeed look beautiful and imposing from afar. It used to receive all the important people in the colony. Now only gravediggers visited there, and I was one of them.

The next day Meneer L— visited me where I worked in the archives building.

"I have been checking if there are any other papers that might be of interest to you, Meneer," he said. "I have four people working on it now. But no results so far, Meneer. We haven't worked out a way to organize the archives properly. Just imagine, Meneer, seven kilometers of documents! Most of them have not been touched by human hands since they were deposited here. There are no schools to train archivists. Everything is worked out as we go, trial and error, using just ordinary clerks. No money has ever been made available for us to go to see how other more advanced archives are organized."

I listened to his complaints and gripes. It was easy to guess that he thought my letter of introduction had originated with an instruction from the governor-general. He was hoping that his complaints would reach Idenburg's ears. A vain hope, Meneer, I answered to myself, as I smiled compassionately. The bureaucracy in the Indies was as rotten as colonial power itself.

"And what makes things worse," he spoke again, "is that much of our material is stored in Buitenzorg."

"Oh, up in Buitenzorg?" I responded, humoring him politely.

"But they don't receive guests there. It is just a warehouse. If we don't train some people to be expert in this soon, then perhaps we will be left with just a pile of paper that will give us very little benefit."

"I can understand," I said.

"It seems you will be coming here often. I hope you will forgive us if we are not able to find what you want quickly. That is why I have told you about our difficulties. Seven kilometers of closely packed papers."

"Yes, I can understand how difficult it must be."

"Thank you for your understanding," and he nodded happily. "I will not disturb you any longer. I hope your work goes well."

As soon as he left De Man added: "You are the only guest that has ever come here with a mandate from the Algemeene Secretariat. Meneer L— has great hopes that you will understand our difficulties. We will all be grateful if Meneer is able to help us solve some of these difficulties."

He returned to where he was sitting yesterday and I threw myself into my reading. I did not need a lot of documentary material. What I had been given was sufficient to give me a handle on things. A lot of what I read made it seem that the neighboring country of the Philippines was located far away, up near the North Pole. I discovered a document from the period of Governor-General Van Der Wijck, dated 1898, which ordered that there be no public reporting on the rebellion in the Philippines.

And there were no other papers that showed whether the instruction was implemented or how it might have been implemented.

There was also another document from the period of Van Der Wijck's successor, Rosenboom, in the form of a recommendation from the Algemeene Secretariat concerning English intentions about Aceh. The note recommended that as the Aceh war came to an end, everything should be done to prevent the English from talking with the Acehnese with the ultimate aim of taking over Aceh. The note suggested that racial solidarity from the English-speaking peoples, both English and American, could not be relied upon. The American pressure on the Spanish over the Philippines might make the English nervous and encourage them to make inroads in Aceh. England had given considerable assistance to Aceh, in the form of arms and advice, both directly and through hints and signs.

It wasn't too hard to understand the English policy because the Netherlands Indies had violated the 1824 London Treaty. This treaty stated that Aceh would be treated in the same way as Siam, as a buffer state between two colonial neighbors. The provisions of this secret treaty were not adhered to. The Junghunn Expedition in Central and North Sumatra found signs that one of the reasons for the Natives' resistance was the supply of guns from Singapore and the Peninsula.

The 1871 Treaty resolved the problems between Holland and England. The two colonial powers made peace by agreeing to divide up their colonial spoils. Holland was free to act in Aceh, and England was free to act in Siam and all its occupied areas with the same rights as the Dutch businesses. The Netherlands Indies had ended England's earlier dealings with Aceh by waging war against the Acehnese. Although the Acehnese resistance was no longer militarily significant, the rebellion in the Philippines might embolden the British to resume their support for Aceh. In assessing the situation in Aceh, it was important not to forget the United States' role in the Philippines.

I felt that I had discovered among all these papers the key to the problem that had been mentioned by Meneer K—, the important colonial figure, in the Harmoni Club. It was like this. Dutch colonialism was worried and suspicious of British and American colonialism. The Dutch were worried that the others might help the educated Natives in the Indies organize a revolt, then swallow up the Indies for themselves, either in part or whole, just as the Dutch themselves did to the North Celebes when the people there revolted against the Spanish.

But there was an important reason why there could be no revolt by the educated Natives of the Indies. There were no higher educational institutions in the Indies. The only exception was perhaps the STOVIA-medical school. I made a special study of the STOVIA. After all, most of those promoting the awakening of Asia were doctors, and not lawyers as was the case in Europe. Perhaps the movements for enlightenment in Europe were motivated by the violation of people's sense of justice. In Asia the awakening was inflamed by the awareness that society was sick and must be cured.

If such a movement were ever to arise in the Indies, it would clearly follow the Asian pattern and not the European. The Indies Natives had no sense of justice, no sense of law. Try taking away the property of a Native. If it is taken by a European or a Eurasian, the Native will not say a word. He does not feel that any of his rights have been violated. They don't understand the meaning of the word *rights*; they understand nothing about law. All they know is that there are judges who sentence them. It was no coincidence that the government made sure there was no big increase in the number of educated Natives so that there would continue to be no defiance. Of course, I don't dare claim all this as definite before all the evidence for my conclusions is collected. These are just provisional notes.

Now Aceh sheltered under the authority of the Netherlands Indies. Aceh would never be a subject of dispute with England. The Philippines sheltered under the authority of America. Many people accurately predicted that this nation, which was so proud of its nationhood, would give America many problems. And this English-speaking people in the North Indies remained a danger to the Netherlands Indies. So all contact between them and the Indies Natives, either directly or through books, needed to receive proper direction.

To the east of the Indies were two other colonial powers—Germany in East Papua and Portugal in Timor.

There was no danger of Portuguese influence seeping outside its territories through the educated Natives. During the last century, Portugal had been pushed out of the European cultural realm by its northern neighbors, Belgium, Holland, and France. Portugal now found itself almost exiled to the African continent, with its money, energy, and life spirit exhausted.

Although Germany seemed very calm at the moment, this country, on the other hand, required special attention. The German people, who had historically always determined their fate on the battlefield, were a people always young and fresh in spirit. I had my own grounds for being suspicious as well. Twice now, the police had arrested and deported groups of Turkish youths. They had been traveling around the Indies, declaring themselves propagandists for Pan-Islamism. They said they were based in Istanbul. When they were interrogated, it turned out that they understood German better than English. They had thought that Arabic would be enough for them to make contact with the young Moslems of the Indies. They suffered total failure. And we discovered that they were all educated in Germany.

The government did not make a fuss over these incidents and decided that they should not be made public. Even the journalists in the Indies never understood the real background to the arrests.

The times had indeed changed; someone like Pitung had no chance today. You could not achieve much with just courage and terror in these

modern times. This was the era of knowledge and learning. Today everything was assessed using that knowledge and learning. It was the era of
leaders who were also great thinkers, who themselves sometimes did not
need to descend into the arena of battle like Pitung. It was the power of
their ideas that provided leadership, not just courage and terror.

Uh, Pitung. *Ziihhh!*

"Do you need something, Meneer?" asked De Man, offended.

"Yes, yes, as it happens. A drink, Meneer De Man. Thank you very
much. Like yesterday—hot milk."

He called an attendant and not long after, my order arrived. The servant put the glass down on my table. And I knew that De Man was watching
me with unhappy eyes.

By my third visit, De Man was making it clear that he did not like
me. I didn't care. Hopefully, today no *ziihhh* would escape from my lips. I
would try to be in control of myself if Pitung appeared.

After four hours of reading through the papers, I came across an instruction of Governor-General Rosenboom regarding the ban on reporting
of events in the Philippines. It was in the form of an order from the Algemeene Secretariat to all governors and representatives of major companies
in the Indies not to publish or discuss the Filipino rebellion in any of the
publications under their control.

And so it was that I sat in the State archives building studying those
papers, document after document, for almost a month. I did not find anything else very important. I would have to look for anything else I needed
in the Dutch and Malay papers. I didn't understand Javanese. I could borrow
newspaper material from the Gedung Gajah Museum library that belonged
to the Batavia Society for the Arts and Sciences. It's true that its collection
wasn't complete. There had once been a call for all publishers to give the
library three copies of everything they published, to be saved for posterity.
The call, however, was never backed up in law and many publishers took
no notice. Apart from the library, my office also subscribed to several newspapers and magazines from the Netherlands, France, and England.

It was from my reading of all those papers that I was able to make the
following notes.

The colonial powers of Europe were experiencing a calm that would
eventually be costly for them. Especially given the emergence of new colonial powers like Japan and America, the calm in Europe was suspicious.
All these powers, except Holland and Belgium, were not satisfied with the
extent of their colonies in Asia, Africa, and Latin America. England had lost
South Africa. Spain had lost the Philippines, Mexico, and Cuba. Meanwhile
it was only natural that Belgium and Holland restrained themselves. Besides,

they would be unable to compete in the battlefield with countries like France and Germany.

Among all the colonial powers, the one that appeared most thirsty for colonies was Germany, which had joined the struggle for colonies late in the piece, having been preoccupied with Europe for the previous two centuries. The Germans were aware that they had been left behind. The world outside Europe had already been divided up among the European colonial powers.

Among themselves the Europeans respected the law, so they had no grounds to start disputes with their neighbors over these colonies. The only opportunity arose when the Natives of the colonies themselves revolted and invited intervention.

It has been said that no matter how clever a Western scholar might be, if he did not understand colonial affairs, he would never understand the world. He would be viewing the world from one floor or another of an ivory tower. Throughout the history of humankind, it was having colonies that turned a country into a whole world in itself. A country without colonies was like a widower who had to do all the housework as well as make a living by himself. The colony was like the wife who went out to work, who was submissive and faithful and obedient. Even though it was contrary to Christian morality (except for the Mormons, of course), the more wives a colonial power had, the more prosperous he would be, and the more desirable.

If this analogy is at all appropriate, then we could go on to say that the wives Germany had acquired in Africa were incapable of doing anything, and its wife in East Papua was a dumb and useless one that not only didn't produce anything but, in recent times anyway, had become a burden.

In order for one country to seize its neighbor's colonies—ah, see how the world was growing too small to cater for what was known as humankind's lust for dominance—without the help of the Natives of the colony, the balance of power between the nations of Europe would have to be changed.

I returned to the State archives to study some more about Papua. Could the Germans use it as a staging post to make moves into the territories of the Indies?

It turned out that Papua had been the subject of colonial interest for a long time. The English tried to occupy West Papua in 1784 but were forced to leave, not just because its inhabitants were too primitive, but because blackwater fever was a terrifying angel of death. Once somebody was struck down by blackwater fever, his urine turning black like chocolate, he was wiped from the face of the earth. The English pulled up camp and left Papua, to be replaced by the Dutch, who established their headquarters at Manokwari.

After one week of solid study at the archives, I concluded that England would regret having departed Papua in 1793. England should have developed Papua into a base to link Australia with Singapore and Malaya. Portugal in East Timor and Germany in East Papua were both too far away from any other base. This was true for the Indies and Holland too. But they all retained these three colonies. No matter how empty, or whether they were profitable or not, the possession of colonies was what made a country great. You could face your neighbors in any gathering with pride while you possessed such greatness.

For three months solid I worked, digging about like this, to get a basic picture of the situation of the Netherlands Indies as regards the possibility of rebellion by the educated Natives, and of intervention by other colonial powers.

When I asked for the papers dealing with Portuguese Timor, Meneer L— once again brought them to me himself. He sat down at the table across from me, looked at me for a long time, then began: "From the papers that you have been studying, I think I can guess how important your work is," he said. "I have shown you everything. I have total control over all this material. I alone know the cataloguing codes. If I say that certain documents do not exist, there is no power that can bring them forth, Meneer."

"Yes, you are a very important man," I said. I was thinking that he was hoping for gratitude from me and some words of tribute from His Excellency the governor-general.

"What do you mean?" he asked.

"I mean it would be very easy for you to refuse to hand over a document if you really didn't want to."

He pulled on his lip, making sure he did not let all his feelings show. He seemed to be after sympathy. He was too lonely, stuck for years in this graveyard of a building.

"Yes, it's true. All I need do is say that *it does not exist*. Nobody would ever ask again. The document would cease to exist. As if I were a magician. Anybody who didn't believe me could try to look for themselves among the seven kilometers of documents. They could search until they had grandchildren and still they would not find it."

"Yes, I can see you have total control over these documents. Thank you very much for all your help."

Now he smiled happily.

Perhaps he was telling me all this as a way of expressing his annoyance at having to provide all this assistance to just a Native, even one with a mandate from the Algemeene Secretariat. Or perhaps my earlier guess was right—he wanted me to lobby His Excellency or the Gods of the Alge-meene Secretariat for more resources for the archives.

"All the important work of the government begins with studies in this building, Meneer," he said again.

"The members of the Indies Council too, yes?" I asked.

"Very true."

"For their own research, or for the committees?"

"The committees, Meneer. So I know how important your work is. And you yourself are an important man, Meneer."

"To be frank with you, Meneer, I don't know whether this work is important or not," I refuted him quickly. "All I know is that there is a task that I have to finish. I know no more than that."

"Do you have any plans for this evening?" he asked suddenly.

"Just family business," I answered.

"Would you like to join me for dinner? At the Tong An restaurant? Eight o'clock?"

"I don't think I can accept your very generous invitation, Meneer."

"Tomorrow perhaps?" he asked quickly.

"I don't think I can, really, Meneer."

"What about with Mevrouw?" he continued to press me.

"Very well, tomorrow, with my wife."

He held out his hand to me, and we shook hands. He was delighted. He went back into his office.

There was very little of interest among the documents on Portuguese Timor. Most were concerned with tribal conflicts on the border. The next thing I had to look at was the question of England and North Borneo and all its oil.

It appears that the most sought-after colonies are those with big populations, but even more so if they are also fertile and rich in minerals. It was precisely because Java had the biggest population that the Dutch set up headquarters on Java. The large population of Java could then be enslaved by cannon, rifle, and bayonet. Dutch colonial power in the Indies was always Javacentric. It was from Java that they saw and evaluated the rest of the Indies and everything that the Indies contained.

In the Tong An restaurant two things became clear about Meneer L—. On the one hand he loved Chinese food, and on the other, he loved to study everything about Java.

"And you have access to so many documents," I said, commenting. "You will be the one who surpasses the achievements of Raffles and Veth in the twentieth century."

"There is no need to try to surpass them, Meneer. They are the great classic teachers who will live forever." He gulped down a brandy after wishing me success and good health. Continuing: "One day, when the Javanese come to learn gratitude, they will put up statues to those two students of Java."

"They will build a statue to you too, Meneer," I added.

"That is too much praise, Meneer. I am not a pioneer. At the most you can say I am finishing off their work. Raffles and Veth's place in this field is guaranteed for eternity."

And it was then that I also understood that this man did not need the attention of His Excellency the governor-general or the Algemeene Secretariat. It was enough for him to be able to bury himself in that mausoleum, still and cold as it was. All the documents that he needed were there and came to him on his command. He could research whatever he wanted and write about any subject he wanted. He would succeed. Why would he need people to pay him any special attention? It would be obvious to anyone that it would be a long time yet before any Javanese could equal him, especially if they did not begin to study Western logic. So why had he invited my wife and me to eat at this restaurant?

My wife was busy talking with his wife. Sitting there under the hundred-watt light, their faces glistened even though they wiped them with their handkerchiefs repeatedly. After the dinner the waiter presented us with a scented wet towel. My wife had never eaten at a Chinese restaurant before and so did not know what to do with that warm, damp, and scented towel. As soon as she saw Meneer L— wipe his face and mouth with it, she gave an understanding laugh and followed his example.

"Why did you choose to make Java your main subject of study, Meneer?"

"There is one secret that I have not been able to discover, Meneer. I am not even able to make a simple hypothesis. See if you can work out the answer. What is the reason for the fact that there are many more Javanese than any other people of the Indies despite the similar opportunities and natural environment? Why does Java have a longer and richer history? Why is its cultural heritage greater, for any particular period of history? The Javanese even surpassed some of the European peoples in certain areas in particular periods. Aha, I see you are amazed at my saying that?"

I was not amazed. Talk of the superior achievements of the Javanese always left me with an irritated feeling. But I knew the time would come when I would need more knowledge and understanding of the Javanese. So I decided to humor him now while he was so keen to talk about Java.

"Isn't that because the Dutch decided to make Java the center of the Indies from the start?" I asked.

"On the contrary, Meneer Pangemanann. The Dutch decided to center the administration of the Indies on Java precisely because of the fact I mentioned earlier. Even before the Europeans arrived, the Javanese had sufficient social organization to make possible cultural and socioeconomic advance."

"Seeing you heap so much praise on the Javanese, Meneer, perhaps you could also explain why they were able to be defeated by the Europeans."

"That's a long story, Meneer." He held up his glass of brandy and clinked his against mine: "May you achieve success as a colonial expert!"

"And may you achieve success as an expert on Java!" I answered.

The lecture about Java was resumed the next day in the State archives before I began my work.

With that irritated feeling still there, I asked: "Do you include among the Javanese things you find so worthy of praise the *serimpi* dance that everybody is talking about?"

"Yes, that too. Of course, the slow, courtly serimpi is not the best example, perhaps it's even the worst. It was born during the degeneration of Javanese feudalism. It was created not to praise the gods or ancestors or a victory over evil, or the depth or greatness of some human emotion. Certainly there is no real drama in the serimpi dance, not according to European criteria anyway. It came out of the process of degeneration, to give Native rulers, great and small, the chance to sleep with the dancers after they had shown off their body in the dance."

"You're making this up, Meneer, aren't you?" I said. "Do you know that for sure? After all, you have probably never left this building, Meneer."

"It's possible to justify any opinion. It just depends from what angle you approach it. And Veth, that brilliant expert on Java, Meneer, he never even set foot in Java. And you too, Meneer. And now you too are studying to become a colonial expert by going in and out of these buildings? You are not throwing yourself into the midst of the people's lives either?" He shook his head but I didn't know what he meant by it, and: "Because documents are more reliable, Meneer. They are more reliable than the mouths of their own authors."

I nodded in agreement. And from that time on, I became friends with him, and my wife with his wife.

"If Java is so great, why was it able to be defeated by Europe?" I repeated my question.

"First of all, there is the Javanese character. They are always seeking similarities, sameness, harmony. They ignore differences in order to avoid social conflict. These are the values to which they submit and obey, sometimes without restraint. And so, as time goes on and it happens more and more often, they end up falling from one compromise into another, finally losing all principles. The Javanese prefer to adjust rather than quarrel over matters of principle."

"Come on, you're making this up again," I said, egging him on.

"You must learn more about Java. Every expert on the Indies begins with this extraordinary people. No, I'm not making these things up, Meneer. The Javanese themselves have left behind the evidence, and not just in the form of stones and copper and empty stories. How did they develop this character? Because of all the wars, one after another, never ending. Everybody longed for peace, and so people gave up their principles. A poet from the time of Hayam Wuruk in the fourteenth century, Mou Tantular, described this compromising personality in a verse of one of his poems."

"A poem?" I cried incredulously.

"Yes, Meneer, a poem written in the fourteenth century. Roughly translated it said: Buddha, whom we honor, is no different from Shiva, the greatest of the gods. Buddha, whom we honor, is the universe. How can we separate them? The essence of Jina and the essence of Shiva are one. They are different, yet they are one, there is no conflict." He gazed at me to keep my attention. "Another poet from the same period, Prapanca, who at that time was also in charge of the Buddhist church on Java, wrote the poem *Negarakartagama*. He wrote from his exalted position, a very responsible position. He also equated Shiva with Buddha. Always in the direction of compromise, where all principles are forgotten."

"But these are matters of religion, Meneer," I snapped back.

"In those times, Meneer, religion was also politics, a matter of power. Wasn't it also like that in Europe in earlier times? Wasn't the eighty-year war between the Netherlands and Spain a struggle by Protestantism to defend itself from Catholicism? And it was this struggle that created a free Netherlands. It was the same in Java. One raja was overthrown by another, because of differences in religion. One worshiped Vishnu, another Krishna, and so on."

I could understand this, but that the Javanese had written poems in the fourteenth century . . .

"They were writing poems when most of the European peoples were illiterate, Meneer. There is archaeological evidence of their writings from the eighth century. The Dutch people were just getting to know Christianity. They were just learning to recognize writing. They certainly couldn't read yet. They even murdered the first Bible propagandist, Boniface. Isn't that so?"

I had to admit in all honesty that this man had a deep understanding of Java, past and present.

"Have you read any of these fourteenth-century works yourself?"

"Of course, Meneer, in classical Javanese language and script." And he was like a snail buried in this graveyard.

"The official thinking of Majapahit at its zenith, as espoused by Prapanca and Tantular, was one of the reasons for the death of the Javanese nation. Society more and more disregarded its principles. It was the same when Islam arrived almost one hundred years later. Everybody looked for sameness between Shiva-Buddhism and Islam. So Islam was accepted in an unprincipled manner too. Only its outward form was adopted. For decades society lived without principles. Then the Europeans arrived, and Europe based itself on adherence to principles. The Europeans were much fewer in number but won because they held clear and firm principles."

"Will you be presenting this thesis for a doctorate?"

"No, Meneer, all I want are better facilities for this office and some additional budget for a few specific items."

"Have you ever submitted a proposal for a new budget?"

"I never get any response. We are operating on guidelines drawn up last century."

I returned to my study of the documents. Were there any signs that Germany had desires to replace Holland in the Indies? I didn't find any. The Germans had lost their opportunity to become a colonial power. I wouldn't find any signs of their wanting to take over the Indies. I did come across some interesting papers about Governor-General Van Imhoff's five-year term in office. In the history of the *VOC* he was the only German and he had brought out a large number of German soldiers to the Indies. Among these documents were many that seemed to be hinting that Van Imhoff wanted to Germanify the Indies. Of course, there wasn't a single sentence anywhere that came out and made a direct accusation. And the Dutch were suspicious of anything remotely German. One thing that I did find that amazed me was a poem, a story in poetry, in Malay, entitled *Syair Himon*, a kind of self-criticism by Imhoff himself, and a flurry of correspondence concerning people's objections to the establishment of a Lutheran congregation for the German soldiers.

I also came across some old, decaying papers from the case of Pieter Elberveldt, a German trader born of a Native woman. That was an interesting case. He had allied himself with the Mataram kingdom against the VOC. His aim was to win the Indies for Germany. The aspect of his case that had become common knowledge in the Indies was the cruel nature of the traitor's punishment. All four of his limbs were torn from his body by four horses.

His body was then sadistically chopped up and his head stuck upon a spear. It was displayed in Pasar Ikan, over the entrance to his own front courtyard. It was clear from these documents, however, that not everything about his activities had been announced at the time. What interested me was the idea of following the trail of any German who wanted the Indies for Germany. And if there had been such people in the past, why not today? Weren't those Turkish boys preaching under the guise of Pan-Islamism also evidence of German activity?

Then I read about the activities of the German missionaries. Were there any signs that they were preparing their region of operation as a base that could communicate with the colonial authorities in East Papua? To be honest, I don't dare come to a conclusion, or make a statement about this. I tidied up the documents and put them away, as if I had never read them. Being a Catholic, I could find dealing with these sensitive issues too difficult to handle.

Taking further material from a number of specialist studies on colonial affairs, I began to write my report about the educated Natives and the possibilities of their coming into contact with other educated Natives from the neighboring colonies. That was the longest report I had ever written. It took me almost one year to complete.

Perhaps I have not made it sufficiently clear what my duties were after I was promoted to commissioner. I had no authority at all. All I did was swim among papers and write. My only power to give orders was to order a messenger boy to buy me some cigarettes or drink. It was different from when I was an inspector. Then I had command over a combined brigade of field police.

After I finished my report, I handed it over to the chief commissioner. Then there was nothing. Every day I returned to my office and sat nailed at my desk. This situation changed under Idenburg. I was given a difficult job, but in line with my earlier research—to keep watch over the educated Natives. And, of course, the figure in the vanguard of the Natives was—Minke. And it was because of this task that I came to know him so well, even though he never knew me.

I carried out this job right up until his exile to Ambon, where I handed him over to the assistant resident of Maluku, as I have related to you. He was kept under house arrest there. He had to report every time he had any contact with somebody from outside the house. He had to submit a list once a week of where he wanted to go and whom he wanted to see. He had to hand in a list of everybody he had met. He received an allowance equivalent to the wage of a new graduate from STOVIA, except that as he hadn't graduated, he received fifteen guilders a month and not eighteen. He could receive letters but could not send any without permission. He was allowed any publication he wanted but could not publish a single word in any publication.

I knew that for somebody who was used to expressing his opinion, such regulations would be terrible torment to him. It would be spiritual torture for a modern person like him.

On the boat trip home, I continued writing in my notebook.

This was the once in my life where I had been present at a historical event, the exile of somebody whom I considered to be my teacher—Raden Mas Minke. He was the first victim of colonialism's effort to prevent the Indies from becoming a second Philippines.

At the end of these notes, I wrote: A Servant of the Government! Somebody who is always responsible to the government and feels responsible to the government, such people never accept responsibility themselves, except to ensure their own security and enjoyment.

When I arrived back at headquarters, my boss summoned me to his office. He congratulated me on a job well done, and told me that I was being watched sympathetically by those higher up. And what official was not happy to hear that his superiors liked his work?

He ordered one of the boys to bring coffee and cakes, as if he were very keen to enjoy the results of my work. I had found out from someone in the personnel section that he was an Anglican, and perhaps he had absorbed some hostility toward my religion. So I must be very careful of him.

He whispered good-naturedly: "There is an official letter for you, Meneer," and he took the letter out from his pocket and gave it to me. He stood up, as if he were waiting for me to read it and as if he wanted to read it as well. Realizing this, I opened the envelope and read it. My head started spinning. Everything went dark. As from today I was being retired! Oh, my God, so this was the boon I was to receive from the government, after I had sold myself, sold my principles, become so contemptible a person.

"You don't like getting a pension?" my boss asked.

"I am still young, Meneer."

"Then there are probably a dozen other letters here for you, Meneer," he said, playing about. He pretended to search all his pockets, then brought out another letter. "Yes, you are young, Meneer. You're not ready yet to be some pensioned grandfather. Another letter, Meneer Pangemanann."

But I had lost all hope. I took the letter and stuffed it in my pocket.

"Why don't you read it now?"

"Thank you, Meneer. But I had better go home."

He clapped me on the shoulder and escorted me out to the office veranda, then ordered an officer to get a vehicle for me. He had never been so friendly.

"Greetings to Madame," he told me, to be passed on.

On the drive home, my heart was busy accusing the government of ingratitude. I had been thrown away like garbage on the road. What was Pangemanann with two 'n's worth without position? And what about his European wife who would no longer be able to protect her standing? Who would Pangemanann be without his police uniform? A civilian and elderly pensioner! The government buildings would no longer open their doors for him. People would no longer bow or tip their hats. He would be just a blank piece of paper without meaning.

Even in exile, Minke kept his integrity, and the government respected him. In retirement, who was Pangemanann without a job in the government? What was left for me now? All my principles had been thrown aside for the sake of the government.

As soon as the car stopped at the veranda, the driver jumped out and took my briefcase straight into the house.

"You look so pale, Jacques!" my wife greeted me. She quickly caught me when she saw I was staggering. My legs felt heavy, my joints weak. What had become of me that I was like this?

The driver helped support me inside and into my room. He bowed and then left.

I sat dispirited on the bed while my wife took off my uniform—a uniform that I would never wear again. Retired, without any kind of ceremony, no special ceremonies or parades for me . . . and my pistol in its holster dropped onto the bed. She undid my shoelaces, and struggled to take off my shoes, then, holding her breath, pulled off my socks, put my legs up on the bed, and laid my head down on the pillow.

"You've been so weak lately, Jacques. Two of your children aren't even grown up yet." She pulled down the mosquito net, came over to me, kissed me, and said, "Don't I love you enough, Jacques?"

"Get rid of that dirty uniform, darling."

She went and did what I wanted. She took out the leather belt and, as she always did, hung it on the hat stand. She put the pistol in the cupboard and locked it. She took the dirty clothes outside. Shortly after, she returned, took off my shirt and: "There is an official letter for you, Jacques. It's still unopened. Why don't you read it?"

My fault, I thought: "Put it in the drawer, darling."

"No, you can't do that!" she answered back. "All letters to do with work should be read straightaway. Why are you so lazy these days, Jacques? Do you want me to read it?"

"You read it. I am very tired."

I heard her tear the envelope open. I closed my ears and tensed my body, also shutting my eyes. I did not want to hear anything!

Suddenly: "Jacques!" she cried out.

I pressed the pillow harder around my ears. She would no doubt start to cry once she read the list of my failures and mistakes.

She rocked me back and forward. For the sake of politeness, I was forced to turn over and pay her attention. She wasn't crying. Her face was shining with joy.

"What is it, darling?"

"Jacques!" she cried out joyfully. "Why don't you say something? A promotion, Jacques. A promotion!" She hugged and kissed me. "It hasn't been wasted, all this exhausting work you've been doing, Jacques. Jacques! Jacques!" she wept in her joy.

She didn't understand Dutch properly. I would receive a pension of 200 guilders. The Harmoni Club would be closed to me now forever. My name would be crossed off the membership list. Total ruination.

As soon as she let go of me, she stood and crossed herself. I couldn't bear to see her disappointment once she realized she had misunderstood the letter. Suddenly: "We will move to Buitenzorg, Jacques. I will like it there. It's cool and quiet, not restless and busy like here. Except the children will have to change schools."

Move to Buitenzorg? Why to Buitenzorg?

"But what a pity, Jacques, you won't be able to wear your uniform anymore. You began your career in such a uniform. Since Vlaardingen, then s'Hertogenbosch, and after that here in Betawi."

"You haven't misunderstood the letter, darling?"

"I understand every single word."

"Are you happy, darling?"

"Who wouldn't be happy, darling, if their husband was promoted to the Algemeene Secretariat . . . ."

I jumped up from the bed. I grabbed the letter from her and read it myself. My wife had not misunderstood a single word. I was being transferred to the office of the Algemeene Secretariat with an increase in salary of 200 guilders. I would have to move to Buitenzorg. A house had been allocated for me.

The Algemeene Secretariat! Just one or two steps from the governor-general!

I dropped to my knees and crossed myself, giving thanks. The government had not forgotten Pangemanann . . .

4

If my wife had not pulled me along, perhaps I would still be standing openmouthed in front of our new house in Buitenzorg. The children raced each other to be the first inside. My wife could not restrain herself any longer; she wanted to see if everything had been put where she ordered.

I was the only one left standing there openmouthed. This house was the former residence of Raden Mas Minke. I should have been happy to live there. Across the street was the governor-general's palace. The house had spacious grounds; you felt you could breathe easily. There were big and well-maintained shade trees, all green, which refreshed the eyes. The house itself was a stone house, large and beautiful too, much more luxurious than our old house.

You had to get rid of Raden Mas Minke in order to live in this house! Yes, you Pangemanann! I could no longer stop my conscience from accusing me.

Ah, I replied, the government wields more power than my conscience. To hell with you all!

Someone was laughing raucously behind me. I turned around. Pitung and Minke were laughing, pointing at me, knowingly passing glances. *Ziihhh, ziihhh, ziihhh.*

"You're starting again, Jacques!" my wife reprimanded me.

The government has defeated both of you. Pitung, Minke, give it all up! And so I entered the house.

That afternoon we were visited by our neighbors, who all turned out to be high officials of the Algemeene Secretariat. They were very cautious and guarded in their behavior, and in their conversation too. They all studied me as if they were watching a gecko lost among real lizards. They stayed no more than a quarter of an hour before leaving.

Another problem arose that evening as the four of us spent our first evening there. It came from Mark. "Papa, we're visiting Europe in three months, aren't we?"

"Ah, yes, Jacques. What about your leave? Will you still get that leave? Or has it been lost with your transfer to your new office?"

The four of us had made many plans. My wife wanted to take the children to see their grandparents in Lyons. Then she wanted to make a pilgrimage to Lourdes and later go on to Rome, where she wanted to see St. Peter's. The children would stay in Lyons, where they would go to the same school that I had attended. I planned to visit my adopted parents, with special souvenirs of the Indies. Nothing expensive, just materials used for traditional Javanese medicines, powders and so on made from leaves, roots, and skins.

I was not at all confident that I would still get leave. And so I said nothing while they chatted gaily about all their beautiful plans.

The next day, Sunday, Meneer L— and his wife came and stayed the night. They planned to return to Batavia on the first train the next morning. Meneer L— would go straight to the office. His wife would go back to their house.

It was good to have Meneer L— as company. At the very least, there were many things to distract me from my own chaotic state of mind.

Sitting out in the garden, as the afternoon wore on, it was I who began: "If you think that Java has always been defeated because the Javanese had lost all their principles due to their mad search for the sameness in everything, then you must think that if the Portuguese had approached the Javanese in a more sympathetic manner, Java could have been Catholic since the fifteenth century."

"You are not wrong," he answered. "The Javanese will accept anything as long as you emphasize its sameness with what is already prevailing. As soon as they see there are clashes of principles involved, they will become suspicious and withdraw."

"You must have a lot of examples of this, of course," I said, digging around for more information.

"Of course. For example, Meneer Pangemanann, you won't read in any of the histories about there being conflicts between Hinaya Buddhism, which was the first to arrive in Java, and Mahayana Buddhism, which came later, despite the fact that they are as different as heaven and earth. They were accommodated to each other through ancestor worship, very much the Javanese way. And so it continued, with the arrival of Hinduism, with all its forms and teachings. These accommodations have been maintained in tradition until now through the teachings of the wayang. Have you ever followed even one wayang story, Meneer?"

"Never."

"Yes, you need quite a lot of time to study the main line of thought in the wayang. To understand wayang is to understand the history of the Javanese view on life and the world. To become a conscious master of the wayang world, Meneer, means to master the Javanese. The mastery of Javanese through wayang is one way to become a colonial expert. Even for a Javanese who consciously mastered wayang, able at the same time to free himself from the grip of the wayang world, it would still be a long journey for him to reconstruct himself as an independent personality, Meneer. The universe of wayang is a world of its own, which cannot be touched by modern ideas. Whether Christian, Moslem, or without religion, the Javanese have all been sucked into that universe, just as Prapanca and Tantular designed."

I couldn't quite follow his lecture, even though I tried hard to understand him.

"When the Portuguese arrived in the Moluccas, the people all rushed to become Christians without the slightest resistance. Yes, there were social historical reasons for this. All throughout their history they have been a colonized, defeated people. They have never experienced national freedom. And all this was because their country was rich in spices. They have mixed with many peoples, from nearby and far away, and never have been able to draw any benefits from these contacts with more advanced civilizations. Then, when in the second decade of the seventeenth century Jon Pietersz Coen pushed the Portuguese out of the Moluccas, they all gave up Catholicism and became Protestants, again without any resistance. They accommodated once again, even though the sources were different from Prapanca and Tantular. They adjusted themselves, accommodating to the power that came and conquered them."

His explanation gave rise to a strange irritation inside me. If he could speak that way about the Moluccas, then he might start saying the same things about Menado! From Catholic to Protestant. I got in first: "Can you prove what you're saying, Meneer? Is it just a hypothesis?"

"Yes, of course. I can't put forward all the evidence in a casual conversation like this. Perhaps one day I can write a full-scale study on this. Don't think that it is only the peoples of the Indies who have developed this trait of accommodating, adjusting, compromising. No, Meneer. It is the trait of all peoples who throw away their principles when they come into contact with more principled peoples. The opposite happened in the Americas. The Indian peoples, when they came into contact with the more advanced and stronger Spanish, were destroyed because they were unable to find a way to compromise and accommodate. They went from defeat to defeat. From being meat eaters, they ended up living on wheat gruel, defeated and pushed onto reservations, where they were destroyed by the cruel treatment they received and by tuberculosis, because they could no longer keep themselves alive. In other words, there are two choices for a weak nation when it comes into contact with a strong one. Such a people must accommodate or flee into the jungles, where their culture and civilization then degenerate, until they fall as low as the sheep in the fields."

The archivist himself didn't seem satisfied with his explanation. Perhaps he didn't feel that his argument measured up to the scientific criteria he himself held to, so he added: "Yes, all this has to be investigated further."

I turned and looked over toward the road. Outside the fence, which was made of painted palings on top of a low cement wall, with hibiscus flowers planted inside, I saw two figures standing one behind the other. Both of them were women. The one in front was still. The one behind was anxiously tugging on her friend. Perhaps they were two beggars who were nervous about coming inside.

The archivist followed my gaze. "And that is what has become of the Javanese, Meneer."

It seems that the two women did not know that beggars were forbidden to enter the area around the palace.

"But as far as I can tell from my reading of the Netherlands Indies history, the Javanese always resisted, right to the bitter end of any battle," I answered back.

"When you start off with the wrong philosophy, Meneer, all that is left is to defend yourself. The Javanese have never gone on the offensive against the whites. All they have ever been able to do is put up a defense, to hold the fort. But they were always defeated, because they held to a defeated philosophy. The more their philosophy degenerated, the more they were defeated on the battlefield. The Javanese people today, Meneer, are not the same people as four hundred years ago."

"So what about the Javanese today?"

"Today? All that is left is that accommodating, compromising character. They can't even put up any kind of self-defense anymore. They have reached a dead end. There is nowhere forward for them to go anymore. It's very sad, but they themselves don't even understand their own situation. They can only do that by comparing themselves with other peoples. Their writings over the last hundred years are the writings of a defeated people who do not want to escape from their defeat. There is no one who will suggest that they learn from Europe. Rather they are told just to serve Europe, or they even pretend that they do not know that Europe has them in its grip. They don't even know that, Meneer. Rather they are proud just to have a European acquaintance. Just an acquaintance! But they don't know how to reap any benefit from that experience."

"You are too certain of yourself, Meneer."

"Yes, I get carried away sometimes."

"There are already Natives starting to study the European sciences."

"I think it is only their brains that are developing. Their mentality remains Javanese, carrying that burden of three hundred years of defeat—dispirited, frightened, submissive—or sometimes the reverse of all this, as a compensation for all these things."

The two women were still hovering outside the fence. Now one of them was tugging on the other, perhaps trying to get her to leave. The other refused to move, without looking at her friend. They were both looking in our direction.

I excused myself from Meneer L—, went into the house, and telephoned the local police station to get them to get rid of the women.

"Forgive me, if I got carried away. Maybe I do not have the personality to be a scholar," Meneer L— went on when I returned to keep him company.

The sun had set. Two police agents arrived and herded the women away with rubber truncheons. They did not come into our grounds. I don't know what happened then, it was already too dark to see any distance. That night Meneer L— and his wife stayed over. They left for Betawi very, very early the next morning.

I arrived at my new office at eight o'clock in the morning. I was taken to meet my new boss. He turned out to be a lawyer, a Frenchman educated in France, Monsieur R—.

He greeted me unexpectedly politely, in French: "I have been looking everywhere for an experienced man who spoke Malay, had a higher education, and understood the modern languages. You are the adopted child of the chemist Monsieur De Cagnie, yes? From Lyons?" He ushered me in. "He has retired from his company now. You have heard, yes?"

"Of course, Monsieur," I answered. "We are actually planning to visit him when my leave in Europe comes up in three months' time."

"Forget about your European leave. Come in!" and he showed me into another room. And in his southern French accent, he began to explain to me my new duties: "You are greatly needed here." It was clear as day that I had lost my European leave. I could not imagine how disappointed my wife and children would be. And myself as well. How quickly our feelings rose and fell because of things outside our control.

"Many people have reported that your Malay is quite good. This is just what is needed for your new work. I want to be able to ask you questions and seek your advice whenever necessary. Your new duty is very simple—all you have to do is answer my questions, not as a defendant, but as an expert. According to what I have been told, you already have years of experience in this. Most of my questions will be about the somewhat undesired activities of the educated Natives, activities outside what has been determined as allowable by the Ethical Policy."

My work would be no different from that I carried out as a police commissioner.

From that day I had the privilege of having my own office, all for myself. There was a big cabinet filled with official documents, both public documents and private ones, about and by educated Natives. I found all my reports for the police there too. The biggest file was that on Raden Mas Minke, who had been the most active during the last six years. There were also newspaper clippings, including ones with those famous initials of the editor of *Medan* at the bottom, as well as clippings from French and German papers quoting from *Medan*. I had never seen those European newspaper reports before. Perhaps Minke never knew about any of this either.

There was also my report of my interview with Minke, and on the submission recommending his exile were the initials of three people whom I did not know but would perhaps soon meet.

Monsieur R— left me in this room, which was as cold as the room in the State archives. A telephone awaited me on my desk, its dial shining, not a scratch in its chrome. The walls were bare and unadorned. There was a small table in the corner, with a white tablecloth, but no flower vase. On a shelf underneath there was an instrument which I did not recognize. I went over, picked it up, and examined it. It seemed to be a simple appliance, with a fan inside, while in the front there was a kind of basket made from woven wire, which could be opened and closed. In the wire basket, and indeed among the wires themselves, there were signs of burning, as if it had been in contact with flames. I put it down when there was a knock on the door.

An attendant in a white uniform, a rather good-looking Eurasian with sharp eyes and pointed nose, entered but seemed reluctant to salute me. He just stood there staring at me.

"Who are you!" I snapped, offended.

Finally he gave a little respectful nod: "Frits Doertier, Meneer, your attendant."

"What schooling have you had?" I asked sharply.

He seemed embarrassed, hiding his nervousness by fixing his hair; then he finally answered: "Primary school, Meneer."

"Why have you entered here?" I growled again.

He scratched his neck and tried to smile, without speaking. "Get out!" I ordered.

He left without saluting. My colonial heart was offended.

A few moments later there was another knock on my door. This time it was a Pure-Blood who entered, fat and not so tall. All his hair had already turned white. He also wore an all-white uniform. He nodded deeply, introducing himself: "I am in charge of housekeeping, Meneer. Nicolas Knor."

"Pangemanann, Meneer Knor. I am a new official here."

"Welcome, Meneer. I hope you like working here. Is there anything you would like me to do for you?"

"Not yet, Meneer, perhaps later. Ah, perhaps there is one thing: Do you know Frits Doertier?"

"Of course, Meneer."

"I don't want him coming in this office."

"I will make sure of that, Meneer. A young boy, Meneer, still in his teens, doesn't know proper etiquette yet."

He nodded very politely, excusing himself, and disappeared behind the closing door. I couldn't help but keep staring at that big, and heavy, door. Who would appear from behind it next?

And I was right. A moment later someone else knocked on the door, slowly and, I thought, very cautiously. I didn't answer. Instead I moved away to a spot where I would not be seen if anyone appeared from behind the door. There was another knock. I still didn't respond. The door handle seemed to move, then the door was pushed inward. A man wearing an all-white uniform peered into the room, stepped into the room, and shut the door behind him. He carried a feather duster in one hand and a flannel cloth in the other.

I took a cigarette and lit it up. I blew out smoke as hard as I could. He did not move toward the document cabinet. He turned to look behind him. On seeing me watching him, he suddenly stumbled and gave an obligatory nod of respect, his face turning pale: "Good morning, Meneer."

"Good morning. Who told you to come in here?"

"I'm Simon Zwijger, Meneer. I wanted to clean this office."

"Who ordered you here?" I asked.

"It's my daily duty, Meneer."

Just at that moment, the telephone on my table rang. I walked across and picked it up. Simon Zwijger's eyes were fixed on me for a moment; then he very quickly made a show of hurriedly wiping down the cabinet. And I felt he was trying to listen in on my conversation. Monsieur R— summoned me to Room A. Straightaway.

"Simon Zwijger," I called to this person whose position I did not yet know. "I am leaving this office. Please leave first."

"But I have to clean this room first, Meneer," he said.

"Did you hear what I said?"

"Yes, Meneer."

"Get out!"

He left with a sullen look on his face. I locked the windows. And I locked the door too, and only then went to Room A.

Several senior officials were waiting for me. Nobody showed any sign of interest in my arrival, except to appear amazed at my presence.

"Good morning," I began.

No one answered. They just nodded indifferently.

Monsieur R— stood and introduced me to them. It was then that I learned who it was that I would be working with in this sinister place. I studied each of them as they were introduced to me. It was these men who among them decided the fate of the Netherlands Indies, its people, the land, and all it contained. And now I was one of them. I later came to realize that together we were the brains behind the Netherlands Indies. The governor-general behind the wall across the way was just a bemedaled uniform who carried out what we thought up.

Monsieur R— did not explain to me what work my colleagues did. The introductions did not take long. They were over in ten minutes. Then the meeting broke up. Only Monsieur R—, Meneer Gr—, and I remained.

"Nah," Monsieur R— started again. "I am sure that Meneer Pangemanann will be frequently working together with Meneer Gr—."

I did not know in relation to what.

"Of course," responded Meneer Gr—.

"So, please, begin, the two of you. Excuse me," and so he left, after nodding to both of us.

We sat opposite each other. I studied him even more closely. Meneer Gr— brushed off some cigar ash that had fallen on his trousers, put his right hand on the back of mine, which I was resting on the table, as if I was his favorite child, then spoke in a soft voice: "Are you happy to get a French boss?"

"I only met him this morning, Meneer," I answered.

"He is very clever, quite smart. It's a bit of a pity though that he vacillates whenever the time comes to make an important decision," he went on. "You received a good French education. We all know that. He is very conservative whenever it comes to anything French. It won't take you long to get to know him." Suddenly he moved on to the main subject, which he no doubt had already prepared in his mind: "Have you been following what has been happening among the Chinese subjects of the Indies?"

"I should be, of course, Meneer."

"You are too modest, Meneer Pangemanann. I am not trying to test you, Meneer. I would like to get your reaction to one question though, even if it is outside your area of responsibility. Is there anything that has caught your attention since China became a republic under Sun Yat-sen?" He waited silently for my answer, but added: "I mean here in the Indies."

For anyone who studied the newspapers and magazines from front to back, including the advertisements, it was natural that they would have at least a few words to say.

"Many Chinese have taken to writing lately, Meneer," I answered, "and translating Chinese poetry into Malay as well, and publishing European-style fiction."

"European-style fiction! Are you sure you haven't made a rather hasty conclusion?" he asked suddenly.

"You are right, no doubt," I answered quickly.

"Have you ever studied Chinese affairs, in the Indies or China?"

"Never, Meneer, especially not in depth."

"Do you understand Chinese or one of the dialects?"

"No, Meneer. I have only read what they have written in Malay and Dutch."

"That's quite adequate."

"If you think my conclusions were a bit too hasty, Meneer, what are your own opinions then?"

Meneer Gr— examined me with his eyes, then: "In my opinion the Chinese do not need to copy Europeans. They were writing at least fifteen centuries before Europeans. They are a people who love the truth even though they have been influenced by Hinduism and Buddhism. What I mean is that they don't need to learn from Europe when it comes to writing. Perhaps it is the opposite that should be happening."

"They have never had a victory over Europe," I said, and what Meneer L— had said about the Javanese suddenly flashed through my mind.

"That's true. In politics and in our lifetime. But in the past, Meneer, they trampled over Europe on their horses. The kings of Europe bowed down in obeisance to the narrowed-eyed victors, who left behind Mongol birthmarks on the behinds of European babies, even until today."

"But that wasn't China. That was the great Genghis Khan."

"The same, Meneer. The same race with the same abilities." He stopped again, and then, like a teacher, resumed his examination of me: "Do you remember the names of the Chinese who are writing in Malay?"

"It's hard to remember Chinese names. I'm sorry, Meneer. If I am not mistaken some of them are Lie K— H—, Kwee T— H—, Tan B— K—. Perhaps I haven't pronounced them properly."

"That's good enough. You pronounced the three of them correctly, Meneer. What do you think of their writings?"

"You mean are there any special traits?"

"Yes, what is of the most interest in their writings?"

"I haven't given this matter any in-depth study yet, Meneer."

"I think we will be able to work together, Meneer. Excuse me, I should get on with my work." He nodded. Before he left, he spoke once more: "We will meet again later today."

I was left by myself in Room A.

The whole room was surrounded by polished brown timber walls. There were pictures of the Queen's family hanging in several places. The tricolor flag was on display. There were silver ashtrays on the table, most already containing ash. The windows looked as if they had not been opened since the palace had been built. I could see through the windowpanes the palace gardens and lawns outside. The kaleidoscope of color of the flowers gave the view some gaiety.

The door was still open. Meneer Gr— forgot to close it. I saw an attendant come and close it from outside.

So what was I supposed to do sitting here in this meeting room alone? But it was so peaceful here. I rested my face in my two hands as I savored the peace and quiet. During the last ten years I had rarely enjoyed this kind of peace. I knew that I would not be able to resist, that I would cross further into the field of mud before me, as a good official, as a successful career man. You can't succeed in everything, I humored myself. To succeed in just one thing already puts you above most other people. And I knew that I had no wish to be an extraordinary person with successes in all sorts of extraordinary areas. My success was already enough. Anyway, what was the real difference between a successful human being and a successful criminal?

They both contained elements of success. The only difference was that one was good at being a human being, the other at being a criminal.

I had lived through half a century now. How much longer would this body of mine survive? Ten years? Fifteen? Twenty? The doctor said there were no signs of anything wrong with my heart. My lungs were in first-class condition. I had ideal blood pressure—120/80. I had a waist as good as any young man. There were no signs of any hardening of the arteries. I should be able to live another fifty years, if everything could be as peaceful and quiet as at this moment. And to make it possible for me to live another fifty years, I did not need all this turmoil and confusion afflicting my mind and emotions.

I was not a person with great passions. I had no unlimited ambitions. I certainly had no great desire to be wealthy. Neither did I have ambitions for great power. All I wanted was the authority justified by my position and abilities. I had no grandiose dreams. As far as this went, I was a normal and balanced person. But there was one plan that I worked hard to successfully implement—to ensure that my children would be equipped with enough education and learning to cope with the new times, their own times, the times they were entering now. Was I sinning too greatly if, for those reasons, I now decided to choose to be only an official?

My hand seemed to move by itself, as I crossed myself: "Protect me. Guide me." It was only then that I left Room A and made my way to my own office.

I had only sat down for a few minutes, when I stood again and opened the windows. Fresh air entered the room, accompanied by a cool and pleasant dampness.

The telephone rang again. Monsieur R— summoned me.

Now that I realized that so many people wanted to get into this room, I locked both the windows and the door before I left.

Monsieur R— welcomed me as amicably as he had in the morning, saying politely: "Put your pistol down on this table."

I took my pistol from under my coat and put it on the table.

"Are you happy with that weapon or would you like a better more modern one?"

"It is all up to you, Meneer."

He took the pistol and put it in his drawer. He took out a smaller pistol and showed it to me: "This is not made in England, Meneer. America."

American products were not generally thought to be any good, so: "Then perhaps I could keep the old one, Meneer."

"You haven't used American weapons yet, so you don't want one," he said. "Anyway, your pistol belongs to the police. Get used to this one first. And here is an additional box of bullets for practicing with. You know where the practice range is?" he put the weapon, the bullets, and the papers down on the desk. "You will come to love this weapon. I myself have already fallen in love with it. You don't need to report the use of the bullets to the police. Just tell me. That's enough." He continued to speak in French. I just agreed to whatever he said. He went off across to a cabinet and took out a big file tied up in tape and the knot sealed with wax. He put the parcel down on the table. "This is your first case." Then he started again: "Take the pistol. Don't carry it at your waist but use a shoulder holster." He opened the drawer again and gave me a black leather holster. "You prefer a pistol to a revolver, yes?"

Bored with his never-ending stream of words, I just nodded.

"Please take all this. To be honest I don't like having that pistol on my table."

I returned to my office with everything he had given me. I opened the window, locked the door, and took off my coat. I tied my shoulder holster on and slipped the pistol into its pouch and then put my coat back on. I was just about to open the sealed file when the phone rang again and I was summoned once more by Monsieur R—.

"Do you realize, Meneer, that you have broken the law?"

"I realize, Monsieur, that I have no papers for my pistol and the bullets. But I was only carrying out your orders as my chief, isn't that so?"

He smiled. "Here are the papers. Put your signature on them; then everything will be legal." I did what he wanted.

"That file is for your eyes only. It must not leave your office."

I returned to my office. Monsieur R—'s nerves were worse than mine, I thought to myself.

"Who said Meneer R—'s nerves were worse than yours, Meneer?"

I looked up from the file. Before me stood that man in his white robes and white turban. His teeth grimaced at me. Two on one side of his mouth were missing. *Ziihhh. Ziihhh.*

But the vision did not disappear, it just grew more challenging, pointing at me: "Meneer is sitting here now precisely because you are worse than R—. In any case, both of you, all of you here, are nothing more than a bunch of sick human beings. You destroyed us because you saw us as criminals. You here are nothing other than official criminals, we were unofficial."

I held the file in front of my face. *Ziihhh, ziihhh!* Get away, you!

"Yes, Meneer, what can I get you?"

"Fetch me a drink," I ordered, unable to see, my face still covered by the file. I shut my eyelids so tight I could start to feel my eyes warm at the edges.

Suddenly I remembered that I had locked the door. I dropped the file on the table and checked the key that was still in the keyhole. I tried the door handle. The door was still locked. The hairs on the back of my neck and up and down my body stood on end. My hands made a cross.

Was I as sick as this?

I opened the door and saw Frits Doertier walking briskly by carrying an empty serving tray.

"Frits!" He glanced back but continued on without answering. His eyes didn't blink. They were dull, like those of a dead fish. Oh, my Lord, I needed a friend here in my office. I longed for the presence of Nicolaas Knor, the chief of housekeeping.

I was about to leave the office to find him when I remembered I had to lock the file away in the cabinet and lock the windows too. So I turned to go back into the room instead of heading off down the corridor. Suddenly my hairs stood on end again. The window and the file seemed far, far away. I was afraid to enter my own office. I stood there not knowing what to do. Or had I in fact lost my mind? Were my nerves in such a bad state or was this room haunted?

How lucky I was that there was no one else in the corridor except Frits Doertier. I knew he was taking his revenge on me. Nicolaas Knor, where was your office? Ah. I couldn't leave this office with the window left open like that. Anyone could get in and mess around, putting their hands on documents to which they had no right. And I could be in big trouble.

I felt as if I stood there for a long time. Frits Doertier appeared with the empty serving tray again.

"Come here, Frits!" I called to him in Dutch.

He stopped in front of me. His sullen face displayed his hatred of me.

"Go and get Meneer Knor."

"Very well," he answered stiffly.

I was not offended. This time I was in great need of his help.

Nicolaas Knor appeared in the distance. His yellow buttons gleamed, and his white head was hardly less shiny. He nodded respectfully, waiting for my orders.

"Please go in, Meneer Knor," I invited him and I followed him inside.

"You don't look well," he said after he sat down opposite me.

"Perhaps, Meneer. The hairs of my neck are always standing on end. Perhaps this room is too damp."

He just cleared his throat and glanced across at the open window.

"Perhaps some hot milk would help me, Meneer Knor."

"Let me get some for you, Meneer. Is there anything else you would like?"

"I would like to talk to you for a moment."

"Good. Let me get you the milk first, Meneer."

He stood, and I stood too. My eyes followed him to the door. He walked down the corridor toward the back of the building. He had been walking a long time and still he didn't disappear from my sight. I felt so ashamed of myself standing outside my door like that. Fifty years old and I was beginning to believe in ghosts? Is this what Pangemanann, graduate of a French university, is going to be like in his period of degeneration?

Nicolaas Knor arrived back accompanied by Frits Doertier, who carried a tray with glasses of hot milk. They entered and I followed. Knor took the milk and placed it on the desk.

"And whiskey, Frits, with three tumblers," I ordered. "One bottle."

Frits nodded happily and rushed off.

As soon as I had sat down, I quickly asked: "Meneer Knor, whom have I replaced?"

"Meneer *Mister* De Lange."

"Did he retire with pension or . . ."

"A terrible thing, Meneer, a terrible thing."

"What do you mean?"

"Suicide, Meneer."

"Here?"

"Yes, here, Meneer, with poison," he said slowly, then pointed to the door. "It was locked. We discovered him at closing time. He didn't come out of his office. I knocked several times. No answer. He was still very young. He had graduated from university only five years ago. Over there"—he pointed to the window—"I went round and looked in from there. God! Meneer De Lange was sprawled out on the floor. I didn't dare go inside. I telephoned palace security. They came and went in through the window. I followed, Meneer. Such a young man. A graduate. Not even married yet! Here, Meneer, in this room!" He pointed to a spot on the floor, near the legs of the table. "He was bleeding from his mouth, and the pores of his skin. Perhaps his arteries had all burst. I don't know."

The extremities of my feet, wet with perspiration, shivered from the cold.

"Why did he kill himself?" I asked.

"Nobody knows."

"Why did he kill himself here?"

"Only he knows that, Meneer."

Frits Doertier arrived with the whisky.

"Sit down here, Frits. Let's the three of us drink to our friendship!"

The two of them became merry after a couple of whiskeys. I drank mine in my milk. When Frits's face started to turn red, I told him he could go, and he didn't seem to hate me anymore.

"I have never heard of any suicides at the Algemeene Secretariat," I said.

"There is no need for anyone to know, Meneer."

"What about his family?"

"He had no family."

"Perhaps love was the motive?"

"Who knows, Meneer? He was a happy man who was well liked by the ladies."

"What was his first name?"

"Simon, Meneer, Simon De Lange."

That was the first time I heard that name, and he was such an important person. I already had a vision of what kind of work he did here every day. And he chose to kill himself here in this room. He planned it! He didn't kill himself at home but here in my office!

"He didn't leave behind any message?"

"How would I know, Meneer? You could find out from the gentlemen at palace security."

"Were the cabinets opened and inspected before I arrived?"

"Of course, Meneer," he answered coldly, as if nothing had ever happened, as if no human being had lost his life.

"They didn't find anything?"

"I don't know, Meneer. Perhaps yes. Perhaps no."

"You don't mind me asking you these questions?"

"No, Meneer. We all know that you were a police commissioner. It's only natural that you ask such questions. Before you arrived, everyone talked about your successes in the police. I am sure that you will conduct your own investigation of this secret incident."

"Meneer Knor, have you ever entered this room by yourself?"

He seemed startled by that question. I had to clear things up: "Others too, perhaps? By themselves alone, I mean?"

"As head of housekeeping, naturally I have been in here often, Meneer."

"I mean after Meneer De Lange killed himself?"

"Of course."

"You never felt there was anything strange about this room?"

"I always found it a bit distressing coming in here, Meneer, especially after such a terrible thing happened."

"When did it happen?"

"Three days before you arrived."

"Thank you for keeping me company, Meneer Knor."

He rose from his chair. I went over straightaway and opened the window, then followed him to the door. Before he left for his own office I added: "Come and visit me often, Meneer."

He just smiled, nodded politely, and left.

I left the window and door open. I startled to fondle the sealed file again. Meanwhile I started laughing at myself: You who have already lived through half a century; what are you afraid of now? You only have a little time left to live. Enjoy what time you have left. You are stupid if you don't do that. Put some zest in your life, go and visit Rientje de Roo occasionally. Yes, like everyone else. Make your life as balanced as possible. You're always anxious and restless. What do you get from being so anxious all the time? Nothing, zero. All you do is destroy yourself and you are afraid to let other people see. Even your own wife.

The warmth of the whiskey was starting to affect my spirits. I took out a pair of scissors and cut the ribbon around the file. There weren't many papers inside. There was a note about the freezing of all the assets belonging to the Central SDI under the control of Raden Mas Minke. This included the building in Bandung where *Medan* was published and all assets, movable or unmovable. The latter included the workers' houses. The rest included all monies, whether in bank accounts or not, the *Medan* kiosks in Bandung, Buitenzorg, Betawi, and the other big towns of Java, the stationery, writing utensils, and office equipment business in Betawi, the *Medan* hotel in Kramat Street in Betawi, and all the contents of Raden Mas Minke's house in Buitenzorg. The company set up by the Solo Branch of the SDI to import raw materials for batik making from Germany and England was also frozen. After reading all that, I went through the papers again and again. There was nothing to indicate that any of this had been done under court order. It was all done outside the law.

I fell into reflection. I couldn't stop thinking, how could Europeans, whose sense of the law is so deep, behave like forest outlaws? If it had been one of the Asian peoples who had done such a thing, I could have understood because their rulers' own capricious, despotic, and lawless behavior meant that Asians had lost all sense of their rights. What they had done to Minke was truly the act of forest outlaws. This was not Europe! And the victim was not even allowed to defend himself! And even before all this, they had stolen his freedom, his liberty, even though in law he had the right to defend himself before the White Courts; he had *forum privilegiatum*.

Ah, why let all this bother me? Wasn't I myself involved in helping to get rid of Raden Mas Minke?

I gulped down what was left in the bottle of whiskey.

His exile had been carried out based on political considerations. There was proof that the person accused had acted against the interests of the government, the governor-general and his authority. And Raden Mas Minke had indeed done all this through his pronouncements in *Medan*. But I had never guessed that they had seized all his property. My conscience could not accept that. No! with precedents like this, there could be no more guarantee of the security of private property. Anybody could be robbed the same way. There would no longer be the certainty of the rule of law. It was back to barbarism. In the end nobody would have rights over their life or their own bodies.

Why should I let all this worry me? It hasn't hurt me, has it? But one day such things could befall you, your wife, or your children.

Hush! Whose side was I on? Did not I myself have the right to rob others while I remained a part of this colonial setup?

I was startled to hear myself give out a cackling laugh. Join in and become a part of colonial power, and I will have the right to do whatever I like to the Natives, even my fellow countrymen up in the North Celebes. Why was I hesitating? Long life to Her Majesty!

I grabbed the bottle again. It was empty. I grabbed the glass. Empty too. Frits, oh, Frits, get me another bottle. But he would not come back. And my laughter cackled on of its own accord.

I went on reading all the papers. I went over and over them. Again and again. All Minke's property had been frozen on the orders of the commission. And the head of that commission—De Lange, Meneer De Lange, who, a few days earlier—had it been a week?—was sprawled out on the floor beside this table, blood oozing from the pores in his skin and his mouth. Why did you do it, De Lange? Couldn't you stand your conscience eating away at you, Meneer De Lange?

I examined the papers again. I studied the signature of the expert I had replaced. There were a few places where there were signs he had been shaking when he signed his name, unable to face his conscience, perhaps? He would have known that all the law that he had studied in university disintegrated into dust when he implemented these acts. Was that the reason you killed yourself, De Lange? Idiot. There was no reason why you shouldn't have been prepared to become a little rotten. Then I wouldn't have had to come up here to replace you. It doesn't surprise me that the detectives have been unable to discover the secret of your death. You chose your conscience rather than your life. Idiot. So all your struggles to become a lawyer were wasted, De Lange.

The bell signaling that the office was about to close rang out. I locked the file in the cabinet. I locked the window and shutters myself, then the door. I pocketed the key to take it home in accordance with regulations. I did not hand it over to the housekeeper, as was also in accordance with regulations.

"Meneer Knor," I said, giving an order, "arrange a car for me and a good driver. I have some business."

The car raced down toward Betawi. Fast! Faster! I must not waste what remains of my life without enjoying its sweeter pleasures. I went straight to police headquarters. No, Meneer Commandant, I do not want to see you.

"You can take the car back now," I told the driver. He nodded respectfully and obediently and climbed back aboard the vehicle, which then disappeared in its cloud of dust and smoke. I went inside. I went straight to the telephone and ordered a taxi.

I was in the taxi now! "Drive slowly," I ordered the driver. "To Kwitang."

The door to Rientje de Roo's pavilion was not closed. As soon as the car stopped at the foot of the veranda, I jumped out and went inside. The young girl was just leaving her room carrying her bag.

"Meneer Pangemanann," she greeted me. "But I am leaving."

"Godverdomme!" I swore. "That is not the way to greet me."

"I have to go to Bandung. I have already called a taxi."

"What is there in Bandung that is more important than me?"

"It's not that, Meneer Pangemanann. Don't be angry. I promised to visit Robert."

"Robert Suurhof? I'll shoot him like a cur. Don't lie to me, I know you have a customer tonight." She gazed at me with her big eyes, hiding behind her eyelashes.

Desire spread through all the glands in my body to the tips of my nerves, as if it were twenty-five years ago. I grabbed the young girl around the waist. "To the devil with those others. Come with me."

I dragged her outside and she locked the door. We climbed aboard the taxi. And Rientje De Roo sat beside me, silent. She was too frightened to even glance at me.

To hell with what people will think. "Tanah Abang Heights!" I told the driver.

"To Panggung, Tuan?" asked the driver.

"Yes, Panggung," I answered abruptly. To Rientje de Roo: "Have you ever been to Panggung?"

"No."

"You're lying. If you didn't know what it was, you would have asked just now."

She didn't say a word. Perhaps she thought that she was about to be involved in some police case. The taxi headed straight to Panggung, a huge timber two-storied house in Tanah Abang Heights, the pleasure house of a Chinese lieutenant.

There were already many people there. There were not just Chinese there enjoying themselves, but Europeans as well. Lieutenant Swie welcomed me, asking: "I'm surprised, Commissioner Pangemanann, you have brought Rientje here with you on an inspection."

"All under control, Babah Swie," I answered drily.

"Enjoy yourself, Tuan," and he left us.

Rientje's eyes were still full of wild suspicions. I grabbed her around the waist and took her over to the cashier.

"Ten half-guilder chits, Bah!"

Rientje glanced at me but did not open her mouth. She thought she had been brought here on police business. That was funny. What was the difference between police and criminal business as long as nobody made any accusations and nothing ever came to court?

I took the ten chits, made from some kind of bone, with red Chinese writing on them whose meaning I did not understand, and said to Rientje: "I bet you can get rid of these ten chits in ten minutes."

She wouldn't speak. She took the chits without a word.

I embraced her round the waist and took her over to the roulette table. She looked pale, this girl no older than my youngest. Even so, it did not detract from her beauty or allure. And I could see many eyes gazing at her full of lust—almost all Chinese, gamblers and adventurers.

"Stay here. Use up all these chits. I will come back later." It gave her no joy to hold those chits. And I could fully understand her unease.

So I left the roulette area, passing by and weaving my way through many old pigtailed Chinese as well as young ones, with their hair cut short, slick with hair oil and neatly combed. Most of them moved aside to let me through.

I found a rattan chair in a corner, where I could sit down and watch Rientje's every move from afar. But all I could see at first were all the people who were peering at me. Nobody approached Rientje. The young prostitute herself was too frightened to look around her. She kept her head bowed down all the time. She was far too conscious that she was being observed by a police commissioner. And the police commissioner himself also knew only too well that he had been retired and was no longer really a policeman.

She lost her first chit and started to bet with a second one.

"Tuan Commissioner." The old pigtailed Chinese man came up to me, bowing all the time and pressing his two hands to his chest in a gesture of respect, so that his sleeve fell back to his elbow exposing his arm, which was nothing but skin and bone. "I haven't seen you for some time, Tuan Commissioner," he smiled, and while he may have grown terribly skinny in his old age, his teeth were without imperfection. "I am so happy to see you sitting here, Tuan. Do you need a drink of *arak*? There's no harm in giving it the occasional try, Tuan. You have never tried it, so you don't believe me."

"How many mistresses do you have, Grandfather?"

"Heh-heh, six, Tuan."

"At your age. How old are you?"

"Eighty years old, Tuan."

"Eighty years old with six mistresses. You are a liar, an impostor."

He only laughed. His sunken, shriveled cheeks stretched sideways and his eyes disappeared.

"The Tuan Commissioner is the only one who has ever said that to me."

"Very well, bring me the arak."

He went away and brought back a small glass on a tray with a raised red dragon painted on it, as if from wax.

"In one gulp, Tuan, just like any other liquor."

I gulped it down without another thought. It wasn't very strong, a bit slow, but left behind a stronger than usual taste. The old man stood there waiting. And I knew he was waiting for payment for the arak. I groped about in my pocket.

"First try, Tuan, no charge," and he took out several keys from his pocket. "Of course, Tuan, you will need one of these."

He laid out the keys on the palm of his hand. Each one had a small bone button with a number on it. My hand flashed out and seized one.

"For that, Tuan, you do indeed have to pay. Five guilders, Tuan, until dawn."

He took his money and paid no heed to me after that. And I could see that Rientje had lost another chit. Perhaps she was bankrupt already. I went over to get her. Even more eyes now looked in my direction. The men playing cards or *mahjong*, the upper class's prostitutes—Chinese, Eurasian, and Native.

Rientje was still busy playing roulette. There were fifty chits piled in front of her—twenty-five guilders. She won another ten chits.

"That's enough, Rientje. Let's go."

She gathered together all her chits and we went to the cashier to cash them in for thirty guilders, about half the monthly cost of my children's education in the Netherlands. I didn't believe this child could be so lucky. Those bandits running the roulette made sure she won as a plan to get all my money later on.

"It's all for you, Rientje."

For the first time there was puzzlement in her eyes, and she still did not speak. She put the thirty guilders in her bag and stood waiting for my orders. Once again I seized her around the waist and I took her up the stairs to the next floor. "We'll go up, Rientje."

As she stepped onto the first stair on the way up, she looked at me calmly as if she couldn't believe that somebody who had just a few days ago treated her as his own daughter was now inviting her up to a room that she usually entered with other men, anyone who was able to pay.

Not the slightest sound came from the carpeted stairs as we climbed them. On the next floor, a long carpet took people to the rooms they desired. Here it was peaceful and quiet like on the top of a mountain. Here and there were open windows, and if you happened to glance down you could see the lights of Tanah Abang flickering like stars that shone on earth instead of in the sky. And the lights from the passing vehicles were like fireflies rushing through the darkness.

I gave her the key. She took it silently and went straight to the door with the same number.

See, I can do this too. . . .

The next day I had not long been at my desk when Monsieur R— came in. He said good morning and sat down in front of my desk.

"The first thing I want to do today is say how much I respect your abilities, Meneer. You have been paying quite a bit of attention to things that I have ignored. You have put aside time to read the Malay stories that the Chinese writers are publishing. Lie K— H— is from the older generation. Did you know he was a Protestant?" I shook my head. "Self-educated. He reads a lot, he has a lot to say. But I am not convinced that he has been influenced much by the awakening in China. Most of the experts say that any Chinese who has given up the religion of his ancestors would not be interested in what was happening in China."

"Perhaps. Maybe you could say that giving up the old religion and beliefs also means forgetting the country of your ancestors, but I am not

convinced of that either, Monsieur. As far as Lie K— H— is concerned, I
have to admit I haven't studied him in depth. There are about fourteen of
these new Chinese writers. Their stories are half journalistic, a bit like elon-
gated newspaper reports, very much like what the Eurasians have been
writing, but in Dutch as well as Malay."

"So you think most of these Chinese are following the lead of the
Eurasian writers?"

I had to agree with what he said.

"And what about the Natives, Meneer Pangemanann? You would
know these even better?"

"The Natives haven't begun writing yet, Monsieur, at least not in the
European sense, in Malay or Dutch, let alone their mother tongues. If there
are one or two, they are exceptions. Haji Moelek's *The Tale of Siti Aini*, for
example, and Raden Mas Minke's *Nyai Permana*. But they are not representative."

"So you think that means that there is no awakening taking place
among the Natives? And isn't Haji Moelek a Eurasian anyway?" he asked,
egging me on.

I realized that he was testing my own knowledge of what was happening among the Natives. This was clearly something that could affect my
position here. I launched forth with all sorts of evidence to show that the
Indies Natives on Java were already beginning to rise up, had already placed
time bombs in all the towns of Java that could explode at any moment,
setting the Indies aflame.

That, I said, was the reason that Raden Mas Minke was exiled, to get
rid of the initiator, the pioneer of a national awakening. He was dangerous!
He himself did not understand that what he was doing was dangerous. The
government was fortunate that it was dealing with someone who did not
understand the possible consequences of his actions.

He listened to me in the same way that I listened to Meneer L— when
he spoke about the Javanese. He looked at me with a clear face as I spoke,
like a school student who was learning for the first time one of the mysterious secrets of nature.

"You have not said a single word that differs from what Meneer De
Lange used to say. Did you know him?"

"No, Meneer."

"It's a pity that he died. You and he would have been able to work
together well. Two people, but one opinion, and one assessment."

It was a state secret that De Lange had done no more than study my
own reports. And I think he also knew that this was the case, but was testing
me to see how solid I was in keeping such secrets. Here in the Algemeene

Secretariat it seemed that I was once again stuck in a mudhole where there were many even more dangerous traps awaiting me.

"So it is your opinion that there are two peoples awakening here in the Indies—the Chinese and the Natives?" he asked.

"Exactly right."

"Two kinds of awakening. Both of them in the Indies where there is only one power—the Netherlands Indies government. It is your opinion that this movement led by Raden Mas Minke has planted time bombs in all the towns of Java. In other words, the government is in great danger. Perhaps you could say something more about the awakening of the Chinese?"

"Now it is Meneer's turn to give his opinion," I said.

And with that, the morning's conversation, where he had been feeling out my opinions, came to an end. He went back to his office. But I knew that he would be back again with another problem sooner or later. I had to be careful not to give an answer that could be used against me at some later moment. My appointment as an expert adviser to the Algemeene Secretariat meant that my opinions would be used in solving or reviewing all sorts of problems.

Monsieur R— came back with a new file, also sealed. In his usual friendly manner and hiding his nervousness, he spoke in his usual French: "Nobody else may read these documents, only yourself, and whoever you approve."

"An honor," I said, no less politely.

"Why do you leave the door open?"

"I can work better with the fresh breeze coming in and out like this, Monsieur."

"Very well, if that is your custom, but make sure you are extra vigilant about who comes into this office. Be especially careful with your papers. Not even a single sheet must ever be lost."

There was no indication of who sent the file or to whom it was sent, just as was the case with the first file. There were no postage stamps. There was nothing to show from where it had been sent. The seal was marked with a simple W with a crown, the symbol of Her Majesty's rule in the Indies.

"I think you had better study these papers as quickly as possible. You have to be able to answer any inquiries concerning your work from anybody who has dealings with these matters, that is to say, everybody who has permission to enter these offices, except of course the attendants and so on."

"Very well, Monsieur."

"How is Madame? Is she settled in now and happy here in Buitenzorg?"

"Of course, Monsieur, providing she does not think of our canceled
holiday in Europe."

"Yes, a great pity. But it was inevitable. I was upset too. But there is
so much work to do, and it all has to be taken care of quickly."

As soon as he left, I opened the packet. I left the door open. There
was no letterhead inside, no accompanying letter. Just a list of the documents that were attached and a statement as to their number.

The first document explained that as soon as the import company
owned by the Solo SDI was frozen, the batik firms went back to buying
from Geo Wehry and Borsumij.

The next document described how this government decision had in-
furiated the SDI leadership. And that they used this situation to even further
agitate the masses.

The third document explained how the decision to exile Minke had
caused an increase in SDI membership in a number of places. The local
Native administrators warned that this was tantamount to a challenge to the
government and that the government should give some consideration as to
how it should react.

The fourth document was a long report from Solo, taking up at least
forty pages, in tiny, packed-together, and beautiful handwriting, but terrible
Malay. The report set out the details concerning recent activities of the SDI
in Solo that had come to the attention of both the Native and white administration. Haji Samadi and the rest of the SDI leadership had issued a
statement announcing the formation of an organization called the Sarekat
Islam, with Haji Samadi as leader. But the whole leadership of the SI was
the same as the old SDI. It seemed that, while avoiding mentioning the
SDI, Haji Samadi and the other leaders were making it clear that as far as
they were concerned, they no longer had any connection with Raden Mas
Minke.

The fifth document came from Semarang and explained that the SDI
membership in the sugar areas along the north coast of Java had doubled.
It was their guess that the increase in membership was a reaction to Minke's
exile.

The sixth document was from Bandung. In several towns in West
Java, including Pameungpeuk, Banjanegara, Ciamis, Garut, and Cianjur,
and especially in Sukabumi, SDI members were behaving with outright
hostility toward government officials.

Documents like these that just reported the facts did not demand much
thought on my part. I took a sheet of paper and wrote out my comments,

concluding with a recommendation that all the reports—and I wrote out several quotations and the origins of the reports—be double-checked for accuracy. The follow-up reports should be submitted as soon as possible. I took my note myself to Monsieur R—.

He was busy examining files and I excused myself.

Back in my office I discovered Frits Doertier quickly glancing through my manuscripts. I realized straightaway that I had been negligent. I was wearing rubber-soled shoes from England. It was only after I was well inside the room that he realized I was there. He moved quickly away from the desk and made to look as if he was about to wipe down the chairs with his flannel cloth.

"What part were you reading, Frits?"

"I didn't read anything, Meneer. I was just putting the papers aside so I could wipe down the table."

"What part were you reading?" I asked again.

"No, Meneer, I didn't read any of it."

And I knew that I could do nothing to him. I had left the door open and had forgotten to lock the papers away before I went to see Monsieur R—.

"Would you prefer to be dishonorably discharged?"

"Don't, Meneer. I haven't done anything wrong. It is my job to tidy up and clean all rooms left open. That's what the regulations here say, Meneer."

"Empty your pockets, Frits."

"No, Meneer, I won't do that. You have no right to do that to me. You need a police order to search a person, or at the very least a policeman as a witness. You of all people should know that."

"Very well," I said. "Stay here, don't leave," and I reached for the telephone and reported the incident to Monsieur R— and asked for somebody from palace security to come and search Frits Doertier.

Monsieur R— arrived with Nicolaas Knor. And the latter immediately thundered his anger at Frits Doertier.

"What about all the advice I gave you? Why have you shamed me like this?"

"That's enough, Knor," intervened Monsieur R—. "And you, Frits, who gave you permission to touch those papers?"

"I had to clean the table, Meneer."

And it was no one else but I who suffered shame because of this incident. But I thought the risk involved was greater than the shame. That I forgot to close the door and lock it was something I had to admit. I had to admit also that I did not lock the files away in the cabinet. But to risk a leak or loss of official documents would be to sin against the government.

A sergeant in the palace guard arrived, listened to my report, and ordered Frits Doertier to take off all his outer clothing, which was then examined. There was nothing except Frits's personal belongings. The sergeant reported that there was nothing found on the person, saluted, and left.

"So what now, Meneer Pangemanann? It is you who must decide now," Monsieur R— spoke in French to me.

"Yes," I answered also in French. "I am very much ashamed of what has happened. I know I was negligent in not locking the door and forgetting to put the papers away. It is up to you, Meneer, to decide which of us you most need to keep."

"You are the more important, of course," he answered. "Do you want him to be dismissed?"

I knew I was in the wrong, and I knew that Frits was also in the wrong. I because of negligence, he out of conscious intent. At that moment, I couldn't find an answer. My mind was working through the pros and cons of what was just.

"Do you feel you should apologize, Frits?" asked Monsieur R— in Dutch.

Putting his clothes back on, the teenager replied: "What reason is there for me to apologize, Meneer?"

"Very well. You need not report here again, Child," said Monsieur R—, while observing me.

"I think that is the best," I said in French.

"A pity, Frits," said Monsieur R— in Dutch. "Leave this office now."

"Very well, Meneer. I will come and fetch my letter of dismissal tomorrow, which should explain that I was not dismissed dishonorably. I have done nothing wrong." He nodded respectfully to Monsieur R—, to me, and to Nicolaas Knor, then walked out of the room.

"Is there anything you want me to do, Meneers?" asked Knor.

Monsieur R— shook his head. He stared at me silently as if he were testing me inside.

"I am truly sorry this has happened, Monsieur R—," I said.

"Nothing like this would happen in the police, Meneer Pangemanann. I am also very sorry. It is a pity you are no longer a policeman. I could imagine that you would take this matter to court if you were a policeman. But here, Meneer, we cannot do that. Nothing that happens here may become public. This office must remain respectable and respected. Nothing must happen that harms its reputation."

Nicolaas Knor returned carrying a bundle of Malay-language newspapers and magazines.

"This is the first time I have brought these here since Meneer De Lange died." He looked straight across to the little table in the corner. Then he left again saying a thank you to me on his way out.

"You will get used to the rules and customs here," said Monsieur R—; then he also left.

I threw myself into reading the magazines and papers that had just arrived, trying to forget all about what had just happened. And anyway, this was going to be my daily routine for the foreseeable future. And I always found it interesting to read this kind of material. From an author's writing, I would construct how he felt and thought, what his desires were, which way he leaned on this and that, his dreams, his stupidities and his weaknesses, what were his particular skills and capabilities, how broad was his general knowledge, and everything was linked together, as if by clear crystal threads. Every piece of writing was a world unto itself, floating halfway between reality and a dream world.

That was the first level at which I looked at things. The next thing I had to do was consider if these little worlds halfway between dreams and reality were in fact bullets aimed at the government. If they were bullets, it would be I who would assess their caliber and speed. And if the speed and caliber were enough, it would be my job to get rid of these particular bullets so they did not hit their target.

Among the writings of note that had appeared while I was away escorting that Modern Pitung alias Minke to Ambon were a number commenting on his exile.

One among them read more or less as follows:

Europe and the West possess a wealth of knowledge and learning that every day grows larger at an ever-increasing pace. It seems that here in the Indies every time a Native gets hold of just a tiny, meaningless speck of that knowledge, he feels so strong that he begins to behave as if he can compete with Europeans. That is not the reason we Dutch have taught the Natives to read and write. And so what will happen as more and more Natives receive a higher education? It will be of no use to them, their people, or the government. They will cause disturbances and problems everywhere. And worse than that, this new knowledge they have will only cause them to lose their own happiness. In the Indies, the happiest people of all are the peasants, precisely because they know nothing of the world and its problems. To broaden the education of the Natives is the same as to rob them of their happiness. An example of this is the current case of the leader of the SDI, Raden Mas Minke, who is now departing into exile. What is the point of a high education if its only fruit is one's own exile? His education has not been of any benefit to him, nor to his family, nor to his people. It has been in vain that the government educated him.

Another assessment:

Raden Mas Minke, the wild man from Medan, has been exiled to Ternate. Only Ternate. None of his ancestors would have escaped with such a nearby exile. They would have ended up in Ceylon or South Africa. If he has any understanding at all, he will realize how generous His Excellency the governor-general has been in allowing him to still have some hope of returning to his homeland one day. And how kind the Netherlands Indies has been in never executing any Natives of the people of Raden Mas Minke. Study the history of the Indies since the Dutch have ruled here. Has a noble ever been executed? In these last three hundred years, it has rather been the Native kings themselves who have often ordered the death sentence for their own people. Are these not all signs of the greatness and generosity of the European heart?

If this wild one, this Raden Mas Minke, possessed just a little real understanding, he would know that what the government has done for his people has been far, far more and of far greater benefit than anything ever done by the Native kings in all their history.

Who was it that abolished forced labor? Not Raden Mas Minke, not the Native kings, but the government in all its glory. Who was it that taught his people, including Raden Mas Minke himself, to read and write? The government, not the kings of Java. Why was it that the cleverer he became, the more ungrateful and rebellious was his thinking? So it is only proper that people such as he are gotten rid of so as to lessen the ingratitude and troublesomeness in society. Is not our aim in life to have security, order, and calm so that we may be sure that all our plans meet with success?

I put these two examples of the reaction aside so I could discuss them later with Meneer L— and Monsieur R—. I knew just too well that they represented colonial thought in its most pure form. They used beautiful words, and presented the honorable face of the moralist, but were totally dishonest about the essence of colonial power. Because the reality was that only the powerful had the right to decide on how life would be lived, and on everything else. It was the powerful who had the right to decide what was wrong and what was right, what was just and what was unjust, what was good and what was bad. Whoever had the power could do whatever they wanted, until someone more powerful came along and reined them in or crushed them altogether. So life in the colonies was not like that in democratic Europe. In the colonies life bowed down before whoever was strong or stronger—in other words, colonial power itself.

Ah, these papers should have been just a bit fairer than that. If they were a bit more honest they would have written that Natives like Minke must learn that they are not yet strong enough, because colonial power comes from the sword, machines, and capital, while the Natives have none of these things.

You have to understand, my teacher, that during the three hundred years of Dutch rule in the Indies they built a pyramid of Native corpses, and that is their throne. I respect and honor you because you have changed the face of the Indies, because as a rebel you have achieved many things. But you did not understand the real inner workings of colonial power. You were too small in the scheme of things to challenge this power. You never saw the pyramid of your people's corpses that has been their throne. If you had seen it, you would have run, run without ever turning back.

And just think, they have done this not just to you whose rebelliousness has succeeded in changing the Indies. Governor-General Idenburg had no qualms at all about exiling Natives who, after studying in Europe, did nothing more than demand equal wages with Europeans. They annoyed His Excellency because they had become so bigheaded as to think that they were the equals of Europeans. An example is Sutan Casayanag. And he is in the same place as you, my teacher, in the Moluccas!

Perhaps Minke himself would read all these excuses. I could imagine so clearly how all these spears would pierce through his heart, and he had no right to defend himself!

I had not yet finished reading the newspapers and magazines when the bell rang letting us all know we were now to go home.

That evening the family gathered in the parlor. The children were reading storybooks. They loved to read everything and anything that was connected with France. Madame sat silently beside me, doing embroidery, looking out toward the main road.

I just sat there enjoying the fresh evening air and smoking my cigar. I had not the slightest desire to think about anything to do with the office. Now that I had passed the half-century mark, I had to be able to bring some order to my life so that I could enjoy these moments of peace and quiet. The SDI could run amok all over Java, but evenings like this were for me alone to enjoy. Someone of my age who did now know how to be calm and how to enjoy the peace and quiet would achieve only rapid, and even more rapid, degeneration. Wasn't it precisely for moments such as these that I worked so hard and ignored my conscience?

Outside in the wider world, there were predictions that before long mankind would experience new, unparallelled comforts brought by electricity. Electricity could already send signals through Morse, and the human voice over wire as in the telephone, and now, they said, you could hear classical music and speeches and news of sensational incidents. It was being predicted that soon everyone would have such an instrument in their homes. You would never need to read again because electricity would read the news, speeches, and lectures for you. What was the meaning of happiness if it was not to savor such moments as these, moment after moment, without your conscience jumping up and down making accusations?

There was no traffic on the road. Except occasionally a carriage rolling past, its driver nodding off as he went. People here didn't seem to like going out much.

Aha—there were those two women again. I watched them walk along, one behind the other, then stop as they did the other day and hold on to the fence. Why were these two beggars always hanging around our house? Why were they afraid to enter?

I got up and went inside to fetch my telescope. I sat down in my chair and looked at them through the telescope. The woman at the back was tugging on the other, trying to get her to leave. They seemed to be wearing quite respectable clothes. They weren't beggars. They weren't carrying any bamboo box. No coconut shell either.

I thought I recognized the woman who was pulling from behind. I stood and looked harder. Yes, I had seen her. And the woman in front. She was staring in our direction with an intense look in her eyes. It was not just a passing glance. She was watching us.

It hit me in a flash and my arms lost all their strength. The telescope crashed onto the glass top of the table.

"Jacques!" my wife cried out, throwing aside her embroidery. The children also stopped reading. Everyone was watching me. I myself hurried across to the telephone. I rang the police station and asked them to take care of those two women!

"And search them."

The woman was none other than Piah. The one in front was the excellent shot with the revolver, the Princess of Kasiruta. That poor child wanted to shoot me. How ungrateful she was. Didn't she know that she owed me? Wasn't I the only one in the world who could prove it was she who shot Suurhof?

My wife chased after me and humored me: "It's just a couple of women looking for work, Jacques. Maybe they want to ask here."

Without answering I went into my study and fetched my pistol. I put it in my pocket. When it came to shooting, perhaps I would come off second best. At the very least I had to be ready to defend my wife and children if she ran amok.

The police arrived, arrested and detained the two women. I heard the argument between them and the Princess.

"Come and see what's happening," I called to my children, who were already about to get up to have a look.

We could hear the Princess shouting abuse at the police and Piah groaning from being kicked. Then there was a scream of pain from the Princess. Everyone in the street was coming out of their houses to have a look. The children didn't come back. They followed the police back to the station.

"Why were you so hard on them, Jacques?" asked my wife.

"They ruined the view, darling. I work hard all day and then my rest is ruined because of them."

She looked at me, completely amazed: "There are many women out of work like that in France, too. Would you call the police to get rid of them also?"

"Yes."

"Yes? Everyone would curse and condemn you."

"Not here. No one will condemn me here," I answered curtly.

"Why have you become so hard these days?" she asked, unbelievingly, more to herself than to me.

I didn't hear what else she said, I didn't listen. I vomited anger all over my insides. And I wasn't angry at the Princess of Kasiruta, but at myself. How faithful was that young woman. She wanted to find a way to have it out with me. It was only Piah who tried to stop her. If she had possessed a gun, she would have come straight in after me. But she didn't. Perhaps all she had was a knife. And so she hesitated.

"Men beating up on a woman, police too, making her groan like that."

No! There was no newspaper that would defend them. *Medan* was dead and buried. No one would speak out for them. Those groans came from the throat of a corpse. Their ancestors had been treated worse by the Company. They were just slightly injured. The police who beat them were no doubt Ambonese or Eurasian. But you, a retired police commissioner, why did you look on silently? Indeed, it was you who ordered that they be arrested, detained, and searched.

My wife's nagging was getting worse. It was as if she was the one suffering. She didn't realize that all that young woman's bullets could come smashing into her head.

Neither of us spoke to the other, as if we had become enemies. The children returned and told us how the two women had been tormented all the way back to the police station.

"Nobody did anything?" asked my wife.

"Everyone just watched," said Mark.

"And what about you, you stupid child?"

"Shut up, everyone!" I shouted an order, suppressing the torment that was inside my heart . . . in my own heart . . .

5

The government had issued an order—Meester Hendrik Frischboten was to be deported from the Indies. The order was then executed. This lawyer much beloved by the Natives—the legal adviser to *Medan*'s legal column—shed tears as he walked up the gangway onto the ship. So did his wife, who was carrying their baby. A crowd of wharf laborers went aboard with them and showered them with thank-yous and presents.

In a broken voice Frischboten told them: "There is nothing more precious than sincere friendship, my beloved friends. Thank you for all your kindness. There is no human being who can live without friendship and kindness, because anything else is not human. Good-bye to you all whom I love and care for so much."

Full of emotion, they all shook hands, as though they were all family. There were no color differences; they did not care where the others came from.

And I descended from the ship with an empty heart. They did not even know each other, but they could be such friends to each other and truly love each other, more than their own families, bound together by shared kindnesses and good deeds. Frischboten had also said: "Permit me to leave behind a message: My greetings to Raden Mas Minke, whom I

have been unable to defend in his difficulties, which have not been overcome. And I say to you all here too—do not forget him. It was your friend
Raden Mas Minke who has been the pioneer, the one who began, because
he was the first to light up the way and lead you all.''

I knew that Frischboten was an honorable man, honest to himself as
well as others. But the pronouncements and actions of honorable men no
longer moved my soul as they once did. On the contrary, they irritated and
annoyed me. And I knew the reason. My own ruination was not only more
and more certain, I was becoming more and more contemptible and rotten.
And the worst thing was that I was fully aware of this.

People were still talking about Minke. And who wouldn't be irritated
and annoyed with that? The SDI did not fade away. My eyes, and of course
the eyes of the government, were now focused on Solo. It was now Haji
Samadi's turn to ascend the stage. The organization's membership exploded,
unlike anything that had ever occurred before in history.

At an emergency conference in Solo, the SDI branches changed their
name to Sarekat Islam. And, yes, it was I who had to work overtime because
of all this. Paid henchmen were gathered together and put under my control
through connections that would protect the government's good name. But
all of them were of no better quality than Robert Suurhof.

But I could not stem the rush of new members to the SI. I understood
that the time had now come when organization had to be added to the list
of the Natives' real needs. It was my task to stop this. It wasn't only I, but
I think all the experts on colonial affairs, who were amazed to see how
quickly the Sarekat Islam developed after the leadership shifted from Minke
into the hands of Haji Samadi.

Even so, my original report was still considered correct, because the
governor-general had been able to take the decision to exile Minke in time.
If he had been late in doing so, then this Modern Pitung might have caused
as much trouble outside Java as well. The Sarekat was growing into
something quite large, but it would not be able to do anything without
Minke's brains.

When my boss, Monsieur R—, gave me urgent orders to come up
with recommendations about how to deal with the continuing growth in
the size of the Sarekat, I set out straightaway to study all the suggestions
and recommendations that had come in from the local administrations, both
brown and white. They were all worried about the attitude Sarekat members, especially new ones, were exhibiting toward government bodies and
officials.

My boss's orders showed that the colonial authorities were nervous
and so was my boss.

And there was no denying it, the organization's growth was amazing. Rough estimates coming in put its membership at between 250 and 300 thousand people. No organization in Europe had ever grown as much in just four years! There was one document prepared by certain officials in Kasunanan that said that these two men—Minke and Haji Samadi—had agreed to transfer SDI headquarters to Solo because it was only in Solo that the Natives had retained their independence, as was reflected in the social and economic life of the town. It was also suggested that the princes of Solo, dreaming of the greatness of past times, were preparing to use their new power to further their own private ambitions. But another view was that the Solo nobility had lost all ambition and would never raise their faces against the Dutch again. This last document said that the Susuhunan of Solo would take a neutral stance toward the Sarekat.

As I read these documents I began to wonder, was it true that there was no brain behind the Sarekat? I was locked in a game of chess against Minke. He was living peacefully in exile while I was running about madly like this. I was playing chess against the man whom I considered my teacher, whom I respected and honored. The game had not ended with his exile, but had only entered its first phase. At the same time, I knew for certain from our surveillance that there was no communication between Ternate and Solo, neither open nor underground.

Then I received a report that I found no difficulty in believing—Haji Samadi was also in a state of confusion. He didn't know what to do with such a large mass following—a mass following thirsty for leadership and action. If he were to work on that problem, his own business would fall into ruins. If he didn't try to do something, he would lose all public credibility. And even if he wanted to give them the leadership they wanted, he didn't know how.

I worked for a week. Every day Monsieur R— came to see me, his nervous tension getting worse all the time. And all the time, more reports arrived, all on clean white paper, and all bearing their own story. In this hurried manner, I finally finished my paper, which recommended that the government let it be known that not only was Raden Mas Minke out of favor but so also were all the members of the Sarekat. And so a decree should be issued forbidding all State employees, from the top to the bottom, to join the Sarekat, and ordering them not to give the Sarekat any room to be active.

"We've issued the instruction as you recommended," said Monsieur R—, "but why so gentle?"

"Taking action against an individual and against the masses are two different things, Monsieur, requiring different analysis and approaches. The masses are more or less easily mobilized depending on the quality of their leaders. Now with Minke gone, whose caliber we fully understood, they might start producing new leaders at the local level, about whom we know nothing as yet. We need time." This new policy did not hit the target either. The government had no legal authority to interfere in the workings of public organizations. And there was no law under which a State employee could be forced to prove that he was not a Sarekat member.

So my recommendations ran into obstacles before they could be fully implemented, even though in some places they eventually had the effect of controlling the activities of a few officials. On the other hand, they eventually caused other people in other places even more aggravation. These people, who basically had no love for colonial authority, were inflamed into even greater revolt. The undeniable result of the government's new instruction was that the Sarekat began to recruit even more members. A European daily, not from the Netherlands, estimated that the membership had reached half a million, had become the biggest mass organization to emerge this century and was active over an area the size of Europe. Another English-language paper from outside the Indies estimated 300,000. Haji Samadi himself never responded. He probably never even knew that these foreigners were commenting on his organization. Perhaps he himself didn't know what the membership was anymore. And my own estimate, based on the official reports of government officers, was between 300,000 and 350,000. But no one knew exactly how many there were.

But what was the point of making such a fuss over numbers? Both from the point of view of the quality of its membership as well as its leadership, it was clear that the organization was unable to raise itself up onto a higher level. The Sarekat would never be anything more than a heap of rocks cemented together by nothing more than private daydreams, not by the shared dreams of all its membership, and so it would not be able to carry out any united action.

This became the basis of my thinking on what needed to be done.

Haji Samadi himself seemed to be affected by the prevailing colonial opinion that he would never be capable of leading half a million members. He was going crazy with confusion. Then another report came in that he was rushing around Java, going from town to town, trying to meet as many educated Natives as possible, hoping that he would find someone whom he could ask to help organize and lead the Sarekat. Our surveillance soon gave us additional information—the type of person he wanted to meet was not only educated but also Moslem with a knowledge of religion, one who had real experience, and not just an indirect knowledge, of modern commerce.

Poor Samadi—if you didn't have an ambition to be a leader, you could be living a nice, peaceful life looking after your business. Now you've become a workhorse climbing up and down mountains, carting things about which don't even belong to you, and are not for your use either.

Sitting at my desk in my office in Buitenzorg, I was able to follow this batik trader everywhere he went, to Betawi, Semarang, and Surabaya, checking out all the addresses he had obtained. It became widely known in all three of these towns that he wished to meet educated Natives who were working for the import-export companies Borsumij and Geo Wehry. It was not difficult to guess what he was doing. The most important thing for him was to find someone who could help him save his batik business in Solo, which could no longer obtain dyes directly from Europe, from ruin. He was really after someone who could help him get his business out of trouble. The Sarekat was second priority.

Then something unexpected happened that was rather unnerving. Monsieur R— came to see me several times in one day, and Meneer G— too, although never together. It seemed that Governor-General Idenburg was in a rotten temper because of an article in an English newspaper that insultingly stated that, compared with India, the Indies was hell. The Moslems of Java, said the article, had organized themselves. All the actions taken by the Netherlands Indies government had failed to yield results. There would soon be outbreaks of unrest if the Netherlands Indies government did not undertake radical reform and leave behind its outdated ways.

There would be no reforms of the government system, said Idenburg. The Indies government would not give up the time-honored ways of doing things that had always guided the Indies authorities.

But I, Pangemanann, who was groaning under this mountain of work, would have no choice but to try new ways.

Monsieur R—, in his usual nervous manner, said: "There is no way the government will bend just because there is something going on among the Natives. The government is strong, and will always be stronger than the Natives. Otherwise, there will be no place for the government here in the Indies."

So I had to order some more severe acts of repression. The game of chess against Raden Mas Minke was entering its final stages. But how could I take such action when there were no legal grounds or means for doing so?

"From what I can tell from your reports," said Monsieur R—, "you've approached this problem of the Sarekat from the outside. What about if you study how it works internally?"

"Is that an order, Monsieur R—?"

"Yes, that is an order."

"Could you put it in writing?"

He promised he would do so and then left.

"Meneer Pangemanann," Meneer G— began as soon as he sat down in front of me, "there was once a governor-general who lost his position because of an incident involving the Chinese community. Do you remember what happened?"

I could not remember the name of that governor-general. I had heard about the incident, but did not know much about its background.

"What a pity you have forgotten his name," he said, "but of course it is not your field. But you remember the year, of course?"

"The Chinese Massacre, 1740," I answered.

"The important thing is the background to what happened. If you have no objection, perhaps I could explain what happened?" And I had no objection even though the task of finding a way out for His Excellency Idenburg's fury still lay before me.

"During the ten years before the incident many Chinese came and settled in the area around Betawi. Restlessness spread like wildfire among them when the Company threatened to evict them. The Chinese who worked in the city, mainly peddlers, craftsmen, building workers, had achieved a high level of solidarity in their struggle against the European businesses that were supported by the Company. The Native bourgeoisie were bankrupt and there was no sign of them rising again. You could count the occupations of the Natives on one hand—farmer, laborer, fisherman, and salaried employee in the service of the government or the local Native rulers, and finally—criminals. All large-scale commercial activity, including inter-island trade, was in the hands of the Company or other Europeans. The Chinese had not moved into wholesale trade like they have now, but they controlled small-scale retail trade and provisions for all public works. The Europeans were just beginning to feel the competition from the enterprise of the Chinese, but the Natives had felt it severely for a long time. There was social envy, agitation—you know the rest."

"The Chinese Massacre," I answered in reply.

"So, what do you think about all this?"

"Well, it's clear from the fall of the governor-general of the time that the incident was generally condemned."

"Things were harder in those days," he continued. "The idea behind the massacre was to prevent the social and economic advance of the Chinese. But they were not stopped. They soon had complete control over all petty and medium-level trade. Then they started to press even further upward, starting to compete with the Europeans and Arabs. The Europeans were able to hold their own, but the Arabs all succumbed. And that is the situation that we find today. And at the beginning of this century they have entered a period of national awakening. If it were confined to China itself, there would be no need for us to trouble ourselves. But this is the Indies, Meneer Pangemanann. Can you imagine what might happen in ten years' time if they continue to progress the way they have?"

And so it was that he placed before me, on my desk for me to analyze, the problem of the races in the Indies—European, Arab, Chinese, and Native—and the relations among them.

"What about the Indians?" I asked.

"They have never played an important role. They have always been in a more sensitive situation. Why, what about them?"

Equipped with rather indirect instructions, and a letter authorizing me to use the documents at the State archives, I ordered a car and driver which took me to Betawi. There was nothing that I needed from them, I just wanted to get away from my office, from the never-ending stream of orders. I needed a more peaceful atmosphere.

Meneer L— was very happy to see me. Once again he quickly served up another lecture about the Javanese. God, it felt as though my brain became swollen every time I listened to his endless lectures. He repeated everything he had said before, adding here and there some additional facts to strengthen his case.

"So it all began during the glorious days of the Majapahit Empire, as told by Tantular. All religions are the same. And as a result religion and all principles themselves disappeared. The Javanese were left without any guide in life. Foreign merchants introduced Islam to them. These merchants were at heart people who needed to gain the friendship and trust of the Javanese so they naturally tended toward making compromises. If some other religion had been introduced to the Javanese at that time, using the same methods, then the Javanese would have adopted it just as easily, along with the friendship of whoever brought it, so as to accommodate to the new situation. They had lost the principles that they had been taught by the religion of their ancestors. They received no new principles from their new religion. This was the period of the spiritual and philosophical decline of the Javanese and this is why they were not able to resist the Europeans."

God knows what else he went on to say. A lot, such a great lot. All that I heard which entered my consciousness was: "Majapahit, an empire no less well organized than the Roman Empire . . . the biggest maritime power in the world during that time . . . destroyed from within . . . it collapsed spiritually, philosophically, socially, economically, and organizationally. . . . Islam could not save the Javanese from their decline. Even up until today. Their decline made them turn their backs on reality . . . they turned to dreams, predictions, magic formulas, mantras, all the heritage of Tantrayana. . . . Meneer Pangemanann, when the Company began gobbling up Java, region after region, using military tactics unknown in Native military history, what was happening in the centers of Javanese life, in the courts of the raja? *Babad Tanah Jawa*. That is the answer. It's a pity you don't read Javanese. This is the book of the Javanese that tells of their downfall, step by step, up until today, though without understanding that they did not suffer defeat only in the matter of losing control over territory but also in the spiritual, philosophical, social, economic, and organizational fields. Since the fall of Majapahit this people have not left behind anything of value to humanity, or to themselves."

"But what about the Javanese today?"

"That's what I have been talking about. We are heading toward the deepest point in their decline since the fall of Majapahit in 1478. There is nothing else to be told about the Javanese since then, except their decline which is leading them toward extinction."

"But aren't the overseas papers talking about the rising up of the Indies bourgeoisie?"

"The rising up of the bourgeoisie? Do you mean like in the early years of the French Revolution?"

"No, you can't equate them like that. The European bourgeoisie awakened and developed Europe, and then started to put pressure on the aristocracy, and then replaced them as rulers. The Javanese bourgeoisie did not develop anything, or do very much of anything else either. They are just beginning to open their eyes. The European press is calling that an 'awakening.' Ah, no, they have not yet awakened. Perhaps you agree with my assessment?"

"The decline of the Javanese has gone too far, Meneer. The rising up of the bourgeoisie should occur in Aceh or Bali, where the people have preserved their integrity, not in Java. Except that the Acehnese and Balinese bourgeoisie are far too weak. When you see how far the Javanese have fallen, from plus to minus, you will realize how any awakening in Java should have taken place in the wake of the resistance of the Balinese and Acehnese. Perhaps the Javacentric policies of the Dutch are the reason the awakening is taking place in Java, if you can really call it an awakening."

"Do you think we can call it an awakening?"

"No, I don't believe that is happening yet. The bourgeoisie in Java are still too weak. They haven't achieved anything worthwhile yet."

"What are your views on the Sarekat Islam?" I asked.

"Well, if you are referring to how big it has grown, I don't think that means anything. I'm sorry, perhaps that's a rather hasty opinion. I think that these days, Meneer Pangemanann, it is not enough to look at the size of an organization but what kind of leadership it has and where that leadership is leading it. How do you evaluate its leadership, Meneer?"

His question put me to shame. It would have been worse if I had to answer it. I, for whom these matters were my profession, had not given these two matters any thought at all. I answered in all honesty that I had not yet thought about these issues. Yet it was the answers to these questions that I was looking for in coming to grips with my new tasks.

I went straight back to my office without going home first. Nicolaas Knor was the only one about as he lived in the palace complex. He ran hither and thither ordering food and drink for me from his own household.

I was able to finish a draft working paper that evening with recommendations that information be sought as soon as possible about the inner workings of the Sarekat. In particular the quality of its leadership and how they worked, the situation regarding its Arab members and a report on their general outlook.

And I knew that the next morning while I was bathing, express orders would be sent via the latest technology throughout Java. Exactly how and to whom, I didn't know. And anyway, that was none of my business. I did not need nor was I obliged to know.

As I walked to the office the next day I could not get rid of the great admiration I had for the foresight of the Hindus when they divided humankind into castes: brahman, ksatria, waisya, and sudra. It was no coincidence the way these castes were ordered either. It was true indeed that it was the brahmans, the priests and holy men who first ruled over mankind; then they were overthrown and replaced by the ksatria, the knights and soldiers. The French Revolution was a classic example of how the ksatria were then overthrown and replaced by the waisya, the merchants and craftsmen.

And the waisya in Java? Perhaps Meneer L— looked at the problem of the Sarekat using these Hindu castes, and saw that the merchants and craftsmen were too weak and small a group to be conscious of themselves as a caste. Be that as it may, I was scampering hither and thither looking for answers. If you could analyze the situation of the waisya of Java the way Meneer L— was doing, then everything would be much easier. You wouldn't have to take into account things like the stage of development they were at, the different ways they started to emerge, and the particular manner in which they expressed themselves. The waisya of Java, weak and unconscious of their own position, were already a threat. And I still could not discover the secret of their strength. Who knew what the secret was? Certainly Haji Samadi had no idea.

I submitted a new proposal, which in essence meant that I would look to Raden Mas Minke to answer this question.

Just on two weeks had passed, during which I was under constant pressure from my boss, and he from the governor-general, when an answer arrived from Ambon. A package of papers, tightly bound and sealed with red wax in ten places, arrived on my desk. I knew for certain this was from Raden Mas Minke. I had no idea how it was obtained.

I locked the door from inside. The windows too. I opened up the parcel. The contents—a pile of notebooks.

Locked in my room like this, I could ignore Meneer Gr— when he knocked on the door wanting to talk once again about the situation of the Chinese. And I was liberated too from Monsieur R—, who could do nothing but show how unnerved he was by the pressure from the governor-general.

There were 123 notebooks. They were all full of Minke's terrible scribble and there were many words and phrases scratched out and replaced. The notebooks were tied together in separate bundles. They were all written in Dutch. The first bundle contained a story that had already been published in Malay, entitled *Nyai Permana*. I put that bundle aside. The second bundle was entitled *This Earth of Mankind*, the third *Child of All Nations*, the fourth *Footsteps*.

Perhaps one day I will write about these manuscripts. In short, however, I can say that after reading through them quickly over three days, I came to realize that the waisya caste and its appearance on the scene in Java was not as simple as Meneer L— thought. There were many aspects to its emergence and it faced many different problems, all interconnected and intertwined, sometimes disguised, sometimes clear to all. Yet I still did not find any definite answer to my problem.

Sometime during those three days while I was reading the notebooks, I received news through the chief housekeeper, Nicolaas Knor, that a Javanese who had been exiled to Ambon had been robbed. I did not inquire any further.

"Perhaps you have obtained enough material to be able to answer our questions now, Meneer Pangemanann. Come, let's go to Room A."

Inside the room there sat six men. Three of them were unknown to me. Monsieur R— introduced them to me as three colleagues whose names I did not need to know. They were all Pure-Blood Europeans.

With the minimum of formalities, Monsieur R— invited the three new men to speak, one after the other. They all spoke about the inner workings of the Sarekat, including the attitude of the members of Arab descent. Meneer Gr— spoke about the awakening of the Chinese. Then Monsieur R— asked that I speak about the awakening of the Javanese bourgeoisie. And so I told them as much as I understood.

"Gentlemen, gentlemen," said Monsieur R—, after I finished speaking. "We have information concerning three groups of people, the Chinese, Arabs, and Natives. The government does not wish to implement reforms to the system of government. And indeed there are no reasons to do so."

I do not dare put down on paper what were the results of the discussion in Room A. At the very least, I can say that the purpose behind Meneer Gr—'s hints and comments about the 1740 incident in Betawi were becoming clearer. I could sense that a project was being formulated. And I joined in of my own free will. The project was named—violence, a new-style Saint Bartholomew's Day. I was to write up and make the final formulations of all the decisions from that meeting. And it had to be finished that day.

After this, Monsieur R— seemed to be becoming even more nervous. The whole office was put in a spin, like a propeller. Attendants were being reprimanded left, right, and center. Nicolaas Knor was running about, back and forth, doing I don't know what. People I had never seen before came and went. This lasted three days.

Orders arrived. I was to go to the Harmoni Club, and to take my first stride up the front steps at exactly nine o'clock in the morning.

At nine in the morning I saw Cor Oosterhof standing on one of the front steps. I went inside and he followed me without saying a word. I sat down and ordered lime juice. When my drink arrived, Cor Oosterhof approached me.

"May I join you, Meneer?"

I nodded. He ordered liquor. While observing people arriving or playing cards, he said: "I am here to find out what has to be done. You know, about it all." He didn't state his name, nor his position, nor where he came from, nor on whose orders he was sent to meet me.

I recognized his face, his name too, from an opium smuggling case fifteen years before. He was a young man of twenty years then. He had matured now, I don't know in what field. I did know that I had come across him several more times over the next fifteen years in various cases.

I have said that he was involved in an opium smuggling case, which means, whether he realized it or not, that he was also involved with the Chinese Tong terror gangs. I don't know how Cor got along after the Tong were disbanded as a result of Sun Yat-sen's efforts. One thing was for certain, he would have a lot of connections among the Chinese and would know a lot about what was happening in the Chinese community.

"You still have many friends amongst the Chinese, Meneer?" I asked.

"In every corner of Java, Meneer."

"Excellent," I said in reply. "What is it that you want me to tell you about, then? Something to do with the Chinese?"

"You know best, Meneer," he said.

Cor Oosterhof was far easier to get along with, far, far easier, than Robert Suurhof. He showed no signs of arrogance. Before he drank his liquor, he bothered to nod to me and his eyes and mouth invited me to join him. He was not at all an awkward or formal person. Dealing with him was like dealing with an old friend, undisturbed by memories of any past unpleasantness.

To make sure that everything would go smoothly, I explained the ABCs of the problem. I told him about the awakening of the Japanese people, which was later followed by the awakening of the Chinese. Both these developments had a great impact on an educated Native named Raden Mas Minke. Making things even worse, these two developments to our north influenced a layer of people among the Chinese in the Indies. The impact on both the Chinese and on Minke pushed both into forming organizations. And every non-European organization, every organization not dedicated to European interests, will in the end, without exception, develop in such a way that it ends up challenging Europe. By Europe I mean the government of the Netherlands Indies. Such organizations as these will eventually subvert the loyalty of the government's subjects.

I gave him the example of the Hwee Koan Chinese school, whose students ended up openly turning their backs on and ignoring the government and were more loyal to China. And it was the same with those people who had become members of the Sarekat Islam.

"Do you know about the Sarekat Islam?"

"Of course, Meneer."

"Excellent."

"But there is a big difference between the Chinese and Islam, Meneer."

"The difference is only in appearance, Meneer; the key thing is that they are both organized. Understand?"

He nodded, and once again listened earnestly.

I explained to him that Minke was an admirer of both the Japanese and Chinese. He had taught his members how to use the boycott after he saw how this weapon of the weak had been able to bankrupt the big European merchants of Surabaya. Sooner or later the Sarekat would use the boycott against the government. Everywhere Sarekat members were enthusiastically talking about boycotts. The government had exiled Minke. But the Sarekat did not die just because it had lost its leader. Several of the leaders of the Chinese organizations had been deported also, but still their organizations did not die. Both of them continued to grow. The government cannot take action against these organizations. Organizations have a different status in some matters compared to individuals. The government has power over individuals but not over these abstract entities.

"Do you follow me?"

"Continue, Meneer."

"Raden Mas Minke was exiled. The Sarekat did not die, and now they have found a new educated Native who is being prepared to replace Minke. His name is Mas Tjokro, an employee of the Surabaya Borsumij. If Mas Tjokro is arrested and exiled, all that will happen is that a new educated Native will appear and so it will go on."

"Yes, I understand, Meneer."

"And this year, 1912," I continued, "perhaps you already know, Meneer? Up there in China they have formed a political party, called the Kuomintang. It means the National People's Party. Do you know, Meneer, what a political party is?"

Cor Oosterhof was silent.

"An organization formed in order to build power. Now that they have formed a party in China, sooner or later we will have them here too, set up either by the Chinese or the Natives, who knows? The emergence of a political party means the emergence of a new challenge to the government, which until now remains the sole wielder of power."

"But there are the police and army to sweep them away!"

"If we had war, then that is what would happen. But there very well might not be a war. And it could even turn out that the police and soldiers join the new party as well. Who knows how the chicken will turn out before it is hatched from the shell? And because there has never been a political party in the Indies, there are no laws covering their activities."

"So what are your orders?" he asked politely and cautiously.

"Oh, yes, I forgot that you are awaiting orders. Do you know Robert Suurhof?"

"I only know of him, Meneer. They say he's under medical care at the moment."

In fact, I was unsure about going on and giving him orders. I ordered whiskey. Two slugs were still not enough to give me the courage to give him his orders.

"You seem anxious, Meneer," said Cor Oosterhof. "Perhaps you should have a few more."

I drank down three more. Cor himself didn't need any.

"There are two things we must achieve," I said then. "First, the exaggerated esteem in which the Sarekat is held internationally must die away. We want people to realize that as far as the Indies is concerned the Sarekat is nothing. There will be no point in the Sarekat hoping for foreign support anymore, dreaming about foreign intervention in the Indies. Do you know what intervention is?"

Cor shook his head and I explained it to him. And as I spoke I could see in my mind's eye those Turkish youths from Istanbul who claimed they were spokesmen for Pan Islamism.

"No one in the Indies should have grounds for thinking that the Native bourgeoisie are awakening." I did not know if Cor was able to follow what I was saying. "Second, we must make the Chinese once again loyal to the government. We must be even more successful than in 1740. Cor, you must set one against the other, Chinese against Native. Don't hold back. Use all your cunning. Do not leave behind any evidence that could lead to a court case."

I watched Cor Oosterhof shake his head. It would not be possible to set them against each other. The Chinese had no hatred for the Natives. They were respected by the Natives because of their abilities. They were admired because of their toughness. The only enmity that might arise was from those Natives who did not feel capable of competing with the Chinese in commerce and who were not able to save in the same slow, steady way. He talked and spoke, argued and refuted.

"Those are my orders," I said to him angrily.

"If those are the kind of orders you have for me, then I may as well tell you now that I can't carry them out!"

"You have heard what I have had to say. So from this moment on, wherever you go, although you will never see them, the barrels of pistols will be watching over you. Understand?" I threatened him.

"I understand."

"What's the point in saying you're ready to accept orders, then when you hear them all you can say is that you can't carry them out?"

"I never thought they would be on such a scale as this."

"You're not some snotty-nosed youngster who doesn't know about the world. So listen—Sukabumi will be your first target. And don't pretend you haven't got enough reliable men. Don't do anything too smart either. Sukabumi first of all, and then on to other towns, more and more, wherever you choose. You have heard what my plans are now. The only thing that will wipe out what you have heard or make you forget it is a bullet. Go now. And remember whom you are dealing with."

This bandit and thug, enemy and rival of Robert Suurhof, left the Harmoni Club. His gait was hesitant. He did not look back. From where I sat he seemed small, bent, and insignificant. Just like me during the meeting in Room A with the six others.

So it was that some months later at the beginning of 1913 I set off in a sedan to visit a town that I had so far avoided—Sukabumi. I had no desire whatsoever to meet Princess Kasiruta. No. To meet her would only make me feel ashamed. After she was arrested in front of my home that time, it turned out that she was bearing no weapon of any kind, gun or knife. She was released three days later with the qualification that she was no longer allowed to leave Sukabumi. Her parents suffered the same ban as well. And truly I was ashamed too that I had chosen Sukabumi as the first target only because I hoped that Princess Kasiruta would end up involved in some way or another, would be found to have broken the law and so therefore it could be determined that the proper place for her for a certain period would be in jail.

"We can't go any farther, Tuan," said the Native driver.

Yes, it was impossible to go farther. The road was packed with people carrying all sorts of things, so many that I could never list them all one by one.

I alighted from the car and set out on foot. I was wearing a white long-sleeved shirt and white drill trousers. I followed those who were marching in procession shouting and yelling. A few minutes later the procession suddenly broke up and people dashed in all directions attacking the Chinese shops right along the street. I was like someone out on a leisurely stroll with no interest in what was going on. Screams and shrieks of fear, shouts and yells of attack. Then just screams and shrieks.

The shouting and yelling died away as people struggled to grab whatever booty they could. And so shops that had been built up with hard work every day, for years, maybe decades, were destroyed in just a few minutes. For a moment I found it hard to believe that Natives who were usually so lethargic could all of a sudden turn into a pack of wolves who could growl, snarl, attack, and tear things to pieces like this. Their eyes were popping out, inflamed with revenge. And wasn't that what the Company soldiers and Dutchmen were like back in 1740? Full of revenge because they were shown to be not as tough as the Chinese and could not compete? Full of revenge because they had lost out in the struggle for the bones from the colonial dinner plate?

It made me sick.

I climbed back into the car. At that moment the whole of the local police flooded out of their barracks, and in no less a fury attacked the rioters.

They beat and bashed, clubbed and kicked. Their truncheons waved up and down in the air, landing with a thud on human bodies. As a retired policeman I knew how they felt. They felt they had been done a personal injury because rioting had befallen their territory.

All that was left for me to do was await the police reports. The car headed off to Cirebon via Bandung. As I sat back in the front seat, enjoying the wind blowing over me, it also pleased me to guess at how many people would be arrested and end up before the courts. And I speculated too about how great a role in the rioting Princess Kasiruta had played. Then any members of Sarekat Islam who had a hand in the riot could be hauled in too.

And, Meneer Raden Mas Minke, you will witness how this youngest child of yours will be torn apart and will lose all credibility in the eyes of the foreign press. How there is no such thing as the rising up of the Native bourgeoisie. And you, Sun Yat-sen, you will soon be setting up a consulate in the Indies, whose first task will be to protest this act of barbarity. And you, Kuomintang, you will think twice, ten times in fact, before you decide to implant yourself here in the Indies!

In just a little while the leaders of the Sarekat would be put on trial as criminals. And you, my teacher in exile, you will be able to do nothing except weep and fill yourself with remorse because of your youngest child, who has now lost its way. There is nothing you can do. You gave away too easily the chance to castle on our chessboard. You now face your own defeat, Minke. See, the Chinese you looked upon as your teachers are being set upon by your own Sarekat. Cry your heart out. This will go on and on until the Sarekat is destroyed, and you will not be able to do a thing about it. Pray as much as you like. The government will still be victorious. You and yours will be destroyed!

The same thing was happening in Cirebon. Nothing much interesting. The car took me back to Buitenzorg.

I drew up a list of what follow-up actions we had to take. The Sarekat leadership had to be discredited as instigators of riots and disturbers of the peace. The Sarekat must be made to shrink up. Reports had to be circulated worldwide and throughout the Indies that emphasized the criminal activities of Sarekat members. It must lose any international esteem it had won. The outside world must forget about the idea that it would be of any importance in the future.

How everything moved when I jerked my fingers! As time passed I became engrossed in this kind of large-scale work. And you, my teacher, Raden Mas Minke, it is I who now decide things, I who have the initiative; all you can do is hold out as best you can. Huh, in fact you can't even do that. Perhaps you are already half crazy, or perhaps you've even lost your mind altogether. And the newspapers will keep visiting you in your study, reporting how the Sarekat ringleaders entered the trap like rats.

One riot followed another—Gresik, Kuningan, Madiun, and so many small towns that I lost count, like Caruban, Weleri, Grobogan. But all remained calm at the Sarekat center in Solo. That was the way it was bound to be. The whole of the economy was in Native hands. There was no competition with the Chinese. But that too was in accord with my plan. There would be nothing left of the Sarekat except its leaders in Solo, nothing else.

Through its own channels the government had already warned Haji Samadi. All that was needed was evidence that the rioting was being organized by Sarekat people. In the trials that followed it would be possible to implicate several Sarekat members.

The Sarekat hastily organized a national conference in Solo. The conference proceeded in a gloomy atmosphere, under pressure from government warnings. The rioting was eventually subdued, as a result of both the government's and the Sarekat leadership's actions. But it was too late—the rice had already become porridge.

Then something happened that completely astounded the organization's European observers and sympathizers. On Haji Samadi's recommendation, a newcomer who had not yet any record of service in the Sarekat was appointed Sarekat president. This person was Mas Tjokro.

And with this incident the organization's European sympathizers lost their interest. The Natives, it seemed, still did not understand democracy. Such a decision could only occur in a Stone Age culture. Foreign interest in the Sarekat dissipated.

But it was only people like me who understood the real reason Haji Samadi was in such a hurry to free himself of the leadership of these hundreds of thousands of people. He did not have the nerve to handle the pressure that was coming from the government. He did not have the steel nerves of someone like Raden Mas Minke, who also had no personal vested interest in the organization.

This all reminded me of what Meneer L— had told me once, just after I had visited him to tell him about a 5 percent increase in the 1913 budget for the State archives. He said there were many European experts on Java who tended to think highly of the level of democracy achieved in Java's villages. If ancient Greece in its time could boast of its democracy and its city-states, then Java could boast of village republics that were wholly democratic, which could be seen today in the fact the villages still held elections for their chiefs. He didn't agree with all these experts; he had his own views. This village democracy was a system that suited weak people and killed off people's character and integrity. As soon as anyone living in this democracy was able to develop his character and grow strong, he would rise out of this democratic environment and, in fact, begin to manipulate it. Javanese democracy was not the same as democracy in Europe today. A mistaken assessment of this will result in coming to conclusions that are no less mistaken.

The Europeans, particularly those I was in frequent contact with, loved to laugh in contempt at the rise of Mas Tjokro. One of them even went so far as to say that it was a general phenomenon in Java that the Natives preferred to surrender everything to leaders, so that they could be free of the need either to think or to take responsibility, because, in fact, neither of these things had yet become traditions in Java. Indeed, the Javanese weren't even acquainted with these things.

When the Sarekat leadership elevated Mas Tjokro as president and announced that the national leadership would be based in Surabaya, people were even more amazed. Wasn't the Sarekat's base of support located in Solo? Why were they deserting their own base of support?

In my report to my boss, I explained it like this. The move to Surabaya was nothing more than a reflection of Haji Samadi's personality. He wanted to safeguard Solo, whose commercial life was well in hand, especially his own businesses. At the same time, moving to Surabaya was in accord with Mas Tjokro's own ambitions, even though it ignored the real needs of the Sarekat.

When I later received a report that Haji Samadi's family had held a big thanksgiving ceremony in Laweyan, it was easy to understand why— he was giving thanks that he had freed himself from all his troubles.

What was the situation in Solo now that the national leadership of the Sarekat, now officially known as the Sarekat Islam, had moved?

I asked Cor Oosterhof what things were like there now. He wouldn't answer. I told him that I was going to see for myself. He said that it was probably impossible to make any headway there. Was it really true that we couldn't stir up Solo as well? I asked. There's no point, he answered coldly.

And so I went by train to see for myself if Solo was no longer the heart of the Sarekat.

This was the first time I had visited Solo. It was so calm, as if there were no great changes taking place among all the restlessness of the modern world. The roads were full of women, all wearing batik *selendangs*, carrying children, or a basket or a bag. It looked as if the whole of the town's business was carried out by women. In the stalls and shops, it was women too who served the customers. It was European opinion that Solo men were the

most backward in civilization. They looked upon women as capital that
would bring them food and clothing. The dream of all the men of Solo
was to marry a Solo woman so they could live simply without ever having
to work. If you married two women, then you were guaranteed food and
clothing as well as money for gambling and cock-fighting. To marry three
women . . . and so on and so on. And everybody was happy with this situation. I couldn't really say whether these insults contained any truth or
not. Perhaps after I'd stayed here a few days . . .

Everything here was done by Natives, even the little riot that occurred
that evening to mark my arrival. Several Chinese workshops, not so many
really, were attacked by a small group of men. Things followed their normal
course—arrests, interrogations, and later, perhaps, to court. And it all had
no other aim than to cause the Sarekat to collapse from within.

Cor Oosterhof was right. There were no opportunities here to get at
the Sarekat. There was not enough basis, or no basis at all, to successfully
pit Chinese against Native in any big way. I returned to Buitenzorg with
empty hands.

Another quite big wave of rioting hit Kertosono, Nganjuk, Pacitan,
Lamongan, then climaxed in Mojokerto, turning back into Central Java—
Kudus. Enough! I said to myself. Enough. My report on all that had hap-
pened was very well received. Once again I could hope for leave to Europe.
Perhaps I might even be awarded a medal next August 31 on Her Majesty's
birthday. Who knows?

And you, my teacher. You would know better than anyone that I was
not happy about any of this. If in the end I am defeated, all that will happen
to me is that I will retire from my office. There will be a pension waiting
for me. While your Sarekat, bloated with too many members, if it falls, will
be crushed under its own weight. That's how the game is played. I will
only lose my job if I am defeated. You will have lost everything. We are
just chess players in a fixed match. And in all this, I have given up my
principles. I can see you now jumping up and down celebrating your victory
in defeat.

Victory or defeat! Modern Pitung, what am I doing now? Planning
what I will do during my leave in Europe. I will stay in the Netherlands
just a few days, to see my children. Then I want to visit the Basque country,
where I can enjoy to the full the dancing of those hot-blooded girls. Don't
be angry, Raden Mas, but my boss has already answered my question unhesitatingly: "You will get your leave after August 31."

My wife was already packing. You can guess for yourself why I'm
getting my leave after August 31. A medal!

And, yes, the man who has taken your place, Mas Tjokro, he doesn't have an inkling about how you were influenced by the example of China. They have founded the Kuomintang. I am willing to take a bet that your replacement has never heard of it and is not interested anyway. Your Sarekat won't turn into a party. No, if in fact it doesn't just close up shop, it will never be anything more than just a social organization, and indeed, it must never be able to become anything more than that.

6

Several years ago a meneer landed at Tanjung Priok. It is not clear who was there to meet him. It's quite possible no one met him. He went to live in Bandung, where he got to know Wardi, who was helping out at *Medan* at the time. There were some who said that this meneer also helped *Medan*, through Wardi, by supplying foreign news reports. He used to summarize them down as much as he could, but this did not keep him very busy because *Medan*'s readers had not yet developed an interest in foreign news. But he didn't do this for long either.

This meneer's name was Douwager. He liked to say that he was a relative of *Multatuli*. He bore on his shoulders the burden of past experience. He had fought with the Transvaal in the war against the British in South Africa.

From the moment of his arrival, colonial society kept its distance from him. Everyone thought he had strange ideas. If the Dutch in South Africa could establish their own nation separate from the Netherlands or England, why couldn't they do the same in the Indies? He dreamed of a South African–style Republic of the Indies.

Meneer had forgotten, the Dutch did not establish a colony in the way they did on the southern tip of that black continent. The Eurasians of the Indies were also very, very few in number. The Dutch were not like the French in Algiers or Canada. But he kept on dreaming.

The Dutch subdued all the Indies by using the Javanese, including conquering Java itself. And you, Meneer, have no authority among the Javanese.

How determined he was, this meneer. He tried to talk to the men at the military barracks in Cimahi, Padalarang, and Bandung. But he received a very cold response. Indeed, they all thought he was a madman.

He should have known (or was he just pretending he didn't know?) that in these Indies, so green with jungle, paddy, and fields, he was really living inside a house of glass. From behind my desk I could even see every individual movement of his eyeballs. Didn't you learn anything from what happened to your friend Raden Mas Minke?

I think the colonial press's warnings were correct. They said you were drunk with a lust to carry out your uncle's, Multatuli's, dream, that you wanted to be a white emperor in the Indies, like James Brook in North Borneo. Be careful what you do next, Douwager!

What was true, however, was that it was not you who had become an emperor but Mas Tjokro! The foreign press had given him, the president of the Sarekat Islam, the title "emperor without a crown," even if only as a rather insulting joke. It wouldn't surprise me if Mas Tjokro thought he was being honored. But any educated person who understood European history and the European spirit would know that such a nickname was not an honor but an insult. How could someone who had not taken part in the organization's struggles, its joys and pains, suddenly find himself its supreme leader? If it was the Sarekat that was his empire, then in conditions like this the Sarekat members would be no better than his slaves. He ruled as an emperor over the Sarekat. This situation did not help the development of democracy as a characteristic of a modern organization. Tjokro's position was no better than that of the head of some primitive tribe.

And that nickname did not at all bother Meneer Tjokro's conscience. With so many members, perhaps he was already dreaming of a real empire.

Tjokro and Douwager brought with them different experiences and ideas. Douwager came from South Africa bringing wounds and defeats. Tjokro's beautiful dreams came from inside a Borsumij warehouse, and now he had inherited a kingdom left behind by Raden Mas Minke—something that could never happen in a public organization in Europe. But that is what happened in these green Indies. And people speak of Tjokro as the *Ratu Adil*, the "just prince," the messiah of the Javanese. And Douwager, on the other hand, was still unable to make any progress.

Tjokro started publishing *Peroetoesan* as a replacement for the still frozen *Medan*, and the Sarekat still did not turn itself into a party. Following

Minke's example, Tjokro's paper used Malay, not Javanese. Douwager also set up a newspaper, *De Expres*, using Dutch. Douwager used his paper to attack what, according to European criteria, he saw as the bad conditions in the Indies. He called out to the Eurasians who were paid less money for the same work as that done by Pure-Bloods. With Wardi's help, he built a paper that spoke with a fiery voice and biting cynicism.

You could never win equal wages without struggle. There could be no struggle without organization, an organization that was courageous, intelligent, and principled. So spoke Douwager. And so the *Indische Partij* or the Indies Party, the first political party in the Indies, was formed just on one year after the Kuomintang was formed in China. The party had three leaders—Douwager, Wardi, and Tjiptomangun. The latter was a doctor, a graduate from STOVIA, in the same class as Tomo, the founder of Boedi Oetomo. Tjipto was lucky. He had been posted to a large town. Tomo, who had fallen out of favor because of his involvement in Boedi Oetomo, was posted to a small, out-of-the-way town—Blora.

I knew that the arrival of the Indische Partij on the scene would mean more work for me. Especially as it turned out that the Sarekat still refused to die, despite the riots, arrests, and trials. Well, one thing was for sure— no matter what kind of new work I would be facing or why, I could say good-bye to any leave in Europe.

If it was true that Tjokro simply took over all that had been begun by Raden Mas Minke, then it was true too that the Indische Partij, at least to some extent, was also extending the influence of the ideas of the Modern Pitung. Douwager himself, and of course Wardi, had both worked with Minke. I had no file on Dr. Tjiptomangun.

These experiences of mine were quite interesting. You could say that yesterday I had faced my teacher. I had subdued him, my teacher. For the time being he had not risen again. But now four new teachers emerged at once! One teacher departed; now I faced four people who were continuing his work. Yesterday I faced the Sarekat; today I faced the Sarekat and the Indische Partij. It will be easier to deal with the Indische Partij, however. To start with, its members and leaders are Eurasians and educated Natives. That means their way of thinking will be more modern. And I won't need to visit Meneer L— so often. Well, let's see if they turn out to be tougher and more successful than our teacher!

"And, Meneer Pangemanann," Monsieur R— greeted me one day, after glancing into my room while passing by the door. "It looks as if there will be a lot of work for you now."

I replied with a smile, knowing that my holidays in Europe were gone, vanishing in the winds of a storm. Meanwhile, my wife was still making all the preparations—collecting herbs, roots, bark, and leaves.

"D-W-T, Meneer," he spoke again. "You are going to have to put in much more effort, Meneer, especially more thought into your work. I don't know if your knowledge and understanding will be up to this new challenge."

"What do you mean, D-W-T, Meneer?"

He laughed, happy perhaps that his puzzle had been successful.

"They are the new commanders—Douwager-Wardi-Tjipto-mangun."

It had annoyed me too, his puzzle—as if he was more expert in these things than I.

And so more and more papers started to pile up on my desk dealing with the Indische Partij, in addition to the Sarekat. Although there were still many more coming in on the Sarekat, it no longer represented a danger to the government. It continued to survive as an organization but no longer as a sword of Damocles. The storm of riots had exploded the time bombs that had been planted by the Modern Pitung, but they had been aimed at another target, while the Kuomintang danger was also able to be contained at least to some extent.

In my eyes, the Sarekat was like a great wave formed by the ocean of life, which had been whipped into a storm by new modern ideas and ways. Then one day the wave crashed, leaving no traces at all. The Indische Partij was different again. It was oriented instead toward uniting all the modern elements in Indies society—the Eurasians and the educated Natives. The size of its membership was nothing compared to the Sarekat. But its level of political consciousness was much greater. As far as political consciousness was concerned, Mas Tjokro would still have to learn from them. But despite this, the two organizations shone like two stars in the blackness of space separated by millions of kilometers one from the other, never attempting to move closer together, let alone actually making contact. One was bloated from too many members and was unable to act. The other had just a few hundred members and was worn gaunt as a result of its wild, limitless ambitions.

Anybody could see in a moment that these two organizations were as different as heaven and earth, different in every respect—number of members, aims, basic philosophy, teachers, language, location, type of members. They would never join forces. . . .

Then one day my request to interview an Indische Partij member, who was involved in a criminal case, was approved. And so it was that, accompanied by a local police official, I visited a detainee in Purwakarta.

Reinard Jansen had accidentally shot dead a Native child whom he

had mistaken for a wild boar. He was a Eurasian and a member of the
Indische Partij.

My brief interrogation proceeded as follows.

"Meneer Reinard Jansen, what is your position in the Indische Partij?"

"Just a member, Meneer."

"What is your occupation?"

"It depends. Sometimes I act as a middleman if somebody's got
something to sell. Otherwise, I hunt."

"And if there is nothing to sell and there's no hunting?"

"I ask for help or borrow money."

"Tell me who has helped you or lent you money."

He quickly rattled off the names and addresses of several of the quite
numerous Eurasians who lived in Purwakarta. The senior police official
who accompanied me confirmed what Jansen said.

"Do they always help you or give you a loan?"

"I have never been refused, Meneer, except if indeed no one has any
money."

I looked at the policeman and then asked the victim again: "It seems
they trust you."

"Yes, that's how it is among us Eurasians. It's difficult. We have no
land, paddy fields or gardens, to fall back on. We're not traders either. Most
of us are just low-level employees."

"You're not old enough to have retired. You're not an invalid. But
you look as if you used to work as an official of some kind." He said I was
correct. "What happened?"

"I was dismissed, Meneer."

"What did you do wrong?"

"I used to be a foreman on a tea plantation. A Pure, still green, just
arrived from the Netherlands, was appointed to the business. He started
bossing me around very arrogantly. He was no better educated than I was.
We both had primary school education. The last time he treated me that
way, I taught him a real lesson. He lost five teeth. And that is the true story
of why I was dismissed."

"Why did you join the Indische Partij?"

"It was one organization that at least understood that there needed to
be a struggle for employment justice. Eurasians should be paid the same as
Pures for the same work."

"Does the Indische Partij also struggle for equality in wages for the
Natives as well?"

"That's for the Natives to work out, Meneer. We're not Santa Claus,
giving out presents at unknown addresses."

"Do you believe the Indische Partij will succeed?"

"Even if we don't succeed, Meneer, at least someone will have tried. That is enough as a beginning."

"What else do you know about the Indische Partij?"

"It's not my responsibility to explain all this to you. The Indische Partij leadership will no doubt be happy to explain everything to you."

"Don't worry," I said. "I have already met them. But I want to hear from an ordinary member so I can see if I get the same explanations. So what is your answer?"

His gaze dropped to the floor. He couldn't answer. Perhaps he didn't know much more.

"Is it true that the Indische Partij is calling on the Indos to overthrow the Pures and rule the Indies in their place?"

"I've never heard that, Meneer." But his eyes told me that he did know about this, and indeed that it was the reality.

"Of the three leaders of the party, there is only one Eurasian; the other two are Natives. What do you think about that?"

"Meneer, if a monkey were to join our struggle for justice, we would accept him, let alone Natives."

"And if not Natives, or monkeys, but the devil himself, would you accept him?"

"Why not? Especially as it is only an 'if'?"

"That is a very cynical answer."

"Because in these crazy modern times, even justice has to be struggled for. The old stories about justice suddenly falling with a bang from the sky, well, that doesn't happen anymore."

"And was justice ever achieved in the past without struggle?"

Once again he went silent, not because he had been lying but because that's all that the Indische Partij had taught him on this question.

I asked a few more questions. He didn't answer, but started to get angry and pound the table, shouting at me to shut up and to leave him alone. And I knew then that our question and answer session was over.

I interviewed three other Indische Partij members who were involved in police cases in other towns. They all gave differing answers but shared the same basic idea. They wanted to get rid of the Pures and replace them as rulers. I was forced to come to the conclusion, though admittedly based on rather limited and inconclusive evidence, that the Indische Partij had an anti-Pure outlook.

Its members probably viewed Wardi and Tjipto as two gods who had descended at the wrong time (or in the wrong place).

The more I delved into it, the more interesting this problem of the

Indische Partij became. I forgot all about my leave to Europe. And the Sarekat was still following the path laid out by Raden Mas Minke; it still used Malay. In other words, it was still trying to address the concerns and serve the needs of the masses from the independent layers of society, the waisya caste, not the ksatria who lived off the generosity of the government, the priyayi as the Javanese called them. The Boedi Oetomo started off using Dutch and Javanese, which were suitable to its task of producing the new priyayi, but it was using Malay now as well. And the Indische Partij? I think it is best described as a party of the brahman caste, because its only capital comprised ideas and enthusiasm. It still used Dutch as its one and only language, as the language of politics, even though it is likely most of its members spoke Malay. Their decision not to use Malay also obviously reflected their intention to consolidate European domination over the Natives. They wanted to rule over the Natives, in the same way the Pures did now.

As we entered the second decade of the century, the newspapers were no longer just the conveyors of news. They tried to analyze, to teach, to guide, to present new ideas. Behind these modern newspapers were not just printing machines, but thinking machines as well. *Sin Po* was controlled by the thinking machine of the Chinese nationalists, *Peroetoesan* by the thinking machine of the Sarekat, and *De Expres* by the thinking machine of the Indische Partij. Through these papers the brain spoke to the other parts of its own body, annihilating distances of hundreds of kilometers. But they also spoke to me, in the same words and conveying the same intent.

And *De Expres* liked to ornament itself with the exultant cries of triumph and victory, like a hero who has just been victorious in battle, and also words of insult and contempt, glorifying itself, always on the offensive, promising better times to come. Yet its circulation never topped one thousand and fifty. *Medan* had overtaken *De Locomotief*, which had been publishing for almost a century. Now it was *Sin Po* that had the highest circulation and it had been going less than two years. In this field, as in many other fields, nobody had yet equaled Raden Mas Minke, let alone surpassed him. *Peroetoesan*, which was the youngest of all, had not yet reached two thousand.

I had not yet completed my picture of all that was happening, the ink had not yet dried on the papers giving legal status to the Indische Partij, when something entirely amazing happened, something very close to a major act of impudence. The Indische Partij requested an audience with His Excellency Governor-General Idenburg. What had possessed them to try this? Perhaps this impudence originated from the rather shallow idea that they could imitate Modern Pitung. Minke used to meet for chats with

Governor-General van Heutsz, who summoned him to the palace several times. No one knows what they spoke about. Now these imitators wanted to clear a path to the palace as well.

Watch out, all of you, because His Excellency is no longer van Heutsz. He was merciless in battle, but amicable in socializing. The current governor-general did not like war but was a bureaucrat of unrivaled excellence. He was very inflexible and would not allow his authority to be diminished even the slightest little bit.

When Monsieur R— came to see me to ask my opinion on this, I answered: "Yes, Monsieur, now the Indische Partij has been given legal status. They have the right to request an audience. And His Excellency will no doubt wish to listen to them, to find out what they have to say, if their ideas and intentions are in accordance with their constitution and documents."

"So?"

"So, is the Indische Partij truly a political party that feels it represents a certain current in society? His Excellency is the supreme political authority in the Indies and, of course, needs to hear for himself. It is different with the Sarekat or Boedi Oetomo or Tirtajasa, which are all social organizations."

"So you think His Excellency should go ahead with the audience?"

And so it came about that all the educated people of the Indies were amazed to hear that Douwager, Soemantri, and Tjiptomangun were going to the palace to be received by the governor-general. For the three of them, this invitation was excellent propaganda for inside the party. For His Excellency himself, he was able to come to his own conclusions—that they were just students entranced by what they heard in some political science lectures, immature and one-dimensional in their thinking.

"You were right," said my boss, Monsieur R—, after the excitement of the audience had died down. "They are nothing to worry about. His Excellency's adjutant said they didn't even know how to be diplomatic as any good politician should. They were quite cocky. Very rough nuggets indeed. What they had to say was as shallow as their pamphlets, just like their own writings in their paper. There were no hidden undercurrents in anything they said."

My boss now came to see me every day, just to get some new angles on things and keep His Excellency happy. He was silent in a million words about my holiday to Europe. And there was even more work still for me as D-W-T became more and more active. They took turns traveling around the big and small towns of West Java propagandizing their ideas. Of this triumvirate, it was Dr. Tjiptomangun who was becoming the most gaunt, because he was doing the work of a doctor, politician, editor, and orator all at once. When did they sleep, these three?

One additional task that I now had to implement was to make sure that the Boedi Oetomo, Sarekat, Kuomintang, and the Indische Partij did not come together. But in fact I never had to put even a centimeter of ink to paper to ensure this. It seemed I might not even need Cor Oosterhof's services again. Another group of Eurasians emerged who were opposed to the Indische Partij and who called Indische Partij Eurasians "goat class Dutchmen"! They argued that these "goat class" Indos were, in fact, dependent on the so-called "first class," the real Dutchmen, for everything— their experience, knowledge, authority, and of course, their blood. If the Indische Partij's ideas were correct, they said, then the Eurasians would have been ruling the Indies long before now. Pieter Elberveldt was the example they used. Here was a Eurasian who did not know how to be grateful. Loyalty to the Pures. That was their slogan. Without the Pures, the Eurasians would be nothing.

It was from among the employees of the big European merchant houses that this new voice first emerged, but then it spread quickly to all the small towns as well. They weren't interested in the glories of politics, which others saw as the *sesame* that could open so many doors. They were happy enough and felt secure enough under the protection of Her Majesty.

"Do you think they should be encouraged to establish a rival organization to the Indische Partij, one advocating loyalty to the Queen?"

"Maybe it would be useful," I answered. "But, Monsieur R—, there would be a risk of things getting out of our control. If a loyal organization was set up, which then challenged the Indische Partij, it is clear another party will emerge taking a neutral stance. And then another will emerge as soon it is clear the three older ones have failed. And this last one might very well decide to approach the Natives and draw them into it as well. And there will be bedlam in the Indies, a tumult of organizations, voices, papers, conflicts, and hostilities."

"So you think we should just ignore the Indische Partij?"

"Let's just wait. Let them be. Let them go on feeling that they are the cleverest, most knowledgeable, the bravest, the most fantastic, in other words, the best in everything. One day these emotions will reach their peak, they will lose control of themselves and will be unable to keep themselves within limits. We just need to wait, that's all."

"You seem to be very sure of your views."

"If you have some better analysis, perhaps it is better we adopt that," I answered.

Whatever else might be the case, I was the expert in these matters and he would listen to me. He didn't discuss it with me for a few days. He seemed to be very busy but I didn't know with what. Then one day he rushed nervously into my office, quite suddenly, just when I was in the middle of studying some new material: "Meneer, I will need everything about the Boedi Oetomo. Within the week, if you can."

I knew that my boss had been reprimanded. Most of my reports up to then had virtually ignored this big organization. As far as I was concerned, it had found the form that suited it and was well satisfied with what it had achieved. I didn't think His Excellency needed to bother himself with it. But an order is an order. While I set out studying whatever they had published in Dutch (I knew no Javanese), I requested a report from the director of STOVIA about the students who had originally been involved in founding the Boedi Oetomo, almost five years ago.

After I had studied everything, I came to the same conclusion. Nothing important was happening. The BO was paying no attention to either the Sarekat or the Indische Partij. During the year so far, 1913, they had founded two new primary schools in East Java. Some of the BO schools, those that had proved that they could sustain themselves and reach a sufficient standard of teaching, were receiving government subsidies, like the Protestant and Catholic schools.

The BO had also sponsored the formation of a youth organization called Young Java, and Scout groups in Solo and Jogja. It had also established a life insurance company. It remained active in social affairs, and was making clear advances. I didn't receive any useful information from STOVIA.

Then, three days later, I received another visit from my boss. Nervous as usual, he gave me orders to prepare a report on the education situation. I put aside my other as yet unfinished work. I went straightaway to see the director of the Department of Education and Culture. I didn't get much out of him except the statement that his department would always be the most responsible implementer of the Ethical Policy, in accordance with the demands of these modern times, no matter whether they changed the governor-general four times in a year.

I knew he didn't like having to deal with a Native like me. And I was not after any statements, but data, figures, and information about what was actually happening in educational affairs. If I had been a Pure that is exactly what I would have said.

"You should have come November last year, or even earlier, if it's figures you wanted," he said.

But I insisted. He summoned the department secretary to help me. And we set off for another office, leaving behind Meneer Director and his office. As we walked along, he whispered: "This director is completely the opposite to Meneer van Aberon."

"Do you mean he is not paying attention to his department's work?"

He stopped and looked at me full of regret and suspicion.

"I didn't mean to say anything bad about my boss. Especially to an official of the Algemeene Secretariat."

"What do you mean?"

"Our department implements whatever policies are given to us by the government, I mean by the governor-general, in accordance with his mandate."

All this made me suspicious that there was something not right with this department. And supposing my suspicions were correct, what was it that was not right? As soon as we sat down opposite each other he began to tell me. The separation of the basic Native schools into Grade 1 and Grade 2 had come to a standstill. The fact was that there were not enough teachers to make the Grade 1 schools Dutch-language basic schools.

But that couldn't be right, I thought. Before the governor-general announced that decision, the number of available teachers and coming graduates from the teachers' schools had been calculated. And that didn't include the teachers who had already received a basic certificate in Dutch. And so I realized that I had been sent here as a representative of the governor-general's lack of confidence in the director of the department.

I asked for the figures. He tried to avoid this, always changing the topic to the amount of subsidies they had given to the Dutch-language private schools. And there would be even more of these subsidies as the number of BO and *Kartini* schools increased.

"It is even the case," the secretary continued, "that there are efforts in Semarang to set up a school for girls that will graduate Grade 1 pupils just as that girl from Jepara hoped for, exactly in accord with the ethical thinking of people such as Van Aberon, van Kollewijn, De Veenter, and the other advocates of the Ethical Policy. De Veenter has made the greatest, the most significant and important contribution. It is probable that this school will be named after him. So we will have to hand out another subsidy, just as we are doing for the trades school being set up by the Soerya Soemirat, which was established by the Eurasians, also in Semarang."

He still refused to give me the material I wanted.

"Well, if you still definitely need it, give me a couple of months to get it ready for you."

The fact that I was not Dutch, let alone a Pure, and only Menadonese to boot, was once again making my work difficult. I had to get the information from somewhere else. But where?

On the journey back, as I contemplated everything that had happened, I rejected my earlier suspicion that I had been given this job because of His Excellency's lack of confidence in the department. The Algemeene Secretariat could obtain whatever information it wanted simply by issuing a formal instruction. Why did he need me? Or was I the one that my masters above were playing games with?

Resting in a drinks stall, I asked myself whether or not I had properly understood what lay behind this new task. Perhaps I had not been keeping my eyes enough on things to do with the general life of the economy? Education! Education! I remembered now an article about the costs and benefits of teaching Dutch in the Indies. Where was that published? I couldn't remember. I had obviously misinterpreted what my boss wanted me to analyze. This was the question that my boss had given me to analyze. And I had misunderstood.

It seemed there were some among the colonials who thought that teaching Dutch to the Natives would cause more damage than it would do good. Children who were taught Dutch would develop more quickly because it would bring them into contact with the new horizons of the modern world. They would be able to peer into the wider world, but without the benefit of a European to guide them. The result would be that they ended up out of place among their own people, a white cock among a flock of crows. And the whiteness of the cock's feathers would frighten the society of crows.

Was this what the government was afraid of? If that was the case, why didn't they review the status of the Dutch-language Chinese schools and withdraw their permits? And why did the Hwee Koan Chinese schools still insist on teaching English rather than Dutch? I had never given any thought to these issues. This was all new to me.

As soon as I got back to my office, I set to work.

A small group of Natives, graduates of Dutch-language primary schools, had indeed burdened the government with much additional work. All the leaders of the Native organizations spoke Dutch. Now I understood why the governor-general was worried. What would happen in ten years' time if all these new private schools, which also taught Dutch, poured out their graduates into society? This was no simple matter!

I still had not finished this job when new orders arrived. I was to analyze what lay behind the disturbances at the agricultural school in Sukabumi. Then in the teachers' schools. It seemed there was something new going on in the hearts and minds of the high school students everywhere.

I was no longer enjoying my work. My masters were chasing me like a great ocean wave, and everything would then crash down upon my head.

Once again, for the umpteenth time, I requested that I be given an assistant and for the umpteenth time my request was refused. I put forward the argument that there was no chance that the amount of work would get less; rather it was bound to pile up even more. Monsieur R— didn't want to know. Meanwhile, his general state of anxiety seemed to be worsening all the time.

With all this work still unfinished, he gave me yet another problem to look at: "Now that the Boedi Oetomo has been tamed, especially with these subsidies, how do we tame the Sarekat?"

"There is no reason to try to tame it. The Sarekat was tamed as a result of all the riots," I answered, rather offended, as if all my earlier reports had no meaning. "They have not been able to set up even a single school, they have no institutions at all, they have not achieved anything at all, except for one factory."

"A factory?"

"Yes, a talk factory, a hot air factory."

"I know you are tired and frustrated. What can be done? You are the only person who has been entrusted with this work. To receive such trust often brings with it heavy and difficult consequences."

In a tone meant to soothe my feelings, he explained that the staff of the Algemeene Secretariat was not bound by civil service regulations and could receive a salary increase of up to 75 percent in accord with the service they performed.

"To be freed from the chaos here at the moment might be worth more than a seventy-five percent salary increase," I answered.

He came up to me and patted me on the back, as if I were still some minor clerk. I closed the files on my desk and got ready to leave.

"Going home," I said savagely.

"I can't do this work without you."

"I still haven't heard anything about my leave, Meneer."

"Yes, well, there is more and more work to do. Native society has begun to change. It is no longer like it was five years ago, Meneer Pangemanann."

"We all know that. And there is more happening than just change; society is in real motion as the Natives adapt to the modern world. Native society has been penetrated by new ideas. The Native people are in motion now, changing both their own form and content. And there is no human force that can hold them back."

"At least we have to come up with more powerful ideas to keep them in check. And we don't seem to have any."

My boss's approach to his work, always full of worry and anxiety, was wearing me down, exhausting me. Things could not keep on like this. I was nothing more than someone he used to secure his position, prestige, and pension.

Seeing that I wasn't responding to what he had said, he then asked, as if nothing had happened between us: "If the Sarekat has been tamed because of psychological factors resulting from the riots, then we could no doubt do the same with the Indische Partij?" He spoke in such childlike tones, trying to say he was sorry without actually saying it.

His childlike manner amused me. I put my briefcase back down on the desk. As I stood there, words that I had accumulated in my storehouse of knowledge all this time started flowing forth: "The Indische Partij poses no danger. It has no mass following it can mobilize. The Eurasians as a social group have never shown that they have what it takes to carry out major actions. The Natives have proved themselves in this area, whether in the villages, the plantations, even at sea. The Eurasians have no real roots in society. They are always under suspicion. In the end, the Eurasians are dependent upon the government, whether or not they oppose the government."

"But there are two Natives in its leadership."

"Very well, let's look at those two! Both Wardi and Tjipto, aren't they both culturally Eurasians? And politically as well?"

"So what you are trying to say is that these three—D-W-T—are no more than three kings, alias a triumvirate, who have crowns but no kingdom?"

Now he was tormenting my mind, this nervous wreck of a man, not just my feelings. "No," I said, fed up.

"You'll explain why that's not right, of course, Meneer."

"First, you know, there is really no Indische Partij. There is only D-W-T. The three of them are not kings, they are no triumvirate. They have no power or influence over anything. They, with their daring, are no more than the broadcasters of new ideas and concepts that have been unknown in the Indies so far. It was necessary to tame the Sarekat, but not the Indische Partij. It is only a shadow party," I said, full of spirit, but frustrated, and I fired another salvo: "They are not politicians in the sense of being the wielders of power. They are just writers and journalists. Even if the Indische Partij had no members, D-W-T would still be doing the same thing. As long as somebody is reading their paper, they are happy with being able to pass on their ideas and feelings. They don't need a mass following. Even if they had such a following, they wouldn't know what to do with it—just like the Sarekat."

"But it's not true that they have no mass following."

"All they have for a following is a bunch of Eurasians who have no roots in society."

He knew he had tormented my mind as much as he could get away with. He laughed happily, pleased to get my answers, nodding all the time. He reminded me of a white-skinned wild pig who couldn't see anything around him except what lay directly in front. He didn't care what I thought of him as long as I was ready to come out with my opinions.

"You must see this," he said, groping in his pocket and taking out a page of proofs from the next *De Expres*. He pointed to one column. "Both His Excellency and his adjutants have made a mistake about the Indische Partij. D-W-T are different from what they think."

The contents of that column were quite interesting. I sat back down in my chair and read and reread the column, thinking and reflecting while my boss awaited my opinion. And he indeed seemed more and more to resemble a wild pig. A question flashed across my mind. Why was he so willing to be dependent on my opinions?

He spoke again: "This column shows very clearly that they are not the young, overzealous university students that His Excellency and his adjutants think they are. They are already hinting about self-government, even though they have no basis for proposing it whatsoever. They would probably just stare at you openmouthed if you asked them to actually explain what this government would be like. Yet they are still hinting about it. A conceited man might just sit behind his desk and laugh at them. Not me. This is something very, very serious, even though they are still just hinting at it."

"So what is your opinion then?"

"They are starting to spread around ideas that are very, very serious."

"They are just hinting at it; they don't have a fully developed idea on this. And there is no ban against people stating their opinions as long as no law is broken."

"But this kind of talk is verging on agitation."

"No, not yet."

He shook his head, indicating his disagreement.

"So what do you want me to do?"

"Make this your work."

"But I have so much other work to finish yet."

"Leave it," and he left the room.

This new work was very urgent. This new development with the Indische Partij confirmed that there were new things afoot and spreading within Indies society. And what about the alliance between the Eurasians and the educated Natives? Especially in relation to this self-government that they were hinting at. No one expected this kind of development. Wasn't it the case that the Eurasians and Natives shared no common origin or social goals?

The Indische Partij had been established only a few weeks and its voice—and only its voice—was screeching out, scratching at the heavens. And this made me suspect that things weren't going so well for the organization itself. Most published, as well as spoken, reactions to their views simply expressed astonishment. But I had another view. The number of Eurasians was too small. And even among this small number, it was only a very tiny segment that agreed with Douwager. In the end he had to turn to the Natives. But the vast majority of Natives took no notice because his language was different, his way of thinking was different, and he had different interests. In the end, his only hope was the educated Natives. And only very few of them took any notice either.

I had to test out my own ideas. I had to make sure I was not exaggerating anything, because that is not acceptable in analytical work. The danger from this was clear—you would start to lose your own critical abilities, and your integrity. So I had to find a way to approach them, to meet them in flesh and blood, and not just deal with their ideas and actions.

I had never met Douwager. Minke had introduced me once to Wardi. He didn't seem to pay attention to what was happening around him at the time, a bit conceited, or perhaps he was one of those arrogant Natives. Maybe he just had something else on his mind and so wasn't paying me much heed. Most small, short-bodied people are like that. They try to give their rather lightweight physiques some substance by behaving as if they were important. If he could grow any hair, he no doubt would have kept a mustache as big as his fist.

It is possible that Wardi could have been carried away by Douwager's stories about South Africa. If that was the case, then he had also forgotten that to leave behind your country and seek your fate in another country was the equivalent of receiving a diploma confirming your courage and ability to set out on a real adventure. The founding of a new country was the prize that went along with that diploma, and such a prize was itself a blessing that came straight from God. Without God's blessing there could never have been a Republic of South Africa. And you, Wardi, you have left only your parents and your village, not your country.

And you, Douwager, you were a failure in South Africa, emerging not as victor but only as a prisoner of war. And you, Wardi, you also failed to graduate as a doctor. Minke may have failed too, but he at the very least succeeded in founding an empire, and pioneering real changes. And all the activities of the modern Natives will follow in his footsteps.

I must find out just what you are made of, before I throw my weight in against you, as it might be an unequal confrontation.

And you, Dr. Tjipto, the daydreamer! You see the world before you, on the surgeon's table. This is the age of the triumph of imperialism, when victory always goes to the strongest. No matter how clever a person is, even if his knowledge would fill a warehouse, he still must bow down to the powerful, the victorious. It is very unwise of you to think that this mighty giant before you is like a patient, whom you can operate on without knowing what the illness is. Do you want to replace the patient's heart with a rubber balloon? And the brain with sago porridge? This giant is not sick, is not asleep, has not fainted. Watch out, Tjipto, he might sit up and fling you away.

I studied that column for a long time, line by line, sentence by sentence. I couldn't find any sign that they had a clear concept of self-government. There were no signs that they were three architects who were trying to construct something. Just big words.

And that was what made me most angry with them. It was my duty to respect anyone who had greater abilities than mine, no matter how different our positions in the world might be! But you three, you give rise to more anger than you do respect. . . .

In accordance with what had been decreed from the throne in the Netherlands, the Indies too was preparing to celebrate the one hundredth anniversary of Holland's liberation from French occupation, or more accurately, Napoleonic occupation. The government, with Governor-General Idenburg's full blessing, had ordered that a big celebration be organized.

The members of the Indies Council were preoccupied by the excitement and bustle of the preparations for the coming celebration. They were paying too little attention to the effect that Western education was having on the Natives. As it happened, I still hadn't finished my report on this so the government had nothing to guide it in this matter.

According to what I could see, even if in all sorts of different forms, and with different degrees of substance, it was clear that a national awareness was growing and developing in the Indies. The seed of nationalism was secretly beginning to grow into an embryo in the womb of Native society. And the Indische Partij was, perhaps it could be said, an imperfectly formed child of this process.

As could be predicted, the Sarekat Islam, and even more the Boedi Oetomo, had no objections at all to the commemorations. The BO even decided that it would mobilize all its pupils to join in the commemorations. That was understandable. The Natives in Java had celebrations only for births, marriages, and Idul Fitri, at the end of the fasting season. If there was going to be another celebration, why object? There was the celebration and nothing else but the celebration.

But of course the Indische Partij had to have a different attitude. Their members were educated people who knew the history of Europe and its colonies. They knew that the commemoration of one hundred years of the Netherlands' liberation from Napoleon, and one hundred years of the Netherlands Indies being liberated from England, had a real political message. Perhaps the Indische Partij would open its mouth on this issue.

Perhaps I was the only person who was waiting for them to do something.

One hundred years liberated from French occupation. One hundred years ago the Netherlands Indies was ruled by Governor-General Herman Daendels, a general and great patriot who was hailed by the Dutch people as a Hero of the National Liberation. In 1787 he fled to France when Holland was attacked by the Prussian army. But eight years later, in 1795, Daendels returned and drove out the Prussian army from Holland. He was hailed as the Liberator. In 1807 the king of Holland appointed him governor-general of the Indies.

It wasn't long after that that an interesting event took place in front of the governor-general's palace in Betawi. There was a military parade, commanded directly by Governor-General Daendels himself. He descended the palace steps in full uniform. Then, accompanied by a drum roll and military trumpets, the tricolor was raised. Hands were raised in salute. Then Daendels himself led the ceremony for the flag to be taken down again, also accompanied by drums and trumpets, played with the greatest respect. The next scene saw the raising of another tricolor—the French tricolor.

This event occurred in 1811 when Daendels received the news that the Netherlands had become a part of France and that King Louis Bonaparte, the brother of Emperor Napoleon, had accepted this annexation. Daendels also had agreement from the Raad van Indie to raise the French tricolor. Daendels, whose mind was full of his military experiences, mobilized the Natives to build many military roads and forts as preparation for an attack from the English who were the enemies of France and who had imperial designs on the rich and prosperous colony of the Indies. There is no way to know how many thousands of Natives died building the military road from Anyer to Banyuwangi or the great fort in Ngawi. Tens of thousands died on the road doing forced labor. And there was no attack from the British navy while Daendels ruled the Indies.

Daendels was summoned by Napoleon to join the attack on Russia.

He left the Indies and was replaced by acting Governor-General Janssens. It was just a few months after he left that England, as France's enemy, came to the Indies to seize it from French hands. Its armada landed in Sumatra and Java. The Netherlands Indies army was thrown into chaos. Janssens was caught and detained. And from that moment the Indies became a British colony.

In 1813 Napoleon Bonaparte of France was defeated by a combined attack of the armies of the European states. The Netherlands was free again. And a hundred years later, this year, that liberation was to be commemorated with great celebrations in both the Netherlands and the Indies. Preparations for the celebrations proceeded smoothly. The celebrations must be even bigger than those for the birthday of Queen Wilhelmina.

Then we began to see the true face of colonialism. As you moved farther and farther away from Betawi, the extravagance became worse and worse as the officials all lusted to be seen as the most loyal and active. Not to mention the corruptors who opened their mouths as wide as they could, hoping to catch that fattest and juiciest of all prey, the unaccountable use of money. The government had allocated funds. But there would never be enough money in the official budget to pay for celebrations that were obliged to be as huge as these.

The colonial newspapers began to publish all sorts of reports about how rotten the French and English were, so that their readers soon began to realize how grateful they should be that the Netherlands was now free of France and England. There was an uncontrollable outpouring of hatred for Daendels. And, of course, the Sarekat and Boedi Oetomo could be counted on to interfere in all this too.

It was only *De Expres* that didn't join in the hysteria. It didn't join in preparing the atmosphere. It only celebrated the liberation of the Netherlands and Indies from the French and English. It did not take part in denigrating the French and Napoleon Bonaparte.

And I was right. As the day approached, there came at last the unpredictably amazing explosions from the trio D-W-T, this triumvirate of the Indische Partij. This team of emperors who had crowns but no empire had their say. Put together as a single statement, it could be expressed this way.

One hundred years ago the Netherlands and Indies were conquered by France. It took just a few years to complete. Then later the defeat of Napoleon Bonaparte returned freedom to the Netherlands as well as the Indies. But why should we celebrate this? Isn't it true that when the tricolor was once again raised into the sky symbolizing the victory of the Netherlands, our own flag was trodden into the ground? Are we to celebrate the trampling into the ground of our own flag? And why should the liberation of the Netherlands and the raising up once again of the tricolor mean that every family must pay the contribution that the authorities demand for a celebration that is not its celebration? And if they do not have the money, do the heads of these families have to pay with their labor? Native laborers must work for four days to pay their festival dues, while hunger has its own festival in the stomachs of his wife and children?

It was impossible to imagine such a challenge coming from the Sarekat or Boedi Oetomo. The thing that amazed me most was Wardi's article, Nederlanders als Kolonialen. It was so beautifully written, full of sincerity, and so moving. Perhaps that was the best thing he had ever written, or would ever write again. Perhaps precisely because it was so beautiful, many people did not sense the anger and rage that he was expressing.

As soon as that issue of De Expres appeared my boss came rushing into my room without even knocking. That was how he behaved whenever he had lost control of his nerves.

"Monsieur," he spoke as usual in French, "it's shameful. You of all people, Monsieur, must understand how I feel about this. After all, I am a Frenchman."

"I sympathize with you," I said to calm him down. "His article gives the impression that France has no honor or glory in its history. It was Napoleon Bonaparte himself who elevated Europe to its present level of civilization. They don't want to discuss anything else except the wars." He began to grumble like an uneducated villager, as if he weren't a lawyer, just because his feelings had been hurt. I watched his face go red because of his impotent anger.

"You have a French education. You have a French wife. How do you feel?" he asked, unable to control himself.

"I, Monsieur?" I was forced to grope around for some words.

"You always have an opinion," he pressed, seeking even more sympathy. "Isn't France too great a nation to be treated like this? As if this is some kind of court where history is being judged. Why don't you say something?" he continued to press. "Very well. You do not wish to answer. Now I ask you. How do you feel as a Dutchman?"

I knew his nerves could not take suffering like this.

"Monsieur, it's a pity, but this is not part of my work."

"Or do you prefer to take the position of a Native?"

I don't know, but for a moment I felt insulted by his question.

"I am sorry, Monsieur. I didn't mean to insult you."

"I see all these things simply as a problem, nothing more," I answered.

"Exactly. So you do not feel the resentment of a conquered Native, heh? Isn't that exactly where the problem lies?"

I could sense that danger was threatening. Was my boss, whose recommendations to the governor-general had always been well received
mainly as a result of my work, now going to pounce on me, just because
his Frenchness was being tormented? Yes, a wild pig. I had to escape this
attack and play along with him.

"Don't just be quiet," he said.

"Your country, France, has conquered and occupied the Netherlands
and the Indies. I, as a Dutchman, have participated in subjugating the Natives. As a Native myself, I have joined the Dutch in their subjugation of
the Natives. What else can I say?"

"There must be something you can say."

"The Indies Natives have not been conquered for just a few decades
but for hundreds of years. The fiercest tiger is thus turned into a big, fat,
tame cat."

"It is true that you have succeeded in taming the Native organizations.
But haven't you also given contradictory advice? Wasn't it you yourself
who once said that the Indische Partij would one day become a real danger
because of its ideas?"

I gazed at my boss calmly. It seemed his mind was off balance as a
result of his national pride being offended. He could easily forget himself
and sacrifice me as proof of his loyalty to the governor-general.

"And now you say a fat, tame cat?" my boss repeated what I had said.
He threw down a copy of De Expres onto my table. "You have studied
this, no doubt."

"Of course, Monsieur." I could hear him panting. Perhaps there was
something wrong with his heart as well.

"What these Indische Partij people have written has only provoked
the colonial press into hurling more insults at France."

"Your national pride has been hurt," I said speaking directly to the
problem. "That is your affair, of course. That has nothing to do with the
Indische Partij, or De Expres."

"No, you are wrong," he cut in. "The more De Expres pursues this
line, the more responses there will be from the colonial papers."

"And so you will be tortured even more, because even more people
will start shouting about how good it is that the Netherlands was liberated
from France. It is not De Expres that is tormenting you but the colonial
papers, the government papers."

"Monsieur," he said, starting to get angry, as if he were not an educated European, "this has nothing to do with my personal feelings. This is
a problem to be analyzed. As far as French national pride is concerned,

Monsieur knows very well about that. The problem now is, how do we stop *De Expres*?"

So now he was showing me his true colonial face. Here was a bureaucrat who was going to use his power to achieve his own personal ends, his own personal victory. And I, as a person with a French education, a product of those liberated and free human beings, educated also to always use common sense, felt ashamed to bear witness to his colonial face. He, a Frenchman himself, preferred to turn his back on all that his ancestors had taught us and was going to use his colonial privileges to achieve his own personal ends.

"Close the paper? The Netherlands has the right to celebrate its victory over France. Why are you so upset? It is not *De Expres* that has decided there should be these celebrations."

"*Tss, tss,* the short of it is that I want you to find a way to put a stop to *De Expres.*"

"But it is not a Native matter. It is not in my area of work."

"There are Natives working on the paper."

And so this new task also fell upon me.

I knew that it would be very easy to silence the paper. And I didn't need any rational excuse either. But that would not be sporting. That would be corrupt and would corrupt me too. When I had to deal with Raden Mas Minke, there was resistance. And if there was no such thing as the governor-general's Extraordinary Powers, then perhaps it would have been I who was defeated. D-W-T did not play dirty. Must I play dirty?

I didn't want to. It would be too easy. And the Indische Partij was just a few months old and had not yet had a chance to show what it could achieve in politics. And now my task, my colonial task, set for me by my boss, was to find a way to take action against them. How contemptible!

A few days before, there had been a number of plantation managers from Central and East Java who had come to the office to see Monsieur R—. It was my guess that they were there to try to buy his services in getting him to influence the governor-general in some decision or other. And it was also very likely that this new, disgusting task of mine had something to do with their arrival.

Just after my boss left me, there was a visit from a delegation of all the West Java plantation managers. Such a big delegation hadn't come here just to chat. Something big was in the wind.

I left a note on my table explaining that I had taken my work home. Then I went home. After I had eaten, I went straight to bed. I woke again at seven in the evening. Not because my wife or children had woken me up, or because I had quenched my desire for sleep. There was an alien voice at the front door.

"Good evening," came the voice of a man, speaking in French.

Nobody ever spoke French in the house except my wife and the children. I jumped out of bed. I knew who it must be. My boss, driven by his anxieties, had come looking for me at home. This wild pig was becoming more desperate in his efforts to treat his wounded feelings. I went into the bathroom.

As soon as I came into the parlor, my boss asked: "So, Monsieur, have you finished your task yet?"

I felt very offended. My wife left the room when she heard the question.

"I haven't even worked out where to begin yet," I answered.

"Disaster!" he cried. Suddenly he changed the subject, asking: "It is hot. Don't you have a fan?"

Just as he finished speaking, Mark walked in carrying a fan and gave his greetings. He put the fan down on a coffee table. Silently, while stealing glances at my boss, he wound up the fan forty times, then left.

Knowing that the fan still hadn't been turned on, my boss stared at me with blazing eyes. He asked stabbingly: "Is that fan broken?"

I stood up and turned it on. The fan whirred. My guest started ahemming threateningly.

"I hope this makes you happy," I said.

I didn't understand why it all seemed like some prearranged drama. Now Dede came in too, and asked: "Would Sir like to hear some music?"

"Thank you, sweetie, that would be very nice."

Dede left and not long after we could hear a popular French song coming from the phonograph. It was being sung by a singer whose fame was rising at the time—May Le Boucq. The song was "My Love Is Afraid of the Sun," a true Parisian song.

My guest was absorbed by this. His eyes no longer reflected anxiety. He bowed his head and mumbled: "Paris! There is nothing man has made that is more beautiful than Paris!" He raised his head and looked at me. "What Frenchman does not know that voice?"

"May Le Boucq!" I confirmed.

"And is there anyone who sings more beautifully than the French?"

"You're right."

Now my wife came in as if she wanted to bring this unhappy scene to an end. She sat straight down in a chair and said: "It's been too long since we have seen France, Monsieur."

"We all miss it, Madame."

"When do you think we will all get a chance to see it again?"

"Well, we all can't see it yet, Madame. I myself will be going back next year."

"And my husband's leave?"

"Aha, that's what you're getting at? I am afraid there is nothing that can be done, Madame. His Excellency still needs your husband's ideas."

"That is exaggerating, Monsieur," I protested. "I can decide to quit at any moment, perhaps today, perhaps the day after tomorrow."

"The day after tomorrow?" My boss jumped up, startled. "Impossible. Our work still piles up."

My wife left, realizing that her little drama had failed.

My boss took out the latest copy of *De Expres*. He asked: "And have you read this?"

I nodded with my eyes focused on the columns marked in red, with notes down the side, and some sentences underlined. "Things have reached a climax. Let's discuss this together."

We didn't finish our discussions until two in the morning. My head started to throb. My boss pressed me to devise some action that could be taken against the Indische Partij triumvirate. I refused. What they had written was to be expected from young nationalists, if we can call them that, a little intoxicated by the freedom that they were still able to enjoy. I was still under the influence of the very moving article of Wardi's that I had read the previous morning. His Dutch was beautiful, full of true literary value. I defended with all my soul my view that what they had written was quite to be expected from people with a European education. If you don't like these sorts of statements, I said, then it is best that Natives stop being given a Western education.

"And it is you who have stopped me from finishing my work on the influence of Dutch-language teaching," I said.

"Meneer Pangemanann, I know you are starting to get angry. And you know too that I am not happy with your work at the moment. But we must finish this task this morning no matter what."

He left in a fury. And my own head was throbbing even more now. I gulped down an aspirin and climbed back into bed. I fell sick. The doctor was summoned that morning. After he left and as things quieted down at home, I began to put in order my thoughts about the Indische Partij triumvirate. But no! It was beyond me now. All I could decide was that they were young nationalists full of romanticism and emotion. And I slept bathed in sweat.

At nine o'clock in the morning, my wife passed on to me a letter of reprimand from the office and a page out of an English-language newspaper. I didn't bother reading the letter.

The newspaper clipping contained an article criticizing the way the Dutch had administered their colony and the peoples of the Indies. According to this newspaper, Raffles did more good for the people of the Indies than the Dutch did in three hundred years. Raffles abolished slavery and began to build primary schools for the Natives. As soon as the English left Java, the Dutch abolished all the schools and allowed slavery again. Even now slavery was rampant in the Indies, except in Java, the Moluccas, and North and South Celebes. It was indeed appropriate for the Dutch to celebrate the hundredth anniversary of their liberation from the French. But it would be even more appropriate for the Dutch to consider to what extent they have really repaid their debt to the Indies Natives, as they are supposed to be doing according to the Ethical Policy.

That article worked wonders in helping to cure me. It was much more powerful than the medicines the doctor had given me. For the next three days and nights, I hid under my bedsheets. I don't know how the anniversary was celebrated. My wife and children didn't go outside either. They were worried about my health. Several letters arrived from the office. I didn't bother with any of them.

The festivities continued for three days. All that I could hear was the occasional thunder of cannon, the very same cannon that subjugated the Natives. What for the Dutch symbolized greatness only reminded the Natives of their insignificance. D-W-T had not violated the truth, even slightly. It was the Dutch who should have been ashamed of themselves, nobody else. The French came, the Dutch were defeated, the English came, the Dutch were defeated. So these celebrations of one hundred years of liberation from the French were nothing more than the celebration of a defeat that had never been brought to an end through victory. These were the celebrations of a people who had never achieved greatness in war.

And Monsieur R— was at odds with himself, caught up in both the cyclone of history and the reality of the present. And I was at odds with myself because of the cyclone of power that was thirsting for victims.

I reflected on my experiences in my work over the last year. There was no doubt that my every step took me deeper into the field of mud. And my footprints sank into its softness. And no matter how completely they disappeared, there was no way I could deny they were mine. Why was all this upsetting me again? How beautiful were my days as a police inspector. I never hesitated to deal with wrongdoing, formal wrongdoing with an iron hand. And I knew that the Natives' wrongdoings were not due to their having a criminal character. Most of this formal wrongdoing stemmed from poverty or was just a result of some injustice they had suffered. But formal wrongdoing was still wrongdoing. There was also some wrongdoing that stemmed from ignorance and superstition, excessive patriotism, or being caught in a dead end, all of which was also the product of a greedy and miserly colonial occupation. And Pitung represented wrongdoing that stemmed from these three colonial products fused into one.

How disgusting was this more recent work of mine, waging war against the best products of European civilization—this very youthful nationalism.

All the time I was sick I could not rid myself of the image of Raden Mas Minke. And Wardi, Tjipto, even Pitung, even though he no longer bothered me as much as he had in the past. Strange. Douwager never came to visit me in my visions.

What must I do now? I didn't know. I felt as if I were about to lose all my willpower. Or was it that I had already become an old man? All that I needed now was spirit. Somehow, something must blow some spirit into me again. Without such spirit, there was no way I could continue my journey across the field of mud that lay before me, nor turn around and leave it behind. Would I die here stuck fast in the middle of this field of mud?

And this necessary spirit was blown into me—by the arrival of His Excellency the governor-general's adjutant. He arrived wearing the full uniform of his position and was welcomed with great respect and honor by the whole family. Accompanied by them all, he entered my room and sat at the edge of my bed.

"Meneer Pangemanann, I have come on the order of His Excellency to see how you are." And with those words, I sat up, attracted by this musical and comforting voice.

"I am not ill, Meneer Adjutant, just exhausted. I think I am beginning to recover," I answered. "I am deeply grateful for His Excellency's concern and kindness. I am sure I will be able to come to work tomorrow."

And so it was. The next day I was sitting once again at my desk. How much I longed that His Excellency would come and visit me in my office, sit down and perhaps say a few encouraging words. Such words would be from Her Majesty and be addressed especially to me.

It was only Monsieur R— and Meneer Gr— and the other senior officials who came to see me out of politeness. Perhaps they would have preferred that I had died, stiffened, and never returned. The most polite of all was my own boss. I could not guess what he had done while I was away.

It seemed he had to wait for me because I was the one with the position of sworn expert.

"It's good to see you're well again," he said and now he didn't seem as stressed as before, perhaps because the wave of hatred against the French had now passed. "His Excellency was truly hoping for your recovery."

He pushed across to me a sheaf of papers, including an unfinished report of his own. It was presenting a case as to why the governor-general should use his Extraordinary Powers to . . . It was at that point that I closed my eyes. My boss wanted to exile the Indische Partij triumvirate, who had been puncturing his national pride all this time. And it would be I who had to finish this dirty work.

I had to complete and fix up his draft, as well as make a copy, because such documents were not allowed to be copied by the clerks, and then I had to sign it. My boss left, saying he would come back later to pick up my work.

I carried it all out while trying to convince myself that I was not doing it of my own will, that I was not responsible. No! No! I am just a clerk who is copying out my superior's recommendations. And I finished it. I read through it again. I was satisfied with my beautiful writing. I could have been a very successful scribe. I had received a score of nine for handwriting ever since grade school. My letters joined together to form words, and the words formed sentences. I always scored high marks for my Dutch as well.

"You don't look happy with this work."

"My headache has returned, Monsieur."

Everyone else had left the building.

Suddenly, as I was reading it one more time, I began to choke, I couldn't breathe. Every word seemed to be squeezing my emotions in its grip. Every single word was another nail in the coffin of those three men, and they did not know a thing about me, yet it was I who was determining their fate.

"You have not signed it yet," Monsieur R— reminded me.

I affixed my signature. I pushed the papers across to him. I picked up my coat and hat. I hurried out of my office. Nicolaas Knor was waiting outside to say good afternoon. I nodded in reply and then left. I wanted some peace by myself, undisturbed by anybody. My feet did not bear my body home. I just walked and walked. I went into the first inn I found and threw myself down onto the bed still wearing my shoes.

What has been the use of my education all this time? Before I realized it, I was sobbing uncontrollably. The tears of someone who should already have grandchildren. Bankrupt! An intellectual bankrupt! It had been a waste of time, all the study I had done. Colonial corruption had corrupted me too, corrupted my soul. Yes, my God. I was no longer a chess player. I was nothing more than a contemptible slave.

My head throbbed and I soon had a high temperature. If death were to arrive now, I would be very, very grateful. How would it feel if it was I who had to suffer what would flow from what I had just written. And what if it was not D-W-T who would suffer all this but my own children? What would I say then? To whom could I roar out how I would feel? What would happen now was the result of the action of men. And I was one of them. And the colonialists and the holy men would say this is punishment from God, pray to Him for your safety. Yes, my God, how easily do they corrupt your name. How much more easy had it been for them to corrupt me.

There was a knock on the door. I had not even had a chance yet to turn on the light. I got up and turned the switch.

"Meneer, Meneer," I could hear a voice calling outside, "Open the door."

I looked at my watch. Three in the morning. My head throbbed as if it would burst open at any moment. Slowly I opened the door. Standing before me was the Chinese man who owned the inn. Behind him stood His Excellency's adjutant.

"Good morning," he began. He was not wearing his official uniform. "It was lucky we were able to find you so easily. Sign this receipt."

I signed the receipt and I was handed two letters sealed with wax. One was for me, the other was for the *KNIL* commander in Bandung. I opened and read mine—my orders.

"There is a car waiting for you outside. You must leave now."

Carrying my briefcase, I climbed aboard the car which bore the special number plates belonging to vehicles of the governor-general's palace. Perhaps I was the first Native to travel in a palace car, carrying out a special task for the governor-general.

The driver was a Pure European, wearing a white uniform and white cap too. Without anyone saying anything, the car sped off in the direction of Bandung, its headlights blazing.

I became dizzy as I watched the trees lining the streets suddenly appear in the lights of the car and then disappear again, swallowed up by the darkness. I had known what was going to happen. I had tried to hide in a little inn somewhere, but they had found me. And I just accepted everything when they found me. I had not the slightest desire to resist.

I woke up when the car stopped in front of the guardhouse at the

KNIL commander's headquarters. I hadn't realized until then that my clothes were a mess. My hair was uncombed and I had left my hat at the inn.

It was six-thirty in the morning.

I received a cool welcome. I was only a Native. All the soldiers were Pure-Bloods, in khaki uniforms, with brass buttons decorated with a picture of a rifle. They wore green bamboo hats as well. One of them escorted me to the waiting room that was beside the commander's office.

I sank into a big divan. Hunger was making me restless now. When an adjutant came to see me, I stood, and I could feel my vision blur and wander. I held out the letter to him, the one addressed to the commander. He accepted it and read the address.

"You look very pale. Are you sick?" he asked.

"I have a bit of headache, Meneer Adjutant."

"Please sit down. I'll call a doctor."

He left. A little while later an attendant brought some white coffee and toast. It tasted so good. Ah, I hadn't brushed my teeth or washed my face yet.

The adjutant returned with a Dutch doctor. They took me to another room. The adjutant left again. A quarter of an hour later he returned, looked at me as if it was for the first time, and said: "I hope Meneer Doctor can help you. He said you were ill. Even so, no one else can carry out this task except you. You must try to hold on for a few more hours. Just wait a while now. The medicines for you will be here soon. Then you must take this letter to the garrison."

My medicines arrived. The adjutant escorted me out to the car. And it took me to the garrison. A captain received me in proper military fashion, asked me to wait, and excused himself from the waiting room.

Then I remembered that I had left my briefcase in the car. How forgetful I was becoming these days. Was I beginning to go senile? I tried to remember what was in it. No, there was nothing dangerous.

And it seemed I waited for so long.

At eight-thirty in the morning a convoy of trucks arrived carrying a company of KNIL, in full battle dress. I was invited to sit in the first truck, next to the driver, an Ambonese corporal.

The convoy started to move. Everyone along the road had to stop and watch us. The convoy traveled quite slowly. We finally stopped in a residential area. The soldiers all jumped out of the trucks and spread out. I stayed inside the truck, by myself.

It wasn't a quarter of an hour later that I saw Wardi walking along the road escorted by the soldiers. Everyone walking along the street at that time stopped to watch this strange scene—a civilian under military arrest! And there were so many military. The one under arrest was a skinny, small, short Native.

The detainee walked with confidence. His chin was thrust out as if he was communicating with everyone who looked at him: "This is how they are treating me. This is how these soldiers with nothing to do are kept busy. Here I am. Wardi! Tell everyone that they have arrested me and with so many soldiers."

I bowed my head. I knew all this was happening only because, on my boss's orders, my hand had scratched some words out onto a piece of paper.

Douwager and Tjipto's fate would be no different. It was I, nobody else but I, who was assigned to witness the arrests. How powerful were words, just scratched out on paper. One company of soldiers is set in motion, a person is arrested. Perhaps as many as a whole battalion has been mobilized to carry out the arrest of all three of the triumvirate. And all because of my signature. My boss had been worried that they might be defended by Indische Partij fanatics. That wild pig! He never listened to what I told him—between the triumvirate and their mass followers there was much too big a gap. Or did he just want to have a display of power? And if they were to arrest Mas Tjokro? Maybe they'd put a whole regiment on display!

On that day I witnessed how heroes were made. On the other hand, this disgusting work of mine did not end there.

As soon as I arrived back at my office in Buitenzorg, I received new orders—I had to devise a public justification for the arrests. A public defense! Not the internal justification! All this was because the Chinese and Malay-Chinese press were roaring demands for an explanation. It wasn't long before the English-language press overseas also announced their amazement and stated their view that the Indies government had over-reacted and abused its power. This was not the Middle Ages. There had to be a justification for everything.

Still feeling sick, I explained that D-W-T were not arrested in their capacity as leaders of the Indische Partij, not as politicians, not as political leaders; they were arrested as journalists whose writings had threatened public order and security.

They would soon be departing for exile. But because of the severe reaction of the Chinese and English press, the governor-general wavered in his actions. They were given a chance to defend themselves with a written statement that was allowed to be published. And they used that opportunity.

When Wardi and Douwager were offered the choice of exile in the

Indies or overseas, they chose the latter and departed for Europe. Tjipto at first chose the former, but finally changed his mind and also chose Holland.

I realized that I could not wash my hands of this, even though I knew this was all the plot of my boss, a mad Frenchman, whose national pride had been offended. The son of a great nation, a nation that had given humankind a great revolution. That was in 1789. In this year, 1913, he betrayed his ancestors—using my hands.

7

It was the year 1914. I was never going to be given my leave to go to Europe. No medals had been pinned to my chest either.

Over there in Europe, the shooting incident at Sarajevo had been turned into an excuse for war whose real purpose was to fight over the colonies which were desired as sources of raw materials for Europe's industries or as markets where they could dump their products. Very, very quickly, every colonial country involved itself in the struggle over the colonies. A great war took place. War!

France was directly involved. My wife and children's dreams of going back there were destroyed. And how stupid it was for civilians to descend into the battlefield.

The government requested the Christian and Islamic spiritual leaders to say prayers for the safety of the Netherlands, Her Majesty Queen Wilhelmina, and her family. And I am sure that had D-W-T not been in exile, their words would have once again given much pain to the colonial authorities. But now, pray, all of you, that the Dutch may rule over the people and earth of the Indies forever!

In this year, I recovered my health.

My boss was transferred to another post outside Java. My new boss was a Pure-Blood of Dutch descent who did not have much to say for himself. He had not been long in the Indies and so had not yet been completely taken over by the colonial mentality.

The overseas press started to call this big war the "world war." Someone had argued that this war was involving the whole world, the whole of humankind, without exception, from those who were being taken off to their graves to those who were just being formed in their mother's wombs. A fortune-teller prophesied that this great war would leave a mark on all the babies that were being born now. They were fated forever to be involved with wars, until they died.

Nobody knew what would be the fate of the Indies, into whose hands it would eventually fall. The colonial authorities would be demoralized. Their thoughts would be preoccupied with the uncertain future. The thunder of the English, French and German cannon seemed to grow more audible every day, echoing there in the background and instilling fear about the future. Once the Netherlands was attacked, all the Indies could do would be to await its fate.

My heart was no longer so tormented. I had found some sort of peace. However, there was no letup in my work. There was more and more to do every day and I still had no assistant.

As 1914 neared its end, there were some developments. Some former members of the Indische Partij formed a new party, called *Insulinde*. But it was pallid, insufficiently infused with blood. It had no paper, no mouth. It had no initiative, it had no will and had no hands. It had no factory of ideas, so it grew like a tree trunk without foliage. Even so, it was another challenge to the Eurasians, who opposed it from the very beginning. Most of the Eurasians had an excessive lust for serving the government, often giving the government itself headaches.

And there was something else. Every town was hit by organization fever. It was almost impossible to count all the new organizations, let alone list them, because they did not seek legal status. They did not develop out of real need; it was just a kind of fever that people contracted—at least, that's the conclusion I rather hurriedly came to.

But what attracted greater public attention was the formation of the Indies Social Democratic Association. Its founders were political exiles from a party split in the Netherlands—Engineer Baars and Sneevliet. Following European tradition, they were quite ready to pronounce their opinions wherever and to whomever. The two of them moved from place to place every day, talking, and talking, and talking, as if they were sure they could conquer every ear in the Indies. . . .

One day my new boss summoned me to his room. He handed over

a file in a sealed envelope. Perhaps it shouldn't really be called a file. It seemed quite a small and thin package, perhaps just twenty or thirty pages.

"War in Europe, Meneer," said my new boss. "Here everything is calm."

I didn't know what he was getting at, and I had no desire to ask. He never spoke in any language except Dutch.

"I think it would be calm in the United States too, just like here in the Indies."

It was beyond me what he was getting at. Several times now, he had tried to get people involved in a discussion about the United States. And what was there that an educated person, schooled in Europe, could say about America? America certainly attracted those who felt confined in their own country. It was criminals and those who were half-starved and never satisfied with their life who fled to America.

"Would you like to read a book about America?" he asked.

"It's something I'd like to do, Meneer, but I have so much work."

"But there is no deadline for your work, is there?"

Well, this was different from Monsieur R—. My new boss didn't want to give me any new work at all. On the contrary, he was suggesting that I read about America. Then what meaning did I have here in this office? Was this a hint that I was about to be dismissed?

"Yes, there are things that have to be finished, Meneer."

"Of course, but why always in a hurry? There is a storm raging across Europe. Why do we need to whip up storms here too? Let's just take it easy. Here"—handing a book to me—"perhaps you will enjoy this."

It was a book about the flora and fauna of America, and about the lives of those Indian tribes that had not yet died out.

"I look forward to reading it."

He smiled, very pleased, and I returned to my office.

There was a note from my boss on the envelope he had given me, saying that I should study the papers inside. God! They were Raden Mas Minke's papers. Who gave the orders to rob him this time? It was not me. Yes, my God, this was not my will. I put them back in their envelope. I realized as I did so that my hands were shaking. This man, exiled and helpless, was still being persecuted. He had the right to write whatever he wished, memoirs, perhaps a confession. He had that right. Only the most cursed of men act so barbarically against him. I say he has the right! Yes, he has!

My two hands rose up by themselves, trying to hold together my head, which was suddenly throbbing again. But no. Someone entered my office, old, skinny, wrinkled; the whole of his head of hair was white, he carried a cane, and wore very, very simple European clothes, but no shoes, just simple slippers. He came closer toward me. He didn't speak.

"Meneer Minke!" I muttered. "Already so old?"

Oh! This was another damned vision. My nerves were going again. I must sit down. I pressed the button underneath my desk. This electrical device had been installed only a week ago. When the attendant came I ordered a bottle of whiskey and a glass.

Who was it who had the heart to do this? I wrote out a note and took it to my boss. By the time I got back, the attendant was standing there waiting. He followed me in and put the whiskey and glass on the desk. By the time I had gulped down four glasses, I knew that the note would by now have left my boss's hands. By the time I had downed ten glasses, messages would be traveling along copper wires borne by electric current in who knows what directions.

I started flicking through my boss's book. What? Colored prints! Was something wrong with my eyes or were these pictures actually colored? I pressed the button. The attendant came back again. I held out the book for him to see, and asked: "Have you ever seen printed color pictures?" He glanced over the open book before him. He looked at me, he looked again at the pictures.

"This is the first time, Meneer." So it was true they were colored. I wasn't seeing things this time. I gave him a five cent tip and he left in very good mood.

I drank and drank again. By the time the bottle was empty, an answer would be arriving for me. I read one page, two pages. There was nothing interesting there. What did it all mean, flora, fauna, and Indian tribes? America! If I had to read about America, I would want something else, not this stuff.

My boss came in, carrying a piece of paper.

"Ah, you have begun reading my book. That's good. There is no need to be so serious all the time, Meneer." He smiled openly as if he were not my superior in this system of colonial power but a friend whom I was meeting on a street corner in Leidishe Square, or a new acquaintance I had made only because we had happened to sit on the same bench in Vondel Park.

"I don't know what this cable means. You will probably understand. Actually, I don't think I want to know either. But I do know that the clerks and other staff around the place, even though they might not understand what it's all about, if they hear something or find out something, they like to sell the information to the press. Did you know that?"

I was reminded of how Raden Mas Minke wrote in one of his books about the Patih of Meester Cornelius's nephew being caught reading papers in the Algemeene Secretariat. But I had not realized until now that it was our own staff that liked to sell information.

"There will be no more storms come from this office," he continued. "I don't want any information from here going onto the market now. The future of the Netherlands itself is in the balance."

He liked to shoot off his mouth. Who else did he talk to like this? Or was it just to me?

"Our job, Meneer Pangemanann, is to make the Indies as calm and quiet as possible, as if there were nothing happening in the world at all. We have already limited the news here about the war. I know there are all these groups forming out there. You call it 'an organization fever' in your reports. But none of this is a danger to us. Let them yap off as much as they like. As long as they have no guns, nothing will ever happen."

It sounded more and more as if I would turn out to be right about nearing the end of my assignment here.

"If you keep taking Sneevliet's and Baars's speeches seriously, you will never sleep. Let them be. A thousand people like them will never change the situation. If we just ignore them, they will end up talking only to themselves. They will never be heroes, just snake oil salesmen."

And would I get any increase in pension from the Algemeene Secretariat when I was retired from this job? And I still had not had my European leave. Perhaps when the war was over?

"We must keep a more vigilant watch over our clerks and attendants. Ever since the first governor-general, Peter Both, this office has always been the source of rumors and a marketplace for information."

In these uncertain times it looked as though the government's policy was to look inward to its own workings.

"Our office will no longer be the source of information for the stock market, press, or other speculation, and no more rumors either. Our situation here in the Indies is going to become more difficult as all our mineral products pile up. Europe's factories don't need our goods now. The only country whose factories keep producing is America, Meneer. And it doesn't need our goods either." He was quite a good orator. "We need new policies to deal with this decline in our markets. Our markets in Rotterdam and Amsterdam are going to remain quiet for the time being."

He laughed, as if he could read my mind. "Throughout its history, Europe has always waged war against itself, and that is how it has been able to rejuvenate itself. That's why it is superior to the other continents. Except America, of course. America has its own way. It won't copy the European countries' fighting among themselves. Once it makes a mistake, it never repeats it. That is America, Meneer. You can see for yourself with that book. The stones, the butterflies, rivers, everything is put down on paper in color for everyone to see. For everyone to see, Meneer. Do you hear me?"

Satisfied with his speech, he left me to my own devices again. He did not even mention the empty whiskey bottle on my desk.

Yes, what's the use of rushing about like this when even Her Majesty's and the Netherlands' future was uncertain? I took out Raden Mas Minke's manuscripts from my cabinet and put them in my briefcase. I would study all these as a fellow human being. No, Meneer Minke, I am no longer your guard dog. Once again I will become your admirer, your student, whose heart overflows with respect for you.

I took the new papers that came in today as well. And . . . farewell to this work of destruction! Good-bye to being a guard dog! I will go back to being the old Pangemanann. No more disasters would befall people because my fingers had scratched something on paper about their destiny. . . .

Quite unusually I received a visit that afternoon from some Menadonese. I really enjoyed that afternoon. I decided I would not start on Minke's manuscripts. I was unacquainted with six of my guests. I only knew my nephew, Pangemanann without a double *n*.

This time my wife sat with us, and my two children, Mark and Dede, also. The conversation was in Dutch, with the occasional Menadonese word thrown in here and there. Then came the real purpose of the visit. It was none other than my own nephew who was their spokesman.

With great enthusiasm and in quite adequate Dutch, he explained that the purpose of their visit was so that I, one of the most prominent Menadonese, would pay some small attention to what was happening in the lives of the Menadonese people in general. Would, yes, would the Menadonese only ever be soldiers and policemen until the end of time?

From the very beginning, I was being put in a difficult situation. From different things he was saying and at different moments, it was not difficult to see where all this was leading.

"Every student strives to become a government servant. Then when they get a job they forget forever that they are still Menadonese. Without the land and people of Menado there would be no Menadonese individuals, no Menadonese soldiers or police. We are not saying that to be a Menadonese is better than being from another people. What is there that we can boast about anyway? What really is there to be so proud about in there being a Pangemanann who has become a police commissioner and a Roemengan who has become a doctor or a Pangkey who has become a lawyer?"

He was in full flight now and I was feeling more and more ashamed.

Suddenly he changed to speaking in Malay. "Why are we speaking in Dutch? Madame understands Malay, Uncle too, and the children."

"Please," I said. "Madame will not object."

"We all know, Uncle, Madame," and he nodded to my wife, "that things are changing. Every day there are more changes. The different peoples of the Indies are starting to organize so as to advance themselves. The Javanese have the Boedi Oetomo, which has already set up many schools. And the government itself has been willing to give some of them subsidies. This year the Sundanese have set up the Pagoeyoeban Pasoenden. The Madurese have formed the Sarekat Madura. The Moslems have the Sarekat Islam. Even among smaller circles, among the nobles of Solo, they have set up the Blood of the Mangkunegaran. We know that you understand all this better than anyone, Uncle. So then, will we just stand by silently, as if nothing is happening, as if there is nothing else in our world except a soldier's or policeman's uniform? We are all agreed that we too should do as these others have done and start to work for the advancement of the Menadonese people."

"Yes, that's a very good idea," I said hypocritically.

"That is what we all hoped to hear. If you agree, Uncle, then everyone else will surely join us too."

I was reminded of the founding of the original *Sarekat Priyayi.*

"It's not that we want our people to set this up just because of Uncle or Dr. Roemengan or lawyer Pangkey. No, we don't want members who are just joining in for the sake of it. What's the use of that? We want to draw in those who truly feel there is a need and who want to work for the organization."

"That is probably the best way. But even members who don't really need the organization can at least tell other people about it," I interpolated.

It was then that I realized how little I knew about running an organization. This young man who sat before me seemed to have such knowledge, perhaps it was even a science, which he had obtained outside school and outside his employment with the government. I began to admire him. I let him keep on talking.

He continued to speak. When you have to work among many peoples with different interests and concerns, then it is important to be good at talking to people. That he was able to get his friends to come here with him was already a sign of organizational ability.

"Uncle, now that Uncle has agreed, we will circulate our invitations very broadly. And if we succeed, what do you think we should call our organization?"

A name? What was the best name? I put my brain to work. How

difficult it was to find a name. Ah, why not copy what others have already done.

"Sarekat Menado."

"That's what I thought you'd say," he said. "But we are not Moslems. I don't think we should use an Arab word like *sarekat*. And *menado* somehow doesn't feel right. Wouldn't it be better if we used *minahasa*?"

God! I had never thought about anything as detailed as that. So what meaning did I have for the Menadonese people, even though they were proud that I had reached such a high position in the police? It was shameful. And my work was in fact to manipulate these Native organizations. Not so that they would develop, but so that they would be destroyed. I had to make sure that they did not travel down the road that they chose, but the one that I chose for them. And now if an organization of my own people were to be set up, would I now have to do the same to them? Shameful.

"What about if we call it Rukun Minahasa? Do you agree with that, Uncle?" he asked straight to the point, unhesitatingly, and it seemed that this was what he planned to suggest all along.

"Excellent. Rukun Minahasa," I answered spontaneously. "That has much more Native Menado character."

As soon as I spoke they all stared at me.

"I didn't mean that as an insult. The word *Native* is not an insult," I said quickly. "You all reject the word *sarekat* because it is Arabic. As far as I know *rukun* is not a foreign word but a general Native word throughout the Indies. Isn't it because you wanted to maintain your cultural integrity that you have decided not to use Dutch or other foreign words?"

And now it was I who opened my mouth! And I explained to them about the anti-cosmopolitan movement that was growing in Europe, outside England, Germany, and France, among peoples who were sick of the influence of these three countries, who felt that their national integrity had been swallowed up by the influence of these three. This movement argued that there should be more attention paid to national development, even down to the question of language. If a nation continued to live in a cosmopolitan manner because of foreign domination, as in the Indies, then its language would become cosmopolitan too; it would fall into chaos, as had happened to English at one time. The rise of national consciousness in England had also required them to eventually put their language in order.

"So," I repeated, "to give priority to Nativeness in finding a name means showing our national character. I agree with Rukun Minahasa."

And during the course of my work, I had learned how to identify certain characteristics of Native organizations by the names they used. For example, those who used their mother tongue were making a statement that they did not need to communicate with the organizations of peoples other than their own. While those who used Malay were opening their doors to relations with all the organizations of the peoples of the Indies.

But I could see from the look in their eyes that they had not really understood what I had told them. These kinds of issues were still beyond the grasp of most of the educated Natives. I began to regret having talked about cosmopolitanism and the national question. So I did not continue. They might misunderstand.

"I support the idea of this organization and its name," I said, ending my speech. "Anyway, I am already old now. The future belongs to you. It is up to you to make use of it and determine what happens now. Old people like me will be of no use then, and those times will not belong to us anymore. It is you who have the right to determine what happens from now on."

"And, of course, you will not object to being one of our patrons, Uncle?"

A patron? I screamed in my soul. Me? A hunter and destroyer of organizations? These children do not understand how things really are.

"I will have to think about that first. An old person like me has to be more careful. I have to be very clear about what constraints there are upon me as a government official."

They seemed disappointed.

"What are your objections, Jacques?" asked my wife. "You have never paid enough attention to your own people all this time, and neither have Mark and Dede."

"Anyway," I said, "you must continue with your efforts. It will be your efforts that determine how things will be, not old people past their prime like me."

And I felt free again once they went away.

That evening I read Raden Mas Minke's papers. My conclusions, in brief, were as follows.

There were letters from Betawi, Solo, and Semarang and several more from Surabaya which revealed that Raden Mas Minke had been carrying out an energetic correspondence from Ambon with those towns. He did not agree with the elevation of Mas Tjokro to the leadership of the Sarekat. Haji Samadi should have consulted him first, before taking steps that would change the character of the organization. These letters also stated that Raden Mas Minke would take back the leadership when he returned from exile, which would be after five years, because exile was always either for five years or for life.

For those who have followed the footsteps of the Modern Pitung, it will be very easy to understand what a simple man he is. He is a man who believes in the goodness of others. His world is free of those feudal intrigues that are a normal part of life in feudal circles everywhere in the world. I didn't believe for a moment that he had ambitions to return as a leader of the Sarekat. He had already shown that he was willing to give up such a position. It was my guess that others were in fact trying to make sure that he did not return to his former position.

It was not the police who had to find out who was spreading these rumors about Minke wanting to be leader again. The police did not yet have units for doing that kind of work. And it still wasn't clear to me who had ordered his papers to be stolen, the second time he had suffered such theft.

So I had to come to the conclusion, based on what material was available, that there was a group that was worried that Raden Mas Minke might return to lead the Sarekat. There was no reason for the government to take action against the Sarekat. In such matters, it was indeed I who decided such things; I knew better than anyone about this. So there was no reason either for the government to intrigue against him. I guessed that the intrigues were coming from inside the Sarekat itself.

It was true though that the government would not like to see the Modern Pitung return to lead the Sarekat. He had given the weak in society the weapon of the boycott. He had given them that weapon. And the government had succeeded in getting them to use it, except not against the government.

In the more recent papers, there was nothing at all to indicate that he was in communication with Java. There was no evidence of that, or at least no one had discovered any evidence. From among the twenty or thirty pages he had written, there were only a few things that I thought were important. I mean they were just his opinions on different things, not actual pointers about what nations should be doing, and some general reflections on several issues.

About language, for example:

We were not wrong. Public organizations in the Indies will only grow and flourish if they use nongovernment Malay, and if they base themselves among the independent layers, the free people who are not tied to the government through their office or service, and those who are tied to the government through their employment. Several times I had to work very hard to convince Samadi of this. He preferred to use Javanese. The more Malay distances itself from the way it is taught in the government schools, from the feudal circles in general, the more democratic it becomes, the more it becomes a truly invigorating means of communication, a free language for a free people. And it is only the free people, the independent layers of society, who will determine the fate of the Indies, because the only way all the different peoples of the Indies will ever unite is through getting to know each other and working together on a democratic basis.

About capital:

It would be good if the Sarekat were to expand into an even bigger organization and bring together into a huge concentration all the capital of the weak. That capital must be able to free them from their dependence. Private capital as a means of freeing an individual from dependence is also good, but not the best way. That kind of private, personal capital also chains you to a new dependence and drags others into dependence as well—it is the European model of capital. The result has been the absolute enslavement of almost all the peoples of the world out the continent of Europe, and the relative enslavement of the European people themselves.

About himself:

I too have made mistakes. I never set aside time to train people properly. The three people closest to me—Wardi, Sandiman, and Marko—were left to find their own way without any real leadership from me. Wardi had no respect for the Sarekat. I paid too little attention to Sandiman, who had real talent, so that he never was able to play the role he should have. And I let Marko drown in day-to-day work and in looking after my security.

There was nothing among any of the papers that gave any more intimate information about his relations with those three helpers of his. And he never wrote about his wife either, as if he had banished that astonishing woman from his heart altogether.

He did not say much more about Samadi or Mas Tjokro, even though he did follow the newspaper reports.

As far as Wardi, Sandiman, Marko, Princess Kasiruta, Samadi, and Mas Tjokro were concerned, I knew much more about them than Minke. It is already clear what had happened to Wardi. He vanished after his leader was arrested. Marko too. The two of them seemed to be involved in the shooting and stabbing of Suurhof and his men. Raden Mas Minke's own writings pointed to that. I could have ordered that both of them be investigated in addition to Princess Kasiruta. But that would have been dishonest. They were faced with a gang acting outside the law. There was no need then for them to be brought before the law. And it was I who held this secret to the whole affair. I would not go hunting for the three of them because of that attack.

Sandiman and Marko fled with their very valuable freedom. Princess Kasiruta was in Sukabumi, where she spent her days just thinking about her husband. She would never be able to wreak the revenge she wanted, a revenge that would eat her up from inside. And I thought that from the point of view of my own safety it was better this way.

Raden Mas Minke was gone from them all now. And of course I won't burden you with all of his last notes.

About the attacks on the Chinese:

How could so many people be incited to attack the Chinese? Are there no educated people in the Sarekat at all? That kind of amok *was nothing more than a statement that they did not believe in the future, as if God in creating Nature had not made sure there was enough for everybody. Yes, there was human greed which made others poor, but there were wiser solutions to this problem than running* amok. *Amok! No wonder the Westerners say that running* amok *is an irrational emotional explosion and flourishes in traditions that are unfamiliar with rationality. Moreover . . .*

My hand, lifting another glass of whiskey, stopped. I turned around. My wife had grabbed hold of my arm.

"That's enough to drink, darling. It's sad. You are drinking more and more. You've been drunk five times now here at home. Have pity on your children. Don't give them an example like that."

Her voice was sad and weary and her sleepy eyes were even sadder.

I realized that she meant well. But strong drink was the only thing that could banish the tension caused by all these thoughts of mine.

"If you didn't want to talk about the Rukun Minahasa, why didn't you just say so? Why did you let the discussion go on and then come in and try to get drunk?"

I stood, embraced and kissed this woman, who had once been young, and whose skin was now wrinkled and whose body was stiff. I could hear her sobbing, perhaps for the first time in our marriage.

"Forget about it, darling."

"Stop the drinking, Jacques. Go back to being the old Jacques that I knew, and that I miss and remember so well. I chose you, I loved you, Jacques, because you were better than most Frenchmen. You never drank, you were a teetotaler. Do you remember what I asked you before we married? Don't you like to enjoy yourself? And you answered that in the Indies you can enjoy yourself without drink. Now you are not satisfied with whiskey and Bols, but drink it pure like this."

Her voice grew sadder and sadder as if the sun would never rise again.

"Don't torment your wife like this, Jacques. It's as if there's no point anymore in being your wife. You don't care about anything anymore. You hardly ever sleep well. These days you often say things that you don't believe in. Like what just happened with your nephew and his friends."

"What do you want me to do, darling?" I asked, forcing myself to continue.

"If it is true that you no longer need your wife and children anymore, let us go back home to France. Here we are probably just a nuisance to you."

"There is a big war going on in Europe."

"Who knows? France might still need me. What is the point of being someone who is not needed like I am now, not even needed by my own husband?"

"Go to sleep."

"How can a wife sleep when she sees her husband like this?" There was protest, anger, frustration, and sadness, fused into one, in her voice. "You never take us to church anymore. You stay away overnight more and more. And no, I have never asked to what office you have gone. You are bored with your family now, Jacques. You don't need us anymore. Your children need you, and you don't even care. You used to read to us all. Now you are not even capable of reading your own heart."

"How must I answer, my darling?" I asked.

"You don't need to answer, you have no answers anymore."

"You are putting me on trial, darling."

"No, it is you who have passed sentence on us. You don't need me anymore. I have become a burden for you. Drink is more important to you than your wife and children."

She kept on talking, all the while in my embrace. Sometimes I could no longer hear what she was saying. Sometimes I just heard a jumble of words whose connection one with the other I could not catch. Perhaps because I was already half drunk.

"Darling . . ." I said, but was cut off.

"Now it is my turn to speak. Every word you speak sprays me with whiskey, that accursed stink. The more expensive the drink you buy, Jacques, the heavier the curse. I will not let my children end up as drunkards. They have to learn to act and think with their own brains, not with whiskey."

"They are asleep, darling."

"Isn't it true that I have never spoken as much as this in all our marriage? Perhaps this is the last time you will want to hear my words."

"Why do you say that?"

"Tomorrow you will be worse than today. And the day after, worse still."

"Forgive me, Paulette, forgive me for making you suffer so much."

"Forgive me, Jacques, I cannot fulfill all your needs. Let me go home. I will feel happier if I can remember you while you still have some goodness left, before you have been ruined totally."

"No, don't leave me by myself, alone."

"No, I have been watching you for months now, thinking it over. I have done everything I could. You are getting worse. Thank you, Jacques, for still wanting to keep me here, but you cannot keep me here anymore. Drink all you like. I am just a nuisance to you."

I grabbed her, and said we should go to bed.

"I want to leave for Europe within two weeks, Jacques."

"No. You must stay here."

"You cannot stop me. I am going to leave. I have told you how I feel. You can continue your drinking now."

"You have never said anything before."

"You are far more educated than I, Jacques. You understand these things very well, but you haven't wanted to understand. Let us go."

"What will you do in Europe?"

"I feel I am needed by my children."

"I can't afford to pay for five people in Europe."

"Don't worry about that. I am used to working, however lowly the work."

"France is at war."

"Whatever else happens, I can still live in the Netherlands."

"The Netherlands' fate is not certain either."

"Let us go. That is all I hope from you."

And she climbed into bed. She didn't want to say anything more. I went back to my desk, I brushed away all the papers, and I went on drinking, glass after glass.

So this was how things were now. One by one I had lost everything. One by one they had left me. Was I fated to lose my own being, my self, as well, so that there would be nothing left at all?

That woman, who had been so loyal and dutiful, was now turned into a mountain of rock that could not be moved. She departed to Europe with the children. I could not imagine what their life would be like in Europe, where war now raged, where everything would be expensive and money worth little. I gave her all that we had saved over the last twenty years. And she accepted it, but with great regret, regret that this was how her marriage was ending. I whispered to her, asking what if I was able to give up the drink? She did not believe that a drunkard could ever reform himself.

The house was empty, still, as if I were a man who had been cursed with impotence. My only friend was the bottle. There was nobody now to try to stop me from drinking. Then I added to this friend several other new friends, one after the other, from among the friends of Rientje de Roo. But my heart remained empty and still, just like this house.

I had been the kind of person I wanted to be for forty years. I was hard on myself. But during these last fourteen or seventeen years or so, another, greater power than I had had given me a new character, one that waged war against the man that had already come into being, that had already been formed. And now this was what I was like today, in tatters, having lost everything, one thing after the other. This is I.

Even while I lived with the bottle and my office and the bought women, I still continued my studies of the Modern's Pitung manuscripts. And as I studied them I began to feel even more strongly how empty was my life, how futile it had all become, how shallow the stream of life that was once so deep, how all my vision was blanketed by anxiety and restlessness and . . . and how I had no future. Even in the middle of this crisis, I kept on with my study of those papers.

I could truly feel his disappointment and sadness. He was disappointed because he thought he had been exiled due to the editorial in *Medan* which, according to him, had struck at the authority and policies of Governor-General Idenburg. He couldn't accept that he had fallen just because of a banana skin. If he had been exiled over some really major issue, he would have been happy to accept his fate.

People become great people because their actions are great, their thoughts are great, their soul is great. The opposite is true of small people, he wrote. *The punishment I received was unjust for such an insignificant article. And so how should I describe somebody who hands out punishment too great compared to the crime? In reality I have the right to use the severest of words. I have too much respect for the paper I am writing on to set down upon it the words that now go through my head. Such a heavy punishment for such a small offense! Something as unjust as this could happen and nobody among the peoples of the Indies feels that their sense of justice has been violated, not Sundanese, Madurese, Javanese, Acehese, or Balinese. I am lost among injustices. And those who have not fallen victim have still not learned to recognize what injustice is. How dark are the Indies. Van Aberon chose exactly the right name for his collection of Kartini's letters, De Zonnige Toekomst, The Bright Tomorrow. It is the duty of every educated person to bring light into the darkness, for the*

sake of a brighter and clearer future, and the schools never teach that. But they are
not learning from this experience either. The Boedi Oetomo has been silent, and the
Sarekat itself has gone mute.

Very well, Modern Pitung, let me answer your questions. You had
planted time bombs wherever there was a Sarekat branch or cell. You were
not aware of what you had done, or, at least, you pretended not to know.
The series of incidents against the Chinese proved that I was right. Those
time bombs did exist. That was not my fault. Your own ancestors did not
know anything about justice either. And time bombs don't need to know
about justice (at least according to Meneer L—). Try to find a word for
justice in your mother tongue. You can look until your every hair has
turned gray, and you will not find one. You only came to understand about
justice from European writings, and then one day you needed it. But the
thing you needed was not available. You will have to wait until all the
peoples of the Indies become the diligent students of Europe before that
item becomes available here. You yourself were not the best of students.
Even though you had only obtained just a fingernail's worth of knowledge
from Europe, your head was already swelling so much that you quickly
grew eager to confront the Europeans.

Was not the Boedi Oetomo more correct than you? Boedi Oetomo
is doing fine and thriving as it hands out the equipment that its people need
to become good students of Europe. You wanted to jump ahead of developments. You had to fall. It was only my generosity that prevented you
from suffering an even more cruel fate. Nah, this is my answer.

You thought that you were exiled because of what Marko and Sandiman had done. That conclusion was without foundation. Your fate had
already been decided. It was just a matter of waiting for you to make a
mistake and then you would be off.

I was exiled because I was considered to have harmed the policies and authority of
the governor-general, he wrote, while those other three emotional hotheads were
exiled just because they made a lot of noise about a celebration! The crime was as
small as the punishment was big. Both they and myself only caused quite a small
commotion! So we can be sure that many more will be marched off to exile in the
future. How happy must the children of Europe be. They could condemn, they could
question policies they did not believe in, and without being punished, let alone exiled.
Both they who were the best of accusations as well as those who did the accusing did
not lose anything—on the contrary it meant that both would advance, each correcting
the other. In the Indies, it was considered an outrage that could not be accepted. But
this was just the beginning.

And I answered, Modern Pitung, it seems you have forgotten what it was like in the time of your ancestors. What do you think would have happened had you criticized or attacked one of them? Even before the last word rolled off your tongue, your head would have rolled off your body. Haven't you ever read the stories about your own ancestors? Don't try to apply European ways to the Indies. Even the Europeans here try to imitate the methods of your ancestors when it comes to matters of justice. You are the only person in the Indies who protests about this.

But it is true that these pioneering efforts of yours have brought upon you a heavy punishment. As time wears on the Indies will get used to people being exiled; even the government will grow bored with discussing and implementing such decisions. That would have been the time for you to go into action. Even so, you made a start, and as a result a new arena has been opened wide for everyone.

You were active for six years before you were exiled; D-W-T must have been even more frustrated. They survived just a few months! Not even half a year!

And you Marko, Sandiman? Where will you go? To jail or finally to exile? he wrote.

Marko! So Raden Mas Minke did still think about those faithful followers of his. You do not know, Modern Pitung, that after you were arrested, Marko as well as Sandiman obtained no protection from anyone. Realizing that the government was about to move against him, Marko set out to establish a new, fertile kingdom elsewhere, complete with subjects. In Solo of course! Sandiman disappeared from circulation. But, Modern Pitung, I think it is Sandiman who is Marko's *dalang*. He lives in the shadows. The Indische Partij could not be home for him. There is no place for a village boy there. Let me find out for you what these faithful followers of yours are doing.

With the little knowledge he learned from working with you, and a sentence or two of Dutch that he picked up from the streets, Marko began to appear all over Solo, speaking everywhere, in the town and the villages, to whoever would listen, and about anything and everything.

Being able to claim your authority, but with his own courage, he still was not able to take over the Solo branch of the Sarekat, although he became one of its foremost leaders. He is not like you, Modern Pitung; he does not have the same economic strength and the same depth of knowledge. He was forced to live both from and for the Solo Sarekat.

Your guess was right. Marko did have his special strength. And it came

from his special sense of justice. He had this power because he could mobilize all his inner strength, all of it, to achieve victory for a just cause. You
must not think that there was nobody in the Indies who protested at the
injustice that was done against you. Samadi didn't and Mas Tjokro didn't,
that's true. It was only your Marko who spoke out. But he didn't speak to
the government. He spoke to the wrong audience. He didn't yet dare put
down his protests in writing to be read by everybody. Perhaps one day that
is where his activities will lead him.

Very well, Modern Pitung, I will set up a special file for your loyal
follower, Marko. And Marko, from this day forth you will join the others
in the house of glass on my desk.

Now I studied once again Raden Mas Minke's manuscripts. It was my
impression that except for *Nyai Permana*, they were all connected. There
was a rupture between *This Earth of Mankind* and *Child of All Nations* on
the one hand and *Footsteps* on the other. I wasn't sure though whether these
were parts of a genuine autobiography or not. For the time being I decided
to treat them as a series of interesting stories, with all their strengths and
weaknesses. I decided that I would put aside some time to check out the
details of the story against the reality of any relevant official documents.
Actually, the decision to write down these notes of mine was also influenced
by those writings, I am not afraid to admit it.

I viewed them as stories, and the first of the manuscripts mostly reflected the modernization process in the thinking of Natives at the beginning of this century. The Native way of thinking and the European way
of thinking came together in this story, either in an explosion or in an
accommodation.

In fact, it wasn't really necessary to have the answer to the question
of whether this was an autobiography or not. As a story with many different
aspects to it, the process of change is most of all reflected in Minke, its
narrator. His values change as his situation changes. There is the influence
of the environment on his personality, and the impact of his personality on
the environment, changes in the means of communication and the people
he communicates with, the role of racial discrimination and the law as its
shadow, Europe as a teacher and a destroyer.

During a discussion once with Meneer L—, he explained to me how
there was an unbridgeable gap between the European and Native way of
seeing the world. Europeans saw nature as something outside themselves
that they wanted to subjugate. Natives saw themselves as part of nature
itself. It was this difference that was the origin of all their different behavior,
and it was here too that the differences could be rediscovered. Europeans

want to subjugate nature. Natives want to accommodate to nature so that
they are in harmony with it.

And if Meneer L— is correct, then does that mean that I can say that
the character of Minke is a bridge between these two worldviews? His
thought world was neither fully European nor fully Native. And the bridge
itself seemed to be more weighted in Europe's direction.

But I mustn't make a hasty decision on this. There is still so much that
I don't know about the Natives. It seems this is a science of its own. Dr.
Snouck Hurgronje had his experiment. The de la Croix family wanted to
make Minke their experiment. But Minke himself seemed to have become
a cultural hybrid. In *Footsteps* he bent again in the direction of the Natives
while still standing firm with his European values. Yet when he worked
and dealt with other Natives, he still did so as a cultural hybrid.

But even so, I still could not help asking myself—were these three
manuscripts an autobiography? For the time being I was unable to answer
this. At the very least, I think, he tried with all his might to depict how
things were during the time the story took place.

As I tried to understand these writings, I was reminded of literature
classes at high school. In my last year, my teacher gave me an assignment
to read Gustave Flaubert's "Un Coeur Simple." It's a pity that I was never
asked to analyze a French work of the same caliber as these manuscripts. I
mean the same caliber in the sense of looking at these kinds of transformations in values, world outlooks, and social life itself. Anyway, I can still
say that I have been taught how to analyze a piece of writing by my teachers
at school.

I don't know whether my comments about these writings will interest
the reader or not. But I think it would be a mistake not to write something
as I am probably the only person in the world who has such an absolute
opportunity to master these manuscripts, which do not seem to have been
meant for publication.

The echoes of the Great War more and more resounded in the Indies.
And I became even more interested in studying these manuscripts.

The third manuscript, which seemed more like an autobiography than
the others, described the growth of the first organizations that Minke
founded based on European concepts, and how they developed, the efforts
to get them going, the difficulties, the victories and the defeats, and how
the further development of these organizations could not be separated from
the development of the press and its trials and tribulations, its successes and
failures. The other thing about this manuscript was that the role of the
individual, be he named Raden Mas Minke or Si Ana or Siti Ainu, was not

important at all. The times guaranteed the birth, growth, and development
of organizations as the vehicle for different ideas and for the ideas themselves. Of course, the individual left behind deep marks, perhaps eternal
ones, on the life of these organizations, but what was more important was
the role of these organizations on the modern history of the Indies, in the
way they changed the Indies and its people, in accordance with the ideals
that had been formulated, struggled for, and developed as the essence of
these organizations' activities.

And the role of the former police commissioner called Pangemanann
was not important either. No matter what he did to hold back the development of these organizations, he would fail. History will march on according to its own laws. Pangemanann was just the representative of the
Netherlands Indies state power. The forward march of history is the movement of humanity all over the world, the life trajectory of humanity. Whoever defies history, whether a group, a tribe, a people, or an individual, will
fail. Including the Netherlands Indies and I myself. I knew for certain that
this is what would happen; I didn't know when, I didn't know whether
quickly, or slowly. . . .

I don't think I need to put down for eternity all my opinions about
these manuscripts of Raden Mas Minke. The echoes of the Great War are
more pressing today than the opinions of a person who will never change
anything.

8

Before Wardi and Douwager left for exile in Europe, I submitted a request to escort the two exiles on their journey and then to take my European leave. But my boss did not approve the request. To forbid things is a colonial hobby that gives a pleasure of its own. It makes you feel more important and more powerful.

I could understand that. I too had experienced that feeling and would still seek to experience it again. To oppress is a part of the colonial character. And the pleasure that you obtain from oppression is even deeper than that obtained from simply forbidding. And Europeans, who come from that democratic society of theirs, after just six months of breathing the colonial air, will quickly be addicted to forbidding and oppressing, enjoying the rights once exercised by the same Native kings that they so love to insult and revile. I agree completely with what Kartini, the girl from Jepara, wrote about this.

My failure to get my leave to Europe deepened further my understanding of the colonial order. At the top, colonial power was supported by a small group of white colonial people who in their turn were supported by colonial brown people of which there was a greater range of kinds and groups. From the top going down, there were bans, oppression, orders, insults, and abuse. From the bottom going up, there were arse-licking, submission, and slavelike self-abasement. And I had my place in this order. And so anyone who heard my boss's reply to my request would just smile. "There is so much work to do these days, Meneer. And you are not allowed to have any helpers or any replacement. You must understand, Meneer, that the work you do is new in the Indies."

Madness! I swore inside while my lips smiled sweetly and politely. Yes, the smile must be sweet and polite, because that is how a subordinate must behave toward his superior, because that is the colonial custom we must always honor.

He also replied with a smile and I could feel the insult it expressed: Ah, you, all you do is write up excuses for arresting and exiling people, and here you are making all sorts of demands. And my smile also took on other meanings: Ah, you, all you do is use my ideas, and here you are so sparing with your generosity! If I go on holiday, you will have to do my work yourself and use your own brain. Isn't that the real problem?

And that was the kind of conversation that took place inside me and continued to take place, haunting me still, a week, a month, and a year later. My wife had gone. My children had gone. My pangs of conscience because of the exile of the Indische Partij triumvirate had also disappeared. Strong feelings of nostalgia for the old days often came to disturb me. I wanted to work once again in the midst of fellow human beings, among and with other human beings, giving up all these documents and this thirst for blood and victims on the part of the government, giving up these documents that are without flesh and blood, and contain nothing but thoughts.

"There's no doubt about it, the Liberals' policies have set off amazing political developments here," my boss said to me once, trying to encourage my enthusiasm for my work. "All kinds of organizations are springing up everywhere like mushrooms, and, you know, they remind me of a fungus too. When do you think the Menadonese will start setting up their organizations?"

"I hope that never happens," I answered.

"But it will happen, that's a certainty," he countered. "And you will have even more work to do as a result, Meneer."

"Well, if that does happen, then you can be sure I will remain loyal to the government. It won't cause me any trouble," I parried.

"We don't know what is going on in the mind of the Menadonese people, your people, Meneer," he said, chopping at me.

I tried to escape him. I couldn't even look into his blue marblelike eyes. He talked and talked like a policeman interrogating a criminal who has just been arrested. And that is how I felt. Not being able to take this any longer, I quickly cut in: "Our people are closer to the Dutch than the other people of the Indies. We are Christians. There has never been a Christian people of the Indies who looked for trouble with the government," I answered. "Yes, there was one Christian people in the Moluccas who fought the Company. They were even led by a priest, a European priest. But I think that was because of the Company's own excesses. There has never been any other incident since then, has there? No, they have been just like the Menadonese, haven't they? They have never sought to make trouble again."

He just laughed and then began another lecture as if he were some neutral professor giving an objective explanation of some problem that was located tens of thousands of kilometers distant from himself. But in fact, these problems were represented by the papers that lay strewn across my desk in front of me then: "But in these modern times, isn't it true that religion is no longer a guarantee of loyalty to the government?" he asked. "Ah, you understand all these things better than I, Meneer. New ideas from all over the world can make their way to the most isolated places, can touch the minds of certain individuals, and turn them into different people, nah? It is no longer religion that determines whether they will be loyal to the government or not, but people's interests or what they see as their interests."

I knew that I had to bring this dangerous conversation to an end. It was very true that in its time religion was also politics. The Christian peoples of the Indies did not seek conflict with the government. But Raden Mas Minke's writings gave examples of how some people could seek conflict with their own peoples—Khouw Ah Soe and Ang San Mei, for example. It was true that one was a Catholic and the other a Protestant but it was not their religion that moved them to try to overthrow the Ching dynasty. They were motivated by something else, called nationalism.

Ah, there was no need for my head to argue myself into a corner like this. Whatever happens I will still carry out my duty as best I can. Sometimes, you know, my conscience can gallop into action and almost drive me insane. But I have been able to keep it under control so far. As time has passed by, I have learned to enjoy the colonial pleasures. I was a colonial god who could decide the fate of others. I was a free man—no wife, no children. All I had to do was send money and all was well. There was nobody to boss me anymore. The enjoyment of all pleasures was now open to me. There was no limit to what I could drink. In the office I was a little god; outside I had unlimited freedom. Every letter and word I affixed on the papers on my desk would be felt directly by the skin, flesh, bones, heart, and brain of the Native nationalists. And they probably had never even heard my name. It was only those nationalists exiled overseas who were beyond my view and observation. As long as they remained in the

Indies, they also remained in the house of glass on my desk.

I wanted to say to my boss: Enough, no more. I knew that I was sinking more and more into the colonial mud, deeper and deeper. I was no longer stepping through just muddy ground, but was clearly and obviously sinking into a stinking and deep mudhole. Yes, my God, put weights on my body, on my head, so that the mud will suck me down even quicker. . . . But no, I would never speak back to my boss like that. All I would ever do is again and again swallow my words.

And you, you, my teacher, you will escape the mud. Your hands will remain clean and your heart will never cry out because of the accusations of your conscience.

But what my boss said was: "Soon there will be organizations set up by the Bugis, the Toraja, Banjar, Dayak, Minang, Acehnese, and so on. And you, Meneer, what do you think will happen in the end? Perhaps there'll be no call for me to worry about it anymore. Perhaps, yes perhaps."

"Why not?" I asked, amazed.

And he just laughed, like an innocent little boy. And I was truly envious of him.

"Don't worry about it for now. You have to study the ones who were influenced by Raden Mas Minke, the ones whom he brought up and pushed onto the main stage. I think that's the kind of work you find very interesting."

And I—this bruised and battered conscience—continued to carry out the orders of my superiors.

It was easy to guess whom he meant—Marko Kartodikromo and Sandiman. From their teacher's manuscripts it was already clear that Sandiman was a mysterious character. Now he had disappeared from circulation. No one knew where he was. In fact, we had lost his trail altogether. It was my guess that he was in Solo and was the brains behind Marko, but I wasn't able to prove it.

With Marko it was different again. As time went on it seemed he lived less and less in the shadow of my power. He began to appear more and more frequently in public. He talked and wrote, wrote and talked, everywhere, in town and village, in people's homes and in the public squares.

Among the papers that were seized from the editorial offices of *Medan*, Braga Street 1, Bandung, were a number of Marko's writings that had never been published. I found one of them in particular very interesting. Perhaps he himself never realized how important it was. It was about the changes that had taken place in the Indies, and in himself as the author, during the last half century.

When he was still under the wing of his teacher, he was "Marko."

After his teacher departed so suddenly, he changed his name to "Marco."
It seemed that his teacher's departure made him feel he had lost a source of
strength. Now he had a new source of strength by changing his *k* to a *c*, so
that it was like the great names of Marco Polo and Marconi, and read more
like a European name, and felt more like the name of an educated person.
Yes—yes, I could see that many of the literate Natives in the towns and
cities of Java would follow Marco's example, having lost faith in the power
of their own ancestors who had always been defeated by Europeans. This
action of Marco's seemed to indicate there was a trend to surrender un-
conditionally to European civilization.

He was very different in many ways from Wardi. In fact, he was almost
the opposite of Wardi. Wardi came from the Javanese high aristocracy and
he understood fully the empty extravagance of his nobility and so he gave
up all his titles. As far as Europe was concerned, Wardi also seemed to reject
it too, even to see it as an enemy. To show his sympathy for the poor masses
he deliberately wore black shirt and trousers, no shoes and a sarong, as if, I
said as if, he had given up priyayi and European clothes forever. That he
was sympathetic toward the peasants did not mean he was interested in
taking up the peasants' occupation. He had a tendency to seek strength in
being different.

It was different with Marco, now with a *c*. He tried to understand and
then go with the flow of history as it picked up speed. He always wore a
white shirt and white pantaloons. His hair was always neatly parted in the
middle. His eyes were always wide open, always, as if he did not want to
miss even one thing that happened around him and in the big world outside
his country. He passed on everything he understood, half understood, or
he thought he understood to whoever was willing to pay him any attention.

In some things they were the same. They both had explosive and
agitated spirits, they were both spontaneous spirits, and both were full of
hatred for the colonial power.

Nah, while Wardi gave up all his titles, Marco followed in his teacher's
footsteps, affirming his, and so in recent times his full name began to appear—Mas Marco Kartodikromo.

From one of his writings, the one that I thought was particularly important, I could see just what lived in his soul. This is the piece I mentioned
earlier, written in very chaotic market Malay. I have copied it out below,
with many improvements.

*Finally he could work no longer. Neither could his wife, who had fallen ill before
him. Only his nine-year-old son still had his health. As could be expected, though,*

the village official then forced the son to go off and do his mother's and his father's quota of work.

The little boy cried and cried all the way along the four-kilometer track. Not just because of hunger—the soles of his feet were covered in ulcers and yaws had spread throughout his body. Among the crowd trudging along the track, there was an emaciated women heavy with child, old people coughing and walking with canes, a man carrying a baby a few months old whose mother had just died of hunger.

A procession of future corpses, and for most that fate would come in just a few months. All walking south. To the government indigo plantation. Forced labor. Forced cultivation! No pay. Cultuurstelsel.

The name of the village was Cepu. Not the Cepu of today. It was a poor village. But that former village was now part of one of the richest regions in the Indies. It was here that I was born. And it was here too that I heard every night the stories of the old people who had to leave every day for months to walk to the indigo plantation, to work for no pay, without any security, left with no opportunity to tend to their own land. And every day some among them died of illness and hunger.

My village was just like other villages. The people should have lived as farmers, hunting for wood in the forest, breeding goats, cattle, chickens, and themselves, and living among big families. But the Cultuurstelsel had split asunder these families and robbed them of rice and spirit.

In short, don't imagine that Cepu was anything like the district of Cepu today. My Cepu was sheltered by very many fruit trees. Today's Cepu district is sheltered by lampposts and telephones.

The nine-year-old had been working for ten days when he was discovered in his empty house one evening. He had laid out on the floor leaves that he had gathered on his walk home. A cold hearth. There was no food, no people. He had called out for his sick mother and father. There was no answer. He went to his neighbor's house. All he found were more sick people. Those who were a quarter sick or half-sick also had been off to work.

As dawn approached his father returned, linked arm in arm with others so that they would not fall, or lose their way in the dark. They were returning from burying the child's mother.

A month later even more were buried like this, including his father.

The child still carried on doing his quota of work. He ate young grass, because that was the easiest to get while he was working. And furthermore the Chinese petai fruit and leaves, though they had more taste, made all his hair fall out, and in a gaunt and haggard state, and hairless, a person looked like Satan.

Then one day the people heard that the indigo plantation had been closed down and forced labor had been abolished. But that village had to endure it for another two years yet. And later I found out that any forced labor that took place after the government abolished it was done for the local officials, European and Native.

I don't know what happened that finally brought it to an end there. Perhaps there had been some dispute over the spoils. But I don't really know. That was the business of the gods above. So people went back to cultivating their paddy fields and gardens that had grown into jungle and wild brush. The number of inhabitants had been halved. So the recultivation of the jungle and brush was never completed properly. And the village government did not improve even after the abolition of state agriculture, otherwise known as the Cultuurstelsel.

Then there were new reports: The government plantations were going to become private plantations, and these private plantations would belong to Europeans. Village people would be allowed to work there, for a wage—a wage enough so that a family could eat.

Meanwhile the child had reached the age of eleven, and was stronger now than three years before. And these reports never turned out to be true. What was true was that both the village's fields and the land of individual farmers were stolen by the government, including five sixths of this village's land, also, it was said, for private plantations. When this happened, these farmers, who were only just recovering from hunger and deaths, rose up in anger.

They were led by Pak Samin, a man from another village. A peasant rebellion took place.

The eleven-year-old joined up with the rebels. But the peasants were defeated, and defeated easily, by the police militia who were brought in from the towns. They did not have to face the army, because, everybody said, all the soldiers had been ordered to Aceh.

The men who escaped returned to their villages. There were fewer still now, many having been killed in battle.

The child turned fifteen years old.

It seemed that there might be peace now and their land would be returned to them. But no. Teak trees were planted on the villagers' land. It was said there were no European companies interested in the stolen land because it was too chalky and infertile.

But it turned out that the star of ill fate still shone. Because then the village people were chased out of the village. An oil company wanted to set up its refinery and offices on the village site. The villagers took their animals and opened up new land to make new fields and paddy and homes. It was said that the villagers were compensated with money for the loss of their village but no one ever saw any of this money which had been promised in unspecified amounts. They were even saying that the villagers were being paid for each teak tree that was planted. These were nothing more than empty reports, nothing more.

My village, once shaded by its many fruit trees, was magically transformed into an open field. The houses disappeared. They built beautiful roads, and buildings too. Everything was beautiful, except they did not belong to the people of the village.

he child lived in the new village. There he married one of the remaining aidens who had not been borne away by death. And I was one of their children.

Later on, much later on, I found out that in just five years the oil company, which had started with just five thousand guilders, had developed into a giant company worth half a million guilders. The villagers who had been evicted from their village never even heard about, let alone saw, any of this huge profit. It was also later on that I found out that the teak grown on this earth of my ancestors was the best in the whole world and became famous as "Java-teak." The best quality teak was not allowed to be used in the Indies; it was for export only. And we never received any share of this profit. Now it was only privation and loss that they dropped down on us from on high.

How strange is the way that profit and this man-made fate we all suffer is apportioned among us. I know and I am prepared to prove that the local oil barons started off as engineers working for the government in Bandung. They came to where I lived, where my parents, neighbors, and relatives lived, to carry out exploration on the land where my ancestors were born and buried. The villagers always gave the visitors a warm welcome, not caring what was the color of their skin, or their religion. We brought firewood, old and young coconuts, and fruits to their house. After they had discovered what resources there were, they returned to Bandung and—resigned. Then they returned to Cepu as giant mosquitoes to suck up our blood, flesh, land, and the oil in the womb of my ancestors' land. Within ten years their company was worth millions, while their former hosts had lost their land and continued to live in greater and greater poverty. And not only that. From being free farmers they had been turned into the coolies of their former guests.

It was while they were drilling in our region that I was born. My father, the boy with yaws and ulcers, was no longer a coolie. He had become the village head. And the oil company was becoming even greedier for land. They were afraid of the competition from other companies that were springing up like mushrooms throughout the region where we lived. They started to pay for the land they stole. Each company was afraid that its competitors would expose the other's criminal activities.

Then we reached the stage where our village no longer had any land where we could graze our animals. If even one of our animals strayed onto company land, the Oil Police would grab it, confiscate it, and its owner would be fined one hundred times the normal daily wage.

I just want to make it plain that in the government, there was also an Oil Government, and the people of our village had to obey both of them.

Now thousands of people from other areas flocked to Cepu, from all races, to seek their livelihood. Soon the district of Cepu, which originally comprised only three villages, had spawned twenty more, turning into a busy town. Crime and indecency were rampant. Syphilis spread through the village, leaving many cripples and invalids for the village to look after.

The farmers almost rebelled again. All of a sudden several villagers were arrested and were never seen again. They were arrested by the Oil Police.

There was no more restlessness after that. It was as if the old sense of security, with all of its deformities, had returned once more. Neither the government nor the companies shared any of their profits with the local people. There were no decent-sized pieces of land left. The village cattle had also disappeared because of the forced cultivation.

If I had been an American, honored readers, do you know what I would have done? I would have drawn my revolver and defended whatever could still be defended. But I was just a Native boy, with no weapons, and no knowledge of the world. I did not even know where the location of the village where I was born was in relation to the rest of the world. Nor did I know where lay the land of these people who came and impoverished us. I had been to school for only three years; I had been educated only to become another coolie for the oil companies who had stolen my ancestors' land. I was educated to know nothing and to obey every order that came from the white-skinned tuans.

When my father was dying, his parting message to me was: "They have stolen all that we have. No, my son, you must not be their coolie any longer. Go to Bandung. There you must serve a man of honorable heart. This man is named Raden Mas Minke. Find him. Carry out everything he asks of you, and take as an example for your life all of his good deeds."

I did not know and had never heard of this man. And I had no chance to ask my father either.

After my father died, someone from the town told me who Raden Mas Minke was. He was not a lord like the other priyayi, I was told. He was a priest, a teacher, they said.

And so I left my village for the very first time on a quest to carry out my father's instructions. All that I had with me were a few cents, a village school education, my father's instructions to me, and three years' training in fistfighting from one of my uncles, who was among those who still wanted to fight back (and who later died somewhere or other). So, honorable readers, you can understand how difficult it was going to be for me to find this Raden Mas Minke. I didn't know if I should board the train to Bandung or not. I didn't have enough money. I had to find some more money. Don't become one of their coolies, my father had said. But there was no work for me to do anywhere in this town. All they needed were coolies, only coolies. I lived off the streets while I tried to get together some more money. Because I could give a bit of a display of fistfighting, the Oil Police liked me. But what was I going to be able to achieve this way?

Then one day at the railway station, I met another boy like me. His name was Gombloh. It was an easy name to remember. I didn't think it was a good name for him. He was clever, perhaps seven years older than I. He liked to read the papers *and he taught me to read Malay. The two of us fought once with a group of black and white sinyos who were harassing some girls selling peanuts. One of the sinyos had his jaw dislocated. I managed to get a black sinyo in the midriff and knocked him down. The village people hid us. They gave us what little money they had and told us to leave Cepu.*

Gombloh left and I didn't know where he lived. I left Cepu too but returned three months later. I had spent the three months in the teak forest with a hunter. He taught me to master the use of a knife. It was with this new skill that I returned to Cepu feeling much stronger, protected, and indeed I was now an adult.

For several more months I lived like this, not knowing what was to become of me. There were many other boys about me who also did not want to become coolies. Then I heard that someone was looking for me. I looked for him, and it turned out to be Gombloh. Do you want to live in Bandung? he asked, making an offer.

It was then I remembered what my father had asked me to do. I cried and embraced him. I knew that I had put off carrying out my father's orders for too long. I looked upon Gombloh's offer as a test from my father himself. Gombloh had suddenly become very important in my life.

We went by train together. In the middle of the journey, he asked me if I had ever heard the name Raden Mas Minke. My heart started to pound as if it might burst at any moment. I just nodded. And he spoke again. We are going to protect him from any and all dangers that might arise. I shivered. Why are you shivering? he asked. Are you afraid? And I answered: Just give me the chance to defend him.

And so it was that I was taken in by Raden Mas Minke, in a big town called Bandung, where I did not even speak the language of its inhabitants. He treated me as his own younger brother. He educated and guided me, and taught me to do good. Do not become their coolie, he said as if repeating my late father's words. Don't make them richer and more powerful because of your sweat. Learn all you can from them so you become as clever as they are. Then use that knowledge to lead your people out of this never-ending darkness.

My honorable readers, we will never return to how things used to be. The sun has set behind the mountains and behind our backs. The sun will now rise before us, bright and brilliant, and will never set again.

I think Wardi read this as well as Minke. That's my guess. It has exactly the same spirit as NEDERLANDERS ALS KOLONIALEN. It has that Multatuliesque spirit. The thing that I saw most of all in his story was the change that was taking place in the Native soul. The theft of their land and of their livelihood and their way of life had made them more patriotic and, more than that, had turned them into nationalists, in the European mold.

Perhaps what he had written was not the absolute truth, although it was clear there were autobiographical elements, as in Minke's manuscripts.

The important thing was that he was able to describe the process of transformation in values that was taking place, and also the economic and social transformations of the time.

God knows what all this European influence, whether through the things it has built or the things it has destroyed, will ultimately produce. After just a few years of mixing with an educated Native, this village boy has been able to absorb the European skill of writing, but uses it to oppose Europe itself. He no longer talks about the world he left behind, with its ghosts and spirits. Now he speaks only about what needs to be written and what needs to be done. What will things be like in another quarter of a century when European education and society have spread even further and the means of communication have become more effective, tearing away the distance and the hierarchy that keeps Natives apart?

Marco's article also reminded me of what Minke wrote about Nyai Ontosoroh, a Native Javanese girl, who could not read or write. After just thirteen or sixteen years as a *nyai*, she was able to manage a large European-style business, and according to what Minke wrote, then chose to become a French citizen rather than a subject of the Netherlands Indies with only uncertain legal rights. Consciously! And not just because she married Jean Marais.

Jean Marais! Wasn't he a student one class below me when I was at the Sorbonne? Perhaps it was just someone else with the same name. Minke probably just chose a name at random.

European influence is an interesting topic. I will make a special study of this one day. Not as an official, not simply as an office assignment. His Excellency the governor-general had sent the letter to the Indies Council asking them about the costs and benefits of giving Natives a European education. The council had not yet given an answer but voices for and against were already making themselves heard in every big town. Luckily I wasn't overwhelmed with this work. And all that was left of these voices were meaningless echoes. All that people needed to do was read the writings of the Jepara girl, Minke, Wardi, Tjipto, and as a side effect of European education, the writings of Marco. Perhaps, indeed, it should be Marco's writings that decide the matter for them.

Modern Pitung did not publish this article by Mas Marco Kartodikromo. I could see that there might have been two reasons. First, the situation was not ready for something like this. Second, Minke was known to be very averse to receiving praise and flattery and it was unlikely that he would want to broadcast new flatteries and praise.

But in reality it was a waste of time joining in beating the drum either for or against more such education. All the arguments were irrelevant to

the essence of the problem. The reality was that the more European companies set up in the Indies, the more need there would be for educated
Natives. I found it more worthwhile to follow the activities of one of the
products of this European influence—Mas Marco Kartodikromo.

This European influence, which he did not receive directly from
school and family, and which he received suddenly when he was already
an adult, made him a rather strange kind of hybrid. I don't mean to say that
this influence did not work good changes within him. It was just that it
affected rather different aspects of his personality, while others weren't
touched very much or were even completely untouched. His development
was unstable and uncertain.

Just recently his photo had appeared for the first time in a magazine
published in Solo and Semarang. He was wearing an open coat and a tie!
This was something none of his teachers or friends had ever done! It was
quite possible that these European clothes, from tie to shoes, were hired or
borrowed from somebody. It was quite likely. But the strange thing was
that he was already striking a European pose. He stood straight and stiff
with his eyes blazing, so he looked quite frightening. The free and easy
American style of posing for pictures was not generally known in Europe,
let alone in the Indies.

Marco was making a statement through his choice of clothes—he was
a European Native. Nobody could tell him from an Indo. If he took off
his shirt and trousers, no doubt we would find many signs of his having
suffered yaws. But that wasn't important either. Yet it was precisely because
of the strange hybrid character of this European influence and the fact that
he had developed extreme characteristics of both the Natives and Europeans
that he was potentially very dangerous to the government. Eastern brutality
and viciousness could fuse with Western rational thinking, and suddenly
we could have a frightening new devil.

This prediction was not far from what happened. He himself was already beginning to announce that he was heading in that direction. He
discovered and began to trumpet the slogan *Sama rata sama rasa! Equality for
all!* which began to spread throughout the Indies, even to the jungles of
Borneo. With this slogan he had succeeded in arousing a new attitude
among the mass of the people. They began to challenge all rich people and
State officials, no matter what the color of their skin. He had planted the
seeds of anarchy. He took the masses back to the ancient idea of village
democracy that was part of the village republic.

And that slogan took him to new heights of fame, unrivaled since the
time his teacher was forced to depart Java.

Now he began to spread on the wind two new code words—*MTWT I* and *MTWT II*. The first meant: *MoTro WuTo,* the blind comrades. The second meant *MuTo WaTiri.* Both these messages were meant for the young generation of the Sarekat. They were a message to purge themselves of those among them who were blind (to their own friends) and were a cause for worry (as regards the safety of their own friends).

This had quite a significant effect. All those members who were close to the government were pushed aside. They were isolated and their rights as members were taken away. Now Marco's influence spread throughout the area as if he were already armed with a real strike-force.

He was actively getting in touch with the *silat* and other fighters around Solo and Jogja.

And the Sarekat leadership itself, both in Solo and Surabaya, did nothing about this at all. In fact, they didn't bother about it.

Then his activity moved northward—Salatiga, Magelang, Ungaran, and Semarang. In Semarang he succeeded in convincing the Sarekat leadership to form a platoon of fighters. And Mas Tjokro went on happily as ever ignorant of the cancer in his organization.

I had prepared a report for my boss recommending how Mas Tjokro might be woken from his imperial slumber. And so telegrams started to fly to and from and between Semarang, Solo, Jogja, and Surabaya. Mas Tjokro held fast to his belief in his own authority and in the Sarekat's dependence on himself. He seemed to be intoxicated by his new car. He was perhaps the only Native who was not a raja, not a sultan and not a prince who owned a car. As a Borsumij clerk he would never have been able to own a car, no matter if he waited until he was bent with age.

Marco too carried on calmly as if there were no such person called Mas Tjokro in the Sarekat. He continued to build up his own base in Semarang, Solo, and Jogja. If no action was taken to stop him, then it was possible he would soon be able to wield real power in other towns as well. Would this be the way the Natives struggled for leadership? Very interesting.

But hold on, Marco! Don't grow too fast. I need time to follow what you are doing.

I understand you now. You should stop your activities, inflaming yourself and your supporters. You should be setting aside the next four years or so for study so that you can overcome your weaknesses. You might be a brilliant success then! But be careful, because for the moment you are under my close observation. You too are in the house of glass on my desk.

Or was it I who was going backward? Here I was forced to study closely the every action of a village boy. Or was it Marco who was the extraordinary one, a village boy who had captured the attention of an official of the Algemeene Secretariat?

The answer from the Civil Registry Office in Surabaya was exactly as I predicted. No Monsieur Jean Marais, as mentioned in Minke's *This Earth of Mankind* manuscripts, had ever been registered. There were forty-two Frenchmen who had lived in Surabaya between 1898 and 1918. It was clear that Jean Marais was not his real name. This was obviously also the case with the family name de la Croix, which he used for the former assistant resident of Bojonegoro.

It was true, however, that there was a Frenchman who had been a veteran of the Aceh War who lived in Surabaya from 1896. He had been a corporal and his name was Antoine Barbuse Jambitte. He lived in Jalan Kranggan, opened a furniture workshop, and lived with his daughter, Madeleine Jambitte. In 1905 he married a former concubine. But the registry had no information on the concubine.

But I was able to get some additional information from the Kapanjen church in Surabaya. It was true that Antoine Barbuse Jambitte had married a Native woman there called Sanikem. But he had used the name Jean Le Boucq, so it was probable he had registered in the army as Antoine Barbuse Jambitte. Many people hiding themselves away did this.

They left Surabaya after they married. The Registry Office listed them as leaving Surabaya for France in 1907, taking with them two children, Madeleine Jambitte and Rono Mellema.

I shook my head in amazement.

I sent a telegram asking how old Meneer Jambitte and Nyai Ontosoroh were in 1905. They answered that Meneer Jambitte was thirty-seven years old at the time of his marriage. They had no information about his wife.

So Jean Marais alias Antoine Barbuse Jambitte alias Le Boucq was not the university student in the class below me. I had only been guessing anyway. Sanikem was thirty-seven years old at the time of her marriage came a reply from the Kapanjen church. So they had really existed and had been in Surabaya.

Had there ever been people living in Surabaya by the names of Robert Mellema, Annelies Mellema, and Engineer Maurits Mellema? I asked again.

The answer returned even more quickly. Robert and Annelies Mellema were the acknowledged children of Meneer Herman Mellema, the owner of a farming business in Wonokromo. We have no information on Engineer Maurits Mellema, they said. There was a Robert Mellema who was listed in 1899 as missing. Annelies Mellema had left Surabaya for the

Netherlands, and had not returned to the Indies to this day. The documents gave the number of the birth certificate and the acknowledgment of paternity from Herman Mellema.

Before she left for the Netherlands, had Annelies Mellema married or been married to a Native?

The registry couldn't give an answer. And that was to be expected. If they had married according to Islam, they would not have reported the marriage to the Registry Office.

The letter I had sent off to the Surabaya HBS got a less than satisfactory answer. There had not been a teacher at the school from the end of the last century for over fifteen years. Documents over five years old were destroyed. Perhaps, they said, I could get some more information from the Ministry for Education and Culture.

I went to the ministry hoping they might have some more information about Raden Mas Minke. The answer I received was not very satisfactory there either—we keep only internal correspondence, or very important documents. Everything else is handed over to the State archives.

In one of Minke's manuscripts, he said he lived in Tuban and went to an ELS. According to a list of all the ELS schools in the Indies, there was none in Tuban, only in the neighboring towns of Jepara, Rembang, and Bojonegoro.

It seemed that in all three of his writings—*This Earth of Mankind, Child of All Nations*, and *Footsteps*—Minke, as the narrator, did not try to portray himself but rather wrote as an intellectual witness to the events of his time. There was nothing revealing about his younger life among the papers in the State archives, except the information that he was a son of the Bupati of Bojonegoro. I didn't really need anything about his life after he left STOVIA.

His father was later moved to Blora. This year he had founded a school for girls, Darmo Rini, meaning "women's duty." Perhaps this was done in memory of his son, who was now in exile. Perhaps it was established as a mark of respect for his brave and courageous daughter-in-law, about whom there was no longer any news.

Very well. It was clear to me now just who this Raden Mas Minke was and from whence he came. He came into the world in the midst of many different situations as the Modern Pitung, the defender of the weak and powerless. He acted as a witness to the times. He was far more concerned with the world around him than with his own situation. It looked as if it was true that he had obtained the nickname Minke while he was at HBS and had used it all the while as a journalist and writer and in all his activities in society. That was not the name that his father gave him. The initials of his real name, as far as I knew, were Raden Mas T— A— S—.

In 1915 I was on my way to Surabaya. When the train arrived at Bojonegoro, it was my intention to get out and stay for two or three days so that I could speak to the family of this Modern Pitung. But intention remained just that, an intention. The stationmaster in his new red cap came running along the platform: "Who is the one named Meneer Pangemanann?"

He was a Pure-Blood European, and did not seem to be pleased to have this extra duty.

I descended from the first-class carriage and found him at the ticket gate.

"Are you Meneer Pangemanann?" he asked, and I could tell from his pronunciation that he was not Dutch, perhaps German.

He gave me a telegram that had been sent over the railway wires.

"I will wait for your reply," he spoke again.

It was instructions in code from my boss. I was to interview Mas Tjokro to find out what he knew about Mas Marco and the activities of the Semarang-Solo-Jogja axis. I was also to investigate the emergence of a surprising new figure—Siti Soendari, a young woman. I was to find out whether this person was really a woman or somebody using a pseudonym.

The stationmaster took me into his office. He was very polite but it was obvious he did not enjoy looking after a Native like this. He patiently waited for me to write my reply in code. He took my note and copied it out letter by letter to make sure he had understood it all properly.

"It will be sent to Buitenzorg within the next half hour, Meneer."

"Thank you for all your help, Meneer," I answered.

Knowing that I was an official of the Algemeene Secretariat, he, of course, had to tell me his name: "If you need anything else, Meneer, my name is Melvin Manders."

Out of politeness I took out my notebook and wrote down his name. Then I returned to my carriage. My new assignment meant that I would not have time to stay over in Bojonegoro.

He escorted me back to the carriage, excused himself with a polite salute, wished me a safe journey, and alighted. Not long after, he blew his whistle and raised up his signal stick. The train moved off and he waved to me as my window passed him by.

His quite pleasing politeness could not, however, lessen my distress at the thought of having to follow after someone called Siti Soendari. How low would I have fallen if it did turn out that it was a woman, and a young maiden at that? What was going to become of me in the end? The next thing I'll be chasing after some street corner soup seller because he could

write well in the newspapers and magazines! And there were so many newspapers and magazines now and more and more all the time. The government had never issued any controls or bans on them. Everybody had the
right to announce how they felt and what they thought. I was lucky, I
thought, that not every student could afford to buy stamps. Otherwise, the
newspapers and magazines would be full of the writings of these students
as well. I would go crazy if I had to follow all that.

An official of the office of the governor of East Java met me in Surabaya
with a car. The governor did not want me to stay in a hotel but at the
governor's residence. I would use this opportunity as best I could. He was
not at home when I arrived. His wife welcomed me very warmly, so
warmly I became suspicious. After I had bathed, she invited me to sit outside
in the garden.

Her first question: "Is it true that you were educated in France, Meneer Pangemanann?"

"It is true, *Mevrouw*."

"Unfortunately I have forgotten how to speak in that language. And
you studied at the Sorbonne?"

"Yes, Mevrouw."

"You were very lucky, Meneer, very lucky."

The governor's wife was about thirty-two years old. She was a bit too
fleshy around the body, a sign that she was not really looking after herself,
no sport or exercise. In a few more years this excessive flesh would become
a burden for her. She would have no waist and every movement would be
accompanied by panting breath. Meneer the governor of East Java would
not be happy with a wife like that.

"I have heard that your wife is also French," she continued. Seeing
me indicate a yes, she went on. "No doubt slim, handsome, and attractive,"
she said in an envious voice. "How many children have you had with this
French wife of yours, Meneer?"

"Four, Mevrouw."

"A Frenchwoman! With four children?"

I wished Meneer Governor would arrive soon so that I could escape
these idiotic questions.

"And what do you eat at home, Meneer, European food or Native?"

"European, Mevrouw. Sometimes Native."

"Your wife can cook Native food?"

"There are a few dishes that she likes, Mevrouw."

"Does your wife like champagne?"

"My wife is a teetotaler, Mevrouw."

"A teetotaler! From France!"

The evening wore on. When I heard a car, I knew the governor had arrived.

"Aha, here is my husband," said the governor's wife. "Would you be willing to help me a little, Meneer?"

"Of course, Mevrouw."

"I hope you will avoid discussing anything that might make him lose his temper."

"Does Meneer Governor lose his temper?" I asked, surprised. As someone who has to deal with many different people, it was not appropriate that he have that kind of weakness, I thought.

"No, no, he doesn't lose his temper very often. But he doesn't like to get extra work once he is at home."

And so I understood that they did not have a happy marriage.

As soon as he arrived, the governor sought me out and welcomed me as warmly as if I were not a Native. He sat next to me and told me of the many interesting things that had happened that day. He took me inside to his office, which was bathed in electric light.

We sat down on a European-made divan. Meneer Governor signaled his secretary, who stood up, excused himself, and left the office.

My dealings with the governor went much more smoothly than I had imagined. He was a very amicable man with not the slightest trace of racist arrogance. I was able to get a very complete picture of the structure and the essence of the life of all the Native organizations in East Java. His opinion of Mas Tjokro did not differ much from mine. "You can talk to him. He gets a bit puffed up sometimes. And he knows how to be cautious. He has never shown a hostile or cynical attitude toward us European officials. On the contrary, when he speaks to us he often likes to speculate about the meaning of different verses from the Quran. Perhaps he thinks that there are no Europeans who know anything about Islam," said the governor. "It's true, he has a lot of pretensions, but I think that is just a result of his great success as emperor of the Sarekat, emperor without a crown. He is not able to cope with his success. I suppose I mean that his own development has not kept up with the extent of his success."

This briefing from the governor would be useful when I interviewed Mas Tjokro.

I called upon His Excellency the governor the next morning in the gubernatorial office as an official act of courtesy. He was just as polite and relaxed there as he had been the evening before at his residence. He introduced me to the various senior officials who worked for him. Then he took me to the library.

I took this opportunity to ask him to obtain for my use over the next few days copies of the Dutch and Malay magazines that had been publishing the articles by the person using the name Siti Soendari.

The secretary who was given this assignment seemed quite annoyed at being given this extra work.

Back at the hotel I read over the last month's magazine, looking especially for anything signed Siti Soendari. Among this huge pile of paper, I only found four articles, in Dutch and Malay. From these writings, those in both Dutch and Malay, it was obvious she was an educated and well-brought-up woman. This was clear from the way she wrote, the expressions she used, and the kinds of comparisons and examples she put forward in her arguments. Her Malay was school Malay. It was quite likely that she had read the writings of Kartini, especially her letters in the first part of *De Zonnige Toekomst*, where every new line guided the reader to ideas and arguments, whose wider meanings were then revealed. If it was true she was a woman, was she old or still a young maiden? And her writing were full of so much wisdom, in some ways the opposite of Marco's writings.

She could explain her thoughts very clearly and did not indulge in excessive attacks. The examples she used, though somewhat limited, were quite learned. She wrote with great enthusiasm but was able to keep it under control, unlike Marco and Wardi, whose writings were marked with explosions of emotion. She obviously had great reserves of strength. Like Raden Mas Minke, her spirit was not subject to instability and turmoil. It was my assessment that she had the outlook of a cultured aristocrat. Would I be correct or not? I would find out later.

Her articles were quite different from those of other Natives, and especially Javanese, in that they did not exhibit any sign of her having any neuroses. So from this I concluded that she had no imperfection in either body or spirit. She was probably quite pretty and lissome.

She had been cradled in her parents' love since she was small and in an environment that had not given her any kind of strange mental problem.

If it was true that she was a woman, then she was different from the girl from Jepara, who seemed to need people's attention more and more as she grew older. This woman was not seeking people's attention for herself; rather she wanted people to pay attention to the reality around them and their own lives, and to learn from what they saw. She was not like Nyai Ontosoroh, as Minke described her in his writings, hardheaded, stubborn, and never at peace. Siti Soendari had a gentle soul and it was her gentleness that was the source of her strength. And one thing was for certain—she was worth ten governors' wives.

You could also tell from her writings that she was pure of heart and was somebody who knew what she wanted. And from within that purity, there was one thing that glowed brightly—her hatred of colonialism.

At first it was only her hatred for colonialism that attracted me. But slowly, this writer, who used the name Siti Soendari, emerged before my mind's eye as the ideal woman, brought into the world for no other reason than to make humankind's life more beautiful. She was the flower that all men dreamed of. She was a goddess compared to the like of Rientje de Roo. The only thing still not clear was whether she had the toughness of spirit, the strength, to withstand the kind of trials that Sanikem had withstood.

The interview with Mas Tjokro did not come off. When I arrived at his house—without an appointment, of course—he was out of town in his new car, heading somewhere southward. I was told that he had gone to Pacitan, a region famous for its Islamic fanaticism, where no church had ever been built.

A dialogue with a middle-level Sarekat member produced the following results.

"Do you know Mas Tjokro?"

"Only his name."

"Does Mas Tjokro often go on tours?"

"Often, Meneer. That is why he bought the car."

"Where did he get the money to buy the car?"

"The Sarekat will provide everything that its top leaders need, Meneer."

"You're exaggerating, aren't you?"

He didn't seem to be very happy with that question. He was a fanatical supporter of Mas Tjokro.

"Where does he visit most?"

"Jombang, Tulungagung, the East Java coastal towns."

"Why does he often visit some places and not others?"

"He goes most often to those towns where there is a Moslem boarding school—a pesantren."

"So, all the pious Moslems are becoming members of the Sarekat?"

"No, Meneer, it's actually the other way around. Most *santri* do not join. They believe only in their own *kyai*, rather than in any outsider. And the kyais have faith only in their own authority and wisdom and do not like to bow down to somebody else's."

"So why does he visit the pesantren towns so often?"

"I'm sorry, but I am not really sure. They say he is often challenged to debate religious matters with the experts that the kyais put forward. He needs to prove his supremacy in these matters."

"So it is just to defend his status?"

"Yes. There are quite a few people who don't approve of him doing this, because it has nothing to do with the organization's goals. There are even those who say that he is concerned only with his personal prestige. But, then, the Sarekat uses 'Islam' in its name, so every Moslem has the right to discuss these matters. I don't know for sure. Perhaps that is how he thinks too."

"Is that is what he is doing in Pacitan too?"

He gave a rather embarrassed smile. And I didn't understand why. It seemed there was something tickling his conscience. It was already widely recognized that Mas Tjokro was following in the footsteps of his predecessor, Raden Mas Minke, in a number of areas—the way he spoke and dressed, in developing and defending his popularity, in always putting forward grand ideas. And the last and most obvious thing was that they both got on splendidly with the ladies. Perhaps the embarrassed smile of this Sarekat member pointed to this tendency on the part of his leader. And this was something not at all out of the ordinary in the life of a Native male, given that women were so dependent on their husbands, on their husbands' income, not to mention the feudal atmosphere in general.

Then I received an express telegram from Semarang replying to my inquiries.

It was thought that this new figure who had emerged and was using the name Siti Soendari was a recent graduate of the Semarang HBS. Ever since she entered the HBS several years before, she had exhibited a talent and liking for writing. One of the HBS teachers from Semarang had recognized her former student's style in a Dutch-language article she had read. Her style as a student and now as a free woman in the community had not changed in its essentials. With several years' experience in society now, she wrote more confidently and had much more to say. If it was true that Siti Soendari was a former student of the Semarang HBS, then it would be easy to find out more about her.

The next letter explained that a fuller dossier would take another week to get together and that it would be sent straight to the Algemeene Secretariat in Buitenzorg.

From Surabaya I went to Malang to see for myself the preparations being made for the coming visit by His Excellency the governor-general, who was to officially declare the town a rest and recreation center for the Netherlands Indies navy. While in that town I received another telegram informing me that Mas Tjokro was still in Pacitan and that he had opened a *tablig*, a religious consultation. It seemed he would be staying there for quite a while.

There was one incident that embellished my time there in Malang. I

had actually expected something of this sort in Surabaya, so I wasn't surprised when it happened. Such an incident was bound to occur now that I
no longer wore my police uniform, displaying my last rank.

As I approached the billiard table, a Eurasian came up and grabbed the
billiard cue out of my hand.

"Who gave you permission to come in here?" he snarled.

My eyes quickly slid down to my white clothes and shiny brown shoes
with their neatly tied knots.

The chief of the Malang police, Meneer Roedentaal, who had brought
me to this place, was talking to somebody in a marine's uniform.

The Indo's words truly hurt me, even though I had often used the
same words against others.

"The chief of the Malang police, Meneer Roedentaal," I answered in
Dutch.

"I don't care if it was an angel from heaven—nobody has the right to
bring either Natives or dogs in here!" he hissed angrily in Malay.

I am willing to bet that my Malay and Dutch were both better than
his. But such things meant nothing in a situation like this. I was indeed just
an Inlander, a Pure Menadonese, even though we had the same status under
Netherlands Indies law.

"Thank you, Meneer," I said in Dutch. "If only you understood a
little about politeness . . ."

The Indo lost his temper and was about to hit out at me with the
billiard cue. It was then that Meneer Roedentaal intervened: "Meneer
Strooman, I don't think this is the way to behave at all. Meneer Pangemanann is a retired police commissioner, a high official at the Algemeene
Secretariat, and is in Malang on special assignment for his Excellency the
governor-general."

"Meneer Commander," answered Strooman, "does that make him no
longer an Inlander? And does that mean that as a dues-paying member of
this club I can no longer insist that all the rules be adhered to?"

"You are not totally wrong," said Roedentaal. "If the problem is one
of being an Inlander, then you as an Indo are half Inlander yourself. It is
true though that you are a dues-paying member. But so am I and I have
no Inlander blood in me. Meneer can be more polite. It was I who brought
Meneer Pangemanann here. And is there something wrong in a police
commander bringing a high government official to the club?"

This was not the first time I had experienced such an incident. That
is the reason why I did not like staying at European hotels if I was not
wearing my uniform. And now I had been trapped here in this club. If I
surrendered to my emotions, there would surely be a disturbance. Colonials

are the same everywhere. Racial hatred is their guide in life. And I had the same attitude too toward anyone who was not Menadonese or European.

I had to accept defeat, and perhaps indeed I was defeated. I left the club, and Roedentaal followed me and never stopped mumbling his regrets. As we walked out of the club's garden he said that a high official of the Algemeene Secretariat should not have to put up with such an incident. He promised he would not let it pass.

From Malang I continued my journey to Madiun, traveling in the resident's car. Madiun was developing into a center of cottage industry. The Sarekat membership here was always on the increase. It never dropped.

I didn't stay in a hotel. The bupati, an educated man who spoke several modern languages, put me up in his bungalow outside the town. It was here that I held a meeting with the bupati and the resident. They both gave me their official assurances that all the preparations for the governor-general's visit were proceeding smoothly. The whole town of Madiun in all its glory was ready to welcome him.

I was given both written and verbal reports about the activities of the various new organizations in the town.

The inhabitants of Madiun were in the grip of organization fever. Besides the very big branch of the Sarekat itself, there were many other local organizations. There was a Coachmen's Sarekat, a Drivers' Sarekat, a Servants and Waiters' Sarekat, a Station Coolies' Sarekat, and another score or so of others. All of them used the name sarekat and no longer syarikat, the name Raden Mas Minke left behind as part of his legacy. It looked as if this term would become a permanent part of the world of organization in the Indies. But the name was not so important. What was important was the question of why was there such feverish organizational activity in Madiun.

I asked at that meeting that telegrams be sent to Malang, Surabaya, and Semarang requesting figures about these towns' geographical area, population, and the number of Native organizations, as well as their membership figures.

"There is an organizing epidemic here," I said.

"As you can see for yourself," answered Meneer Resident.

"Who is behind all this? It's obviously not all happening by itself," I said.

Neither the resident nor the bupati could answer. I left the room to give them a chance to overcome their confusion and consult without my presence. When I entered my room, I stopped in my tracks, nailed to the floor. Over in the corner, on a grass mat, sat three women. On seeing me enter the room, they knelt down before me and made their obeisance.

This was one of the customs of Native officials that had also ruined the reputation of the Bupati of Rembang.

I closed the door and walked across to them. Although they ceased with their obeisance, they kept their heads bowed.

Every government official who had ever been on an inspection tour knew exactly what this meant. So one by one I lifted up their chins. One of them was a European Indo. Her Native dress could not disguise her bloodline. They all seemed about the same age.

"Who sent you here?" I asked in Malay.

"*Ndoro Wedana*," one of them answered.

She no doubt meant one of the bupati's subordinates.

"Who was sent here by Tuan Resident?"

"I, Ndoro," the Eurasian one replied in Javanese.

One of them hurriedly began to polish my shoes with her selendang. And the aroma of flowers and hair oil wafted up from their heads. I was not used to all these kinds of aromas. The smells were heavy, narcotic, and binding. And the three women were all attractive, young and full-bodied. I left the room again without saying any more to them.

The resident and the bupati both studied my face for any changes in its appearance. It didn't look as though they were in the middle of deliberating or had just finished chatting. It seemed they had been relying on the influence of the women in that room.

"In fact, we haven't given you all the background to the whole issue of who is behind all this activity. We're not really sure that we should tell you the rest," said the bupati.

"And why aren't you sure?" I asked.

"Not all that has been reported can be believed. Some of it is like a fairy tale."

"Like a fairy tale!" I cried drily.

"Yes, Meneer. I still don't believe the reports we have been getting," the resident followed on. "And I am sure you won't believe them either."

"Tell me, then, so that we can think it all over carefully."

"It shouldn't be taken seriously yet, but the fairy story is that it is all being propelled along by a woman."

Soendari! That was my guess. Siti Soendari. There was only one woman who was hurtling brilliantly through the Indies universe at the moment. Just one person—Siti Soendari. Now I will find out who you are, *Noni!*

"A woman!" I repeated. "She is a young woman, no doubt."

"No husband yet."

And I saw before me a beautiful girl, educated, clever, interesting, supple and intelligent, refined and alluring. There was an extraordinary inner beauty reflected in her writings. Perhaps this was how beautiful her face would be. And if it was true that she was pretty, she would never, of course, have been successfully tempted with flattery and seduction. If it was true that she was pretty, then there could be no doubt that she would have a very strong personality.

"Beautiful, of course," I suggested.

"That is what has been reported. Whenever she speaks with officials, they never hear what she is saying. They are only impressed with her beauty and charm, her smile, her gleaming teeth, the supple movements of her body, her red lips which are always moist."

And it was Meneer Bupati who spoke those words.

Was it possible that she was using all these as weapons to move her people? I thought.

It was at that moment that the Madiun chief of police arrived on his Harley-Davidson. He was a European Pure-Blood and his face was pinkish-red because of the heat. His brown bamboo hat looked very old. He saluted Meneer Resident, nodded to Meneer Bupati and to me.

The resident ordered him to sit down and tell us all he knew about Siti Soendari.

He took a handkerchief from his pocket, wiped his face, and politely blew his nose. He said in Dutch: "As for the woman called Siti Soendari, I myself have seen her."

"You haven't mentioned that in your reports."

"The last report was submitted a week ago, Meneer Resident," he struck back. "Yes, I have seen her, but even then I didn't believe what I saw. She is too young. It's such a waste for one so young and pretty to use this beautiful period of her life for this kind of work. She should be the raden ayu of a bupati in one of the very rich districts."

"You haven't made a mistake with her name?" I asked.

"As far as I know, Siti Soendari is her name."

I realized at once that these officials from Madiun did not follow the Indies newspapers and magazines. They needed a reprimand.

"The first time I saw her she was wearing an unpleated batik kain. Her face is like that of a betel leaf, as the Natives say. She had beautiful golden skin, thin but full lips. Anyone watching her speak would be totally captivated by her lips."

"That's not what I want to know," I reprimanded him.

Meneer Resident laughed happily. Meneer Bupati frowned for some reason or other.

"We still know very little about her, Meneer."

"Does she live in Madiun?" I asked.

"No. But it seems she visits here often. Always during the holidays. She always stays in the same place, with a teacher who lives on the outskirts of town. There are reports, which haven't been confirmed yet, that she herself lives in Pacitan."

I hid my smile, perhaps the same kind of embarrassed smile displayed by the Sarekat member in Surabaya a few days ago. Pacitan!

"Then she is not with the Sarekat Islam," I said. And I said to myself that if she was a Sarekat member, then she would be busy organizing for Mas Tjokro's current visit there, but the police chief had seen her here in Madiun during the last week.

They didn't respond. They didn't know enough about what was happening.

"Why do you think that?" the resident asked.

"She is probably too well educated to want to be a Sarekat member," I answered carelessly.

The three officials seemed surprised. Perhaps they thought that I knew more than they did. They sat silently watching me. And I knew they were filled with worries that the governor-general might decide to cancel his visit because their preparations were inadequate. They could lose all chance of a promotion just because of a small lapse. These colonial bureaucrats. And they were sitting there hanging on my words.

A police inspector arrived and handed the resident a big envelope. Without waiting for orders, the policeman then retired from the front parlor where we were sitting.

The resident took out several telegrams from the envelope and handed them across to me without reading them.

There were telegrams from Malang, Surabaya, and Semarang. They contained figures for the population of each district, the geographical area, the number of Native organizations, and the size of their memberships.

"Aha," I said after studying them, "the organization fever here in Madiun is greater than in Malang, Surabaya, or Semarang." I put the telegrams down on the table. "You can read them for yourselves."

Very painfully the resident and the bupati read through the cables. They had to agree that what I had told them was true.

"So what do you think is the quickest thing we can do, before His Excellency arrives?"

"There is no way His Excellency will be visiting Madiun as long as you are unable to control the Native organizations here."

"We will take whatever action is necessary straightaway."

I didn't answer. I just said good night. They stood and left, disappearing into the evening darkness. I could still hear the roaring of their cars and motorbikes. The caretaker came and asked me in Malay if I still needed any dinner. I told him no, but ordered him to bring me some liquor. He asked again whether he should lock the doors and windows now. I told him yes. Then I went into my room.

The three women were still sitting on the mat in the corner. There were two bottles of liquor on the table. I called them over and ordered each one to take a gulp. They each tried a bit, spitting it out all over the place.

I laughed at this funny scene. And they laughed too, pinching each other good humoredly.

According to Meneer L— the custom of presenting women to the Javanese elite originated in much earlier times. And now as the Native officials became even more corrupt and incompetent, they became more and more extravagant in their offerings to their superiors. A newspaper once accused the Bupati of Rembang of corrupting Christian morals! I will never forget that case. And now here before me was a Eurasian girl sent to me by Meneer Resident himself, a European Pure-Blood. So who was it who was violating Christian morality? Colonialism itself or this colonialism from Europe which never bothered to outlaw this custom among the Native officials? And wasn't this custom one of the strongest pillars shoring up the Native officials' authority and preventing them from being exposed for their incompetence and corruption? Yes, it was probably true that that particular accusation was the most daring ever made since the time Europeans first set foot in this region three hundred years ago. And it is clear that the European officials too have enjoyed the pleasures of this custom and so they have never taken the issue to the courts. And if there was somebody else who had raised concerns about this custom, that person was Haji Moeloek in his *Tale of Siti Aini*.

And you, Siti Soendari, are you aware that such a custom prevails among your people? You will shudder at the thought. I too shudder—or at least I used to. But not now. And I think such things occur throughout the colonial world. . . .

When I got back to my office in Buitenzorg, I found a very changed atmosphere. Von Hindenburg was noisily preparing the German army, so all we heard were reports and more reports about the war. His Excellency Governor-General Idenburg canceled his tour. There was a military call-up throughout the Netherlands Indies. The press—colonial, Malay and Chinese—just waited to see how things would develop.

In the midst of this rather claustrophobic, quiet atmosphere, something happened that suddenly startled everyone awake. A Semarang paper published one of its readers' letters:

Not long ago everyone was commemorating the Netherlands' liberation from France. Now the Netherlands is threatened again, this time by a Modern Bharatayuddha. *Who will the Netherlands ally itself with? Will it emerge a victor? After hundreds of years of doing without an army, except its colonial armies used to oppress its colonies? Will the Netherlands fall into the hands of Germany? And then in another hundred years, will there be more commemorations, this time of Holland's liberation from Germany? At the time of the last commemorations, Douwager, Wardi, and Tjipto were exiled—who will it be in a hundred years' time?*

The government ordered the newspaper closed until it was able or willing to inform who the author of the letter was. The letter, written in Dutch, was signed with the initials SS. I guessed it was Siti Soendari, but I didn't tell anyone. I let them all rush about trying to solve the mystery. If she was the author, she should have used the initials StS. And the letter didn't really have that much to say, except that she wanted to humiliate the government in its impotence. But it also led me to speculate that she had probably been a member of the now deceased Indische Partij.

The investigations revealed that the original of the letter had been destroyed, changing into who knows what form. The typesetters who were questioned all stated that they knew for certain that the letter had been used by one of them to wipe his inky hands. It had then been thrown into the rubbish bin. The bin itself had been emptied as soon as the presses started printing.

Most people were speculating that the author was most definitely a Eurasian who was dissatisfied with his position in the bureaucracy. Or some rebel from the Indies Social Democratic Association. Everyone knew that no member of Insulinde would write anything like that. First, because they were so cautious, and second, because they were so loyal.

Anyway, I didn't move a finger. It was obviously Siti Soendari's writing. She had written it fully conscious of what she was doing. She was trying to give the Natives courage to face colonial power. My God, I do not want to go hunting after her, the first woman to appear on my desk, to enter the glass house. I still have some honor, even if only a little! No, my God. I will not persecute this person! The first woman to appear in the public arena and to lead people! She was a thousand strides ahead of the girl from Jepara! A thousand strides in advance of Nyai Ontosoroh. She must not meet too hasty an end inside my house of glass. She deserves the chance to enjoy her beauty, youth, education, and intelligence. Let her develop in accordance with her true nature, let her full beauty bloom. And I myself was interested to see for how long a Native could continue to rise. Of course she would never be a Native Joan of Arc, but she still deserved to get more out of life yet.

Debate and discussion in my office became more and more intense. They were all still discussing the letter to the editor. They all thought it was excessively vicious. There were no laws forbidding people to ask questions, someone said, and all that letter did was put some questions to the faceless and anonymous readers. Others replied that the letter was doing more than just asking questions, that there was evil intent in the letter, very conscious evil intent. Still another asked the question, who can prove evil intent before any criminal acts are actually carried out? If intent, just intent, was sufficient for others to take action against people with such intent, then at the very least half a million Moslems would have to be arrested every time they finish their prayers, because their praying is suspicious and almost certainly they are asking their God to destroy colonial power.

The debate and discussion spread everywhere, even into the offices of the plantation administrators up in the mountains.

Eventually the word got out, I don't know from what source, that the author of this vicious letter was a Native woman called Siti Soendari. The rumors, which in this case seemed more or less accurate, also reported that she was an HBS graduate, and still quite young as well as beautiful. And precisely because the suspect was a woman, a beautiful young teenager, the tension began to relax. People began to ask whether the colonial authorities would be able to bring themselves to take action against such a young maiden. Educated as well. Just because she put forward some facts and asked some questions. Then new rumors began to blow about. There was no way the government could take action against her because not only the original letter but also the envelope had been destroyed. And I myself made my own contribution to these rumors. There were too many people whose name began with S. And also there was no way any Native, and especially a woman, would have the courage to publish anything like this. The only person capable of writing something like that was the girl from Jepara, and she was dead.

The debate and discussion subsided. On the other hand a similar debate emerged in another place—among the Indo Eurasian housewives. If Native women were already starting to behave so impudently, then just imagine what we can expect from their men! So far only one or two people among the Indos had begun to write. And now here was a pure-blood Native writing like this! There were opposing voices: But you all have the freedom to write and to express your anger. The Indo housewives answered back:

We don't know how to write. Then get someone who does know to answer her. But who is able and also willing?

Silently and secretly, I kept watch on this young woman as her star rose higher and higher, shining brightly in the firmament. The higher she rose, the brighter she shone. And for me her writings contained a timely warning—Germany! Germany! Arise, you nationalists, and be vigilant!

And this coded warning seemed somehow to be picked up by the Netherlands Indies government. German activities in East Papua and the surrounding waters were closely monitored. All of the Indies' warships left Java to guard the waterways throughout the archipelago. Surveillance of all the young Turks who had been openly entering the country was intensified. They were harassed too. The spy services that had developed separately in the provinces were coordinated and made official. The main concern was to ensure that Native organizations had no contact with Germans and Turks.

Meanwhile, more and more material piled up on my desk, all confirming my earlier guess that organization fever was overflowing into the villages. There was also more and more material about Siti Soendari herself.

In her file I already had a photo of her. I could do nothing but confirm that she was indeed handsome. Her beauty lay in the simplicity of her appearance. Her face was like that of a betel leaf, just as the Madiun police chief had said, with a pointed chin. A pair of big, shining eyes peered out, full of compassion and concern, as if studying everything that humankind was doing, all its excesses and extravagances. And it seemed that she was indeed a gentle and refined person. I say "it seemed" because in her brain there was a burning white-hot nationalism that could move hundreds, thousands of people, men and women, into action.

Siti Soendari had in fact graduated from the Semarang HBS. She was born in Pemalang. From the time she entered school, she had been an activist in Young Java, also in the Pemalang Association, and in a Native students' organization, and she was always to be found among the leaders. She was in charge of her school's wall magazine, and there wasn't a week that passed when she didn't write something, and not without commendation from her teachers either. Her Dutch was good, while her English, German, and French were adequate. And these good marks that she obtained in the modern languages were nothing other than her key to open the door to European science, knowledge, and civilization. In Europe, school marks meant nothing, they told us nothing. But in the Indies, such marks were always noted down, because here they determined what salary the colonial civil servant would receive. And there were so few educated people in the Indies, among Indos and Europeans, let alone Natives. So school marks also spoke of what kind of future the Indies might have.

After graduating she taught in a nongovernment primary school.

A few months later, she resigned and moved to Pacitan where she taught in a Boedi Oetomo primary school. The move from Semarang to Pacitan surprised many people, especially as her family still lived in Pemalang, which was much closer to Semarang than Pacitan. For me, who knew the real motives for her move, there was no need to be surprised. Her beauty had attracted the unwanted attentions of many young Indos. She didn't like it at all and decided to move to a smaller town.

She remained a member of Young Java, but never joined Boedi Oetomo even though she taught at one of their schools. According to her own words, which someone had heard and so they had found their way onto my desk, Boedi Oetomo moved like a snail. Its long antennas were not there to help it move fast and hit the right target, but were just ornaments, because it wasn't really interested in going anywhere fast anyway. It seemed this girl had absorbed the European rhythm of life, a dynamic one.

Then she began to be active as a propagandist for the Insulinde. Because this party had no strong leaders, like D-W-T, she herself became dispirited. The Insulinde itself apparently saw her as having quality, because she was offered a seat on the Central Governing Council.

But she could never accommodate to the anemic and tired atmosphere in Insulinde, which had no thinker, no initiator. She was fed up too with having to mix with all these apathetic Indos. She needed a teacher, someone with ideas. And indeed, it is not at all impossible for a person in such a state, dissatisfied, longing after action, to make a big unexpected leap in consciousness. Yes, make that leap, Soendari, go on, do it! In fact, she had already made that leap. She had made a big leap and had ended up beside and unable to get out from under the wing of Marco.

Isn't life strange? I had already put Marco inside my house of glass. And now you, sweet maiden from Pemalang, you have joined him inside too. How was it that you, a graduate of the HBS, could end up under the wing of that village *garuda*? Yes, and so it was that these two young people, objects of my study, ended up together standing behind the banner of the youth wing of the Sarekat.

Soendari, just a while ago I wrote that you were a thousand kilometers ahead of Sanikem, the innocent girl from Tulangan, Sidoarjo. And I wrote too that you were a thousand kilometers ahead of the girl from Jepara. And now all of a sudden I find that you have gone no farther than under Marco's armpit. And that is as far as you will ever go, you will never develop further. Even so I will still be watching you, Noni, pretty maiden from Pemalang. Be careful. Don't let disaster befall you because of someone else.

And I will use all my abilities to make sure that I do nothing to harm you, Soen. My pen will not decide your fate. You are the second woman after Kartini who has a right to speak out. I feel a moral and intellectual responsibility for you. I have given you the chance. Now what will you be able to achieve? I want to see if you develop the reach to grasp your goals or will you only be able to scratch nearby itchy spots? It's up to you.

The other information I had found out about Siti Soendari included the following.

She came from an educated family. Her father was one of the STO-VIA's best graduates and was now the director of the Pemalang State pawn-brokers, as well as a successful landowner. The pawnbroker service was a new government agency in the Indies. He had been entrusted to be the founding director in Pemalang. Only Natives were allowed to avail themselves of the service. And who else would be wanting to pawn things apart from the Natives? There were people who said that her father also had shares in a sugar mill, but that was too fantastic to believe.

She had been brought up by her father, who loved her. Her mother had died when she was just seven months old. And her father, who loved her so much, could never bring himself to give her another mother, whose feelings could not be guaranteed.

Soendari's father also had a son, Soendari's older brother. After graduating from HBS in Semarang, he was sent to finish another five years of HBS in the Netherlands. Then he continued his schooling at the Advanced School for Commerce in Rotterdam. All at his family's expense.

And you, Soendari, you must understand that as long as your father works for the government, you, as a Native, remain tied to what is in the interests of your father. You must realize this, sweet maiden, before someone else replaces me. And as concerns that, in the meantime it was as if my work would never end. Problem after interconnected problem arrived on my desk.

The political exiles from the Netherlands were giving us new head-aches. A number of them turned out to be very good organizers. Even though they knew nothing about Javanese and Malay customs, and with a completely noncolonial outlook and tradition of their own, they were quickly able to win over a group of educated Natives, and to integrate with them. And without realizing it, the Natives began to learn the European way of organizing, in terms of both form and content. This development resulted in all the formerly quiet and experience-starved sarekats turning militant. The big workers' sarekats began to appear—the State Pawnbrokers Employees' Sarekat, the Sugar Mill Workers' Sarekat, the State Teachers'

Sarekat, the Tram and Train Employees' Association . . . and a few score more.

And I was still not assigned any assistants, nor did I ever get a more expert boss.

My new boss, the replacement for the Frenchman, was already distancing himself from me. He began to behave very formally toward me and was soon treating me as if I was just chief message boy. Very well, that is exactly the kind of behavior to expect of colonial officials. They became very pretentious under the protection of their position and power, believing that this would prevent their stupidity and incompetence from being exposed. They put on a fearsome and superior face. But Pangemanann with two *n*s knows all about this, gentlemen. And perhaps you gentlemen on the other hand do not realize that Pangemanann will be replying in kind, only pretending to do great work, pretending to work diligently.

One of the attendants, Herschenbrock, was just putting another pile of letters and telegrams on my desk, when my new boss, along with my old boss, the Frenchman, came in. My boss got rid of Herschenbrock as if he were kicking out a cat. He was suspicious of his lesser subordinates. And there were no doubt good grounds for these suspicions. Herschenbrock's eyes wildly surveyed the scene, grasping for any information that could be sold outside.

But Herschenbrock was back again a few minutes later. The adjutant-general had summoned my boss. I was left alone with my former superior.

We sat opposite each other, divided only by my desk. And that was the first time that I saw clearly how my guest's eyes drifted about everywhere, full of anxiety and nervousness, as if he could no longer maintain his gaze on any object or spot. His nervous problem is getting worse, I thought to myself. I studied him again. Yes, it's the same nervous problem he was suffering before.

"Are you happy working outside Java?" I asked, being polite.

"Who can ever be happy in this trouble-ridden world?"

"So how do you plan to get away from it all then, Meneer?"

He shook his head in confusion, took something out of his coat pocket, then put it back. Then he fumbled around in his trousers pocket.

"What can I do for you, Meneer?"

"Who else is on the list to be exiled?" he asked suddenly.

There was a tightness in my chest as I was assailed by so many different feelings. Yes, that's right, the exile of the Indische Partij triumvirate was indeed the idea of this mentally unbalanced man. I copied out and improved his submission with my own hand, crossed the *t*'s and dotted the *i*'s, and then I signed my name to it. I don't know what other letters from my boss or others accompanied that submission to the adjutant and then on to His Excellency. Then came the implementation of the recommendations with me in charge of supervising everything.

The knowledge that the triumvirate's exile was the idea of a mentally unbalanced person disturbed me greatly. And how many other cases, how many other ideas from unbalanced people have become part of colonial policy and its implementation?

I began to doubt myself too. Have I lost my reason as well, or lost most of it anyway? My former boss had forced me to look at myself in the mirror. And I knew that I needed to use all my determination to keep a constant eye on how my mind worked and how I behaved.

Herschenbrock entered again and informed the Frenchman that he was wanted elsewhere. I said good bye to my old boss but told Herschenbrock to stay.

"You are an Indo?" I asked.

"Yes, Meneer, my father was an Indo."

"Are you a member of Insulinde?"

He immediately became vigilant.

"As it happens, no, I am not," he answered hesitantly. "Is this an official interrogation?"

"Do you have any objections?"

"No, not at all," he answered nervously.

"Is your father a member of Insulinde or Indische Partij?"

"No. Neither."

"A member of the Sarekat perhaps?"

He laughed contemptuously.

"Why do you laugh?"

"We are Protestants, Meneer."

"You're no doubt an honest man."

He grinned.

I pulled across a pile of papers before him. I asked: "When you see a pile of papers like this, how much are you able to remember? What do you think?"

He looked the other way. His face went suddenly pale. But he didn't answer. There was something on his mind.

"Whiskey!" I called out loudly, turning around to check the look in his eyes. And there was a moment when I saw a bit of a glint.

"You want me to get you a drink?" he pretended.

"You are the one with whiskey on his mind. What kind of whiskey do you like?"

He became cautious again.

"You haven't answered any of my last three questions."

He shook his head. "I am confused, Meneer."

"What are you confused about? Whiskey?" He wasn't going to answer. "Matches!" I ordered.

He rose from his chair and went over to the corner. He fetched a tin can, brought it across to me, picked up all the papers on the floor, and put them in the tin. They were set aflame with the matches. He carried the tin across to the window, fanning away the smoke. A few moments later the papers were ashes and the smoke was being blown out the window.

This work took less than half a minute. But I had been able to prove to myself during those seconds that I still had my reason. I had been able to see into Herschenbrock's character with just a few questions. Yes, he did like to browse through any papers that he found, and perhaps he did indeed sell information outside for money to buy himself a good time.

He came back across to me, opened the bin to show me that all the papers had indeed been destroyed by the fire, turned into ash, with nothing left.

"You can go now!" I said.

He put the bin down under the small table in the corner, nodded at me, and headed for the door. Just as he was about to turn the handle, I called him back. He came back across but I didn't invite him to sit down. I needed this game of cat and mouse to consolidate my self-confidence.

"Meneer Herschenbrock, do you prefer to drink by yourself, with a group of friends, or together with a single good friend?"

"Let me invite you, Meneer, to come and drink with me," he challenged me, refusing to be the mouse to my cat. His eyes gleamed.

He left under my continuing gaze. I studied the way he walked, the way his waist and hips moved, his neck and his elbows. It was true, I thought, I still have my reason. I was able to make him realize his dignity and mine as well. No, I would escape the terrible fate of my former boss.

And you, Siti Soendari, do you know that Pangemanann, the man drawing up all the government's plans for you, is as sane as sane can be?

9

The political exiles from the Neth-
erlands, Sneevliet and Baars, were becoming more and more active in East
Java, especially in Surabaya. They were making speeches everywhere, as if
their throats would never grow dry. Having run from internal divisions in
the Netherlands and now arrived in the Indies, they seemed to think they
were the acme, the best there was, without rival or opposition, as if the
Indies were the same as back home in the Netherlands where political
activities were protected by democratic laws. It was lucky for them that
they mixed only with Dutch-speaking groups, usually of low status and
living very discontented lives.

Because they were Europeans, it was not my task to deal with them.
Even so, their contempt for colonial authority also offended my own sen-
sitivities. If they were Natives, they would be in my hands and I would
have prepared a hangman's rope as the most appropriate tie for them to
wear. Their speeches turned the best European values on their heads, and
they did that here in the Indies where people were not even acquainted
yet with those great European values. They were from among that accursed
group of people called nihilists. They were very capable and logical speakers
and thinkers and they were able to argue people into a corner where they
were helpless to argue back. It was clear they were from a school of phi-

losophy with which I was not yet familiar. Or more accurately, a school of philosophy that I had heard of but had since forgotten.

It was not only their daring and their brazen and outrageous activities that amazed me but also that so many people were willing to listen to them. And the numbers kept growing all the time. Without even bothering about legal status, they set up an organization. Perhaps they were deliberately showing their contempt for Indies law. They made Surabaya famous by setting up their headquarters there. The Indies had no law that withdrew the right to organize or to freedom of assembly. These men knew this very well. Also, as Europeans they did not have to worry about being brought before the Native Court. They had the right to defend themselves and be defended before the White Court. And I had no doubt at all that they would not hesitate to hire a defense lawyer from Europe if necessary. That prospect alone had the legal authorities here shaking in their boots. They had never had to deal with a European-style political trial. Sneevliet and Baars were exploiting this situation to the maximum, full speed ahead.

Even though they were Europeans and did not fall within my bailiwick, it was inevitable that in the end they became involved in my business as well. They had chosen Surabaya as their base because that was where the Sarekat Islam had its headquarters. They wanted to influence, directly or indirectly, the Sarekat. And it was my job to ensure that Mas Tjokro, the "emperor" with the childish politics, was immune to their influence.

I had to make sure he would lean more toward his own religion than to the radicalism of these secular Europeans.

After being harassed in various ways by my boss, I finally prepared a detailed plan as to how to immunize his majesty the emperor. And in fact it went beyond just normal harassment. My boss even started shouting and threatening me, as if I had some plan to deceive and trap him.

"How do you know they are trying to influence the Sarekat? Where is your proof?"

These pronouncements of his which questioned my abilities in these matters offended my dignity. He should have been able to be a little more diplomatic.

"Actually," I said, emphasizing my words so as to return the pressure, "you are the one, and not I, who should be doing the analysis and putting forward the evidence. They are Europeans, not Natives."

"But you are the one submitting this plan."

"I should withdraw it, then?"

"Such a project must have some kind of starting point. That's what I am asking about."

"So Meneer hasn't had time to read it? Well, if you had said that to begin with I wouldn't have been so startled."

"Get to the point, Meneer Pangemanann."

"Everything is explained in the proposal."

"What is your objection to answering my questions?"

"I have answered that question in my proposal. I am not going to repeat it."

He glared at me, full of frustration. And I stood firm. Just this once I would smash his colonial head and brain, which only seemed to get bigger every day, almost as big as a coconut. He said he was sorry and left my office. That wasn't very colonial behavior on your part, I said to myself. But I didn't care; in fact I felt quite good that I had done it.

If he had done just a little of the work he was supposed to do, he would have known that these European scallywags had never pointed an accusing or critical finger at the Sarekat and its emperor. They had never done anything to cause it any trouble. Yet it was impossible that these European rascals were not aware of its existence. It was the biggest organization in the Indies, perhaps in the world. They should have been attacking it. But no, they didn't. Rather, they pretended not to know it existed.

My proposal was concerned only about how to keep them away from the Sarekat, far enough apart so that the Sarekat would avoid their influence. I found out later that my suggestions were implemented a few days later without my knowledge. But then came a memorandum from my boss. He was not satisfied with just keeping them apart. He wanted to see them drawn so far apart that they would start fighting each other.

It is such an easy task to find a way to get two groups to fight each other when their ideas and way of looking at things are already different. But there were likely to be troublesome consequences. Any hostility on the part of the Sarekat to Sneevliet and Baars would have a strong anti-European character to it. This would flow on to strengthen anti-Dutch feeling as a whole. In addition, the Marco wing, which so far had been denied an arena in which it could show its strength, would use this opportunity. If he broke away from Mas Tjokro's leadership, he and his followers could become a dangerous force. Such a rapid development in that direction was not what we desired.

I replied to my boss's minute on the same day as it fell on my desk. He was soon in my room, spraying his anger and frustration all over the room: "Are you refusing to carry out orders?"

Because I knew that his initiative could not be implemented without a supporting submission and signature from me, I had a way of confronting him.

"If you arrange first for my title as 'Official Expert' to be rescinded by the government, then I will carry out these orders immediately, Meneer. Meanwhile, I have the right to reject them."

His face was scarlet red with anger. Yes, yes, that's right, Meneer, I am mucking you around. Let's see which of us can hold out the longest.

But he didn't press me further and left grumbling. Then another memorandum arrived, this time raising suspicions that I was a sympathizer of one or another of the two organizations concerned.

He obviously didn't know who this Pangemanann was. Once Pangemanann was appointed an official of the Algemeene Secretariat, it would not be easy for anybody to budge him even the tiniest bit away from his duties. I stored his memorandum safely away and did not reply to it.

The time had at last arrived when he would busily set out to find fault with me. I began to go through in my mind everything I had done between 1912 and 1915. There was only one thing that I could be charged with doing incompetently—my analysis of Raden Mas Minke's manuscripts. I had written that they were valueless. I kept the manuscripts at home and made them my personal possessions. The shoddy papers I wrote about them might provide him with the opening he needed to accuse me of covering up facts or hiding my views.

Well, what could I do, anyway? I decided I would continue to preserve the manuscripts as my private property. They were not for public view. If anybody ever asked, I would say I burned them in my wastepaper bin. Even so, from now on I must be prepared for anything.

Malay translations of Sneevliet's speeches began to appear in the papers in Solo, Semarang, Madiun, and Surabaya. Baars's speeches began to appear also. He was fluent in both Malay and Javanese. But the West Java and Betawi papers continued business as usual. These two men's influence could now be easily discerned in Native drama. Their influence spread in a way somehow similar to the way the use of the wheel might have spread. Once people became acquainted and familiar with their ideas, they began to become a necessary part of their lives.

In Solo their influence on Native drama performances was very obvious. The play that was being performed at the time was *Surapati*. And who was it who played the leading role of Surapati? Yes, from the same old gang—Marco!

I prepared a map showing where their influence was growing. Within a week, it became clear that their influence was spreading like an ember crackling and sparkling its way from port town to port town throughout Central and East Java, finally scattering more embers into the hinterland, the regions of the sugar mills—into every place where there were sugar mills.

These developments caused the Indies Council, so people were saying, to ask the governor-general to formalize the status and role of those police who had developed an expertise in monitoring and dealing with Native politics. They asked that wherever the local police had formed a section to deal with these matters, it now be given official status. They also asked that a coordinating body be established that could help in the consolidation and formation of such sections. The justification for this request was the increasing level of Native political activity, which was growing during a period of weak relations between the Indies and the home government in Europe. Even if there were some plans to send military assistance from back home, it was impossible that it would ever actually be implemented because of the war. So the council also recommended that the Indies armed forces be expanded so as to be able to cope with any unforeseen developments.

The recommendations about the military had no important implications for me. In fact, it wasn't really any of my business. But the proposal for a special branch in the police force clearly threatened my position in the Algemeene Secretariat. If such a special branch was established, then it could well be that my service here might come to an end. I would be kicked off one of the top rungs of the colonial ladder, where mighty power was located, falling from a great height.

I could expect my boss to come to see me about this development anytime now. Or he would send me a memo with the Indies Council proposal attached. Or he would turn up ready to blast me again, knowing that these proposals severely weakened my position. He certainly had an interest in getting rid of me. My recent defiance was obviously undermining his standing here. He would, of course, get rid of me in his capacity as a loyal and dedicated colonial official. Huh!

Very well. I was ready to face him and I would not be yielding. And this was not just because I had come to love this work—there was no work in the world as interesting as this. There was another reason too. I dreamed that despite having lost so much to this job, I would one day be able to write for the public about all these colonial issues. And not just memoirs like these I am writing now and something different too from Francis, Tan Boen Kim, and Pangemanan (one *n*), all of whom only wrote crime stories. Yes, it is only proper that Pangemanann too be read by the world!

But during the first week after the proposals surfaced, there was no visit from my boss at all. And there was no memo either. But among the Indies elite there was a great discussion of the idea of a special branch within the police. It was possible that my boss was busy lobbying for the successful formation of such a special branch. And Pangemanann was the only person available to be stabbed in the back by my boss. But if that's what you are up to, then you'd better be careful. You don't know what it's like to confront me directly.

Finally, on the tenth day, he came to see me. He wore new clothes of white drill with a bow tie. His face glowed with victory. It looked as if his conspiracy with the colonial press might be about to succeed. He was fully confident that I was about to be kicked out. He held out his hand to me.

"Meneer Pangemanann, let's forget our past quarrels," he said.

"I have no quarrel with you, Meneer," I answered.

"That's even better," he went on.

A moment later Herschenbrock came in carrying a pile of newspapers. Some parts had been underlined in red. I was being asked to study those. And my boss also placed on my desk a memo, along with a copy of the Indies Council request to the governor-general.

So it was about to begin, I thought.

"This task will have a big role in determining the future of the Indies, Meneer. I am sure you will be more careful and thoughtful this time. Many of our newspaper editors support the Indies Council proposal, even though they haven't made their views public yet. Good luck."

I did not care what people said, whether privately or in print: I would not be dislodged from my position here as an expert. I prepared quite a long submission, arguing that it was not at all necessary to form such a special branch. There was not all that much work involved in monitoring Native politics and there were no grounds for a special force to carry it out. The establishment of such a special force would mean a considerable expansion of the police budget at a time when the State's finances were in a parlous state and were likely to get worse as long as the war in Europe continued. The Indies was totally dependent on Europe for trade.

Also, I wrote, the increase in political activity in the Indies was a direct result of the government's own Ethical Policy and therefore there was no case for the government to arbitrarily decide to eliminate this activity. It would be more appropriate for the government to hold out its hand so as to offer guidance, rather than attempt to destroy this activity.

With the correct guidance, all these new Native organizations need not cause any trouble for the government. In fact, they could become a help to the government, as was clearly the case with Boedi Oetomo, Tirtajasa, and the Association of Government Priyayi. The only action that could be justified was that aimed against extremist individuals. And these extremists, that is, those who are politically conscious, could be counted on one's fingers.

I knew my boss's eyes would pop out when he saw this. But there was nothing he could do about it.

That evening, just as I was about to go home, I was fetched by one of His Excellency's adjutants. And this was the first time I had been brought before the governor-general himself.

I was taken to the library. My boss was there alongside the director of the Algemeene Secretariat.

His Excellency entered wearing his civilian clothes. We all stood to honor him. His fingers were ornamented with diamond rings. An adjutant followed along behind as well as a secretary.

"Let us begin, gentlemen," His Excellency took charge.

And so my trial began.

Both the director and my boss tried to box me into a corner. His Excellency just listened while all the time studying me. I myself remained fully confident in my abilities as an analyst of Native affairs and politics. And indeed that was the reason I had been appointed, on oath, as the Algemeene Secretariat's sworn expert.

The two of them, with obvious intent, kept referring to my Menadonese origins. And so, yes, it's true, my ancestors were not European.

Just when the tension was at its worst, His Excellency asked: "What education do you have, Meneer?"

Just one question, and the whole atmosphere changed.

"The Police Academy, Your Excellency."

He nodded.

"What high school?"

"I went to high school in Lyons, Your Excellency. And also spent two years at the Sorbonne."

"Your last position was as a police commissioner, yes?"

"Quite correct, Your Excellency."

"And how is that you have rejected such an important suggestion from the Council of the Indies?"

I repeated all the arguments from my earlier papers. Then I added: "Such are my views as a sworn expert, Your Excellency. If Your Excellency has other things to consider, then, of course, my views as an expert can be put aside."

"You are not likely to change your opinions?"

"No, Your Excellency. None of us knows when the world war might end. Perhaps it will even get worse. The Dutch businesses do not want to risk making big shipments to Europe. The insurance costs are too high, and meanwhile the decline in the worth of government employees' wages is undermining their loyalty. And there are signs that the government is planning to reduce the number of its employees. The plantations have already begun."

My director was immediately ordered to check with the Algemeene Landbouw Syndicate and the Sugar Syndicate to see whether the plantations were laying off workers. As soon as he put down the telephone, he reported that 6 to 7 percent of laborers had been let go, and about 0.1 percent of administrative staff.

The director was ordered to collect statistics on the number of criminal and political cases the police had dealt with this year in comparison with last year. Meanwhile: "Meneer Pangemanann, you are aware, are you not, that there is going to be an increase in disturbances to public order and security over the coming period? Have you taken this also into account?" asked His Excellency.

"Indeed I have, Your Excellency."

The director reported that there had been a very obvious increase during the first half of the year.

"Ah, now, Meneer Pangemanann, what do you have to say to that?"

"This increase has occurred because the Indies is experiencing social phenomena that are completely new for us. And every time such a thing happens, criminals always try to take advantage of it. So if the figures are going up, it is not because of the larger number of organizations but because of the increased opportunities for criminals. The thing then is not to increase the power of the police or give them an even wider range of matters to look after. Their ability to control these developments will improve with experience. Perhaps the best response to these new developments would be a police school."

I couldn't tell what His Excellency was thinking. I guess he was mainly interested in seeing how firmly my views were held and not so much in what they actually were. And the audience was over. In the end, they depended on my signature. The special branch must not be established. I must retain my position, and I would be in a stronger position as well.

There were no signs that the fighting in Europe was lessening, rather the contrary. More and more European countries were becoming involved and their soldiers descending into battle. All the European countries with colonies were betting the future of their colonies on the outcome of this war. The British increased the size of their fighting forces many times over, especially their navy. On the other hand, the Netherlands, which had no chance of being able to defend itself against attack, strained with all its energy to remain neutral.

It didn't seem there was much likelihood that the Indies would be a second Philippines. The transfer of a colony from one colonial master to another was no longer possible without the assistance of a native educated elite which had some mass support or at least influence. And the educated Natives of the Indies, those with mass support or influence or both, had not developed any interest in other colonial powers. What interest they did have in the outside world was limited to the Netherlands. Unlike their counterparts in the Philippines, the educated Natives of the Indies were still preoccupied with matters of sex. There was plenty of evidence that they were busy working out ways to win European women, or their Eurasian descendants. For most of them, organizations were a new toy. It was a new realm for them, where they could follow in the footsteps of their ancestors, who for centuries spent their time clawing at each other, killing each other, and slandering each other in order to obtain a woman.

So I was as convinced as I could be that there was now no chance of the Indies changing hands. Both the Royal Netherlands government and the Netherlands Indies government went out of their way to make sure that no other power was given any pretext to intervene to replace the Dutch. And for Europeans it was always a necessity to be able to use a pretext. To act otherwise was immoral.

A little while ago the question of the Indies becoming a second Philippines had been a major concern for me. Now the idea seemed a load of rubbish. The Indies would survive the war as a Dutch colony.

I had a second audience with His Excellency. I remained firm in my opinion. And I was victorious. The proposal for a special branch was dropped. The proposal to strengthen the army was also dropped. Meneer Director and my boss would now understand that my appointment as a sworn expert still meant something. All this gave me time and freedom once again to return to my surveillance of the two stars in the house of glass on my desk—Marco and Soendari.

Together they were the very incarnation of the Native organization epidemic. Marco was in a whirl, just like a propeller, and the busier he became, the less substance there was to what he was doing and the cruder his methods became. Perhaps this was a result of the poverty of culture he carried or because he was preoccupied with the challenges from both his friends and enemies. And it was the crudeness of his methods that made him the object of dislike, even hatred, among all the officials and priyayi. And so he often found himself in jail for a few days just because of very trivial incidents. And, Marco, you should know that it has not been me steering you off to jail. You are doing it to yourself because you refuse to learn from experience. And you are getting wilder and wilder too, teaching all sorts of ridiculous things to your friends. Is it true that it's empty talk to say that you love your country, empty talk to say that you're leading your people, if you have never been in jail.

The rise of Marco in Solo amazed me quite a bit. And it was precisely because he was a village school graduate that all the other village school graduates followed him. They too started appearing in public and in and out of jail they went, always ready to become heroes, whenever and wherever. They were more adroit and energetic than their European-educated compatriots, and were more willing to risk making mistakes. Then they joined the other epidemic. They all started using European terms and concepts even though they did not really understand what they meant or when and where they should be used.

The educated Natives enjoyed humiliating and making fun of their ignorance. The educated Europeans and Indos just sneered. Neither of these two groups realized that all this was in fact a real process of Europeanizing people's way of thinking. These new terms and concepts were something new altogether, products of a civilization that they had never experienced in their villages. And like gold and diamonds these new products of civilization were worn like jewelry around their necks. They wore them to bed, when they ate, when they bathed, and they freely handed them out to whoever was willing to take them and use them. They forget that every new word that people pick up along life's road fills their mind with many new concepts, bearing them gradually further and further away from their place of origin. And perhaps the day would come when such people would leave behind both the educated Natives and the educated Europeans and Indos.

As the month passed by, more and more people went to jail. I saw that this was a new fad. People wanted to "attack" the jails. And I saw too that these people consciously went about trying to influence the criminal prisoners. It was possible that some new relationship of mutual influence might develop between the criminal and political worlds—a new danger emerging from today's prisons. It was true that some local authorities were already separating the political prisoners from the criminals. But this was no guarantee that they were not getting in contact with each other. And when a political player consciously sets out to take over the leadership of criminals, you can be sure that some transgression is bound to take place. And a criminal who consciously absorbs political skills and experience can be even more dangerous. It was the Malay newspapers that did best out of all this.

Their reports about the activities that ensued were very popular.

But this was none of my business, and I did not intend to make it my business either. If I were to set out all the background to this here in these notes, then one day people would be sure to remember what I wrote here, namely, that this society was bound to witness political games being played out by criminals, and criminal ventures carried out by politicians.

It is true that you shouldn't find criminal activities going on in the jails. But jails, no matter where they are to be found, are always universities of crime. Or also politics?

The thing was that the nationalists came to think of jail as some kind of stopping-off station where they could expect to be visiting and leaving on a regular basis. They began to look upon time spent in jail as no longer a humiliation but, on the contrary, a place where national dignity could be restored. And I could fully understand this. And this was a different attitude from that of the corrupt officials who preferred to hang themselves rather than suffer the humiliation of being sentenced to do public community work. These were greedy people who were frightened stiff of losing all they had, and especially their fake honor and dignity.

The strange thing was that none of the relevant authorities realized what was going to happen. After their release, those criminals influenced politically while in jail would start to be more choosy when selecting their marks. Now they would make sure they hit the government and the European plantations.

Siti Soendari traveled a different road.

Unlike Marco, who liked having his photo published in all the magazines, she seemed afraid to be recognized. I had one picture of her, but it was of poor quality and she was too young. I had issued instructions that a photo be obtained from the local photographer where she lived. But it turned out that she did not like having her photo taken.

In one of the reports I received she was described something like this. She was always dressed neatly, in a kain and *kabaya*, with black velvet slippers, embroidered with flowers. She wore her kain down to her ankle, nothing higher or lower. She wore her hair in a traditional bun, decorated by an ivory hairpin, as well as a silver *keris*-shaped pin. Her kain was always from cotton and made in the Netherlands. As was proper for a Javanese woman, she always wore rather expensive gold jewelry. She even wore sapphire earrings.

She was always well dressed, whether at home or in public. She was always very polite and genteel.

The report was rather detailed. They were the orders that I had issued. Five agents had been employed to gather the necessary information, including the opinions of the local people of Pacitan who knew her.

I'm sorry for you, Soendari. You perhaps do not realize that even your bathroom walls have ears and eyes.

The report continued to tell how the people viewed her as the ideal Javanese woman, a model for others. She was able always to dress properly and was so gentle and refined. She was very adroit in all company, was always ready to help people in difficulty, never shirked either rough or refined work, was very able to cope with anything that she had to do either in public or at home. But all this praise came mainly from the young nationalists. And if what they were saying was true, then it meant that some big changes in social values had taken place. Because it was the young nationalists who had taken the European woman as the ideal woman for the coming period.

Women among the priyayi held another view—Siti Soendari was a delinquent young woman who didn't know what was proper, a Dutch woman in Javanese clothes, an old maid who was all in a dither because she couldn't find a man. They refused to have anything to do with her, afraid that she might steal their husbands. They weren't even interested in speaking to her. And after all, they didn't have anything in common to talk about. And they were all of one opinion—that's what happens when a girl gets too high an education; the cleverer she gets, the more likely to turn out a sharp-tongued squirrel.

The santri of Pacitan looked upon her as no better than a prostitute or street woman, showing off her wares while on a constant prowl for victims. She was very pretty and very alluring, they said, but that was unimportant while she did not have the qualities needed to make a good wife.

When she walked down the street, said the report, both men and women could not but be dazzled by her appearance. Rarely did any of the men goggling at her even dare bother her, as if she were an angel just descended from heaven. Whenever one of them tried, her reaction was always the same. She would walk up to her molester and ask firmly: What is it that Meneer wants from me? Usually this question left him rudderless. And if he continued to bother her, she would speak again, just as politely but in a loud enough voice for people around her to hear.

There were a number of educated Natives who said that most men were afraid of her. Who would want to take as a wife someone as well educated as that? And, they said, the real motive behind all her extraordinary activities was her desire to catch a high official for a husband. Others rebutted that view. She would never find any high officials among movement people.

Wearing a hypocritical smile and pretending to be polite, my boss asked jokingly why I needed so much information about her. She's just a girl, he said.

What an idiot, I thought. She was the first educated Native woman to appear on the public stage in the Indies, a very important social phenomenon absolutely worthy of study. I pitied my boss. Colonial power had blunted his mind and dulled his vision. His humanity and scientific instincts had been pushed aside by the glory of being a colonial ruler.

All I said to him was that in such difficult times as these any action taken against the educated Natives needed to be considered very carefully. As a government that conformed with European values, ours must always be able to justify its actions. We needed to have enough material to make sure any actions could be properly explained. Otherwise any action that was taken would be no different from that taken by the Native rajas of the past.

I knew he was offended by this lecture of an answer. He could have continued the argument if he wanted to defend his position. Except he didn't know how.

So I continued to gather together more information about my target. At the very least it would be useful for my own studies.

In the next report I wrote, I set out the following information:

She was teaching in a Dutch-language Boedi Oetomo primary school. Once a week she took the students from the most senior class to the rice fields and farms where she finished teaching the Dutch-language class. This made the students even more enthusiastic about their Dutch lessons and also brought them closer to their teacher. She didn't use the official textbooks, but used the natural surroundings all around her. She advised her students to study the textbook themselves at home.

The principal reprimanded her several times. And the principal was reprimanded in turn by the school inspector because the school was receiving a government subsidy.

Soon everyone in Pacitan was saying that Siti Soendari was being watched by the authorities because of her activities and that none of her students would ever be accepted for employment in government service.

The parents and guardians of the students started bringing their concerns to the principal. So in the end the inevitable took place—Siti Soendari departed. She took her leave in front of her class, watched by the principal. Everyone knew that she loved her students. Whether or not her students loved her—well, you can figure that out for yourself.

My very good children—she spoke gently as was her way when saying good-bye to students—it has never been my desire that you should imitate me. I have never taught or suggested to you to do anything other than study hard and well, have I? Today I will be leaving you all and this school. Outside school we will often meet and have the chance to chat and discuss. Perhaps some of you would like to come and visit me from time to time. You would all be very welcome.

Children, I often took you out into the open for classes. Why? For no other reason than that you should get to know the environment around you, in which you will live and grow. You must love the environment around you because it all belongs to you. I will be so happy if just one of you truly learns to love the world around you and understands that it belongs to all of you, and no one else.

Now I am going. I have never hurt even one of you, have I? In my heart, I am sure that I have never done anything to harm any of you. And I know too that none of you have ever done any wrong to me. And that is what is making this good-bye just a little easier. Yes, children, you must all study hard. Love your parents, your teachers, and the land and world of your own people.

She seemed to wipe away a tear as she walked down the steps at the school entrance. But she kept all of her poise. She said nothing to her students about having been dismissed by the school principal. She left her students behind without their ever learning what the real problem was.

Although the reports I received didn't give me a complete picture of what happened, it was enough to move me greatly. For the umpteenth time, I once more acknowledged that she was fully emancipated, and in the European way. She was liberated. For me she was the most beautiful woman to emerge as a product of the beginning of the modern era in the Indies. And this is something I myself am witnessing!

But if she is destroyed because she is ahead of her time, it will be I who feel the greatest loss, even though, yes, even though it is obvious that this is what will happen. She is a historical guinea pig. She will try to drag her people forward with her, but they will only pull her back. And ultimately this will exhaust her. Perhaps they will tear off her hand as she tries to drag them forward. And when her energy is drained away, she will be pulled back and she will disappear again in the midst of her people. Or perhaps she will become bored with her fruitless efforts to drag her unwilling people forward. Then she will let go of them and travel forward by herself, like Nyai Ontosoroh in the story told in the manuscripts of the Modern Pitung.

Yes, alone, without friends, and then suddenly one day she would realize that she was alone, by herself, in silent solitude. There would be no one there to listen. There would be no extra hands to give aid to her fading strength. She would be swallowed up by that new jungle called the modern age. And the whole world around her would seem new and strange and different from how she imagined it, because every new advance brings forth other advances in other fields, and every new product of civilization brings with it new laws, laws that are more and more binding. And there will be loneliness in the midst of tumult, and joy in the solitude of an isolated soul. The modern person indeed stands alone in a lonely world, a world increasingly alien to everybody. But this is still a better fate to befall her than to be ruined by falling in among all the criminals.

It is a great pity that Raden Mas Minke's manuscripts were written before she appeared on the scene. Perhaps if those criminals had not ransacked his home-in-exile so early on, I could have read what his views about her were. (Actually, I still considered that theft as contemptible and totally improper.)

And was there ever any relationship between Raden Mas Minke and Siti Soendari? Of course there was. Among the various reports to me that came in from around Java, there was one that wrote: In March 1912, Meneer Raden Mas Minke visited his old school friend, Siti Soendari's father, in Pemalang.

It wouldn't make very interesting reading to quote directly from all these reports, so I will just set out here some of the material, but in my own words, of course.

It was in July 1912 that Raden Mas Minke finished his tour of Java, explaining to all the Sarekat branches his plans for it to expand beyond the shores of the Indies. He propagandized for unity between all the Malay-speaking peoples of Singapore, Malaya, Borneo, Siam, the Philippines, and, if possible, also in Ceylon and South Africa. With his six years of experience in Java it was quite possible he would have succeeded had not the government sent him into exile. And had he succeeded, it was clear that he would have created disturbances in all the colonies—Dutch, English, and French.

It is true he didn't always note down what his ultimate intentions were. But it was impossible for him to fool someone like me. I knew that in his own way he wanted to show that colonialism was not simply a local problem but an international one, and he wanted to respond to that by building international solidarity among the Malay-speaking people.

But he always forgot his own weakness—he was never a good judge of people. He looked on everyone who was close to him, who knew him well, as having the same abilities as he, the same sincere intentions, the same honesty and goodness. He truly thought of them all as being much like himself. Each time he had to choose somebody to undertake a task, he inevitably made a mistake.

It was possible that in the future people would laugh at him for taking an initiative that did not stem from a Congress decision. But that's how the Native organization operated during that time.

The last place he stopped during his tour was Pemalang. He had often stopped and stayed overnight at the house of his old friend, Siti Soendari's father.

At the time of his last visit there, Siti Soendari was at home on vacation. Her older brother was no longer in the Indies. He had gone to Holland to continue his education. This time she used the opportunity to talk with her father's friend about many things, as a student before her teacher, as a child before her father.

I don't know for sure what it was that they discussed. I am trying to get more complete reports. I will try to get more material, even though the agents there will wonder why I need such personal information.

The main thing is that there was contact between Siti Soendari and Minke. Did they correspond? I don't know. No doubt I will find out about that one day too.

As the war in Europe intensified, the Indies began to experience strange things, as if it was becoming cut off from the kingdom. What was impossible a few years ago now occurred as a daily event—workers began to ignore the orders of the plantation administrators and office staff and even began to challenge them. These officials no longer felt so much at ease and secure under the protection of colonial law but began to carry sidearms with them everywhere.

The situation was becoming more and more interesting. The decline in the country's income, the drop in employment, the increase in food prices, especially with the failure of many rice crops and the import of old, stale rice from Siam, all helped produce a great wave of dissatisfaction in the towns. In Kediri, workers would have burned down a sugar mill if the authorities hadn't intervened in the nick of time. The Europeans no longer felt safe among their own workers.

And Siti Soendari's star rose too with the floodtide of dissatisfaction.

The government was lucky that all this took place only in Java. Only Palembang, in southeast Sumatra, seemed to be experiencing the same turmoil. I had originally thought that the contract laborers on the east coast plantations would use the current situation to rise up and seek revenge for all the suffering they had undergone. But no, nothing happened. It seemed the English administrators had succeeded in domesticating them by bringing in gambling, *tayub*, and prostitutes.

The strength of the police and army was not increased. They had to work even harder as payment in kind in return for not having their wages decreased like everyone else.

There were more and more ethnic organisations—the Sons of Bage-
lan, Rencong Aceh, Rukun Minahasa, Mufakat Minang, and the Banjar
Association. The organization epidemic was spreading ever more virulently.
And all of this was just because of the appearance of one player on the Indies
chessboard—Raden Mas Minke in 1906.

The colonial government had good reason to be concerned. The government in the Netherlands was even more worried. If the situation continued like this with the colony teetering on the edge of collapse and the
world war didn't soon end, the island of Java could explode into volcanic
ash. Just look, here in Betawi there was now even a Drivers' Sarekat that
had unilaterally raised fares for Europeans.

For me, these were all signs that the Natives were at last lifting up
their heads to look in the eyes of those who were their teachers, masters,
and oppressors all at once. Teacher, master, oppressor . . . how did the Javanese call them? Yes, *Durna*. Some little-known writer from somewhere or
other had first used that name. Yes, yes, a new age, a new way of living
with new demands, new concepts, and new names. These are the signs that
things are coming to life, moving forward.

I was completely fascinated by all these developments. Not as an enemy to these changes, like the white and chocolate colonial masters. I studied all these things purely as social phenomena in which I had no personal
stake at all. It was true indeed that there was no reduction in the amount
of work that came to me. It was always possible that my boss would bring
me another plan to crush some other organization. But I always refused to
sign my name as the official expert. Indeed, I usually laughed in his face,
telling him that these useless plans could not turn back the tide.

"But you agreed with and signed the plan to take action against the
Indische Partij?"

"Then there were only one or two organizations. Now there are tens,
scores of them. If you try to force the situation now, you will only produce
the opposite results to those you desire. The organizations will continue to
survive, but they will be cleverer and more cunning and the government
will therefore have to spend much more money in order to control them."

And of course, predictably, a great debate ensued. But I remained firm.
He could say whatever he wanted, but I would not sign my name to his
proposals.

"No matter what you say, you still have to do something, Meneer,"
he finally said.

So I devised two classifications of organization. The first were the
Indies-oriented organizations. The second were the ethnic-based ones. And
instructions went out that government officials should use all available

means to support the ethnic organizations and to encourage them to compete against each other. And that way things would be made more difficult for the first kind of organization. In the end, Indies nationalism was much more dangerous than ethnic nationalism. The first kind of nationalism united people; the second set people against each other.

My boss was almost ecstatic when he received my proposals with my signature at the bottom.

"So it is your opinion, Meneer, that the more ethnic organizations there are, the more opportunity there will be for people to organize, and the better things will be for the Indies, because eventually European democratic ways will find their place in the Native world and thereby change the Natives' feudal ways?"

"At the very least they will study how to decide things collectively. And so these organizations will also be open and above ground and we will be able to peep in through their doors or windows whenever we like."

This was the most substantial and wide-ranging submission I had ever written, perhaps my best piece of work—without having to use any of the material or ideas from my private studies.

So it was clear that these new developments did not threaten me at all. These were natural and reasonable developments, even though they were occurring with more enthusiasm and energy than had occurred in Europe. If there was an exception to this in Europe, it was in France just prior to the Revolution.

And the social transformations taking place in Java were no less interesting. The higher nobility, whose status today was based on their high position in the colonial state, obtained those positions purely because of their aristocratic rank. Now the lower ranks of the aristocracy, desperate for any position in the colonial hierarchy, were eagerly studying all sorts of subjects as long as it finally led to a job in the colonial service. They entered all the vocational schools, which were avoided by the younger generation of the higher aristocracy.

At the same time, once forced labor ended in the villages, young village people started flooding into the towns looking for work, and there they found all kinds of new and different experiences—a thousand times more varied and new than the experiences of their ancestors a century and a half before.

They became acquainted with all sorts of machines and learned to study the laws that governed the operation of these machines. As workers, they became familiar with all those new elements in modern life—electricity, steam power, petrol—and many became first-class motor mechanics, achieving levels of skill far greater than the children of aristocrats ever achieved in their areas of work, aristocrats before whom they used to bow and scrape.

They worked on building steel bridges, put up telegraph cables, drove motorcars and steam engines. They built cement dams. They constructed small and large factories. Then, using all this experience, they started to open their own workshops. And there were among them those who achieved considerable wealth, either because of their skills or because of their enterprise or both. They became far wealthier than the nobles and aristocrats who for centuries had ruled over their ancestors.

It was obvious from the huge rush of the children of lower nobility into the vocational schools that it would be they who would emerge as the leaders of their people. The agricultural, medical, trade, teacher, and veterinarian schools were all taken over by these children. And as well, when that phase ended, it was also clear that the farmers' children who were being transformed into skilled tradesmen and merchants would also have the chance to lead society in the future. They would eventually leave behind the aristocracy, high and low, in life's race. And in the end, being a member of the nobility would no longer mean anything. And then the government, which had based its rule all this time on working through the nobility, would also have to change its ways, would have to accommodate to the new social situation. If it did not do this, it would collapse along with the aristocracy itself.

In my eyes, any educated person who was not interested and not impressed by all these changes was not a truly educated person at all. It was also because of these developments that I watched over Siti Soendari—also a child of a lower aristocrat. What would happen to this maiden? If she were a man, I am sure she would agree with everything I am writing down now. But a woman? I didn't know what would happen to her.

But then Marco, the son of a peasant, should have emerged only after Siti Soendari disappeared from the scene. He contradicted my theory. And the problem was that he emerged earlier than Siti Soendari simply because he was older. Perhaps he represented a phenomenon that was before its time: He was at least fifteen years too early.

This theory also contradicted the Hindu caste system. It should have been the children of the merchants who emerged once the nobility had fallen. But generally speaking, most of the merchants' children never really fully matured, in the way that they did in Europe. The Native merchants gave birth to children who didn't seem to have any real will to achieve anything in life except to be merchants like their parents. They didn't have the energy to reach out for anything more than that or to step out into new arenas of activity.

The way Siti Soendari and Marco each dealt with the question of noble titles seemed to confirm my theories. Soendari, like Wardi before her, dropped her titles, perhaps in recognition of the coming demise of the aristocracy. Marco, on the other hand, who previously had no title at all, adopted the title of *mas*, the lowest rank in the Javanese nobility. Perhaps this was a sign that he felt he had jumped over a necessary phase and because of that enlisted himself among the lower ranks of the nobility.

Perhaps these are all the thoughts of a crazy man, but these are what I think.

And, both of you, if anything happens to you, it will not be because of Pangemanann. You are both very interesting objects of study. You face a friend here in the Algemeene Secretariat, a friend who has neither face nor substance for you, but who, my two friends, does indeed exist.

Then faintly I once again began to hear of vague, difficult-to-pinpoint noises, like out of the fairy tales of children—our own government! And now too! It was the voice of the Indische Partij speaking from its grave. . . .

Marco continued his career as a writer, public figure, orator, journalist, publisher, and jailbird. And there was one thing that many people didn't know—he was also a great writer of letters, especially to Siti Soendari. A number of his letters that were detected by the Solo Post Office were now in my hands.

And Siti Soendari? Even with her refined ways and her adroitness, and bolstered by the warmth of Marco's enthusiasm, she was soon the target of great hostility from among the colonial establishment.

"So, Meneer Pangemanann, now we have no alternative," my boss told me. "His Excellency has been very quick to reprimand us during this last period while we have been so inactive. Now the people in Non-Native Affairs have just reported on a pamphlet that has been circulating which reflects exactly the themes and ideas of the young generation activists in Solo. The style and vocabulary are exactly the same as the open letter signed SS some time ago. I want you to study it. And if it is true that the two documents have been composed by the same person, then you know what you must do, yes?"

He wanted action, not advice. "His Excellency has read this pamphlet himself," he added.

"What did he think of it, if I may ask?"

"He didn't say a word. Just frowned. A sign of a storm looming."

And so I studied the pamphlet. And there was no doubt it was the work of that beautiful girl with the complexion of a betel leaf. I didn't know what her relationship was now with Mas Tjokro, but it was clear that Marco had fallen hopelessly in love with her. And now I had to take action against her, a woman, the one and only Native girl whom I admired with all my moral and intellectual being.

It's not because I want to do it, Soen. The Algemeene Secretariat is in a panic because His Excellency has frowned! This apparently means that the Algemeene Secretariat has been too lax—and so now my pen, and my ink, must interfere in your life, still so young and beautiful.

Very well. You must forgive me if you suffer because of what I must do. I will prepare the most moderate proposal that I can. And so this is how things then unfolded.

The governor of Central Java first of all indicated to the assistant resident of Pekalongan that he should speak to Siti Soendari's father about exercising more control over the behavior of his daughter. Both the governor and the resident agreed with my advice. It would be a great embarrassment to the government if it had to arrest this lovely girl just because she held beliefs and opinions different from the government's. It would be different if she were a man.

The resident of Pekalongan then instructed the Bupati of Pemalang to apply gentle pressure on her father to find her a husband. This was the same procedure that had been successfully used twelve years ago in the case of the girl from Jepara. The Bupati of Pemalang summoned the unfortunate father, who was then given two choices—he could be dismissed without honor and without a pension and also lose his daughter, or he could make his daughter happy by marrying her off honorably while keeping all his positions and his pension when he retired. If he did not have a candidate husband in mind, the government could provide a list of the sons of bupatis and of medical school graduates. And if the father chose the first option, there was a chance too that his son would be expelled from the Institute of Commerce in Rotterdam.

He was a proud father, respected because of his children's success, taken as a model by educated Natives in neighboring towns, envied by certain Europeans and Eurasians. Yet coming from the middle ranks of the aristocracy, he could not live without his official position and status. He was from the older generation of aristocrats who could not yet fully accommodate to modern ways, who could not yet liberate himself to become a free and independent individual. He was an educated man from the older generation who believed that honor and respect could only be gained as a blessing from the government. In his own way and with his own style, he made the same choice as the father of the girl from Jepara—he chose his position. He was too afraid of the government's wrath.

His hands trembling, this parent raised them clasped before him in obeisance to His Excellency the bupati, requested about two months in which to arrange things, and hurriedly set off home. Back in Pemalang he asked to take some time off work.

He hired a taxi and, taking only a small suitcase, traveled to Pacitan. When he arrived at his destination, an old woman greeted him at the door with the words, "Forgive me, Master, Lord, it is so that mistress Soendari has moved from here."

He set off again and turned right, heading for where his daughter was a teacher.

"Yes, Meneer, Juffrouw Soendari left our school a little while ago."

The father now became very worried. From Pacitan he sent a telegram to his relatives in Malang. Back in the inn, he received a reply: "Yes, she had called in on her way to Surabaya but did not leave an address."

Traveling in the same taxi, he went to Surabaya, where he stayed with a friend. He let the taxi go, paying in full. He and his friend spent the whole of the next week looking for his daughter. It was as if Soendari had vanished into thin air.

He set off to return to Pemalang by train very dispirited. He had to stay overnight in Semarang. After alighting from the train, he hired a horse cart to take him to an inn. Up on the horse cart, he watched the hubbub on the streets—wait, yes, wasn't that Soendari? The woman was walking, slender, in fact a bit thin, and her face was pale. Such a pretty girl, who knew her mother's love for such a short time! The father hesitated. His love for his daughter was very great. But his fear of the resident was even greater.

Soendari! Did you have to be the source of your father's fall, and would you be the cause of your brother being expelled from his course in Holland?

He knew that his beautiful daughter wanted to be a free and independent woman, working for her people and country. It was he himself who had taught her this.

And so it was these events that were brought about by the ink from my pen which had dried on the stationery of the Algemeene Secretariat. I had written that any action that was taken should be well advised and should avoid at all costs any harsh measures. Perhaps if I had proposed such harsh and severe measures, her father would not have suffered so much. He would suddenly be confronted with a new reality and would soon adjust. He suffered in the same way, I thought, as the girl from Jepara's father must have suffered when he was ordered to marry off his daughter against her will. And I, as a European-educated person, could sympathize with such suffering.

Would this father regret embarking on such a course for the rest of his life just as the father of the girl from Jepara had? That was a secret that only he himself would be able to answer.

For those few moments of thought, he was unable to speak and the horse cart kept on moving. But his head remained fixed in the direction the young woman was walking. He had traveled another ten meters before he was able to cry out: "Ndari! Ndari!"

The driver stopped the horse cart. But Soendari kept on walking.

The rest of this story was not reported to me by the bupati's office but traveled from mouth to mouth among many people. Perhaps it was spread by Soendari's friends to protect her from the tentacles of the colonial authorities, because there are many gaps in the story.

Just at that moment, the father found himself without the strength to climb down from the horse cart. He said later that he felt as if there were a hundred-kilogram sack of rice weighing him down. That was the weight of the sins of a father who had become the weapon of colonial power against his own beloved daughter. Whether this actually happened or whether it is only half true or even if it is a total fabrication, I can still feel his suffering.

He asked the driver to help him down. But when he at last stood on the ground, he could not walk. He asked the driver to chase his daughter and call her back. Meanwhile he sat on the step up into the horse cart, holding on to the door.

The driver called out: "Mistress! Mistress!"

The pretty but now skinny and pale woman walked on so gracefully, not turning back, her eyes straight ahead, as if nothing was happening around her. The driver chased after her and she accelerated her pace.

"Your father is calling you, Mistress," said the driver, trailing behind her.

Now Soendari was almost running. The driver was afraid of leaving his horse and horse cart unattended and so turned back. He helped his passenger climb back aboard.

"Follow her," and the horse cart turned around and followed her.

It was getting dark. The father saw his daughter enter a *wayang orang* theater that was filling up, perhaps for the evening performance. But there was no sound of a *gamelan* inside. More and more people were arriving. But there was no crowd of people gathering around the ticket window. There was no one collecting tickets at the door. And there was hardly a woman accompanying her husband.

The driver refused to help the old man get inside. With the aid of two young boys whom he paid a few cents, he was assisted inside and sat down on one of the few empty seats. The two boys sat on either side of him.

It turned out that there was a public meeting under way. It was a meeting organized by the Tram and Train Workers' Union, the TTWU, which had its headquarters in Semarang.

Soendari disappeared in the midst of all the people there. The father anxiously watched a man ascend the stage, give a speech, and then come down again. Another followed. Then, yes, then he shuddered. It was Soendari, his beloved daughter, one of the very few women present in the building, who climbed the steps to the stage accompanied by the tumultuous applause and shouts of the crowd. All eyes were on her, this beautiful girl, even more beautiful once she stood there on the podium, despite her being obviously pale and tired.

Then once again the father heard his daughter's gentle voice, even though it was a gentleness that shouted loudly. And it was the first time too that he heard his daughter's voice speak in her school Malay. At home they spoke Javanese and Dutch. Now she spoke Malay. When had she studied that language?

Assisted again by the two children, he moved up closer to the stage. Everyone looked at him, thinking that he was an old man, hard of hearing, trying to hear what Soendari was saying. Perhaps there were people thinking to themselves that even sick people needed to come to hear Soendari speak.

When they saw this, the crowd shouted and clapped even louder. The cry of "Long live Juffrouw Soendari!" echoed in salute to her.

A member of the committee brought over a chair for the father.

No one knew who it was that was being honored with a seat in front of the stage. But the father knew that all the people there respected and honored his beloved daughter.

And so he sat there, this father, head bowed, listening to his daughter's voice, a daughter whom he himself had educated, listening to each of her words, discovering in them echoes of what he himself had once taught her, finding out just how fully had the seeds he planted in his daughter's soul now grown and blossomed. He was now in the grip of his own daughter's spell. And even her mother's smile at the peak of her beauty was not as beautiful as Soendari's smile. And she moved so quickly and surely!

The young woman's fist would be raised for a moment, sometimes a finger pointing. And those soft palms of her hand would even come crashing down onto the lectern. Her pale face was now glowing red, all tiredness disappearing from her countenance. Her face literally glowed. The way she moved, with such authority, made him forget to listen to what she was saying. All of Soendari's being was like a twin of her mother. But Soendari's mother had never raised her fist, her fingers had never pointed jabbingly into the air, her hands had never thumped down onto a lectern.

For a moment he remembered how her mother was during her last moments before her death. He had held her hand, and that woman had spoken her last words: "You must never hurt my child Soendari, Mas. Do not ever do anything to make her afraid or lose heart. Love her even more than you loved me when I was still healthy and beautiful."

And he had never done anything to hurt his daughter. He had always granted whatever she asked. Everything. And now too it was Soendari who had paralyzed him for a while like this, he who, because of the government's scheme, had been blown into the midst of all these people who wanted to hear her. None of them knew who he was. They were just there to hear his daughter, that is what they wanted.

He didn't hear his daughter's words flow forth. All that he could catch was the rise and fall of her beautiful voice, loud even in its gentleness and softness. What would her mother say if she saw such a scene as this?

Suddenly he heard a piercing shout come from his daughter's throat. He didn't hear what she said. And the young woman's head was bowed, showing her respect for her audience. Applause and cries of "Long live Juffrouw Soendari" kept coming from everywhere, as if there would never be an end to it all, while she descended the stairs from the stage.

Her parent's hands shook as he greeted her: "Ndari! Ndari!"

The sparkling beautiful eyes found her father.

"Father!" whispered Soendari, and she continued in Javanese, "How happy I feel to know that Father has been willing to listen to his daughter's speech."

"Yes, Ndari. I needed to come to witness all this myself."

"Has there been anything that pleases you, My Father?" she asked in Dutch.

"Well, it was wonderful, Ndari."

A speaker closed the meeting and the crowd all moved to encircle Soendari and her father.

"Long live Juffrouw Soendari!" people cried.

"Long life! Long life!" they cried.

Hearing that people so respected his daughter, he felt very, very much ashamed and he didn't know what he would say now to His Honour the Bupati of Pemalang. Would he tell the bupati that he was proud to have a daughter like Soendari? It was precisely these sorts of goings-on that the honourable government hated most of all. What was clear was that he was ashamed because he had brought Soendari up to become the moon, the sun, a shining star. And now that her time had come, he was supposed to condemn it all. He was ashamed of himself.

The people escorted Soendari to a horse cart, and as if they were all drunk, they lifted her up high and put her straight into the carriage. And the horse cart itself could only move slowly along, because of the crowd of people around it all shouting: "Long live Juffrouw Soendari!" Many people also tried to shake hands with her father and congratulate him on having such a wonderful daughter.

The tumultuous crowd escorted the horse cart all the way to the TTWU headquarters. The small front grounds of the office were packed with people. Everyone was happy. The whole atmosphere was happy. Only Soendari's father was bathed in a cold sweat.

Perhaps he had forgotten to pay the two children for helping him.

Father and daughter were taken inside, where they sat down on a simple old rattan divan.

A young boy, probably short for his age, in long trousers and short-sleeved shirt, all in white, quickly and efficiently served them tea. After putting down the glasses, he stood up straight and in fluent Dutch welcomed the father to the offices and congratulated Soendari on her success on the podium that evening. After that he bowed like a courtier in one of the European palaces and introduced himself: "My name is Samaoen. I will always remember this glorious day with great happiness. No doubt you will too, sir." He addressed these last comments to Siti Soendari's father.

The fear of the fate that awaited him (and who was it that created this fate if not that unknown god named Pangemanann?) and the great waves of pride in his daughter kept crashing up against each other. The father felt as if he were floating backward and forward between heaven and hell.

The formalities did not take long.

That night the TTWU executive organized a taxi to take Soendari and her father back to Pemalang. Her father had convinced her to go by telling her that something had happened in the family.

Semarang at that time had already set up a Political Investigation Unit unbeknownst to Betawi. Nothing went unnoticed by them. The very next day after Soendari spoke to the railworkers, a new regulation was issued— underage children were forbidden to attend public meetings and visit the offices of any organizations.

This new regulation stemmed from the authorities observing the two young boys help Siti Soendari's father into the wayang orang building and because of the young boy Samaoen's presence in the TTWU office.

It did not surprise me that Semarang took such action. Several times after I had sent telegrams asking about something, I would notice that some related action would be taken. Now they were trying to lead the way in handling these matters. The result was that people who had never been trained for this sort of work, who couldn't even write a proper report yet, had been assigned to carry out this kind of very complicated surveillance and intelligence analysis. The other result was that the reports that came in from Semarang contained a whole range of different kinds of information, but their reliability was very suspect.

Take for example how they reported the conversation between Siti Soendari and her father before they left for Pemalang:

Father: *Tonight, Ndari, we must return to Pemalang tonight.*
Daughter: *Forgive me, please, Father, but my work has just begun.*
Father: *I know that, Daughter, and I respect you greatly for it. And I thank all you men here too for helping and guiding my daughter. But you must forgive us now for there is an urgent family matter that we must resolve. Forgive me if this disturbs all your work a little. I hope you all won't object to giving us a little time to deal with our family affairs.*

"Forgive me, Comrades," Soendari rejoined. "I have not finished my tasks yet. Comrades must decide this themselves."

"Go with him, Soendari," one of them decided and all the others chorused their agreement.

Colonial people, white or brown, who have never studied the Native way of thinking and relating to each other, might indeed swallow such a report as the truth. I myself didn't really believe it. The way the report told it, everything unfolded according to the European way of thinking and relating to each other. I suspected it was probably written by a European.

But I had to be cautious too about this evaluation of mine. What if the report was accurate?

In that case, it would be a very appropriate subject for a short story or novel, written in the European style. Just imagine, a Native, a young woman, dedicating her life to her chosen work, putting that ahead of her dedication to her father, a father who sincerely loves her greatly. And re-member, in a Native family the father is nothing less than a maharaja whose decrees have absolute authority. Just imagine too, there was her father, a man used to giving orders to those below him, more or less negotiating with his own daughter's friends, and in front of his daughter too! What a position for a father like him to be in! How must he behave?

But I must admit I tend not to believe that such a conversation took place. Maybe in Europe—in France, for example—but never here in the Indies.

But let me tell you now how the Bupati of Pemalang reported what happened after he spoke to Siti Soendari's father himself.

They arrived in Pemalang that same evening. The next morning before leaving to go to see the bupati, the father told Soendari to wait for him at home and not to go off anywhere.

And so the father set off to see the bupati to seek his guidance on what he must say to his daughter in accord with the will of the government.

He was asked to come in to face the bupati. By coincidence Meneer *Kontrolir* was also present. The father nervously with head bowed reported on all that had happened in Semarang. The kontrolir without interrupting started taking notes. It was only after the father had completed his report that the kontrolir spoke: "Good. I would like to hear from Soendari herself about her work and her ideas."

So they devised a plan whereby, unbeknownst to Soendari, she would talk while others secretly listened.

That evening her father took Soendari to visit a friend's house. And the young woman did not know that the kontrolir was listening from the other side of the bamboo wall.

As soon as she had seated herself, the woman of the house greeted her in Javanese: "Wah, *Jeng* Soendari, it's been so long since we've seen you. I have missed you greatly, Jeng."

"Yes, there are many difficulties in finding ways to make a living, *Ibu*. Forgive me."

"Why are you worried about making a living, Jeng? Your father can give you all you need and want. What else is there that you want? All you have to do is wait for a husband to come along, but you are out there doing all sorts of things! Your father would be much happier if you stayed to look after him in the house."

"Forgive me, Ibu. I did not spend ten years at school and two years working just to sit and wait for a husband to come along."

"So what else is it that you seek in this life, Jeng, if it is not happiness? And where is there a woman who has achieved happiness without a husband?"

Up till then, her father had avoided saying anything. He knew that behind the wall sat a representative of the State, hiding like a burglar, following everything being spoken. Perhaps the old man was also repulsed by the thought that there were Europeans who were prepared to listen in to other people's private conversations.

I myself never thought that a European would be prepared to resort to such low and contemptible behavior. It's true, all that I knew about Europe were its great achievements, its high civilization, the things in which it was superior to others. In the Indies all the contemptible and humiliating work is delegated to the Natives, such as my work. But now I find there are Europeans who volunteer to do such filthy work themselves.

"But I am certainly not going to just sit and wait for a husband."

"But in a few more years, Jeng, it will be too late to find one."

Then the conversation suddenly turned very serious. Soendari explained her views without hesitation: "Since I was little I was brought up by my father to become a free and independent woman. My father never once forbade me to do anything, as long as it did not bring danger or dishonor to the family or myself. My father's love shed its light on my family and on me. My beloved father has always been my strength."

And now the father was forced to say something too: "Since she was little she has never known the love and affection of a mother. I have been her father and mother together. When she was little she slept in my bed, and I gave everything to her, because she had lost so much that was important; she almost never even had the chance to suckle on her mother's breasts."

"You have suffered so much, Jeng."

"I have never suffered any real difficulties. The star of good fortune has always shone down upon me."

"That's very beautiful, Jeng. For myself I have never been to school. But what difference does school make when the issue at hand is life itself? What is the meaning of life without devotion? Jeng, your father has asked me to help him explain to you the situation, should he ever be in difficulties. You are a clever girl and grown up, Jeng. Now your father needs you to show your devotion to him."

"Here I am, his humble daughter. Have not I always shown my devotion to my father? Am I not speaking the truth, Father?"

The father did not know what to say when he heard this completely unexpected question. Finally he answered slowly, very slowly, and cautiously: "Yes, Ndari."

"Ah, ah, well, it's not so much because you have not shown devotion to your father, Jeng. But think about this. Your older brother is still studying and so has not been able to present a grandchild to your father. Is your father now not old enough to cradle a grandchild? If you yourself one day reach your father's age and are not able to cradle a grandchild of your own, what bitterness will you then feel, Jeng. I am only explaining to you what your father cannot bring himself to tell you."

Siti Soendari glanced at her father for a moment. She saw the chicken-claw marks that had started to appear at the corners of his eyes. She bowed her head and whispered in Dutch: "Father has never before talked to me via a third party. What is happening, Father? Has Father lost his faith in his daughter?"

"It's just that I have been unable to bring myself to say these things, Child. I have never lost my faith in you." He stood up and walked out into the front yard.

"You can see for yourself, Jeng, your father cannot bring himself to continue with what he was saying."

"Is the intention that I be forced to take a husband like the girl from Jepara?"

"No one is forcing you, Jeng. Your honored father wants you to do this of your own free will. Look how your friends are all married. Only one of your friends is unmarried, and that is because she is insane."

"There are three others who did not marry, Ibu. Because they died young. So I can be equated with a madwoman and dead people, is that what you are saying?"

"No, I don't mean things that way, Jeng. Forgive this old person who so easily says things the wrong way."

"Two others died after they married, Ibu. One in childbirth, and another died of a broken heart when her husband took a second, younger wife! Only one among all my friends has not seen her husband take a second wife."

"No one knows how their fate will unfold, Jeng."

Siti Soendari was quiet for a moment, then continued cautiously: "Even if this was indeed what my Father desired, it should not be you, Ibu, who tells me." She observed the old woman suspiciously. "There is something wrong here, Bu."

"Why, Jeng? This is how it is now. I would never speak like this to you if it were not your Father's wish. Forgive me, Jeng, if what I have said has angered you."

Then there flowed forth those words that I had so eagerly awaited, words that would throw light on the relationship between Siti Soendari and Raden Mas Minke. She spoke like this: "I think something bad is going on here, Bu, forgive me."

"How can you say something like that, Jeng?" the old woman asked, startled.

"Listen, Ibu, perhaps Ibu has never heard the name Bendoro Raden Mas Minke?"

"I have heard that name, Jeng. Didn't he visit your house once? Everyone was talking about him then."

"During his last visit to our house, he made a request to Father and Father agreed to carry out his request."

"And what was that, Jeng?"

"Standing before Father and also me he spoke this way: Mas, this daughter of yours, he said, pointing to me, never prevent her from gaining an education. While Mas can afford it, always be prepared to pay whatever it costs. Father made this promise in front of me. Then Bendoro Raden Mas asked another thing: Never force her to marry. Never make her suffer what the girl from Jepara suffered! My father also made that promise. Indeed, he even went on to say: No one will ever force her to go against her own ideals. The tragedy of the girl from Jepara will never befall her. Since she was a baby she has never known a mother, so she must have everything else. Believe me, Minke, I will give her the freedom to become whatever she wants. And I will give thanks just to see her become a person useful to others."

"That's right, Jeng. And you have been of great help and comfort to your father. And how much better would it be if you were able to present him with a grandchild, a grandchild that he longs for. . . ."

The assistant resident of Pekalongan was very satisfied when the kontrolir of Pemalang reported this conversation. He considered that it was a very good first step. In the end any Native girl would cease all her goings-on once she had been taken to the wedding bed. But the resident of Central Java didn't think the meeting amounted to anything, just stupid village talk between a pimp and the next victim.

But the reality was that more and more of Soendari's writings started to circulate, even though she herself didn't appear in public anywhere. The Post Office had been instructed to keep a surveillance on her mail. But it turned out that she never used the post anyway.

The articles that she wrote while she was shut away in seclusion in Pemalang got better and better, all written in school Malay. Even though her name never appeared on any of them, she could not fool me. She had a writing style of her own. So far no newspaper had fallen victim to her— a fine of thirty guilders and closure for three days awaited anyone who published her articles.

And as was the case with the father of the girl from Jepara—at least according to all the rumors—now Soendari's father was also confronted with a list of possible sons-in-law. They were all quite impressive future priyayi, all educated and well-schooled young men from the Pekalongan district. But as the Bupati of Pemalang reported, Soendari refused to co-operate.

"Father has bestowed upon me an education, much learning, and much love. Was it all just for this? Why has Father abandoned me now like this?"

"It is not your father, Ndari, it is not me who wants this. I have given you all the freedom that is mine to give. You have to try to understand just what the real situation is. I would be in the wrong if I did this just because of my own wishes."

"If all that was ever expected of me was to choose a partner, what was the point of my spending ten years studying? What was the point of my using up so much of your money for that? What was the point of all my efforts and striving? I should now be able to achieve more than just the choosing of a husband. Does father not know that since the late girl from Jepara, I have been the only woman to come forward like this?"

It was when I heard this that I realized that Siti Soendari had come forward consciously, as if she were balancing the deficiencies of the girl from Jepara. She didn't want to be pulled down only because of the love of a father. And this was something that made me respect her even more. It was clear that she was indeed the spiritual child of the Modern Pitung, a fighter and a person of action. The words of the Modern Pitung obviously lived on within her. She answered consciously, unmoved by her own personal feelings.

And I could understand too how her father became trapped between two forces—the unlimited power of the government and his love for his daughter.

Then one day her father saw her receive a telegram from a neighbor. As a European-educated person, he did not want to know what was in it. He must not have any suspicions. So he left to check on the rice fields. When he returned home, his daughter was nowhere to be seen. And she had not returned by nightfall either.

Once again he hired a taxi and traveled to Semarang. As he entered Semarang, his taxi was stopped by the police and he was taken to the police station. A police inspector, full-blooded European, pink-skinned, invited him to take a seat and warned him straightaway: "Try to stop your daughter from speaking tonight. She has already caused us a lot of trouble. If more women followed her example . . ."

Semarang was in the middle of a transport strike. One of the colonial newspapers equated this strike with one of the big European strikes. The streets were silent, because even the horse carts refused to work, and the buffalo carts as well, not to mention, of course, the motorized public transport. That was why it was easy for the police to identify the father's taxi.

The father didn't know how to answer.

"Look, Meneer," said the inspector, "your daughter is even playing dirty."

"Playing dirty?"

"Pemalang itself has always been quiet. Meneer himself knows that. Then as soon as your daughter comes back to live, what happens? The sugar fields are burned down."

"My daughter would have nothing to do with anything like that," the father rejoined.

"Don't say it is impossible, Meneer. We'll soon see."

"My daughter never left our house."

"How can you say that? She is in Semarang now."

"That is why I have come here, to get her. And anyway, there have been no sugar fields set alight in Pemalang."

"It happened while you were on your way to Semarang. Fifteen hectares were destroyed, Meneer."

"Impossible! Impossible!"

"Very well then. You find your daughter first, Meneer. You know where to find her? The same place as before. The wayang orang building."

On leaving the police station, the father was surprised to find that his driver refused to take him any farther. He had to pay the driver what was owing.

Before leaving, the driver needed to express his regrets: "Forgive me, Ndoro. I know, Ndoro, that you are the father of Jeng Soendari. I should take you to your final destination. But this is not possible in Semarang. Especially after your being brought here by the police. And if Jeng Soendari saw that I was working, she would be unhappy with me. A thousand pardons, Ndoro. My prayers will always be for your safety, Ndoro."

And the taxi roared off. The father walked on toward his destination.

It was about twelve midnight when he arrived at the wayang orang building. And he could hear his daughter speaking from the stage. He should have been covered in a cold sweat. But he wasn't. Every now and then there was an outburst of applause.

Suddenly one of the men seated in the front row stood up, raised one of his hands, and walked up onto the stage. He approached Soendari and spoke to her. No one could hear what he said to her. And that beautiful young woman came down from the stage.

The man stood on the stage. Now he held up both his hands and signaled that the meeting was over.

The audience stood, moving only slowly, unhappy to see the meeting end so soon.

As soon as Soendari came out of the building, the father spoke: "Quick. Ndari," he said. "They are going to arrest you," and he ushered his daughter into the dark of the night.

No one knew where they went. The police agents given the task of following Soendari lost her tracks.

Two days later we found out that her father had withdrawn all his savings from the Javaache Bank. Since that day we heard no more from Soendari. She made no more public appearances and wrote no more articles.

In her house in Pemalang, we found letters from Marco. And there was more in them than discussions of organizational matters and politics. And they were all written in the tone of a man courting the woman he loved. So the rumors that had been reported to me were true.

10

Ten days after the wayang orang theater incident in Semarang, Marco, that other spiritual child of Raden Mas Minke, was released from the Solo jail. There were scores of people there who greeted him at the prison gates with applause and shouts. He was lifted up on their shoulders, carried across to a car, and taken off somewhere or other.

The next morning he was seen moving around Semarang. Three days later he had disappeared again. then it was reported that he was seen in Pacitan. His clothes were filthy. He was traveling alone and wearing a new pair of leather sandals. His eyes were somewhat sunken. He looked like a sugar field foreman who had just been sacked.

Then he disappeared again, only to reappear in Pemalang.

It was obvious that he was looking for Soendari. Having just been released from the jail in Solo, he was also free of suspicion that he was involved in the recent arson attacks on the sugarcane fields. He no doubt felt a certain emptiness at not being on the verge of being dragged before a court again. In Pemalang he was seen wearing a clean white buttoned-up shirt, white trousers, and shiny black shoes. He wore a gray felt hat on his head as if he were a Eurasian on holiday. He carried a cane walking-stick and strode along dashingly. His big eyes and his rather pointed nose did make it more likely that people would think he was a Eurasian. The way he walked and the confidence he radiated all served to disguise his fears.

He was seen visiting Soendari's father's house dressed this way as well. And nobody ever found out what the two of them discussed.

Several days later, still in Pemalang, in a rather disheveled state, he was seen trying to sell his pocket watch in a Chinese shop. He was seen once more after that day sitting under a tamarind tree, his clothes filthy, barefooted, no more cane, and then we lost all sight of him. It seemed he was also unable to trace Soendari's whereabouts.

It was several days afterward that I received news that he might be arriving by freight train at Gambir station in Betawi at ten o'clock that evening. I wanted to meet this new kind of Indies man. I needed to hear for myself what he had to say, to see what gleam there was in his eyes, and, if possible, to exchange ideas with him.

The car carried me slowly down from Buitenzorg to Betawi. I went by carriage from my accommodation to Gambir. The freight train pulled in and stopped, but there was no sign of Marco.

Back in my office the next day, I reread Soendari's letter to him, which we had seized from Marco's pockets when he was arrested almost eight months before.

What I want to do, Mas, what I still want to do, even now, is to continue like this, to keep doing his work until Tuan Minke returns from exile. How inspiring it would be to learn from him how to manage the publication of a newspaper by ourselves, and to handle all the other related aspects as well. Just see how even today there is no paper that has ever been as successful as Medan, that has been able to understand so well exactly what the readers want. Mas Tjokro's paper, Oetoesan Hindia, hasn't been able to do that. None of the papers have had the kind of influence that Tuan Minke achieved. We need to study all these things, and of course I am sure you will not be disappointed that I have chosen this as the topic for my letter to you, Mas.

If this letter was written to reflect her real intentions, then it was probable that Siti Soendari was waiting for the return of the Modern Pitung. Perhaps she was waiting even now, even though we had lost all trace of her movements. It was as if she had vanished into the emerald sky. It was clear, though, that she was hiding away, living off her father's savings. And with the news that Marco was heading for Betawi, the thought arose that she might be hiding somewhere in the capital of the Indies too.

Was it true that Siti Soendari was in Betawi?

It was four more months before I had the answer to that question. She was in Rotterdam in the Netherlands. A few months later there came further news. Marco was in Rotterdam too.

Three people all closely connected with Raden Mas Minke now found themselves in the same country—Wardi, Soendari, and Marco. And the Modern Pitung, their spiritual father, remained in exile in Ambon.

The three of them had escaped from my house of glass, and were no longer under my magnifying glass. Wardi had been exiled by the Netherlands Indies government. Soendari had escaped to Holland by herself. Marco had followed her.

As political people they would be safe from harassment from the Dutch government as long as they did not get involved in any criminal activity. They all had the right to hold their own beliefs and to propagandize them or, for that matter, to stay silent about them. They would be swallowed up by European life and they would become little lilliputians with the minuscule knowledge that they had brought with them. The land where they now found themselves was not the muddy rice fields of their own country, but a more arid place, where nothing could be produced without much knowledge and science and the application of many advanced skills.

And the situation in the Indies continued to develop, leaving behind those who were outside.

My boss never mentioned anything to do with my leave anymore. I never raised it either. What was the point? Europe was still at war. My children and my wife preferred the Netherlands to the Indies and me.

Then one day my boss came in to see me. His face was shiny. There was never a sign that he had ever grown a mustache or beard, which was very strange, as if he were some fresh-faced college graduate. As time went on he was less and less able to hide his great enthusiasm for America. It seemed that he was trying to change himself, to turn himself into a new person, someone who was open and easy to get along with. I didn't really understand what was going on inside him. Perhaps that was what Americans were like, as he so often explained it to me. In more recent days it was very easy to see that he was trying very hard to change, to make sure he didn't act anymore in a colonial manner. Now he was like a businessman trying to win the heart of a new client.

I think I have the right to suggest that my opinion in this matter is not far wrong. He was continuously trying to change, and this transformation sustained itself because of an even more astounding person, the great American inventor, renowned throughout the world. This was Edison. And in the Indies his invention—the lightbulb, invented several years before—finally started shedding its light in the towns of the Indies.

But I don't want to tell you all this kind of detail. That day he said to me very politely and amicably in English: "Mr. Pangemanann, could you tell me a little of the history of the Boedi Oetomo?" And before I could open my mouth, he continued: "Excuse me, sir, perhaps I am asking too much. But I think you, sir, understand more than just a little of its history. Indeed, you probably know more about it than the Boedi Oetomo members themselves. Moreover, I consider that you have mastered the history of all the other organizations as well."

I studied his words and his face very closely, not only because the changes in him were happening so thick and fast, but also because I was not so used to conversing in English.

"No, I only know a little, Meneer," I answered in Dutch, "because we do not study history in this office but investigate particular cases."

"Would you mind speaking in English?"

I ignored his request, and began to explain: "Meneer, you should have known that Sneevliet would start attacking the Boedi Oetomo. You must have had some idea about this."

I realized then that he had come to see me not only to practice discussing more complicated issues in English but also because he was incapable by himself of carrying out his own duties. Sneevliet's and the ISDV's activities did not fall under my jurisdiction, because they were not Natives.

In his regular lectures in the Marine Club in Surabaya, Sneevliet had begun to attack both the Boedi Oetomo and the government at one and the same time. It was his view that this big and stable organization did not understand what its real tasks were. It seemed, he said, that the Boedi Oetomo was more concerned to serve the colonial authorities than the people of the Indies, whom it claimed it wanted to lead.

The Boedi Oetomo set up primary schools under its name, but despite the fact that it claimed to be an organization for the Javanese, these schools did not teach Javanese in their curriculum. On the contrary, the students were taught Dutch right through from Grade 1 to Grade 7 just as in the State schools. The government had established special high schools for Chinese children. But what had they done for the Natives? Not a thing! But it was in fact the duty and the responsibility of the government to provide such schools. And why was it the Boedi Oetomo who alone provided European schooling for the Natives for so many years since 1909 and not the government? Why had the Boedi Oetomo taken over the responsibilities of the government?

Of course, the government was very appreciative of the services that the BO had provided. And now the BO had developed a very swelled head because it was receiving so much attention from the government. Was it for this that it was founded? Wasn't it set up to lead its people forward? Was the Boedi Oetomo prepared to become a kind of subdepartment of the Netherlands Indies government? Didn't it understand that all its graduates would be soaked up by the Indies civil service? Go ahead and ask all the students studying in the BO schools—what will you become after you graduate? They will one and all answer—government priyayi! In one or two years' time when they all start graduating, we will see them march off in search of government positions.

Pity on all those members who handed over money to join and have been paying their monthly dues all these years. The children have not been taught to love their country and their people but to love the government offices instead! Pity on them all! It's so very sad!

The Boedi Oetomo's head was swelling more and more because the government was embarrassed at how little it itself had achieved. It was a full five years after the BO had set up its first school that in 1914 the government set up an HIS for Natives. And in another seven years' time, when the HIS schools started vomiting all their graduates into society, the BO students will be very hard pressed to find work in the civil service, where Dutch was essential.

The Boedi Oetomo had to study the ABCs of the modern world. To be a modern man means more than just to know Dutch! Don't all you gentlemen from BO really understand that all your graduates will not work for the people at all? What is the use of striving so hard just to deliver more tribute to the government in the form of Dutch-speaking manpower? And in that way help strengthen Dutch imperialism's hold over your people? Isn't now the time for Natives to be more concerned about their situation? Especially now with war raging in Europe?

All Native organizations should decide not to imitate the senile idiocy of the Boedi Oetomo. And where is there a Native organization that is really working for its fellow countrymen . . . ? That was what Sneevliet had to say about the Boedi Oetomo.

If he had been a Native instead of a European it would have been easier for the government to take action. And he was not just any European. He was also very well equipped with the means to do battle in any court of law. It wouldn't be possible to get rid of him just like that as could be done with Natives. And to drag him before a court just because he was undermining the authority of the government with his speeches could end up boomeranging into the face of His Excellency, reflecting on his ability as an administrator of the Indies.

His speeches in the Marine Club in Surabaya were a two-edged sword. "The Boedi Oetomo will be very upset with these attacks," I said, ending my history of the organization. "They have always claimed to be working for the people, and indeed have worked very hard to try to do that. They have never been subjected to this kind of criticism before. Their pretensions have been torn to pieces in full public view. They have been accused of working with all their might only to achieve the opposite of their own ideals."

My boss listened to this very attentively as if he were a humble university student, as if he weren't my boss, as if he weren't one of the gods that helped decide the fate of the Indies.

"The great disaster, sir," I continued, but no longer in Dutch, "is that these criticisms emerge from a different way of thinking, one that is unknown to both the BO and the government, one that is based on quite new values. Sneevliet looks at everything from the point of view of the government's responsibilities to its subjects."

"Mr. Pangemanann, in your opinion, are Sneevliet's opinions correct?" he asked, very politely.

"It depends from whose point of view you look at the problem and what kind of thinking you analyze it with."

"Your own opinion, as a private individual, not an official," he said, again in English. "I know already the views you argue in your official capacity."

"If I were in Europe, I would be of the opinion that Sneevliet had the right to express such opinions, sir. As to the correctness or otherwise of what he has to say, well, people can put forward their own views, and they can be debated."

"It seems you are very cautious when it comes to expressing a personal view," he said, with a biting smile. "Yes," he went on to say, "the easiest opinion to have is the official position. I understand that. Behind the official opinion stands power and so on one has to worry about being right or wrong." Then he laughed. "This is in fact what has made me unhappy working here. So tell me then—what do you think, you yourself."

His words worried me more and more as they became more and more friendly and amicable.

I had to find the right path here: "In my opinion, sir, it is all very simple. Even now the Indies Council has not finished its deliberations over the governor-general's request for its views on the costs and benefits of giving Natives a Western education. It seems that they are deliberately delaying giving an answer. That doesn't mean that they won't give an answer in the end. But I think it is only right that the government be ashamed that its responsibilities have been carried out by Boedi Oetomo."

"But isn't it true that the government has given subsidies, even if not very much, to many of Boedi Oetomo's schools, wherever it seemed appropriate?"

"That's true as far as it goes. But what is fifty guilders per school for the Netherlands Indies government? It doesn't mean anything. Fifty guilders collected from among the membership, however, is worth a million times as much."

"You haven't told me what you really think of Sneevliet's ideas," he said, watching me even more closely now—as if I were some Menadonese Edison.

When he spoke, his head as well as every other part of his body was made to move about as if he were putting American democracy into practice within his own body just as he used to explain it.

It was amazing just how much Edison had changed him. And how ironic it was. Edison's work was to bring to life dead objects, and our work was to kill that which was alive. He was asking about the Boedi Oetomo because it was his job. I answered for the sake of my own security. He was anxious because BO had been attacked by a European, and I was anxious because as a Native I had to face these criticisms as criticisms directed at all Natives.

Our discussion went on for over two hours, something that had not happened for many, many years.

Realizing that I wasn't really answering his questions and that we were just arguing in circles, he very politely, and still in English, requested me to put my views down on paper as to what action the government should take following from Sneevliet's attacks on the Boedi Oetomo.

For two days I studied all the available documents and the telegrams that came in from the regions. There were no signs that the Boedi Oetomo was making any attempt to reply to Sneevliet's attacks. All the material that had come in to me made it more than clear that the BO leaders were in a panic. They were faced with a way of thinking that their priyayi brains could just not comprehend. For the first time BO now faced a way of thinking that was able to launch a completely unrelenting attack. Its silence was proof enough for me of the correctness of Sneevliet's views. This made my work easier. I was able to work on like a machine.

The only thing was that Sneevliet's attacks also hit the government right in the heart as well. And anyone sharing the same interests as the government would also be stung by these criticisms. That went for me too. But I decided I would say that Sneevliet was right. My own position was not important. It wasn't very difficult to prepare the report, even though so many things clashed against each other. The Boedi Oetomo was a tame organization, one on good terms with the government. The one attacking the BO was a European. And it was the government that also provided me with my livelihood. But the criticisms were correct as long as they were looked at from the point of view of the truth and not that of power, or of my own position.

From the very first sentence I made it clear:

It has become a European tradition to be always discarding old outdated thinking. It was this tradition that has kept Europe young and fresh. Sneevliet is somebody carrying on in this historical tradition. What he has been saying about the ethical duties of the government is no different from what Baron van Hoevell said half a century ago, or even what His Excellency Governor-General van Heutsz actually started to implement.

Sneevliet was pointing out the kind of deficiencies in the institutions of the colonial government that the Liberals in the lower house in Holland have long been criticizing. The activities of Mr. Van Aberon, the former director of education and culture, the formation of the Jepara Committees and their campaign to set up schools in memory of the girl from Jepara, and even the offer of help by Mr. De Veenter to help establish a girls' high school for Natives in Semarang, all serve to reflect the dissatisfaction of the radical wing of the Liberals with the Indies government's implementation of its Ethical Policy responsibilities. So to give any recognition to Sneevliet will be tantamount to the government slapping itself in the face.

The old view that Sneevliet and his friends are just a gang of radical extremists may need to be reviewed and more serious and careful attention paid to what he has been saying. From his more recent speeches it is also becoming clearer that he has brought a new kind of logic with him from Europe, a kind of logic that is as yet unknown here in the Indies. While it has always been this new logic that has given them the reputation for being extremists, more effort now needs to be put into studying this new logic.

The only pity is that these attacks have been made in public. They should have been quickly brought before the members of the Indies Council in closed session. The methods used by Sneevliet and his friends will only serve to shock society and greatly discourage the Boedi Oetomo.

For those already long annoyed that I had reached such a senior position as this—and I knew very well how the colonial mind operated—this report of mine would provide them with an ideal opportunity to accuse me of defending Sneevliet. But that was their problem. It now seemed that my responsibilities as an intellectual were at last going to lead to a clash with colonial interests. I would defend my opinions.

After I had finished writing the report and handed it in, my boss was still not satisfied. He returned the report to me with a note: "It seems you have forgotten that we need to work out what action to take. This is not supposed to be just an academic study. The Algemeene Secretariat is not a scholarly institution."

He was right. On the other hand, he did not reject what I had written. Before I had a chance to comply with his wishes, he was back in my office.

"As far as Sneevliet goes," I said, "it is better if the government just leaves him alone."

Then I repeated to him what I had repeated many times over the last few years, namely, that there was no need yet to introduce laws against the freedom of association or the right to hold public meetings. It was true, I said, that the governor-general could also always use his Extraordinary Powers, but the situation was different today. Especially with the Netherlands still at war. Those Extraordinary Powers would be better put in reserve for situations that could not be handled in any other way.

"That's not what I want to know, Mr. Pangemanann. Everybody understands that these days. And I would prefer that the governor-general not have to ask the question himself as to what action the government should take and what attitude it should display toward such a loyal organization as Boedi Oetomo."

"Oh, so that's it!" I cried, somewhat startled. And I was truly startled, because this would be the first time in the history of the colony that the government wanted to display a sympathetic attitude toward a Native organization.

"If that's the case, then the government is about to start a new tradition in dealing with Native organizations. I have never seen any mention of such a possibility in any government documents."

"Ah, but not all documents are available to be read, sir."

He was right. There are many documents written to be read only once and then destroyed.

"It's enough that I tell you," he continued, "that the government does indeed consider the Boedi Oetomo to be the one and only loyal Native organization."

"But the government has banned the priyayi from joining it in some regions."

"That's true. But those bans have been issued not because of the Boedi Oetomo itself but because in some regions the local leaderships have set out on their own independent path and have displeased the local authorities in the process."

"Aha!" I cried. Now I knew for sure there were documents about Native affairs that I was not allowed to see. "Well, if you say that your words on this will have to be enough, very well. Let me get on with it."

This additional task was not as easy to carry out as I thought it would be. I didn't have very specific information about what the government was actually thinking and I had to work from supposition. There was always the danger that I might fall into a trap and make a mistake. And that would provide another opening for my possible demise. Neither could I really quote what my boss had told me verbally. It was not absolutely certain that he was telling the truth. It was always possible that he was setting a trap for me.

So I had to think over this question for quite a long time. I studied once more all the documentary material I had. In the end I had to admit that my boss was right. It was only then that I put pen to paper once more, indicating that the government did indeed need to make it clear that it was displeased by the attacks on the Boedi Oetomo, but without saying so in so many words. The Department of Education and Culture, which had been providing subsidies to BO schools all these years but never saying much, should approach the organization. These attacks had left the BO standing alone like a little child in the rice fields. No one was listening to its sobbing. And whoever approached it at this moment and showed it some sympathy would be looked upon as even more precious than its own mother. The time had now arrived when the government should make an approach to this little child.

The best step for the government to take would be for the Department of Education and Culture to summon the leadership of the BO to meet with the head of the department. I suggested also that the people chosen to be summoned should be those who were active as teachers, because at least it would be certain that they would be proficient in speaking Dutch and thus there would be greater certainty that neither party would end up disappointed or embarrassed by the meeting. If this meeting was satisfactory, it could be taken a step further and an audience granted with His Excellency the governor-general. The other qualification was that no press reports of these meetings be allowed to ensure that no new material was provided for another attack by Sneevliet.

Not more than two days later the Boedi Oetomo leadership was received by the director of education and culture at his house. Naturally I also attended. The meeting was held in the rear grounds of the house and took the form of tea in the gardens.

The guests showed themselves to be the most obedient and subservient of Javanese priyayi, all hanging on every word spoken by the director. They never initiated discussion on a single issue, always waiting, responding, and answering.

I could see that the director was slowly becoming bored with their attitude. The meeting could turn into a failure. I whispered something to him. Taking a lead from my whispered suggestion, he invited them to come forward with any questions they had or any suggestions as to how the government might be able to help the Boedi Oetomo with any of its difficulties.

It didn't appear that they had prepared themselves for such a question. Just to get the invitation was so sensational that they were all off on cloud nine. As soon as the opportunity arose for them to come forward with questions or proposals, they were left not knowing what to do or say. Finally someone asked that positions be made available in the teachers' colleges for graduates of the Boedi Oetomo schools. Another asked for guidance as to how the BO might start setting up its own high schools and its own teachers' colleges. Still another asked if Boedi Oetomo teachers, most of whom were not trained teachers, could be provided with some additional training by the government.

The head of the Department of Education and Culture did not actually promise anything, because his guests had not really explained to him what their difficulties were. And neither side mentioned Sneevliet's attacks, even though it was obvious that everyone was in no doubt that the meeting was taking place precisely because of the attacks, which could not be let pass without a response.

The departmental secretary noted down all the suggestions.

It was also obvious that the director himself was not used to mixing with Natives. He was still unable to hide his arrogance. Just at the moment he stood up from his chair to announce that the meeting was over, one of the BO leaders asked whether or not it was time for the government to increase the representation of the BO in the Regency Councils, where the local bupati also sat.

But the director had left his chair. The allotted time had ended. And he was wise enough not to deal with this issue, which was in fact in the jurisdiction of the director of the Department of Internal Affairs.

And so that was how I elevated the Boedi Oetomo to new heights of glory, where it could revel in its new prestige and its own performance, so that it would feel immune from Sneevliet's attacks. And Meneer Director did not feel that the audience needed to be taken a step further, up to the governor-general.

One day after the meeting, my boss came in to see me very early in the morning. "You have won," he said amicably, his body moving in all directions. "The governor-general has instructed that we invite them here. Could you make the necessary preparations so that things aren't as awkward as yesterday?"

And so I began to make the necessary preparations. I summoned one of the Boedi Oetomo leaders to my office that very morning. He arrived wearing Javanese clothes and carrying his briefcase. He wasn't so tall and was a bit fat.

As soon as he entered my office, he stood, bowed forward a little, and proceeded to announce in a style reminiscent of a school assembly speech: "Representative of Boedi Oetomo, Mas Sewoyo, here fulfilling the summons of the Algemeene Secretariat." His Dutch was fluent and flawless. He had virtually eliminated his Javanese accent.

I went over to him and greeted him: "I am very pleased to meet Meneer General Secretary of the Boedi Oetomo. Please sit down, Meneer Sewoyo."

He sat down on the chair and placed his briefcase on the floor. I picked it up and put it on the desk. I caught a glimpse of his slippers, which were of poor quality leather.

"I did not see Meneer Sewoyo at the audience with the director of education and culture yesterday," I opened the agenda.

It turned out he was in Jogja when they received the invitation and was unable to get to Betawi in time.

"No doubt you were busy in Jogja discussing Sneevliet's attacks, yes?"

"Well, you might say busy, but not really, Meneer, but, yes, perhaps, you could say we were a little busy."

"And so what is Boedi Oetomo's response?"

"We are not going to answer him with just empty words. We are going to answer him with deeds," he replied as if speaking to a confidant.

"That's no doubt the best way. What deeds, for example?"

"We are going to work even harder."

"Quite right, Meneer Sewoyo. He's just a yelping dog," I said and watched his rather inscrutable face, which at the same time could speak so openly, as if to his own father.

Facing a colonial official like me, his answers revealed how backward he was as an organizer. He would never be able to defend himself if he ever had to face Sneevliet. His Dutch was excellent but his way of thinking was just as flawed as his ancestors' had been. He seemed a sincere and honest person and no doubt it was those strengths that enabled him to work so tirelessly for his organization. There was obviously no personal gain in it for him.

"I'm sorry but I have forgotten, Meneer. What was your last position with the government? A school inspector or a teacher at a teachers' college?"

"Forgive me, Meneer Pangemanann, I prefer to be thought of as a

Boedi Oetomo man," was his answer, which I thought was a rather boastful answer. "The work of looking after the younger generation of Javanese is what is most important to us."

"Of course, Meneer. Who else will pioneer this work if not the Boedi Oetomo? Everybody who recognizes the backwardness of the Javanese will realize that they must follow your example. The Javanese people should be very happy to have such leaders as yourself, Meneer."

"Ah, that's far too high praise, Meneer."

"It is a person's right to receive justified praise, Meneer."

"Thank you."

I then told him that His Excellency the governor-general wished himself to meet the Boedi Oetomo leadership that evening at five o'clock. It was hoped that the discussion would not go over the same matters that were discussed the day before. It would be better if they could indicate what were BO's most pressing concerns at the moment. And I also reminded him again that there must not be a single word about this leaked to the press.

He expressed his enormous gratitude that the government should concern itself this way with the Boedi Oetomo, and I then let him go home.

I escorted him outside the building, where once again he scraped and bowed in that traditional Javanese way that attempts to pay respect and give thanks at the same time.

I concluded from this meeting that Sewoyo was trying to convince everybody of Boedi Oetomo's conviction that none of the leaders was involved out of concern for private gain. If the BO could make even a small contribution to the younger generation's progress, then all the officials of the organization would feel happy and contented.

But if he had to debate Sneevliet, he would be challenged with the question: But in what direction are you taking the young generation? His Excellency the governor-general would not be like that. He would nod his head full of understanding and sympathy.

Sewoyo and his friends tried with all their might to speak on behalf of the organization. It was not as it was at the audience the day before. Meneer Director of Education and Culture also attended but did not say a single word. It was even possible he had been warned by the governor-general to try to be more affable. That evening the governor-general went out of his way to be friendly and polite and tried hard to tell various jokes that he had probably prepared beforehand. But he did not mention Sneevliet either.

Closing the audience, Governor-General Idenburg told them that he hoped that there would always be mutual understanding between Boedi

Oetomo and the government and that this meeting would be a beginning of something that would benefit the people they represented. He hoped that this good beginning would be continued by those who followed in their footsteps.

Tomo, one of the most important founders of the Boedi Oetomo, and now a doctor in a Mission Hospital in Blora, was never mentioned in all these discussions. Neither were any other of the founders.

And after that audience Mas Sewoyo's name rose to new heights in the colonial ferment, his name was on everybody's lips. . . .

11

Governor-General Idenburg's term of office ended. The rumors circulating that he would be appointed for a second term, like Governor-General Van Der Capellan, because of the world war, were contradicted by reality. He was going to be replaced.

And then his replacement arrived: Van Limburg Stirum.

The hand-over ceremony was a very simple affair in accordance with the general atmosphere of restraint and anxiety that prevailed in the colony, and reflecting too the special concerns of the government of the Netherlands Indies. Java was beginning to move. There was wave after wave of strikes. In every sector where goods and services were produced there were people who emerged to teach that human labor was the most important thing, not machines and not money either, and so human labor had to be recompensed in a fair and just manner. The strike waves were all demanding that wages be made fairer and more just. The government faced more and more problems as these actions resulted in a decline in the national income.

And Idenburg's departure was not surrounded by the same festivities as in the past.

I was among those who accompanied him to the port. And I saw Meneer Sewoyo there too. He looked fresh, in his Javanese dress, moving adroitly among the bupatis and residents. Meneer Idenburg also looked fresh as he busily said good-bye and spoke with all those who had come to see him off.

When the ship's whistle began to screech, people started to say their final farewells and leave the ship. Finally only the staff of the Algemeene Secretariat were left, including myself. He used this opportunity to thank us all for the help we had given him in maintaining law and order and he asked us to work even harder to help the new governor-general, His Excellency Van Limburg Stirum.

The ship departed.

And standing on the dock, I too, just like everyone else, waved good-bye, wishing him a safe journey. The family of the former governor-general stood at the ship's rails and answered our waves with their own.

The ship dwindled more and more into the distance. The black clouds of smoke from its funnel thinned out to disintegrate into the Indies sky.

Idenburg had gone. And he had left behind in the Indies a new custom—holding audiences with Native organizations. Yes, he had wanted to leave behind a good impression, that he knew how to reward as well as how to punish. There had been punishment for Raden Mas Minke, Douwager, Wardi, and Doctor Tjipto, and there had been a reward for the Boedi Oetomo in the form of his willingness to receive them in audience for an informal chitchat.

But he also left behind new work for us, caused in fact by the teachings of Sneevliet and his friends and their new logic. The situation was not getting any simpler at all. New figures emerged and then disappeared. But there were also names that did not go away—Soerjopranoto, Djojopranoto, Sostrokardono, Sostrokartono, Goenawan, Gunadi, Soekandar, Soekendar. I could hardly tell one from the other—Soematri, Mantri, Soeman . . . no less than ninety names! All involved in their different activities. All making it very clear that they did not like the government. All with their own followers. It was only the servants of the State who had not yet been on strike.

Magazines appeared like mushrooms everywhere. In Solo, Semarang, and Jogja. There were more magazines appearing in those towns than in Surabaya, and even Betawi itself. They began appearing in the small towns too, except they weren't printed but mimeographed. They were full of all sorts of different ideas, clashing one with the other. Almost all of them, especially where they were magazines published in common Malay, reflected enormous confusion as they tried to amalgamate the European way of thinking with the traditional way. And as far as their attitude to the government was concerned, they more or less shared the same outlook—they were hostile.

And of course, it was none other than myself who had to rush hither and thither trying to follow all this. Sometimes a magazine would come out only once, then appear again in five or six months' time, even though it declared itself to be a monthly or bimonthly. And most of them took no heed of the Museum Library's call for them to deposit copies with it.

In nearly every magazine there were attacks on their rivals or replies to attacks. The amazing thing was that among all this debate and polemics I never found any clashes over religion. The main issue being fought over was the meaning of the homeland and livelihood. Some glorified the notion of the homeland. It was the homeland that brought into existence the nation of people who possessed it, and whose task it was to look after, develop, and defend it. The others said to hell with the homeland. Even if we were living at the South Pole, if it gave us our livelihood, then that was our homeland. Our homeland is nature itself. The arguments and polemics never stopped.

For the first time the questions of nationalism and internationalism entered into the Natives' ideological world, even though they did not use those terms. And all of this was the echo of the conflicts taking place over there in Europe.

That's how things were—and I remembered then Meneer L—'s lectures. Everything that is born here on Java is nothing but the echo of what happens on mainland Asia, and now Europe too, but without being based on real principles.

Perhaps I can use Meneer L—'s words as a guide for the time being. But perhaps too Sneevliet intended to teach people how to hold to principles. And Baars too was no longer confining himself to speaking in East Java but was roaming about Central Java too.

And all of this had to be dealt with by Governor-General Van Limburg Stirum. And we were the ones who would have to come up with the schemes and plans of what had to be done.

He entered the palace.

In East and Central Java people were shouting for wage rises while refusing to work, or "staking" as the Dutch say. Pawnshop employees in several places refused to go into the shops and stayed outside joining the crowds who wanted to pawn something. Then plantation laborers joined in.

A businessman from one of the big European companies lost his temper and called the workers "pigs": "You push them, you pull them, they won't move, they just 'mogok'—stop work." Since then the terms "refused to work" and "staking" were replaced by "mogok" as the word everyone used for "strike."

Of all the areas of Native activity, it was journalism that was considered to be the most important. Of course, by journalism I don't mean European-style journalism, but I mean writing in public with your name right up front, either your real name, pen name, or initials. This new phenomenon certainly originated with Raden Mas Minke. He once told one of his friends that a person can be as clever as all the world but as long as he can't put pen to paper he will disappear into society and from history. According to the girl from Jepara, to write is to do work that is eternal. And the Indies style of journalism was a natural mixture of the Natives' need for leadership and eternity.

New public figures were not looked upon seriously if their words could not be read on paper. The same applied to the Natives in the Netherlands. Wardi did not write, but Sostrokartono launched himself into the Dutch journalistic ferment. Even though he used a pen name, people knew who he was. Then Djojokartono arrived and stated in an interview that he would follow the example of Sostrokartono, who, by the way, came from Jepara. Djojopranoto himself, a German citizen, had left Germany after finishing his military service, escaped, and now resided in the Netherlands.

There is something interesting about this Djojopranoto. Like me, he too was the adopted son of an apothecary, but a German. And just like Raden Mas Minke, he was a brilliant student at the Batavia Medical School. His writings were full of youthful spirit, both in German and in Dutch. He wrote quite differently from Sostrokartono, whose pieces were calm and convincing.

In Java Sostrokardono seemed to be copying Sostrokartono's style. Every sentence groped for substance and poise.

Marco did not publish anything at all in the Netherlands. What could he have published with his poor Dutch and limited knowledge? The one I was most sad about was, of course, Siti Soendari. She too didn't write. I don't know whether she continued her studies there or not. If she used her time there to study and then returned to the Indies later, she would become a writer with real substance and ability.

Now that they weren't writing, Marco and Siti Soendari disappeared off the chessboard. But I, Pangemanann with two n's, still kept note of what they were doing.

And in Java too the names of those two people were slowly being forgotten. Goenawan and Sostrokardono seemed to be emerging as the new centers. Soerjopranoto was the motor, always seeking new ways to bankrupt the European companies and cause more losses to the national revenues.

During the first days of Governor-General Van Limburg Stirum's administration, he didn't seem to want to know about any of this. The staff at the Algemeene Secretariat were very worried and tense. There was more and more turmoil outside the palace. The pro-government organizations seemed to be unable to go on the offensive. We all suspected that the new governor-general was uninterested in what was happening. And if that was the case, then perhaps the Secretariat itself needed to take more initiatives of its own.

A week had gone by and the governor-general had not met anybody. From his servants, we heard that he and his wife were busy arranging their furniture. A whole week! Meanwhile the plantation administrators and the European businesses were all more and more worried. They were all hoping for a new and firm policy, one that meant harsh measures to stop these developments.

It was nine days after His Excellency's arrival that my director was summoned. A little while later, the governor-general, accompanied by his adjutants, came to our offices. He inspected them all. He did not seem at all menacing. He smiled a lot, and didn't speak much. His eyes shone with a certain calmness, but his somewhat bald head was often nodding, though never shaking.

Two hours after he left our office, the word started to spread—Her Majesty's government in the Netherlands was very concerned with developments in the Indies and in Java in particular. The policy he brought with him was to continue with the recent new initiatives in the Indies as well as Europe. The increasing aggressiveness of the Native organizations must not be tackled head-on. The situation must not be allowed to deteriorate, which might be the result of a frontal assault.

And that meant that our office would soon be flooded with European businessmen. They would want to bring Van Limburg Stirum under their influence. And it wasn't something impossible either! There were many governors-general kept in the Algemeene Secretariat's grip for as long as big business's tribute to our high officials was considered adequate.

I could just see how the game was going to unfold. And because I was in charge of Native affairs, I held the key to the whole situation. Just one yes, a scribble of my signature, and I would be rolling in money. . . .

So the days passed and there was less and less work to do. I was like a spider waiting in the center of my web for my victims to arrive. It would be at most a month and then the businessmen would start arriving at my door. They would be very polite and engage in quite entertaining chatter, offering me this and that. I would be able to get anything I wanted, everything would come flowing in, whatever I desired and longed for. I would play hard to get with all my superiors. My signature as the official expert must be able to produce at least a hundred or two hundred times my monthly salary. How easy life would be, how happy I would be.

With there being so little work, I used the time to return to my study of Raden Mas Minke's manuscripts. My nights were free now too, so I had time to enjoy myself and all the pleasures of the world.

The evening arrived when I had arranged for Rientje de Roo to stay over with me at my house.

I must, of course, note down something about this remarkable young prostitute who was the most expensive and popular girl in Betawi.

She was perhaps no more than eighteen years old. If I have estimated her to be younger than she really is, it is only because she has a natural talent to keep her youthful look, or is very clever in looking after her body. She was very respectful, clever at conversation, and very clever at seeing to a man's needs. The Dutch have a saying that good grapes need no wreath of flowers. And indeed, she never needed to advertise herself anywhere. And she never had a free day, she was always in demand. If I had not been such an important person or as generous, I would probably have to wait a month at least.

Earlier in the afternoon I had ordered my servant to clean up my bedroom. The mattresses had to be changed. I myself sprinkled the sheets with eau de cologne. There were wreaths of flowers in every room that she might visit that night.

That evening after bathing, I inspected myself before the mirror. My stomach was beginning to bulge. My cheeks were beginning to droop. There was one more chicken-claw mark at the corner of my eyes. But at least, thank goodness, my skin was not yet wrinkling up. Who knows how much longer the skin on my face will hold up? How quickly time passes.

But I felt that I was on top of everything. Was it really possible that I would suffer the same fate as other people? That experience called death? At the very least, I was sure I would reach the age of eighty years. I felt as if I had lost none of the strength I had when I was eighteen years old. Many women wanted me—Pure-Bloods, Eurasians, let alone Natives. And while a man feels he is attractive, he can never grow old! He will always remain young! Eternal youth. See, my skin is not at all dried out like my wife's.

If Rientje de Roo were not a prostitute, I am sure she would want to be my wife. And what if she were my wife? Would life be merrier? At the moment that beautiful girl belonged to whoever could pay. Even though I knew that was the case, I preferred her to the Japanese or Chinese, or Natives. I had lost all interest in European women.

Looking into the mirror, I also conjured up the image of Rientje, her skin, the way she treated me. Not a single flaw. For a moment I was reminded of the beautiful girl that Raden Mas Minke had described. Her name had been Annelies. And if the Modern Pitung praised a woman's beauty, there could be no doubt that she would have been incredibly beautiful. And perhaps Rientje could have rivaled her. But I wasn't dreaming of some beauty while hiding behind Minke's name. Minke wasn't here now, and this was my own dream. Except I did not need to dream about Rientje. There was no need to win her as proof of my manhood as Minke had been challenged to do by Robert Suurhof. It was enough for me to summon her, and she would come.

There is something else that is worth noting down here about this woman. During the last few years, stories had circulated that since Suurhof became an invalid, two other men had died fighting over the chance to be with her. Three others had been severely injured. A merchant had gone bankrupt trying to outbid another client. But Pangemanann needed only to summon, and she would surely come.

I put on a long tie—they were just becoming fashionable in the Indies. The deep blue tie stood out peacefully against my white shirt. Then, before I had put on my trousers, there was a knock on the door. Without waiting for my permission, my servant, cheeky as usual, came in and said: "You have guests, Tuan."

"I'm not seeing anybody tonight, not until tomorrow. Tell them I've gone."

"But it is the police, Tuan, from Betawi."

"The police?"

"Tell him I am not here."

"He's already sat himself down, Tuan."

"Jesus Christ!"

I hurriedly pulled on my trousers and left the room without looking back.

A police agent first class was squatting on a low bench some distance away from the divan. His hat was lying on the floor. He was wearing leggings but no shoes. He jumped up and saluted when he saw me come in.

"Sarimin!" I knew his name.

"It is I, Meneer."

"Who gave orders for you to come here?"

"I have some business, Meneer, very, very important business."

"Come on then, tell me. I am busy tonight."

"She won't be arriving, Meneer."

"You're a cheeky bastard, aren't you? Where do you get the cheek to speak like that?"

"That is why Police Agent First Class Sarimin is here, Meneer. Noni Rientje won't be coming."

For a moment I was quite startled and then I studied his face very closely.

"Who is Noni Rientje?" I asked.

"She lives in Gondangdia."

"I don't know her."

"You have been with her eight times," he said firmly.

What was this mad policeman up to? Was he here to question me?

"Sit down, Sarimin," I ordered, and he sat down. "Now tell me clearly who was it that told you to come here."

"I am on a case, Meneer."

For a second time, I was caught off guard. My mind's eye began to picture Rientje de Roo being interrogated and telling about me and Robert Suurhof.

"Stop beating around the bush. What case?"

"Noni Rientje, Meneer."

"What about her?"

"She's been murdered."

He told me what happened down to the smallest detail. She had been last seen with a young Chinese man.

"Why are you telling me all this?"

"Because your name was also mentioned."

"My name?"

"Mentioned eight times in relation to eight meetings."

"Who mentioned me?"

"It's all here, Meneer." He took out a red leather notebook. "It's all written down here, Meneer, all important people, Meneer, including you."

"Let me see that book."

"This book is not leaving my hands, Meneer. Only Police Agent Sarimin has the right to read this." He spoke without looking at me, his head bowed.

"So Rientje is dead? Really dead?"

"Dead, Meneer. But the book she left behind is not dead, Meneer. A prostitute who kept a notebook. I have never come across this before."

I knew that my reputation was in danger. I knew that I could not be connected to the murder. But it was almost certain that Robert Suurhof was involved, and if my connection with him became known it could do me a lot of damage as well as shame me. "What does it say about me?"

"It is all here, Meneer."

"Let me read it."

"You don't need to read it," he said. "Do you know Noni Rientje de Roo's handwriting?"

"No."

"Then I'm right, you don't need to read it."

"Has anyone else in the police read it?"

"Only me, Meneer, just me, really."

"Very well. How much money do you want, Sarimin?"

Only then did he look at me. Just for a moment. Then he bowed his head again.

"One of our children is getting married soon, Meneer."

"You're not marrying anyone off. You're just going to gamble, that's all. You never win, but you go on playing anyway. Fifteen. Enough?"

He laughed, the rotten blackmailer.

"Twenty?"

"You get about a thousand a month, Meneer, maybe more."

"Who told you that?"

"It all costs money, Meneer. Even the taxi to bring me here."

"Is there any mention of Robert Suurhof?"

"Everything Meneer can guess is in here," he said, patting the note-book as he spoke. Then he put it back in his pocket.

"Twenty-five."

"You remember the name Princess Kasiruta, Meneer, I'm sure. Her name is in here too. You needn't worry, Meneer."

"Who is this Princess Kasiruta?" I asked, pretending to be amazed. No doubt Suurhof had talked about the time she defended her husband with a pistol.

He didn't answer. He stood up, ready to excuse himself.

"Fifty, Sarimin."

"Useless, Meneer."

"I will pay you in lead."

"Lead will be repaid with lead, Meneer."

"One hundred! That's eight months' salary for you."

"My duty is worth more than eight months' salary, Meneer. Even three times that amount would not make me betray my duty."

"When did you learn to blackmail people, Sarimin?"

"You should be able to answer that question better than I, Meneer Pangemanann." He began to raise his hands to salute good-bye. "Your job should be worth more to you than nine times one hundred guilders."

He wanted nine hundred guilders, this filthy blackmailer in his police-man's uniform. Rientje de Roo never got more than twenty guilders from me, on top of food and transport. But Sarimin knew that I would lose everything if that book became public—position, money, and reputation. While I also knew that I could not afford to pay that much.

"How much do you want, Sarimin?"

"Nine hundred."

"That's a great deal."

"Just by picking up the phone you can get ten times that amount."

"So you say!"

"You received all the wealth and belongings of Raden Mas Minke."

"Who said that?"

"Everybody."

God! Everybody. This is a rumor spread by the supporters of the Modern Pitung! That's the only explanation. Perhaps Sarimin is one of his admirers too.

"Who do you mean, 'everybody'?"

"I will only say in a court. Isn't this Raden Mas Minke's house?"

The rumors are as bad and evil as that. I wanted to smash his head in.

"You're a member of the Sarekat!" I accused him. "I will have you investigated!"

"Very well then, Meneer. We will face each other in court. Forgive me. My taxi has been waiting a long time."

For a moment I thought of calling the palace security and getting them to help me seize the book. But it was impossible. That way even more people would know about the book's existence.

"Sarimin!" I called out.

He stopped, but did not come back. I was forced to walk out to him.

"Very well, Sarimin. Nine hundred. But I don't have that much on me. You'll have to take three hundred as a deposit."

"Very well, Meneer. But the book will have to stay with me."

"Come back and I will give you the money."

But he was too clever to come back inside. I was going to threaten him with my revolver. I was forced to use what was left of my month's wages—three hundred guilders. He refused to give a receipt, and even seemed a bit reluctant to take the money, and he said: "You will call on me at my house in one week's time to pay the rest and get this book."

"You are a real bastard, Sarimin!"

"I think there are worse bastards than me, Meneer. A lowly policeman, that was me, perhaps until I was pensioned off!"

He bowed, excused himself, grasping the three hundred in his hand. And I had no idea how I was going to get the rest of the money within seven days.

Back inside the house, I collapsed onto the sofa. Impotent in my anger, I felt all alone in the world. Everywhere I looked I saw a threat. I felt like the girl from Jepara's father must have felt, and Siti Soendari's father. I was afraid of losing my position, which meant losing everything. In the old days, I had never once been confronted with an extortionist. Now even a lowly constable dared do this to me! Perhaps I was no longer walking in the field of mud, but had sunk completely beneath it!

Then a thought came to me. A smile came to my face. Why should I be afraid? I too can do this! I can blackmail people who have far more than I, rich people, people who have more than they need of everything.

I jumped up. I must not waver. I must carry through this idea. What evil is there in blackmailing as long as nobody finds out? My name must not be soiled.

"Food!" I shouted at my servant.

As soon as dinner was put before me, I lost my appetite.

I felt empty. I remembered that Rientje de Roo's body would not comfort me tonight. She had been turned into a forty-nine kilogram heap of flesh that was probably already beginning to rot. How strange life was. Yesterday all the wealthy and high-class men were lusting after her. Today not a single person would make the visit to see her.

How fragile was human life. Yesterday people were prepared to die to be with her. Now she was just a memory to a few people who would be too ashamed to tell their families of their acquaintance with her.

The news of Rientje de Roo's murder was the number-one news item in all the papers in Betawi and Bandung the next day. After I read them all, I went straight to my boss, intending to ask for a loan from the office cash. But I was too ashamed to ask. All that came out of my mouth was the question: "Are there any files for me to work on?"

"Quite a few, but they don't need to be worked on yet."

Finally I asked for two days' leave. He had no objections. I went straight to the Javaache Bank. That was the first time I ever borrowed any money. One thousand five hundred guilders. I jumped into the taxi and headed off to Betawi. And it wasn't that easy to find Sarimin. He was out on duty all day. I sat and waited for him in his house. His wife became worried by my presence. I excused myself and said I would come back later. I left, and spent the next few hours pacing the streets. I came back but Sarimin still wasn't home. I left again and bought an afternoon paper. There were even more sensational reports about Rientje de Roo. I bought another paper. No less fantastic. I bought a Chinese-Malay paper and its news was even more sensational. All this could spell disaster for me. All of it!

When I returned for the third time, Sarimin was at last there.

"The newspapers are getting more sensational all the time, Meneer."

"Where is it?" I asked straight away.

"If you have brought your goods with you, then, okay, we can go for a walk to a certain place."

We left. I swore to myself that I would be on my guard all the time and would keep my eyes open for any opportunity.

Walking along a dark lane, I whispered: "I should shoot you in the head right here. Nobody would ever know."

That was what I really wanted to do. But I would never dare do it before I knew for certain that he had the notebook with him.

"Yes, that's exactly what I was thinking I should do to you," he answered insolently.

My blood began to boil.

"Don't get me angry."

"I know your type, Tuan," he answered. "If I slipped my knife into you now, Tuan, then you too would know who is Sarimin. But we are just conducting some honest business. I need money. You need to protect your name. You need position and rank. What haven't I done for you? I could have handed this book in to the authorities. You would be in big trouble then—your children would be ashamed of having a father like you."

"Very well, let's deal with each fairly then."

"How have I been unfair to you?"

We went into a satay stall on the side of the road and ordered something to eat. We ate but all the time he was sneaking glances at me.

"Let's get this over with," I whispered in between mouthfuls.

"Let me count what you have brought first."

While continuing to eat, I took out from a rather heavy bag twenty-five silver coins. One at a time, again and again, I counted them out until it reached one hundred guilders.

"You're still short," he reminded me. His eyes watched me closely as he pulled off another piece of satay from its skewer.

"A hundred should do you. I'll be bankrupted."

"Do you want me to up it to a thousand?" His eyes watched closely.

I brought out four more coins. I piled them up on the bench where we were sitting, between my legs.

"Where's your capital?" I demanded.

He took out a red book from a calico bag.

"Here," he said. "But this is only a copy."

"A copy?" I stopped eating and put down my spoon.

"Don't worry. I have the original. I don't want anyone ever to be able to have anything on me, anything at all."

"You bastard!"

"Nobody better to say that than you, Meneer."

My suspicions reached a climax—was he playing some trick on me?

"I want both the original and the copy."

"I will burn the copy here before your own eyes, Tuan, if we can resolve everything properly," he answered frustratingly.

"Here!" he called to the satay seller. "Fetch me some kerosene." He threw him a few coins.

The satay-man went outside and the stall was left empty.

He took a silk bag from his pocket. There seemed to be a small but quite thick book inside.

"You will get what you want, Tuan, as soon as you put what I want in my calico bag. If you don't believe me anymore, that's fine too. You'll lose the three hundred guilders you have paid me, and we needn't have anything to do with each other anymore."

It looked as if I was not going to be able to cow this rotten bastard. If I had been able to use him instead of Suurhof for my other work, perhaps I would have met with more success. I was really sorry that I was meeting him only now.

"Very well then. Take the money before the satay-man comes back."

He took the parcel of money and counted it into his little calico bag.

"It's all here, Tuan. There's honor among bastards after all, heh, Tuan?" The words tripped insolently from his tongue. He handed over the small silk bag containing the small book. "Here it is, Tuan. I hope you are happy now." He held out his hand to finalize the deal.

"Just a minute." I refused to take his hand.

I took the book and flicked through the pages. It was indeed the writing of a woman. On the first page there were the words, "Rientje de Roo," as well as place and date. On the other side was the handwriting of a man ordering her to note down all the details of the clients she went with. She had to note down their rank and position, as well as date, time, and place. And I recognized the handwriting. It belonged to Robert Suurhof. This was the real thing all right.

I held out my hand. We shook hands. The satay-man returned with some kerosene. Sarimin burned the other red book, the copy, in front of us. Then he gave the *warung* owner a shiny silver guilder.

The satay-man just watched everything we did without ever seeming to want to ask any questions.

"Nah," Sarimin began again. "You wait here for five minutes, Tuan; then you can leave. Five minutes, Tuan, just to ensure your safety, heh! You won't forget, heh?" His voice descended to a whisper. "If you leave before the five minutes are up, Tuan, I cannot guarantee your safety."

He stood, nodded his respects, and walked into the darkness of the night. He vanished.

Even during the taxi trip back to Buitenzorg, I could not throw off my amazement that the Natives could produce such a fantastic criminal! As soon as I arrived home, I telephoned police headquarters in Betawi to check on his background. It was soon revealed to me that he was the adopted son of a Eurasian family, who had all since died of tuberculosis. He proved himself to be quite a capable policeman, rising more quickly than most to the position of agent first class.

He had absorbed European cunning, I thought. Such a crime as this had never before occurred in Native criminal history. Anyway, whether cunning or not, he had certainly cost me a lot of money.

My name was, in fact, mentioned eight times in Rientje de Roo's diary. Some of the other names may have been false, but there were several that I recognized and whose positions I knew. They were all high officials. Robert Suurhof's name appeared only once. This was on the first page where he had written out his order that Rientje note down everything. Rientje's diary actually contained only the names of the men she slept with and how much they paid. It also noted how much she handed over to RS, no doubt initials that stood for Robert Suurhof. These amounts had grown larger from the time Suurhof was laid up in the Bandung Hospital until the last entry.

During the last six months she had been receiving more and more Chinese, and last week there were even more. During the last month of her life, there were only Chinese. My name, the last name to be mentioned, was the only exception. The last entry was on the day of her planned visit to Buitenzorg. She died just before she was to leave to come to me.

I was silently grateful that I had been able to get hold of this book. Although there was nothing in the book that would have had too evil consequences for me, it would still have caused me great public embarrassment. I would now be short of money for a few months, but I would remain the same unblemished Pangemanann as always.

Rientje! How short was your life. Woman! You passed briefly into my life, bringing with you a different story than others. But you always remained a woman. And womankind was created by God for men. And men for women. You trod your own path in giving yourself to men. Different from Madame Pangemanann. Different from the way Annelies gave herself to Minke. Or Ang San Mei to the Modern Pitung. Was it true that the Catholic Ang San Mei could give herself to the Protestant Khouw Ah Soe and then to the Moslem Raden Mas Minke? And then there was San-ikem who gave herself to Herman Mellema. How numerous were the different paths that bring together men and women. And is it correct to describe all these relationships as women giving themselves to men?

Madame to Monsieur Pangemanann was based on mutual affection, each giving himself and herself to the other. It was the same with Annelies and Minke. Rientje gave herself to whoever could pay the money that she asked for, but the essence of the surrender was the same. Sanikem gave herself because of *force majeure*, because of a stronger force that acted against her will. And what about Ang San Mei? Why did she give herself to Minke? I could understand what bound her to Khouw Ah Soe—they shared the same ideals for the liberation of China. This thing they shared between them strengthened them together. But why with Modern Pitung? I would try to find out whether this story (a somewhat unconvincing story) was true or not.

And Rientje and Suurhof? She even looked after him financially all this while, even while he was an invalid in hospital and could not engage in his usual banditry.

How great in number are the secrets between men and women which I would never know? Well, in any case, the reality is that Rientje will never give herself to me again. Never. She had died, without my feeling any loss. Madame Pangemanann had left, and I had felt no loss then either. My children went away and I felt no loss about that either. So why was it then that I would feel a loss if my position was taken away and my reputation soiled in public?

You have become an asocial being, Pangemanann. You think only of yourself. You have begun to get used to the world centering on you, only for you. There is nothing else but you alone. All your knowledge and learning is now mobilized for one purpose and one purpose alone—to justify yourself and your passions. You have made yourself a god. You no longer have any value even to yourself, Pangemanann. Even Sarimin, a scummy little bandit and blackmailer like that, has defeated you! These are the fruits of your life! You didn't need to go to university just to become such a person as you are now, Pangemanann! An illiterate village child could have done just as well. Probably even better! Even Oblomov, who dreamed of paradise on earth as well as in heaven, all without having to work and strive, was perhaps even better than you. He did no harm to anyone but himself, just becoming the butt of everybody's jokes. You are kaput, Pan-gemanann! Kaput! Kaput! Kaput!

The newspaper reports on the Rientje de Roo case took up more and more of the front page. Every paper in the Indies—Dutch, Malay, and Chinese-Malay—broadcast her name, reports on the murder, and the names of all those involved. The reports reached fever pitch when the matter was brought before the court.

Fifteen days is not a short time. I lost my appetite for the whole two weeks. I couldn't think. My heart no longer beat regularly. There was just one sentence that I sat waiting for—the sentence that would involve me in the case. Just one sentence, a sentence that could result in my heart bursting, and this life would be over. And I would follow after Rientje into the next world. Each day I had only one prayer, the same prayer that mankind always prays—save me, yes, do not betray me, Sarimin. Please don't betray me. Save my honor, even though it is the honor shared among bandits. Yes, Sarimin, save me, Sarimin, Sarimin.

It was the writings of Tan Boen Kim that set my heart racing most. He used traditional police methods to get his material—research, interviews, and on-the-spot inspections. Step by step he moved closer to where I was lurking.

I quickly requested a report on him. It turned out he was a young, poor, local Chinese who lived in a Chinese temple in old Betawi. All he did was write, nothing else but write. No one knew who taught him to read and write. Differing from Lie Kim-Hok who received a special education from the priest, Hoornsma, Tan Boen Kim did not write general articles but specialized in crime stories.

"I don't want to see anyone today," I told my servant. "I do not want to be disturbed by anyone. I've got enough of a headache as it is. . . ." I could imagine Sarimin spying on me, and Tan Boen Kim peeping over the fence. "Even if the police come, tell them I am out, understand?"

"Your servant, Tuan. But Tuan must not drink so much. I am tired of mopping up the floor."

"Isn't that your job?"

"Of course. But there is so much washing to do as well," she protested.

"Do you need some help?"

"No, Tuan. I can handle it by myself."

"Enough then. Leave me alone; I want to do some work."

I took out the manuscript of *This Earth of Mankind* and was about to start reading it again for the umpteenth time. Long pencil strokes in the margin on some pages indicated the passages that I had to reread. These were all about the change from the Native way of thinking to the European way of thinking. The different ways that the change made itself felt, the transformations in tastes and views. And it always came back to Sanikem.

I did once discuss this extraordinary woman with Meneer L—. Was it possible for somebody to jump from one era to another, somebody from a primitive society? He smiled as he observed me. And his smile reminded me of a sentence out of the manuscript by Modern Pitung himself. Never underestimate the abilities of another human being. And Meneer L— explained that with fifteen years of education even somebody from the Stone Age could achieve the same levels of learning as in the West. While in these Indies, Meneer, he went on, it is precisely women who have been behind Native society's great achievements. It could be proved that the greatness of Majapahit was because of none other than Gayatri, the founding princess of the Majapahit dynasty, who made possible the birth of Gajah Mada, and who blessed and defended his actions.

"I have locked the sideboard, Tuan. No more drinking until tomorrow." I could hear my servant's whisperings in my ear. How much power she exercised over me now. Sanikem wasn't like this, that's for sure. She was a dominating woman . . . and this woman wanted to dominate as well. Was it true that women had a natural tendency to subdue men and keep men in their grip? And what about Surati in *Child of All Nations*? And Surati's mother? And Ang San Mei? And Minem? And Minke's mother? What was her name? Meneer L— says that it was women who were behind all the great achievements in the Indies. But everybody in her life had forgotten the name of Minke's mother.

I stood up. My thoughts would be plagued forever by all this confusion.

"I have the key to the sideboard, Tuan. I will not give it to you."

Hell! She had been standing behind me all this time.

She still wasn't going to give me the key.

I stood over her, hands on hips. She wasn't the least afraid.

Not the least.

"What is your name, tell me."

"Tuminah, Tuan."

"Don't you have a husband?"

"Lhoh! Tuan is asking things like that, about husbands and everything?"

I took Modern Pitung's manuscripts into the bedroom, locked the door, and for the umpteenth time examined myself in the mirror.

You are getting old, too, Pangemanann, Jacques. There is no one else in the world who cares anything about you except Tuminah. It is she who is taking care of all your needs in this last lonely part of your life. Everybody outside this house is trying to slash you up and swallow you.

Ah, this little life that is left me. Why do I have to live so miserably? What for? Sarimin might even try pressuring me again. And Tan Boen Kim might one day receive a whispered message from the spirit of Rientje de Roo so that my name too would be announced in the papers. I began brooding, with myself as audience.

The trial would continue, and you, Pangemanann, might find yourself seated there not just as a witness but also . . . Didn't anybody know that you had an appointment with Rientje de Roo on the day of her death? You might have a dozen alibis, but it is not you in charge of the case! It is the prosecutor! There! He has a savage look on his face, and he is pointing and shaking his fist. Yes, he could do that to me! Him! And the judge grimaces, showing his canines. And Jan Tantang, Khouw Ah Soe, Darsam, the de la Croix family, Kommer, Sanikem, Surati, Minke—they all give evidence against me, accusing me, crying out and shouting.

"God! God!"

Then suddenly the court disappeared. There was a knocking on my door from outside.

"Tuan! Tuan! Get up. What's the matter? Tuan!"

My chest was heaving with panting. I climbed off the bed. My whole body was weak. I could hardly stand. I stumbled, wobbling, across to the door and opened it.

"What is it, Tuan?" She was startled to see my condition. "What have you done to yourself?"

"Get me a drink."

She grabbed hold of me and led me back to the bed.

"I will fetch some, Tuan. But no hard drink."

"Brandy! Fetch me brandy!"

"I will bring only water, that's all, Tuan."

"Do you want me to kill you? I'll shoot . . ."

"Then I will leave here."

"No, no. Bring me brandy."

"Water."

"Brandy!"

"Water."

"Brandy!"

"I want to leave here, Tuan. Give me my wages."

"Help me to the telephone."

And she helped me across. She kept hold of me while I was telephoning the doctor, somebody who knew nothing about me at all. But even though he was a doctor, he was still paid help. He had to do whatever he was told. But he would help anybody who was in my condition, whether the patient could pay or not. Only I and my friends live off other people's suffering.

A woman's voice answered. Tuan doctor was not at home. I left a message, along with my address. Tuminah then took me back to my bed. She pulled the blanket over me and pulled down the mosquito net.

If Paulette were here, or Dede . . . No, not Rientje, she would probably leave me here. What about Annelies, what would she do?

My throat was so dry and my bladder was so full. I had to go to the toilet. How weak and feeble my body was. Were these the signs of my approaching death? My hands groped toward the edge of the bed.

"Yes, Tuan." I saw Tuminah wake up from her place on the floor under the bed. She pulled open the mosquito net, just like a mother looking after her favorite child.

"I have a piss pot here, Tuan. And water."

"Brandy!"

"I have had a look, Tuan. The sideboard is empty, Tuan. There is only water."

She helped me over to the corner of the room, where I had to go.

"Turn off the lights!" I ordered.

"Tuan is not embarrassed because of me, surely not, Tuan? Aren't I the one who's been looking after you all this time?"

After climbing back onto my bed, I looked once again at this girl whose name I had learned only today. She was young, strong, and perhaps kindhearted.

"How much do you get paid?" I whispered in her ear.

"When the mistress was here—two *rupiah*, Tuan."

"What do you mean—when the mistress was here?"

"I haven't been paid anything since then, Tuan."

"God!" How many months has it been since Paulette left? How many? God! I couldn't count anymore. . . . "Brandy!"

"The sideboard is empty."

"Go to the shop! A note! Fetch pen and paper."

"Go to sleep, Tuan. It's almost daylight." She pulled the blanket over me again. She rubbed my fingers and toes. "You're so cold, Tuan. Will I make you some herbal balm?"

Suddenly there was the indistinct sound of voices.

"What is it?"

"The front door, Tuan, someone is knocking."

"Who is it?" Tan Boen Kim? Sarimin? Pitung? Modern Pitung? She mustn't go. "Don't open the door."

She went to leave the room. She said it was the doctor. I didn't believe her.

"No, don't go. Don't go. Don't open the door! Noooo!"

She went and my heart began pounding. . . .

The doctor ordered me to stay at home for two weeks. The news
reports about Rientje de Roo's murder became fewer and fewer, then
disappeared altogether.

Tuminah was the only person to look after me. And she never relented
from her refusal to give me drink. She did everything. I don't know where
she got money. The food she cooked was very plain. Sometimes there was
no meat or egg or even oil. Just rice and a few greens. I amazed myself by
eating so much of this goat's food.

The office cashier came around to the house to pay me, minus what
I owed to the bank. I also asked him to arrange for money to be sent to
my wife and children in the Netherlands.

"You won't have enough left for the doctor, Meneer," the cashier
said to me.

He was right. I never had money troubles when Paulette was here.
Not even during the early years of our marriage. Not even after our youngest was born. And now the only person who was here to help me was a
village woman and even her Malay was still full of Sundanese words.

As long as sex wasn't involved in the relationship, said Meneer L—,
one day you too would discover an extraordinary Indies woman, someone
who stood head and shoulders above any man. This has been the case since
ancient times, Meneer. What praise has not been heaped on the just rule
of Queen Shima? And now the world finally stands in admiration of Tjuet
Njak Dhien for her leadership in the Acehnese struggle against the Dutch.

Meneer L— was bound to believe in Sanikem. I never mentioned
Princess Kasiruta to him. I never talked about Siti Soendari. I never talked
about Rohana Kudus from the little village of Fort de Koch in West Sumatra. The areas outside Java also gave birth to pioneering women. And
here, beside me now, there was Tuminah, illiterate, from a village, understanding only the language of her mother. She has never read a book in all
her life. Her education consists only of the legends of the Mahabarata and
the Ramayana and the village superstitions. And she had given to me everything she knew about kindness. And she had in fact given herself as well.

Did not life and living get stranger and stranger? Or was it I who had
become so strange, to myself as well as everyone else? To heaven and to
earth.

Ah, perhaps I knew why I was so restless. I had not been doing any
reading all this time. I wasn't allowed to read. And Tuminah tore from my

hands everything I started to read. The village woman was wielding more power over me every day, making me more and more dependent on her every day. Perhaps this Tuminah was like Queen Shima in ancient times, or was Queen Shima like her?

I had given her ten guilders. I asked her what she did with so much money.

To pay the grocery debts, Tuan.

Oh, God! And it was all for me. And I couldn't give her any more. I was bankrupt for the rest of the month.

This house, this house of Minke's, was perhaps an accursed house. I left the house and walked to my office. My office was silent and dust covered all the furniture. Gloom filled the room. De Lange had once lain at the feet of the table after drinking poison. He had taken the easiest path to end his existence. Perhaps death was the most appealing of comrades. Perhaps. Death ended everything. But believers thought that death was in fact the beginning, the beginning of a new life in the hereafter. And my education had made me into a believer. If De Lange had chosen a new birth because he could no longer deal with this life, would he choose a new birth again because of boredom with death?

Nicolaas Knor entered and apologized that my office was so dirty.

"None of us dared enter without your permission," he said. "I'll get the papers brought in soon."

I sat down in my chair. And Knor came back with a pile of newspapers. He very politely placed them on my desk. On top of the pile was a big envelope addressed to me personally. I found three copies of the book *Si Pitung* by J. Pangemanan. I should have been happy. But no, I hadn't the slightest desire to read even a single page. There was also another announcement in the book: Soon to be published—*Nyai Painah*, by Kommer. Perhaps he was the same Kommer who was Minke's friend in Modern Pitung's writings.

I suddenly became interested in this Kommer. I had heard a little about this man. I quickly wrote a memorandum to be sent to Surabaya seeking more information on who this Kommer really was.

After three hours of reading through the Malay papers, a reply arrived from Surabaya. Kommer, the journalist, had just recently died in Surabaya in an accident. One of the snakes that he kept had wrapped itself around him and crushed his arm and his backbone. He had left all his animals to the Surabaya zoo.

He had created something before he died that he could leave behind. And what about me?

Death! Death! What was better, death or a life like this? I too can give something to the world. I called an attendant and I ordered him to put the *Si Pitung* books into an envelope. I wrote Raden Mas Minke's address on the envelope and ordered him to post it off.

Meanwhile, a representative of the Sugar Syndicate had been waiting for me in the reception area.

He was young, slim, clean-shaven, and his face was yet unmarked by the slightest crease. He held out his hand to me, and I could see in his face all the signs of arrogance as he began his dealings with a Native.

"People have recommended that I come and see you, Meneer. I have been trying to see you for several days now. But you have been ill. You still don't look very well."

He rested his hands on the desk. He wore a ring with a big diamond surrounded by smaller stones. It sparkled with a bluish-white light and somehow stirred an empty, anguished feeling inside me.

"You like diamonds?" he said suddenly.

"There is something that you want to discuss?" I asked.

He had spoken with my boss about the troubles in the sugar plantations in East, Central, and West Java. And I couldn't follow everything he was saying. It felt as if there was a great rock banging into my forehead. He spoke for more than half an hour. I just listened, only half understanding.

"It seems you're not really recovered yet, Meneer. I might come back tomorrow or the day after. Excuse me."

He excused himself and left. And my head throbbed. Sentences rebounded back and forth inside my throat like bouncing balls. I knew that I did not have to suffer like this. Wasn't it true that I had lost all faith in myself? Wasn't all that was left inside me just a lava flow of lust, ready at any moment to explode into freedom? Yes, the lust for respect and reputation, that was the source of all the things that I needed so much and that oppressed me. My body was just the vehicle in which different lusts struggled for supremacy. There were no slivers of my old faith in myself there to fight back. Everything had been destroyed.

I went home before the office closed. It was none other than Tuminah who was there to greet me. I used to always be greeted by Mark's dog, Ivy. Who knows where that dog is now? Dead or alive, who knows? I never thought about it anymore.

Then quite unexpectedly the young man from the Sugar Syndicate drove up in his flashy car. The carbide lamps glinted in the afternoon sun. The wheel spikes were made not from wood but from metal, and shone brightly. The nuts in the hubcap too. He came by himself, without a driver.

"How are Madame and the children in Europe?" he asked, setting the agenda.

Such questions could kill me now. And he would kill me with a smile on his face.

"My colleagues in the banks in Betawi, Meneer," he went on, ignoring my dread of all responsibility for my family, "have answered my queries about the situation. You do not have a cent deposited with any of them."

"Meneer!" I cried in amazement.

"You forget who I am, Meneer, the representative of the Syndicate."

"So even the locked door of the bank opens for you?"

"The main thing, Meneer, is that you do not need to worry about your family in Europe anymore. You understand, no doubt, our good intentions for you. Just send us your doctor's bill. Everything will be taken care of. Everything will be fine, as long as you don't leave Betawi and the Indies in these difficult times for us."

It was a very straightforward conversation, and proceeded in a very straightforward manner, but brought me gain that was by no means straightforward.

As soon as his car disappeared from sight, I understood that all my faith had now completely vanished along with any illusions that I would be saved by any miracle from God. I knew for certain then that I had surrendered myself completely to the laws that governed relations between men and the laws of nature itself. I had found strength in these laws. I would never fall sick again because of the conflict between what I had been taught and the realities of life.

Outside my house and office the movement that in so many ways resembled that preceding the French Revolution glowed brighter and brighter as if it were about to reach the moment of explosion at any minute. But the difference from the period before the French Revolution was that here in the Indies no great thinkers arose. There was no concept behind all the activity, no philosophies emerged. Since the departure of Minke, there had been no Native leaders who thought about making contact with the outside world. They were like frogs cooking in the oven of their own isolation. The idea of seeking the intervention of another power never occurred to them. The struggle for leadership among them was no less vicious than that usually fought over leadership of a country. Not having any clear ideas to guide it, the movement degenerated into a race toward nihilism.

His Excellency Governor-General Van Limburg Stirum still took no action. My boss and I had developed a plan to make him realize just how bad the situation was. But he did not awake from his indifference. The two of us had conspired to make sure that the police took action against the Native nationalists at every opportunity. But the courts were never as severe as the police themselves. We were greatly disappointed to find out later that His Excellency had actually summoned the director of the Department of Justice and instructed him not to be too harsh in any case dealing with the Native movement. There were to be no excessive sentences, every act of sabotage was to be dealt with as a normal criminal case, and every offense was to be dealt with strictly in accordance with the law.

Two weeks later all these questions vanished from my mind. The Rientje de Roo murder trial was reopened. A day before the trial began, Sarimin decided to come to see me to reassure me: "Your name will not be mentioned, Meneer. We both might be crooks, Meneer, but there is honor among crooks too, heh?"

People were now calling me a crook without a moment's thought and I didn't feel even slightly offended.

Throughout the Indies, the newspapers set aside a lot of space for their coverage of the Rientje de Roo sensation. And it was true, I was not mentioned once. I was still a respected high official. And there were several other important names in Rientje's diary that were not mentioned. It would not have surprised me to find out that Sarimin had made a profit from all of them. The extortionist was now no doubt rolling in money. And because of the very weak tax system in the Indies, he would be able to enjoy his money free of any accuser or accusations.

And in the midst of the chaos arising in the wake of Van Limburg Stirum's indifference, something quietly and calmly took place in Jogja— yes, in Jogja again. . . . And this something began a new chapter in the life of the Natives. Soerjopranoto had established a primary school and high school that completely turned its back on the government curriculum. This school, which was given the name Adi Darma, meaning "beautiful task," consciously—let me stress that again, consciously—wanted to educate its students to refuse to be the servants of anybody, to be free and independent individuals, and to be the masters of their own lives. With the emergence of the Adi Darma school, the fate of the Boedi Oetomo was sealed. Sneevliet needn't bother attacking it anymore.

12

Until several years ago the Native peoples of the Indies still resisted the power of the government with arms, with patriotism, with religion. And they were defeated every time. But during these past few years, not a single drop of blood had been spilled upon the rice paddies or the fields, the valleys or the tundra, upon land or water. This government that represented Europe now confronted a product of Europe itself—an awakening and exploding nationalism.

In the past the Natives had offered armed resistance in the villages. Now with their nationalism they were rising in the towns and wherever large European companies were to be found.

Europe with its capital now faced the Natives who had no capital but just their labor. Europe with all its science and understanding now faced its own pupils who had more ambition than knowledge—the ambition to become a new nation. Two interests were coming into confrontation— Europe, which had lost its moorings because of the Great War, and the Natives, who were discovering themselves for the first time. And these Natives were not armed with swords and spears, nor with patriotism, and not with religion either. Today their weapons were nothing else but speech and pen.

I don't think I'm wrong in saying that this was a new period in the life of the Natives, the period of the birth of a new nation, with all its limitations in the area of science and understanding. And it was strange too to see a nation formed by speech and pen alone. In Europe, the formation of nations had always been by blood and sword.

Outbreaks of unrest occurred wherever there was big European capital, perhaps more vigorous than those in France against Louis XVI. It seemed people were taking advantage of the government's weakness because of the world war. None of it was organized by me. No, this time there was only unrest that I had not organized—the illegitimate offspring of Raden Mas Minke.

I was so glad that Marquis and Dede were no longer at home. They were question factories that not infrequently pushed me into a corner. This new generation was sharper than my generation. They could see what lay behind reality, once they had tried to get to know that reality themselves. My generation had accepted everything that our elders told us, as if the older generation were the controller of all truth.

And as an official I also had the typical personality of an official. I stamped as forbidden, immoral, and heathen everything that was in conflict with loyalty to the government of the Indies. People must submit and be obedient to the government as the authority approved by the Almighty Father. Otherwise the government would have collapsed long ago. But often even I could be seduced into having more down-to-earth thoughts, that the government, which seemed to stand abstractly above society and which we came to know only through feeling its actions, was nothing more than the manifestation of supreme power, yet it was still a power wielded by humans, and human error was in turn an essential feature of humankind's own imperfection. And my children, this younger generation, paid more heed to the human character of the government—in other words, the things that weren't right, its weaknesses, its mistakes.

I could in fact put together a list of their questions, which would not be too long. But I won't put them down here. They will only disturb my peace of mind as an official. Perhaps some other time, when my resolve is stronger, I'll be able to note them down. At least my children's resolve will equal that of any among the young generation of educated Natives, even though none of the European colonials believe that the Natives will ever advance beyond the level of their ancestors.

But I am a Native too! And I am an official. But as far as the Natives are concerned, I tend to agree with the colonials, that the Natives are trapped forever in a never-ending atavism. Exceptions like Minke can come along and change the situation, but the personality of the majority of people, which gives a people its character, does not change.

The movement that emerged as a result of Minke's strides forward, and all the unrest sweeping the country now, were no more than a movement of bandit gangs desperate for leadership, because they are incapable of leading themselves. I couldn't see any signs that they were continuing the ideals that the Modern Pitung had brought forth. There were new leaders emerging, but no new ideals. The things that they thought were advances were nothing more than ornamentations compared to what Minke had achieved. For example, they thought that the disappearance of European lawyers from positions of responsibility in the Native and Chinese newspapers was an advance. None of them understood what the disappearance of these people meant. They hadn't even written a single short article about it.

It wasn't long ago when Marquis had asked me why there were so many European words in Malay—even very basic words like *buku* for "book," *lampu* for "lamp," and *bangku* for "bench," let alone all the names of machines and their parts. It was even true for words about agriculture, even though the Natives were themselves a farming people. I answered by repeating what Meneer L— had told me once, that the collapse of the Majapahit empire meant also the collapse of Native civilization.

This nation, which once had carried on a busy trade with the great civilizations of Asia, was no longer capable of defending its seas. Slowly it enclosed itself in its own ignorance, cut itself off from the great civilizations, became more and more backward and poor, until finally it was left with nothing except dreams and illusions. Even until today.

So now when the Natives wanted to get close to Europe they had to borrow words from wherever they could. It's so sad, hissed Marquis. Yes, it's very sad, I agreed with him.

And it was sad too. All these foreign words meant that people often ended up speaking only to themselves. Those who had learned to read and write in the village schools never really knew what their leaders were telling them. And these great, impressive foreign words seemed to take on the power that the mantra of their ancestors once contained and became a new mantra. And as was the case with the ancient mantra, the new mantra would not produce results either. And even the leaders, who themselves did not have sufficient schooling, often did not know the real meaning of the words they used. Inadequate knowledge, unclear concepts, were all passed on to followers who themselves were not yet ready.

The Indies was not Europe. A little European education produced only confusion. The government and Europe didn't have to worry about all this. But for me, the confusion and unrest that were occurring were all a result of the confused thinking of the leaders and the even greater confusion of their followers.

The situation in the Indies was very uncertain. The still hand of Governor-General Van Limburg Stirum, who seemed reluctant to move even his little finger, demoralized my boss completely as far as his work went. He hardly ever gave me any important cases anymore. And he hardly ever gave me any orders either. Whenever we talked now, his growing longing for America was more and more obvious. He longed for America, the new continent or the continent of freedom, as he called it, which he himself had never set eyes on.

"It won't be long now, Meneer, and the world will have to sit up and take notice," he said once. "When America entered the war in Europe, everyone was amazed to see their weaponry, and how well they were equipped, as if they weren't heading off to war, but to business. And they will be victorious in Europe. Europe is a barren place now. There is nothing left except the lust to kill and to become corpses. While America brings new, improved automatic weapons. And wheat! Wheat! And all that is left of Europe's wheat is a few weevil-chewed grains."

Having lost hope in the Indies, and his own Europe, this educated man had now turned to America and made himself one with America, just because of the inspiration one scientist, Edison, had been to him. He had subordinated his mind to his emotional needs. How could such a well-educated European man change so much just because of one American scientist, whose achievements were limited to only one sphere of human activity anyway? He had forgotten the other aspects of America, the negative aspects.

I myself was reminded of the American Indians who had been systematically annihilated—conquered, Christianized, and turned into farmers. Then, after they had grown accustomed to eating European food based on farm produce, they had their land stolen from them and they were pushed into reservations and surrendered to tuberculosis and were destroyed.

And my mind wandered to the big plantation fields of America and the Negro nation who slaved in those fields to feed the other Americans, those with white skin. Their fate would be no better than the Native Javanese and West Sumatrans during the Cultuurstelsel period. And I remembered also how in the waters off Menado the American ships of 150 to 200 tonnes swept down upon my fishermen ancestors of only one or two generations ago and stole them away to work in the belly of the earth, digging mines in South America.

"Where every man can live freely and lives to be free!" my boss told

me again, this time with even greater enthusiasm. "There is so much freedom there that there is none left for outside America."

"Don't you feel free here in the Indies?" I asked.

"I feel free here in the Indies—free to oppress the Natives. But this is
a different kind of freedom than the freedom to truly make something of
yourself, to become a millionaire who knows no limits to his wealth, who
knows no limit to his power and influence, whose influence will be felt in
every corner of the earth. That can only happen in America—a country of
freedom with a freedom that is unrivaled anywhere. With its armed forces
entering the war in Europe, it means the war will soon come to an end.
Only America, with its unrivaled technical abilities, can defeat Germany."

"Yes, but when the French began using the machine gun, all the other
countries started making them too. And the English introduced their secret
weapon, the tank. People didn't know what a tank was to start with. They
thought it was a water tank, but it turned out to be a steel fort that could
move. But it didn't take long for Germany to be able to make them too."

"But they will not be able to make more than American can produce."

"Now Germany is using a new weapon, Big Bertha. They have to
use a railline to haul it."

"I am sure if it's just a matter of iron and steel, America can do much
better," my boss interrupted. "Giant cannon like that will be across from
America within a month. Germany will be able to make one cannon at the
most."

"Germany has developed balloons from which it can drop bombs."

My boss laughed, and said that those balloons would be just toys in
the eyes of the American scientists and industrialists. "And they will make
them in unlimited numbers."

There was nothing more I could say to this fan of America.

"Here in the Indies where the people are still children and the authorities arrogant and spoiled, all we can expect to see is oppression."

"But the Natives are moving forward, Meneer," I said, fishing.

"Yes, that's true. We can see that in the way they're fighting the
government. But just imagine what will happen if they succeed—though
I don't believe for a moment that they will. They will realize that they're
incapable of doing anything except fighting each other. They'll end up
fighting among themselves; that will be the outcome."

It seemed he had decided he would answer his own questions this
time. Then he stood up and came across close to me, bent over, and spoke
slowly to me: "They will fight us, Meneer, that is clear. And it is your task
to make it clear to His Excellency just what their main aspirations are. And
please don't take too long about it."

"What do you mean, 'their main aspirations'?"

"Yes, the aspirations that most represent the whole movement." He left me and it was I who had to go to work.

And so I returned to my old work, reading cables and files. And once again I realized that the Sarekat, in its present condition, was not going anywhere because it did not know where it wanted to go. People who were used to just echoing the will of the government now waited in silence for His Excellency to show what his attitude was. The Insulinde was paralyzed even before it got going. The ethnic organizations were busy proving each was superior and more arrogant than the other.

There were only two issues left to discuss. First, there was the slogan once whispered by the Indische Partij: "For self-government!" But nobody whispered that anymore, not even in a weaker whisper. And then there was the Boedi Oetomo, which was campaigning for a broader membership in the local government councils and for the establishment of high schools for Natives. I handed in my report to my boss without presenting any conclusions.

Not long afterward we heard from His Excellency the news that the government of the Kingdom of the Netherlands was still very concerned about the situation in the Indies.

I was startled awake from my indifference. I became very concerned. I studied again the report I had handed in and regretted that I had not done a more thorough job. There had obviously been some connection between my boss's instruction and the news from the Netherlands.

And it was true that the situation in the Indies for the ordinary person was already intolerable. Unemployment was everywhere, crime was on the rise, and unrest and rioting multiplied. The people had nothing left to pawn in the State pawnshops. And things were not helped by the fact that the discontented pawnshop employees also preferred to join in the strike waves.

This closed off the opportunity for the people to obtain a little credit with low interest and so they were forced more and more into the hands of the moneylenders. The State pawnshops were becoming warehouses full of unsalable goods, except for a little gold and silver. In the towns, both big and small, people did not have enough to eat. In the villages the farmers, who produced all their own needs, weren't buying goods from the towns.

There was trouble everywhere. People even began stealing telephone wires and the railway telegraph wires to get the copper. Desperate people, despite the danger of being caught, began forging coins from nickel, copper, and silver.

I was very unsure whether the government would be able to manage all this. The police and army would not be enough. I didn't know what use my work could be either.

"Meneer," I began a conversation one day with my boss.

He sat down in his chair, looking like an emperor who had lost his crown, and without taking his pipe from his mouth.

"I am not satisfied with the last report I wrote. I would like to prepare another."

His eyes were shining, I didn't know why. He gazed at me very amicably, took out the heavy ivory pipe, then smiled. And didn't say another word.

Back in my office, I read a report in the paper that pushed all other news off the front page. Czar Nicholas of Russia had been overthrown. The world press condemned the insurrection for helping the Germans because Russia was in the middle of moving its army into the field. There was a quote from one of the insurrectionists that said that it felt the same to them to be oppressed by Czar Nicholas as by the Germans and they rejected both and preferred to choose freedom from both sides.

Once again I was confronted with a new kind of logic. It felt and sounded crazy, but it had become a reality and had manifested itself concretely in the overthrow of a czar whose power had never been challenged before.

Just a few minutes before the office closed for the day, my boss came in.

"I have a special assignment for you, something you might enjoy."

"Something to do with America, perhaps, Meneer?"

He laughed happily but didn't answer. I saw that he had brought his office diary with him. The same book had been used since the day of my arrival here. Then: "How long has it been since Raden Mas Minke was sent into exile?"

"I haven't been keeping count. Five years! How time flies!"

"And it was you yourself who escorted him into exile. Tell me what you discussed with him during the journey."

"He always refused to talk to me," I answered cautiously. Then I changed the topic: "Well, Meneer, will I be able to review that last report I handed in?"

"Don't you like talking about Minke?"

"Very well, Meneer."

"There is no need to change your last report. His Excellency has already read it. He himself made a few changes and then it was telegrammed to the Netherlands."

"Telegrammed to the Netherlands?"

"Yes, a report based upon the views of the Sworn Colonial Expert, Meneer Pangemanann . . . everything is under control. The report has reached its destination."

My heart began to pound when I heard what had happened. Such shoddy work had been sent to the Netherlands! With my name on it!

"Why have you gone pale?"

He could read my thoughts. He opened the office diary at a particular page and then read aloud, in a clear voice, word by word: "All action taken by the government against the Native movements has been based on the general line of the reports prepared by the Colonial Affairs Expert of the Algemeene Secretariat, Meneer J. Pangemanann. No policies have been implemented without his knowledge and agreement and without considering his suggestions and advice. This is in accordance with the verbal instructions of His Excellency the Governor-General on November 22, 1912."

He stopped reading and watched me for a moment to see how I was reacting. Then he went on: "You are a very competent expert in these affairs, Meneer, and I think your desire to reexamine or rewrite these reports that have been already sent on to the Netherlands can only have arisen because you are worried by something outside your work. You must forget such things, Meneer."

"What things outside my work?"

"Forgive me, but this is just my own opinion, just subjective desires and opinions. It doesn't matter; forget all that, Meneer. Let's get back to our present work. In one week's time, Meneer Raden Mas Minke will be arriving in Tanjung Perak port in Surabaya. It will be your job to meet him and also your job to obtain from him a signed undertaking that he will not become involved in the affairs of the Sarekat Islam for as long as he lives."

I sat there in my office pondering. Now I was reaping the harvest of my own hard work: a bitter harvest. Again I would have to deny my own feelings.

I had developed very detailed policies to make sure that this great organization was kept in sterile conditions, free from infection from new and dangerous ideas and teachings. Because of its sterile condition it was incapable of taking any initiatives. The Sarekat had not been able to establish even one school. It had not even been able to take one action against its own youth wing, based in Solo, Semarang, and Jogja. I had succeeded.

Now its founder was returning, the only person who truly understood why and for what the Sarekat was founded. Once again I would have to face him. So we would no longer just be playing chess against each other from afar. He had never surrendered his principles. He had only lost his freedom. During these last five years I had lost everything: principles, wife and children, my honor—and I had become the bought slave of the Syndicates, the Sugar Syndicate and the Algemeene Landbouw Syndicaat. . . .

I would have to face him in all his greatness. He had not been defeated in any way at all. He had lost all his property and the bank deposits that had been frozen as illegally earned money by the De Lange Commission. Cruelly he had been separated by divorce from his wife who loved him and whom he would never meet again. Princess Kasiruta had been ordered to leave Java a year ago and it was probable that Minke would not be allowed to leave Java once he had returned. He too had lost everything, except his honor and his greatness.

The government and its apparatus had created a situation where it was impossible for him to hire a lawyer who could demand his rights. He might be able to get help from the Sarekat if the government turned out to be unable to keep him apart from the organization. There had been one Eurasian lawyer—a graduate from Amsterdam—who had tried to take up Minke's case. He had been warned and then threatened in various ways so that it had become clear that it would be very difficult for him to open a practice in the Indies if he continued with his intentions.

How great were the consequences that flowed from the thoughts of this colonial affairs expert named Pangemanann! And the other Jacques Pangemanann, the husband of his wife named Paulette Pangemanann, never dreamed his ideas would be used to justify such shameful thefts. Minke's organization had been manipulated and maneuvered into a situation where it was incapable of defending him, or protecting him. And this was not only because it lacked any sense of law and knew nothing about the law, but also because we had succeeded in completely taming it in its dealings with the government.

Now I would have to confront him again. As his escort and host! As a civilized man educated in one of the world's leading institutions of learning. I would have to meet and escort him, a teacher and man whom I admired so much, but who had lost everything because of me. I would go and meet him and he would be like a crab whose legs I had cut off. This meeting would be a great humiliation for me; it would burst my insides because I would be meeting with everything that is my opposite.

In just one week's time! In one week I would be meeting with a teacher so rich in experience but no longer able to teach.

I sat down and began the painful task of composing the statement that he would later have to sign. I knew that I would have to take a very, very sympathetic approach. And my boss gave me full authority to handle everything, just as he gave me a very meaningful look, a look that made me cringe. His glance pierced right inside me. Perhaps he also saw me go ghost white.

In his textbook English he said: "You have always tried to behave like a responsible and rational human being. You seem to want to try not to act in the colonial way. I can sense that you are beginning to become fed up and sick of this colonial prison. I can understand the conflict that you must be suffering inside."

"Thank you, Meneer. Perhaps that is also the reason why you prefer America?"

"You are not very wrong there, Meneer."

"But there is oppression too in America," I added.

"It is not so much that there is oppression, I think. There is freedom to oppress, yes, that's true. But there is also the freedom not to be oppressed. Here there is only the freedom to oppress. There is no freedom not to be oppressed."

Who would have guessed that he could talk like that? Someone so close to His Excellency the governor-general? And I was even more amazed when he said: "You needn't worry. As long as I am your boss I will always approve your ideas, Meneer. The only condition is that they are within the guidelines of colonial policy, because that is today's reality, even though they may become the source of humiliation in another time."

I studied his face. He was much younger than I. His front teeth were brown from tobacco tar. There was no mustache or beard. His face was smooth like a young girl's. His nose was slightly longer than usual for a European, but it was straight and not crooked. He had crystal-clear gray eyes that gave the impression that he could see right inside a person's brain. But his own thoughts were difficult to guess, always a puzzle and somehow uninteresting.

"You regret the work you have carried out in the past because it hasn't benefited the Natives enough, or didn't benefit them at all. Isn't that so?"

My heart shriveled up inside me. I could hear myself sobbing inside. What had I become? What meaning did my life have or my existence?

Then the day arrived. The ship had docked. The sky was beautifully clear. And the sun seemed to be overjoyed at welcoming him. Seven minutes past nine o'clock. There were other people at the docks to meet their families. As soon as the anchor had been dropped and the ship moored, the gangway was lowered onto the wharf.

Along with the families and some government officials who were also there, I went aboard. I obtained Modern Pitung's cabin number from the purser—Number 22 in second class. I hurried to the cabin, not caring about colliding with all the passengers impatient to get off the ship. His cabin door was open. Raden Mas Minke was sitting on the couch smoking calmly. His destar looked old and worn and so did his vest and his batik sarong. His right leg was crossed over his left leg. He was wearing new slippers. His mustache was still luxuriant, black and twirled upward. He looked much older than when he had left for exile.

I knocked slowly on the open door.

He looked at me without interest. "Good morning, Meneer," I said in Dutch.

"Morning. I don't want to rush off yet."

"Are you alighting here or in Betawi?"

He stood and somewhat inhospitably took hold of the door as if he were going to forbid me to enter. He didn't recognize me. "I'm sorry. I'm not sure. Perhaps here, perhaps in Betawi."

"I think you should alight here, Meneer Raden Mas Minke," I said.

He was startled. There was a sudden glint in his eye and he became very wary. He studied me closely. And I nodded, giving my respects.

"Oh, Meneer Pangemanann with two ns," he said. "You are not in uniform."

"I am retired now, Meneer," I answered, and he still didn't invite me in.

He still held on to the door. "Retired," he repeated unbelievingly.

"I think I should inform you, Meneer, that I am once again your escort. You may alight here or you may go on to Betawi. Whatever you prefer, Meneer. But I think perhaps you might like to have a look around Surabaya?"

"I should go on to Betawi. If I am permitted to have a look around Surabaya, I would of course like to take that opportunity."

"Good. Then let me escort you."

"I am to be escorted? So I am still not free?"

"You are free, Meneer. But there is still a formality that has to be taken care of. Until that is completed I will be your escort."

"Thank you. What formality are you talking about Meneer?"

"It's nothing much. You will find out yourself in Betawi."

"Perhaps, Meneer, I will have to bow and scrape before you in Betawi, is that it?"

I performed an amicable laugh, and he still held on to the door.

"You will never be below anybody else, Meneer," I said to put him at ease, "especially not this Pangemanann here, Meneer Raden Mas."

"You are making fun of me."

"No, Meneer, certainly not," I said convincingly. "The Indies has

changed, Meneer; it has all changed since you left. And it was you who
brought about all these changes."

I could see him warily sharpen his observation of me. I think he was
trying to see behind what I was saying.

"The Indies is a smoldering cauldron now."

"A smoldering cauldron? Then I have come back at the wrong time,"
he said, pretending that he didn't understand what his role in all this had
been.

"His Excellency Van Limburg Stirum brought a new policy with him.
He is not the same as Idenburg. Under his administration all exiles are being
returned home."

He was lost in thought for a moment. Perhaps he was thinking about
his wife and father-in-law. But he didn't ask anything.

"Let's go, Meneer. Let's have a look at Surabaya."

He locked the door without getting anything from inside the cabin
first. We walked to the purser's office and handed the key to one of the
clerks, a very old man.

"You are going into Surabaya, Tuan Minke? Don't be late coming
back," the clerk reminded us. "Have a good time. Don't go across to
Madura; then you will be late for sure."

In the taxi, he said: "I'd prefer to do my sightseeing alone."

"Of course, Meneer. So would I," I responded. Then to the driver:
"Drive slowly, driver." Then to the passenger beside me: "Meneer Raden
Mas Minke . . ." I saw the driver try to get a look; I could see his face in
the rearview mirror as he tried to see us. "Meneer Minke"—I raised my
voice and glanced again at the mirror—"where will we go?"

"HBS Street," he answered briefly.

The driver turned in the direction of HBS Street. I glanced at Minke.
He was lost in thoughts which I could never know. I was reminded of
This Earth of Mankind, and even though I did not believe he had graduated
from the HBS, it was possible he had some beautiful memories connected
with the school. Perhaps he once had a loved one—no doubt a pretty
girl—at the school, someone who still had a hold on his heart, but whom
he had not been able to obtain for his wife.

The school was quiet because lessons were under way.

I couldn't help thinking of *This Earth of Mankind*. Minke had written
about his experiences as a student who had been expelled from this school
that he was now looking at. He was defended by the resident of Bojonegoro; then he graduated, gaining the highest or second highest marks in the
whole of the Indies. It was the story of a child's resolve to be his true self.

And it was clear that the resident of Bojonegoro at that time was not de la Croix. Minke would not have dared use his real name. Not enough time had passed yet. Minke had to use another name for the resident.

The taxi drove slowly past the HBS. My neighbor in the taxi still did not move from the window. It was only after we were quite a ways past the school that he sat back again, drew in a breath, and closed his eyes.

Yes, in exile all that you could do was remember and reflect on the past, and so the past did not seem so far away at all. As someone who had been a police inspector, I could understand that. I remembered the conversations of so many prisoners. It was as if they had no present and no future. I could understand.

"We still have plenty of time, Meneer Raden Mas. More than enough time. There is still time to change your mind and catch the train to Betawi."

He kept his eyes closed, and I regretted having disturbed his memories. What could be done? He looked at me, his eyes open now.

"Yes, you can't travel about much if you go by ship," I said, repeating a sentence I remembered from one of his manuscripts. "If we go by train we can stop off at various places. Perhaps you would like to see your parents . . . ?"

He turned and looked out the window again. Then he bent over close to the driver.

"Kranggan," he said.

The taxi turned right.

"Perhaps you would like to know, Meneer, that your father has established quite a good school for girls in Blora."

He looked at me but said nothing. He had written about that in *Footsteps* but I didn't try to discuss it with him.

He bowed his head in silence. He had no interest in the passing scenery, nor in the traffic. It seemed that he wanted to meet only with his memories of the past, things that were forever out of his reach now, vanished forever from reality but eternal and always disturbing him in his thoughts.

"Slowly," I ordered the driver when the taxi entered Kranggan Street.

I knew that he glanced at me but I pretended not to notice. When I glanced back at him, he was gazing at an old house. It was in that house that a Frenchmen had once lived, whom Minke had named Jean Marais and described as a former student of the Sorbonne, a painter, and a veteran of the Aceh War. My research had shown that his name was not Marais but Jean Le Boucq. And he hadn't been a student at the Sorbonne either but at the Catholic University in Louvain in Belgium.

"A Frenchman named Le Boucq used to live there," I said, while stealing another glance at him.

He took no heed of me, even though I saw his eyes blink warily. He didn't ask anything, as if he had no interest in any of this, yet I could feel too that in his heart there were so many questions that wanted to burst forth.

"He was an invalid with one leg, Meneer. It's said that people here in Surabaya have great admiration for him because he was able to marry a nyai, a Native woman who was very, very wealthy." Of course, he knew better than I all about that story. I said these things to him to show him that I was completely familiar with what he had written in *This Earth of Mankind*.

I saw him draw in a deep breath. And I am sure I would have heard him sigh, had it not been for the droning noise of the engine. He was no doubt remembering that fortunate Frenchman.

"There used to be a boardinghouse next door. You can see it's a warehouse now. It used to belong to an Indo. He was a veteran of the Aceh War also."

I watched him take out a handkerchief. His chest was heaving. But I pretended not to see. I understood his feelings. He was wrestling with his past, with the time before he had become acquainted with colonial power, when he was young and the future looked bright and full of possibility and all sorts of hopes for the future, when everything was beautiful. Today's reality was rich with bitter experience and power games. It was a reality where he was just a mouse in a cat's world.

He wiped his eyes. I knew he was shedding tears and he was hiding it from me. Yes, weep, Modern Pitung, because this is the only way you can honestly speak with your past. I can just imagine how it was when you were studying, how you would open each page of your books, fully believing that all you transferred from those pages into your own self would become your strength as you set out to cross the fields of life. You were such a simple person then. You didn't realize that life would not be as simple as you imagined. But even so, you did set off across those fields until the moment arrived when you had to face me. Even now you are, in certain ways, in my grip. But in other respects my hands and fingers are too weak to keep you in my grip, and more than that, you are too big for me ever to be able to hold you in my grasp.

The taxi arrived at the three-way intersection where the right-hand turnoff led to Pasar Turi.

"Take me to see Mas Tjokro." He suddenly awoke from his past.

His request startled me. He was challenging me, announcing that he was not afraid of me. He had leaped into the present. He could not hide how he missed his youngest child—the Sarekat. He still believed that the law would protect him. He should have given up all belief in colonial law by now—he who had had so much experience of it. Or is this just a challenge?

"I think not, Meneer. It will only get you into more trouble."

"So this freedom that I have been promised, freedom Van Limburg Stirum style, is just the old-style one, heh?"

"You are not free yet, Meneer. And perhaps you are right—here in the Indies there is no freedom like that you have read about in the European books. Here only His Excellency the governor-general is fully free."

He looked at me with unbelieving eyes. I could see disgust in that look, I don't know if with me or with the whole world under European occupation. Suddenly he turned away and looked straight ahead. Meanwhile the taxi turned right in the direction of Pasar Turi.

"Very well then. Take me wherever you like. I am still not free anyway."

"In that case we will go back to Kranggan."

The taxi turned back to Kranggan, driving along slowly as if bearing newlyweds who had to be seen by everybody.

"There is so much of what we studied in the books from Europe, Meneer, that does not apply in the Indies," I said, trying to be friendly. "European taught me to honor and respect those who are my superiors and to love those who are less fortunate than myself. Europe taught that all the great men are humanity's teachers. That is Europe. America teaches that whoever succeeds in life should be your leader. Japan teaches that a man who has many friends is a man who has mastered life and such a man is a good man. None of this applies in the Indies. You are my superior. You have had much misfortune compared to me. You are a great man. You have succeeded in life. You have very many friends. But just look, Meneer. I know all this, yet I am also the one who had to arrest you, and even now I am still your host and escort, but in the worst possible sense."

He cleared his throat, looked out the window, and spat outside.

Yes, I felt so small beside him, yet his action was clearly intended as a very crude insult to me. I could hear the blood rush into my ears as I seethed with rage. As a European-educated man, I had to control myself. And he was within his rights to insult me, as was Sarimin. What was I compared to him? If I took him to Contong Square and let him get out, people would be swarming about him in no time and he would be welcomed as a hero. And if I took him to see Mas Tjokro, that "emperor without a crown" would probably dissolve before him. And nobody would ever have any respect for Pangemanann. That was the reality that could happen at any time and that could be verified.

I suppressed my feelings of humiliation and returned to the subject of his past. "Yes, Le Boucq. As a soldier he took the name Antoine Barbuse Jambitte. He was a strange man, Meneer. He was a painter, an educated man, but also just a Company soldier. There are many Europeans who become bored with Europe and try to reinvigorate themselves by living in primitive societies. They try to forget Europe and everything it teaches just when these societies are longing for European knowledge and learning. What do you call that, Meneer Raden Mas? A mutation? Or an irony of civilization?"

He didn't answer. I don't know whether he was listening or not, whether he was submerged in the past again or was continuing his reflections on the present. In the house that belonged to the man that Modern Pitung had called Telinga, there stood a beggar, a woman holding her skinny, dehydrated baby. My guest beside me seemed amazed that there should still be beggars in this area. And I wanted to whisper in his ear that if it was beggars that he was thinking about, then he should know that their numbers will always increase, because a beggar is always a beggar, and a beggar family gives birth only to more beggars, and a beggar never mutates into something other than a beggar. There was even a whole social group—all those thrown out of work and forgotten because of the world war—who now stood on the edge of destitution.

"Right!" I ordered the driver.

And so the taxi now headed off in the direction of Wonokromo. But just fifty meters past the turnoff, Minke ordered the taxi to stop—in front of a row of stalls and shops. He gripped hold of the window edge with both his hands. He was watching a pockmarked woman leading a small child and escorted by a broad-shouldered, strong, and handsome-looking youth.

"I need some eucalyptus oil," he said and, paying me no heed, opened the door and climbed out.

I followed him, went into the stall, and saw him pocket a bottle of eucalyptus oil. But his eyes remained fixed on the pockmarked woman standing in front of him, busily choosing clothes. He went over to her and I heard him clearly ask the first question: "So you live in Surabaya now, Surati?" he asked in Javanese.

The pockmarked woman seemed startled and studied him without fear. Her lips quivered with an unasked question.

"This is your littlest?"

It was then that I remembered Painah, a character in Kommer's work *Nyai Painah*, who might have been based on the story of Surati in Minke's manuscript *Child of All Nations*. Kommer's work was published just before he died, a thin little book that was very pro-Native. The two of them talked and I couldn't follow what they were saying because I didn't understand Javanese. But I did hear the names Sastro Kassier and Tulangan, names that were also mentioned in Kommer's work as well as in *Child of All Nations*.

I saw Surati kneel and pay obeisance to Minke. But he shook his head and told her to stand up; he caressed the cheeks of Surati's littlest, then started to talk with the older boy. It was obvious they were enjoying their conversation. I stood close to them. To avoid suspicion that I was eavesdropping, I looked the other way across the road; then I moved away closer to the taxi. When Minke came back to the taxi, his eyes were shining brightly. The car started up and Minke's eyes still shone.

"What a fantastic woman!" he hissed. "I have met so many fantastic women in my life."

"Yes, an amazing woman. Her name was Surati, yes?"

"So you know her story?"

"Kommer wrote a little book about her. Do you know Kommer?" I pretended I was ignorant.

"An extraordinary Indo journalist."

"Yes, a man who loved the Natives and the Malay language," I said. "It's a pity he died just recently."

"Ha? He always looked healthy and active."

"An accident, Meneer. He was crushed by one of his own snakes, a giant python."

He muttered something, in Arabic perhaps, and I didn't understand.

"I would like to see his grave."

"I don't think that is necessary, Meneer, and we don't know where it is either. I think not. You can do that later, after you've been to Betawi."

"Where do we go now?" he asked, somewhat amicably.

"Wonokromo. Don't you think you should see how that village has grown into a town with many impressive buildings?"

He didn't answer. Perhaps he had submerged again into his past.

I still had doubts as to whether what he had written in *This Earth of Mankind* was true or not. So I watched his countenance closely. Was it true that he had once known somebody called Annelies Mellema? Was it true that he had married her? Was it true that he had been on very close terms with Nyai Ontosoroh? Were these writings nothing more than his fantasies? Or did he know about them from other people?

He kept his gaze on the left-hand side of the road. The taxi traveled slowly. It was as if he were counting every house that we passed.

"If you had been to Surabaya before, you would notice the changes. There are so many houses along this road now. The rice paddies and other fields are being pushed farther and farther back. Who knows what it will be like in another ten years?"

He took no notice of what I was saying. He didn't pay any attention either to the crowds of people heading for Surabaya.

"That used to be a brothel," I explained. "Its old owner died in Kalisosok jail."

He pretended not to hear. But I kept on anyway, as if I were leading him back into his past, so full of beauty as well as bitterness.

"That must be the house that once belonged to a famous nyai. She was an extraordinary nyai, wealthy as well as beautiful. I wish I had been able to meet her."

"It is a beautiful house," he muttered.

"It must have been even more beautiful before. The architecture is quite marvelous. Do you recognize the German features of the building, Meneer?"

Again he ignored me. Yet I was able to guess that he didn't know anything at all about European architecture. I continued to tantalize him with all the fantasies that he had written about in his book.

"Every part of Europe that has ever been under the influence of Germany has houses just like this one. The Natives here have never built houses like this."

He nodded.

"Did you notice, Meneer? This whole road is asphalted now."

My neighbor stretched out the window and looked. He nodded.

"The main streets in Betawi too. They've started asphalting all the main district roads in Java as well. You won't recognize them today. There are so many cars in Surabaya these days. It's much more comfortable in a car than by carriage, especially if the horse has a stomachache!"

Again he was studying the houses along the left-hand side. Perhaps my words were humoring him in his loneliness.

"If you traveled along this road in the past in a buggy or horse cart, your whole body would shake as the wheels fought with the street stones. See how the houses are all trying to outdo each other in beauty?"

We had passed the house of the famous nyai and the taxi continued on slowly. He still watched the left-hand side closely, as if he were looking through an old photo album whose photos were already fading. But I still wasn't able to be sure whether he did indeed once have close and intimate connections with the area.

"You can see the forests over there behind all the tiled roofs." I spoke again. "It's probably a good place to hunt for birds or wild boar or deer," I said, trying to awaken his memories of Robert Mellema.

But my hopes were not fulfilled. He still didn't react.

"If we keep going, we'll eventually come to Sidoarjo. It's said that Sidoardjo is famous because . . ."

"We'll go on another ten kilometers," he said.

The asphalt road was hemmed in by small fields, and on the right there were rice fields stretching out to the foot of Arjuna mountain. Here and there you could see little black spots of groves of trees. It was in among those trees that you would find the farmers' hamlets. But Minke kept his eyes on the left-hand side. And the crops sometimes ran up against fields of reeds and thickets of underbrush standing under the dark umbrella of all kinds of trees. Sometimes we would see a bamboo hut or humpy. And Minke kept his gaze pointed to the left.

Perhaps he had become bored, or perhaps there was another reason, but the driver began to speed up. My neighbor in the backseat told him neither to slow down nor to keep it up.

"Stop!" he said suddenly.

And the taxi came to a halt.

We were surrounded by fields of wild reeds to the left and right. They were perhaps two and a half meters high. As I followed Minke's gaze, I came upon a big iron gate, about three meters wide. Above the gate there hung a huge zinc sign, with the words BOERDERIJ WONOCOLO.

He climbed out of the car, examined the steel posts that were embedded in concrete slabs in the ground, and gazed again and again at the sign. Then: "Driver!" he called.

The driver turned off the engine and got out of the car. The three of us looked down the three-meter-wide road that led through the field of thick tall reeds. There was a bend in the road in the distance and all you could see was reeds.

"Is there a village in there?" asked Modern Pitung in Malay.

"I am not sure, Tuan T— A— S—."

The driver, who had been silent all this while, had recognized his passenger. He had used Minke's real name, his name since birth.

Minke looked at the driver for a long time. His eyes shone—he had made contact with the world that he had left behind five years ago. He just nodded. Then: "Has this farm been here a long time?"

"A long time, Tuan."

"Who owns it?"

"I don't know, Tuan."

"Chinese or European?"

"They say a Madurese, Tuan."

"A Madurese runs a farm? And they keep dairy cattle there?"

"Of course, Tuan. They say three hundred head."

"Enough. Let's go back to Surabaya," he said.

As soon as we climbed back into the car, it turned around and headed for Surabaya. Minke leaned over close to the driver and asked: "So you don't know the name of the owner, driver?"

"No, Tuan. Who would ever remember the name of somebody who lived in the middle of fields of reeds like that? All that is known is that he is a Madurese. There is a story, I don't know if it is true or not, that he was once the head guard at a farm owned by a nyai. Ah, that's a story from long ago, Tuan. Nobody remembers anymore. I don't know how the story went. The nyai was defeated in some court case and then built this other farm there together with the Madurese. After the farm was going well, she married another Dutchman and left for his homeland and has never returned. She gave it all to the Madurese."

Minke threw himself back into the seat. Now his eyes were closed. I still couldn't be sure that the Minke sitting next to me now was the Minke he had fantasized about in *This Earth of Mankind*. Was there a real relationship between reality and fantasy? He seemed at least to be interested in these things.

"Where do we go now?" I asked.

"Back to town." He closed his eyes and went silent.

As we entered Surabaya town I asked: "Don't you want to do some shopping?"

He didn't answer and pretended that he was asleep. I looked at him from the side. He did look older now as he approached forty years. Five years in exile was too heavy a punishment for a person who believed in the need of educated people for freedom. And the freedom that he chased had resulted in his losing everything, including his basic freedom, which was his basic capital. All that faced him each day was the prospect of gazing across Ambon harbor in between reading his newspapers and books. In a few more years he would need glasses, just like the old people. And he still had not gained anything for himself.

As someone who had spent so much time mixing with Europeans, I found his profile distinctly Native Javanese. If he were wearing baggy black pants, an old singlet, and had a sarong hanging around his neck, he would seem no different from any other Native. Even with a mustache twirled upward at the ends. But it was precisely this profile of his that drew my admiration. He was an innocent who did not understand his own strengths. If he had been fully aware of them and been able to use them to the maximum, he could have turned the Indies upside down. Armed with so little knowledge and learning, he dreamed of an Indies nationalist awakening without understanding how it could happen.

And this was a Javanese, a Native Javanese, wearing Javanese clothes, but no longer a Javanese at all. He was not like his parents, or his ancestors. He was a European who based his life on reason, and not on Javanese illusions, on Javanism as he himself called it, including its artistic form of wayang and gamelan—the "mountains" where his people sought refuge after the fall of Majapahit. According to Meneer L—, they sought refuge from centuries of defeat, and it was in these mountains that they found peace and contact with the glories of bygone days, glories that would never be repeated again.

This man sitting next to me was perhaps the only Javanese who had thrown off all his illusions, both as a Javanese and as an individual. With his still inadequate knowledge and learning he groped about, clutching at every straw, hoping somehow to awaken nationalism in the Indies.

It is said that there is a great, unexpected power that can emerge from under the ocean, or in the explosion of a volcano or within individuals who truly know what is the purpose of their life. Wasn't it Minke himself who so often said never denigrate the ability of any individual? And it would be no exaggeration if I were to say that the individual sitting next to me also had the same power that moved oceans, or caused volcanoes to erupt. If he had not been such an innocent, if he had properly understood his own powers, perhaps the Indies too would have had an Asian president to follow after Sun Yat-sen and Aguinaldo.

To be a Javanese who had freed himself from Javanism also meant being able to understand the world of Javanese illusions and to reject it. Such a person preferred to see the world as it was and to accept it and to deal with it as it really was. And a Javanese who was not a Javanist was a revolutionary in these times in which I lived. I knew that he had never studied Western philosophy. Only his common sense would be able to help him escape from this atavism.

Perhaps he was the first Javanese realist.

My thoughts were borne willy-nilly back to Meneer L—'s discussion of the Javanese personality. From time to time, he said, a Javanese will come forward who will seem to be a personality of strong integrity. We see such people at the time they achieve worldly success. You can see this in their leaders throughout Javanese history since the time the Europeans arrived, from Sultan Agung through to the rajas of more recent times. But as soon as these people have been tested in life, their integrity collapses, they lose all faith in themselves, surrender themselves to illusion, and try to suck power from the supernatural world, from trees, devils, spirits, demons, ogres, from their ancestors, from animals . . . and when I heard this I recognized the truth in what Minke had written about the behavior of Sastro Kassier when he was being pressed by Plikemboh.

If one day you get the chance to talk with an educated Javanese, get him into a conversation about wayang, and keris, then praise the sophistication of the gamelan and Javanese dance, said Meneer L—, and then tell him how advanced Javanese philosophy and metaphysics are. If he reacts with enthusiasm and agrees with all your praise, it means he will never achieve anything despite all his education.

In the end every victory of human over human is in fact a victory for a particular philosophy, a particular outlook and spiritual attitude toward humankind, toward oneself, toward society and nature. Java has been continually defeated. Someone who is taken in by such praise is somebody blind to what has been happening all around him for a long time. Such a person will be defeated at his very first test. Study Javanese history, Meneer L— told me: There have been too few leaders who have died on the field of battle defending their beliefs. They all wavered, then surrendered to the Dutch, and by doing that admitted the superiority of Europe, of the European philosophy and outlook, and not just its knowledge and learning.

Do you know what the Javanese people's favorite story from history is? All I could do in my ignorance was sit and listen to Meneer L—. And he continued to speak, full of his own enthusiasm. He told me. The story of *Surapati*, Meneer. The Javanese themselves cannot explain why his story is so popular, but I know why, Meneer. They all dream and long for a leader who is prepared to live and prepared to die for what he believes in, like Surapati. Surapati's attitude, wasn't that itself a philosophical statement? And nobody like Surapati has since appeared. Surapati was the one and only such figure. Now he is just a dream. The reality is that every Javanese leader since then has failed the first test he has faced.

The peoples of the world today, Meneer, he went on to say, are competing to make some meaningful contribution to humanity, in the field of science, learning, philosophy, engineering, medicine, including the Negro and Indian peoples, and there is not a single contribution from the Javanese people. They have degenerated to a situation far worse than that of their ancestors, and live in their shadow. Today's Javanese, and I hope you'll forgive me for using this kind of comparison, but today's Javanese are just like grass living off the richness of the soil. Nothing more than that. They are low grass creeping along the earth they suck their nutrients from. They do not see the giant trees and timber around about them.

I knew that every time Meneer L— talked about the Javanese I felt that I was somehow involved as well, and I began to study my own people, the Menadonese. I think that there is no gap between the Javanese and the other peoples of the Indies, or at least it is a very small gap. Their universe is also a universe of illusions.

The man next to me opened his eyes again, and his gaze went straight to the right-hand side of the road.

"The Japanese Garden," he said to the driver, then closed his eyes again.

What did he want at the Japanese Garden, the neighborhood where the Japanese prostitutes used to live? Was he once involved with one of them and now wanted to witness for himself the ruins of the past? There was one name only that was mentioned in his manuscripts—Maiko. After seventeen years that woman would be just a lump of rotting flesh. In Minke's story she was said to be infected with Burmese syphilis.

As usual, the Japanese Garden, which had slowly grown into a center for soldiers of fortune and enterprise, was rather busy.

He opened his eyes and kept a very close watch on the business signs as we drove by. I ordered the driver to slow down.

"Stop!" he ordered suddenly.

Without asking my permission first, he jumped out of the car and went over to a shop that had just a small thick glass display window. There were roots, various kind of medicinal barks, and dried leaves on display. Written across the rather modest sign was the word MOLUKKEN, and underneath TRADERS IN INDIES SPICES.

He walked straight inside, once again not asking for my permission first. I went inside too. There was nothing at all of interest. It was just an office with a few people working at their desks.

Standing a little way back from him, I watched him speak to one of the employees, who then took him across to another room. Minke knocked on the door and stood there alone waiting. Someone opened the door and invited him inside, but Minke didn't go in. Perhaps he wanted me to be sure that he wasn't going to try to escape. Then the door opened wider and a skinny, pale Native wearing European clothes, somewhat shorter than Minke, emerged.

I did not try to get closer. I just watched from a distance, about seven meters. I ignored the amazed stares of the employees.

The man just stood there in front of Minke. Suddenly he raised his two hands, grabbed Minke, and embraced him. And I could hear his voice sob like a little child: "Mas, Mas, you've come home, Mas. Forgive me for not being able to help you in your difficulties," and like a little child, he wept, kissing and embracing Minke.

Everyone turned to watch what was happening. I went up to one of them and asked him in Dutch: "Who is that man?"

"Meneer Darman."

And I remembered the name from Minke's writings. This must be the company he referred to as Speceraria.

They conversed in Dutch.

"I tried to find Madame Minke, but I didn't succeed. Your mother and father also tried, but they didn't succeed either. Forgive us all, Mas, forgive us all."

"I just wanted to see how you were."

"We can talk about that some other time, Mas. Come on inside now."

"No, I will have to go in a minute. How are your wife and children?"

Meneer Darman hesitated.

"Where are your children now?"

He let go of his embrace and turned away.

"How are relations with Europe?"

"Smooth and orderly," he answered, as if reporting to a supervisor. "When will you be freed, Mas?"

"I am not free yet." Minke looked at me and Meneer Darman followed his gaze.

I turned the other way and walked outside. Not long after, Meneer Darman and Minke also came out. I don't know what else they talked about.

Meneer Darman came over to me and in very good Dutch asked whether Minke could stay the night with him as the ship was not leaving until the next morning. He also invited me to stay at his house. I refused. And Minke himself also turned down the offer.

Meneer Darman was still standing in the door as the taxi drove off.

"Where to now, Meneer?" I asked.

"Wherever you like," he answered somewhat rudely.

"Wouldn't you like to dine somewhere?"

"I want to be by myself in my room," he answered, and this time he was being rude.

He was upset. He was probably angry at Darman for not making a success of his family. Things didn't seem to be quite right with Meneer Darman. . . .

During the voyage to Betawi, Raden Mas Minke was shifted to a first-class cabin. He didn't organize it himself and it was definitely not the work of the government. Meneer Darman had obviously arranged the move. He came to see Minke off and tried to give him a suitcase. I don't know what was in it, but Minke refused it. Minke occupied a cabin by himself. He continued to wear Javanese clothes, even in his cabin. He would not see me.

And so it was that we sailed to Betawi without the exchange of a single word.

I was truly shocked when we alighted at Betawi. His luggage consisted of nothing more than a tin suitcase, small, old, dinted and dented, and most of its paint missing.

"Nothing else, Meneer?" I asked.

"Yes."

"Let me get it."

"No need. I've brought it all in my head."

"Oh, I understand."

He didn't need anything from me. Perhaps he thought that his businesses would still be operating the way they were five years ago. He didn't realize just how fast the times changed in the Indies. The hot climate and humid air meant that everything rotted and broke down very quickly—people's bodies too, and their lives. It looked as if he had not been informed about the confiscation of all his property by the government. And I knew why. The government was ashamed of what it had done. It was none other than the government itself that realized that its actions were deceitful, cruel, and uncivilized. And he didn't know either that paid agents of the government were spreading rumors in the Sarekat that the return of Raden Mas Minke would bring disaster on the Sarekat and its members because it was Raden Mas Minke who was responsible for the attacks on the Chinese that had taken place four years earlier.

And it didn't stop there either. Government agents also whispered everywhere that he had been involved in defrauding a bank and that was why all his property had been confiscated. Government spies, so the whispers went, were seeking out everyone who had ever been close to him, because the government was reopening the investigation into the riots.

And nobody knew better than I that the further the whispers spread away from me, the dirtier, darker, and more threatening they became. I knew that it was a foul, evil thing to do. But this person must be separated from his sheep. The Sarekat must remain totally loyal to Mas Tjokro.

But don't be angry at me, Modern Pitung. This was the kindest thing that I could bestow upon you. And if you knew anything about the past, you would know that such little presents as this were often bestowed upon your people by the Company when your ancestors still wielded some power.

You could succeed in whatever you wanted if you understood your own strength. You had awakened your people who had been stunted and ruined by their illusions. It was so true that this people did not fully understand who you were, even though they had listened to your every word and had carried out your every order. But they remained stunted and ruined under the oppression of such illusions. Even during the next quarter of a century there would probably be no other Native able to free himself of these illusions as I had done. The government needed their illusions, and did not need people who had no illusions, such as you, Raden Mas Minke.

I don't think he slept at all during the voyage to Betawi. He looked tired, and seemed to be getting older. I took the way he had answered me back in Surabaya as a sign that he wanted to be free of me and everyone else. And his meeting with Meneer Darman was the first bitter harvest of disappointment since his release. There would be many more such harvests.

Perhaps the way he had answered me was also a way of showing the servant of the government, this Pangemanann, that we could not rob him of everything. He had a big plan. And that plan was still inside his head.

I had to listen carefully now to his every word, just as I would listen to every word of the government and the governor-general.

The car that was there to pick us up took us straight out of the harbor without having to bother with any of the formalities. He stared full of fascination at everything he saw around him. He didn't speak at all.

I tried to remind him of his first visit to Betawi, which he had described in his manuscripts: "The horse tram still runs, Meneer. When you rode it for the first time you may have already heard the prediction that one day they would run without horses and without spewing out smoke. The engine wouldn't run on petrol or steam, but on electricity!"

He hissed. I couldn't tell whether he had been listening to me or not. But I needed to put him in a friendly mood so as to ensure success in the task I would soon have to carry out. I had to keep talking.

"People are still hoping that all sorts of miracles will be possible with electricity. Electricity outside the human body, Meneer . . ." I stole a glance at him and our eyes suddenly met. He was waiting for what I was going to say about electricity in the human body.

I didn't continue.

The car sped past the jungle and swamps of Ancol. He still didn't speak.

All around Gambir Square there now stood buildings that were not there five years ago. He studied them one by one. Gambir Square looked beautiful that morning. We could see in the distance the Dutch ladies taking their babies for a ride in their strollers, accompanied too by their older children. The older brothers and sisters were running about on the open lawns like little goats. Then I saw his gaze being drawn to the music stand in the corner. He had often listened to the music along with all the lonely nyai, he and his friends from the medical school.

Once again he was faced with the past. There must have been all sorts of thoughts passing through his mind. I could just imagine. Every time you are reminded of times past, you are also reminded of just how fast life passes by, and then you start hesitantly weighing up what you have achieved in all this time. And in Minke's case, it was obvious that he had achieved a great many of his ideals. I too had achieved a great deal, except it was not and now never would be what I had hoped I would achieve.

The car made its way slowly into the compound of Police Headquarters. When we stopped in front of the office veranda, we were welcomed by two police officers in official police style. Minke seemed not to be interested. He knew the salute was not for him, but for me.

We escorted him inside. He was quickly served with coffee, milk, and his favorite cigar. The two police officers tried their hardest to be as amicable as possible. They were both Pure-Blood Europeans. Minke seemed to be trying to smile as much as he could. Yet we all had a good idea of what might really be going on in his mind.

For a quarter of an hour the little drama continued, we playing the friendly host, he putting on all the smiles. He drank a quarter of his cup of coffee and then stopped. We talked about all sorts of things. But he still didn't speak. Then at last he opened his mouth, and we went silent and listened to him. He said in Dutch, quickly, softly, almost hissing: "Good. Enough. Now what is it that you gentlemen want from me?" His eyes swept over us one by one as if issuing a challenge.

"Meneer Raden Mas Minke," I said, "to be frank with you, there is one thing, a very small thing, that we need from you. Just a very small thing, just your signature, and then you will be free."

"He-he. What is it that you want me to sign? Is there some new law or regulation about this?"

"No, Meneer Raden Mas. All we want is a bit of a statement from you. All you have to do is sign it. We have the statement here ready."

"There is nothing that I need to sign. Isn't the governor-general's decree releasing me enough?"

"If that is the course that Meneer thinks is the wisest course, then that certainly is up to you," I said, threatening him, "but perhaps it is best that you also study this statement."

He glared a challenge at me, then at the other two policeman, each in turn. They were both silent. They didn't interfere because this was not their area of work.

Minke nodded and then grumbled: "There is nothing that I need to study if I do not wish to."

"Very well, but at least Meneer Raden Mas should know what is in it."

"You can arrest me again whenever you want. I don't need to know what is in it."

"Very well." I spoke again. "It is my duty to ensure that you know what is in this statement. Because you are not prepared to read it, I will read it aloud to you."

I read out the statement, which of course I had written myself, word by word. The two policemen listened attentively while watching Minke. But Minke himself didn't show any sign of being interested at all; instead he just twirled his mustache as if he were back in his own house.

"Nah, so now you have heard what is in the statement. It has been witnessed by these two police officers. So we now officially consider that you know what is in the statement."

"A promise not to become involved in politics or organizing," he hissed. "Very beautiful. Just like in a palace comedy. Have you ever watched one of the palace comedies?" He shifted his gaze to each of us in turn. "So the idea is that only the government can get involved in politics or organizations?"

None of us expected such a sharp refusal or such a question as that. We were all dumbstruck.

"Not allowed to get involved in politics or organizations," he whispered to himself. Suddenly his lips were pulled back into a smile, and his voice struck out clearly: "What do you gentlemen mean by politics? And by organization? And what do you mean by 'involved?' "

We were all still dumbstruck.

"Do you mean that I have to go and live by myself on top of a mountain? Everything is political! Everything needs organization. Do you gentlemen think that the illiterate farmers who spend their lives hoeing the ground are not involved in politics? The moment they surrender a part of their little crop to the village authorities as tax, they are carrying out a political act, because they are acknowledging and accepting the authority of the government. Or do you mean by politics just those things that make the government unhappy? While those things that make the government happy are not political? And tell me, who is it that can free themselves from involvement in organization? As soon as you have more than two people together, you already have organization. The more people there are, the more complex and advanced the organization becomes. Or do you mean something else again by politics and organization?"

The three of us were still dumbstruck.

"From the time of the Prophet until today," he lowered his voice, "no human being has ever been able to separate himself from the power of his fellow human beings, except those who have been shunted away because they were insane. Even those who become hermits, who take themselves away into the middle of the forest or the ocean, still take with them something of the influence of their fellow human beings. And while there are those who rule and those who are ruled, those who exercise power and those who are the objects of that exercise of power, people will be involved in politics. While people live in society, no matter how small that society, people will be organizing. Or do you want me to sign my own death sentence without there ever having been any trial, just as I was sentenced to exile without any trial? Or is this ridiculous letter another part of the governor-general's Extraordinary Powers? If so, let me see proof that such new regulations have been introduced. I want to see them."

He knew we had lost our tongues, and he put out the cigar in his ashtray and smiled victoriously.

"We do not have to answer," I said.

"Who then? Me?"

We were even more cornered now.

"Don't be angry, Meneer," said one of the policemen.

"It is not a question of being angry or not being angry. You gentlemen are servants of the law. If I sign that letter, it will bind me in law. But the letter itself has no basis in law. I think it is better if you gentlemen sign it yourselves."

When he saw that we were still unable to say anything, he asked me as if he were the governor-general himself: "Meneer Pangemanann, am I still your official guest?"

"Where will you go, Meneer?"

"Anyway, there is no need for me to be escorted."

"So you will not sign this statement?"

"Forget it, Meneer."

"Very well. Today you feel you cannot sign it. Tomorrow or the next day, you might change your mind," I said. "We will keep this letter here. If at any time you feel you need it, you will find it here."

"As a guest to his host, I thank you for everything. Good afternoon."

He picked up his suitcase, which did not seem heavy. Then he strode proudly outside and walked to the main road.

One of the policemen jumped up in amazement, while the other jumped up to restrain him.

"A stubborn clever man," he commented.

"If I were he, perhaps I would have the same attitude," I said.

"What will we do with this document, Meneer Pangemanann?"

"There is nobody who can force him to sign it. It was the wrong procedure. Even His Excellency couldn't force him. Not the whole police force."

From the office window, we saw him hail a carriage. He climbed aboard. The carriage headed off in the direction of Senen.

A few moments later five police agents in civilian clothes emerged from the police compound on bicycles and followed his carriage.

13

According to my boss, His Excellency the governor-general was very impressed with Raden Mas Minke's attitude. He had listened to the report, nodding, and then had said, laughing: "Any self-respecting European would have done the same. Meneer Idenburg shouldn't have taken such harsh action against him. It has only made him harder. Isn't it true that he was not like this during van Heutsz's time? Van Heutsz knew how to handle him."

It was His Excellency Governor-General Van Limburg Stirum's view that it was not only improper but indeed immoral to use the governor-general's Extraordinary Powers except as a last resort. Even so I don't think it was right for him to criticize his predecessor because Idenburg faced a different situation during his rule. The world war was changing a lot of things in the Indies. Very well. Perhaps from now on the government will rely on the courts to decide these matters.

"No person shall be punished without a decision from a court of law."

So he spoke, for the first and last time.

These words of his were enough to make the staff of the Algemeene Secretariat ashamed of themselves. It meant that De Lange had died for nothing. It also meant that His Excellency would review the decisions of the De Lange Commission, if he came to know about them. And if that

happened, there might be several Algemeene Secretariat staff who would
decide that they should resign because of the embarrassment.

I myself would be facing no lesser difficulties. If the government per-
severed with these policies, then there was a real possibility my services
would soon no longer be needed. And what was the meaning of a Pangemanann with two *n*s if deprived of the opportunity to serve the government? The attempt to work together with the Syndicates failed. Not only
did my boss have no interest in the idea, but he was also busy preparing to
leave the Indies to migrate to America. In another five years, he would be
able to become an American citizen. He spent most of his time sitting
daydreaming, and it seemed the whole of the government was following
his example, sitting daydreaming.

To safeguard my position, it was necessary that I show how busy I
was. The situation regarding my future did not look good, but on the other
hand there had been no changes to my official status or the mandate that I
had been given. And so I worked on as if I were somebody very important,
as if the whole Indies depended on me, as if the Indies itself would have to
close up shop if there were no Pangemanann.

The voice of His Excellency Van Limburg Stirum was like the voice
of an angel from heaven. But here on earth, in the Indies, things would be
different. . . . And this was plain from the journey of one human inhabitant
of this earth named Raden Mas Minke, a journey described in detail in
many reports, which were in turn studied minutely.

He had left us and traveled by carriage in the direction of Senen. But
he stopped the carriage before arriving at Senen Markets. Carrying his suitcase, he alighted and paid the driver, who received it without protest, a
sign that the payment was adequate, perhaps even more than adequate.

He turned into an alley, walking briskly. It seemed he knew this area
well from the days when, fifteen years ago, as a medical student, he wandered these alleyways. My men almost lost him. He moved quickly in and
out of alleyways, obviously not looking for any particular address; then he
came into a market. If he had stayed in the carriage he would have arrived
there long before. It seemed he was trying to shake off any surveillance.

He went into a covered stall and, sitting among the market coolies,
devoured a meal. He sat there for some time, smoking his favorite cigar,
and chatted with the coolies who all admired that cigar. Because he did not
have enough, he could hand out only three of them, which the coolies
then took turns at smoking.

There was nothing important discussed in their conversation. He set
off again with his old suitcase. One of the coolies offered to carry his bag.
He refused and walked off alone in the direction of Kramat. Several times

he fixed up the twirl of his mustache. And the suitcase seemed very light, as if it were empty.

He walked quickly, looking neither to left nor right. He crossed a five-way intersection with one hand holding his suitcase and the other the bottom tip of his sarong. He headed for a building on the right. Without looking at the sign on the building, he went straight inside. In the reception he asked: "Where is Mas Kardi?"

One of the employees, who looked as if he were of Arab descent, answered: "Which Mas Kardi? We have a Mas Kardi who is a painter. Or do you mean one of the guests?"

"No, Mas Kardi the manager of the hotel."

"There is no Mas Kardi who is manager, Tuan. I manage this hotel."

"So where is Mas Kardi? The old manager."

"How would I know, Tuan?"

He seemed confused. He looked around the room and his eyes became fixed on the name of the hotel attached to the room keys. He asked hesitantly: "Isn't this Hotel Medan?"

"No, Tuan. It used to be called that. But it came into my hands at an auction."

"An auction! Who said it could be auctioned? I never gave anyone the authority to do that!"

Now it was the hotel owner who was startled. He asked: "Would you perhaps be Raden Mas Minke?" Because there was no answer, he continued: "It seems that you did not see the sign outside, Tuan. Please sit down. Or perhaps you need a room? Please sit down. And welcome back from a place which was no doubt far away."

He seemed confused now that he had lost his hotel and lost the room that he prepared for himself in his mind long before he arrived back in Betawi.

"Neither I nor any of the people working here at the hotel have done any wrong against you, Tuan. I myself was once a member of the Sarekat, Tuan. You can stay here as long as you like. We truly did not know that you were unaware of the auction."

The Modern Pitung left the hotel that was no longer his realm, still carrying his dilapidated case and holding the tip of his sarong. He was grinding his teeth and his face was drained of blood. He turned to read the name of the hotel which read, in big letters, HOTEL CAPITOL. You could still read the fading traces of the old paint—HOTEL MADEN—and underneath were the words: ESTABLISHED PRIMARILY FOR THOSE LEAVING FOR THE HAJ.

Now he walked hesitantly in the direction of Kwitang, turning to the left. Several tens of meters along from the five-way intersection, he stopped to look at the very first house he had ever rented. And across to the right, quite some ways away, and not visible from where he was standing, there stood the hospital complex and the medical school where he had studied for six years.

Now he hailed a carriage and climbed aboard without bargaining for the fare first. The carriage headed straight for the house of Dr. Sindu Ragil. The front door was closed—there was no private practice there. He climbed down and paid the driver, then walked down the side of the house, where he met the doctor's wife.

"Mas, ah, Mas Minke! Don't be angry. Forgive both of us. We have been warned not to receive any guests during this week."

"Who warned you?"

"Come on, Mas Minke, of course you know who. A thousand pardons, Mas. There is nothing we can do."

"Am I on the list of guests that you are not allowed to receive?"

"It just so happens that is Mas who has arrived."

And so the Modern Pitung left the house of Dr. Sindu Ragil, where he often used to visit whenever he was in Betawi. He walked out of the front yard and stood silent for quite a while, holding on to the iron lattice of the front fence of his friend's house, and he shook his head. His body was wet with sweat and he had not wiped his face.

He hailed a horse cart and headed for Sawah Besar. He seemed to be lost in thought and did not take any notice of the traffic around him. The horse cart took him to a certain shop. When the horse cart stopped he hesitated because there was no sign on this shop that read MEDAN OFFICE AND SCHOOL SUPPLIES SHOP. And when he saw that there were no books and stationery for sale inside, he was even more startled. The shop now sold various steel products.

He seemed to be realizing now that a mysterious wall was surrounding him. He ordered the horse cart to go straight on to Gambir Station. Pity on this Modern Pitung. He intended to go home to his house, my home in Buitenzorg.

There were no reports about how he behaved in the train. And then what had to happen happened.

It was four o'clock in the afternoon. I was in my study in the house. From the study window, I saw a horse cart stop in front of the house. Then a man in Native clothes climbed down. I recognized him straightaway. It was Raden Mas Minke. He carried his case and walked into the front yard. He no doubt imagined that Princess Kasiruta would be there to greet him. You are mistaken, Modern Pitung, it will be I who greet you.

I went out to meet him dressed in casual off-duty clothes. He was at the veranda by the time he recognized me.

"Please come up, Meneer Raden Mas."

His face was tense, pale, dry, like paper. In the end I will have my triumph over you, Modern Pitung.

"Please come in, please. You are here no doubt about the statement."

He was trying to keep control of himself. As his paleness disappeared I could see his eyes aflame with anger, his two arms shivered so that he dropped his bag.

"I am not here to sign anything! I have come home to my own house!"

"You are mistaken. Let me take you home. You seem to have forgotten that this is not your address. What is your address now?" I saw him bite his lips. The left-hand side of his mustache was drooping now. Perhaps the wax had melted because of the sun.

"Please come in," and I descended from the veranda, coming closer to him on the ground.

"Of course, I am mistaken," he said, regaining his composure. "It's just that I was so surprised to find you here, Meneer Pangemanann."

"Please come up. You must be thirsty. As it happens my wife is not home, but you need not worry. You must be tired. You can use the guest room."

I suddenly recalled the time I had visited here, but our positions as host and guest were reversed then. I quickly added: "We have met before in this house, haven't we, Meneer Raden Mas? We are not new acquaintances, are we? It's just that our positions are different now."

He swallowed saliva, then: "Thank you, Meneer Pangemanann. With your permission, I shall be off."

"Where do you want to go so late in the afternoon?"

He gave a nod of respect, picked up his case that had fallen to the ground, and left.

I knew then that I had turned into a sadist. And how great were the costs you pay for becoming a sadist—I felt no regret about what I had done. I had even felt honored to be able to torment him like this. And in the Indies anyone could be a sadist as long as they were among the powerful. But for those who have no power, only punishment awaits them if they indulge. Having tormented him like this made me feel even more important and powerful, and I felt even more disgusted with what I had become.

Raden Mas Minke would no doubt spend the evening seeking out his old acquaintances. If that was the path he chose, he would be destitute by midnight. I knew that he did not have enough money with him. As soon as he had received the letter from the governor-general ending his exile, he had handed over all his possessions in Ambon to his maid, even the allowance that he had saved, one *ringgit* per month for five years. The maid, Auntie Marientje, had accompanied him to the ship, crying all the way. When the ship's whistle finally cried out, she had to be forcibly escorted back to shore. The third and final whistle was accompanied by her hysterical screams. She wailed and cried out over and over as the anchor was hauled in and the ship began to move. People began to disperse and make their way home.

She remained there by herself weeping. The ship disappeared from view and so, still sobbing, she made her way back to the house in Benteng Street where Minke used to live. She would start life anew, never to look after the Modern Pitung again.

So my guess was that he had no more than four ringgit left.

He shared a taxi to Bandung with four others. He asked to get out in Braga Street. It was already night. He inspected the old *Medan* building, peeking in through the windows. There were a number of workers from the printers who went in and out. He didn't recognize any of them. Then he left, walking off in another direction.

It was ten o'clock. He visited the Frischbotens' house. He was greeted by the barking of a guard dog and was forced to check the name plate on the fence. It was no longer the Frischbotens' house.

Like a bird with a broken wing, he wandered along in a daze until he found an empty bamboo night watchman's shelter on the side of the road and went inside. . . .

Alone in a roadside shelter in the middle of the night, he would surely be remembering the past once more. And he would be thinking how miserly his homeland and his people have been to him. He, who had been so famous five years ago, had now been forgotten, thrown away like a piece of rag. He who had lived and could only live through leading his sheep, now there would not even be a single sheep for him to lead.

Even so, Raden Mas Minke, you are a teacher, a teacher to every person with a European education, because Europe was able to convince me that every person, any person, who had succeeded in what they had set out to do was a teacher who added to humankind's knowledge and learning. And it is because of your status as such a teacher that I decided to be so lenient toward you. But it was impossible for me to be any more lenient than this, although your departure from this transitory world would have lessened the never-ending effort I had to expend in protecting myself and my job. If you had decided to sign that document this morning, perhaps His Excellency the governor-general would have even offered you a position. But it is too late; the rice is already porridge now.

322 PRAMOEDYA ANANTA TOER

It was reported that three days later he traveled in a third-class carriage to Betawi. He did not find what he was looking for in Bandung. Nor in Sukabumi. If he found anything it was just stories of bygone times.

He sat at the train window, watching the passing scenery chase off into some uncertain world. He was leaving behind him a past full of glories and the farther behind he left them, the more beautiful and poignant they became. Where was his wife, Princess Kasiruta? All he had found was the news that she had been ordered to leave Java for the Molucca Islands and no one could tell him on which of these fifty or so islands she might be found. How solitary was his life now. But he was still young; there was much that he could do yet. But would he be able to do more? Let us watch.

He got out at Gambir Station. He sat for a long time on the station bench. His suitcase, his single possession, rested on his lap. I don't know what was inside. Nobody recognized him. He didn't seem to see anything about him. Perhaps it was only his mind's eye that was dwelling longingly on past glories that others were already beginning to forget. Yes, how quickly do the people of the tropics forget that even the hardest of bones are destroyed by the tropical humidity.

Then at last he got up and left the platform, walking slowly like an old man. During the last few days reality had truly been tormenting his soul. It was all more than he was able to bear. So this is the freedom I have prepared for you, Modern Pitung, my teacher!

He didn't have the money to hire a carriage this time. He made his way by foot. He walked and walked. His head was bowed, peering toward the ground. It was so moving to see how faithful he was to his old decayed suitcase, which probably didn't even have anything in it. . . .

I knew it was unnecessary and excessive to continue the surveillance. Freedom was turning out to be an even more extreme exile for him. But I ordered the police to continue to follow him.

For several weeks he wandered from market to market. It seemed he had decided that he would avoid any contact with his colleagues, his old friends. Then finally he was taken in by one of his oldest comrades, Goenawan, who had been pushed aside in the Sarekat Islam after Mas Tjokro took over.

Everyone had believed that these two friends would never get together because of a disagreement that had happened between them six years before. But they were wrong.

The two men had met in one of the little side streets in old Betawi. It was Goenawan who saw Raden Mas Minke and then watched him for a while. He was walking along when he saw a man with a big luxuriant mustache twirled up at the corners. This man was standing reading a poster that somebody had pasted to a shop wall. He was carrying an old suitcase, wearing a torn calico shirt and scrappy Macao calico trousers too, but he was reading a Dutch-language poster. After he read it, he seemed to pause and think for a moment while his eyes darted left and right without actually seeing anything. Then slowly, he started walking again, walking and walking. He seemed exhausted and sucked of all his strength.

Out of curiosity, Goenawan followed him. He was sure the man was an educated person going through hard times.

The mustache had reminded him of Minke in his days of triumph. Goenawan increased his pace to overtake the other man. He stopped fifty meters ahead and stood underneath a tree, waiting.

Raden Mas Minke was walking very slowly. His face was ashen. He was paying no heed to anything going on about him. Sensing he was being watched, he held his head down. From underneath his forehead he stole a glance at Goenawan, whom he recognized. The person in front of him had not aged at all during the last five years. He pretended not to recognize him and kept on walking slowly.

Once Minke had passed him, Goenawan followed him from one meter behind. He wasn't wrong. He walked faster and came up beside Minke: "Mas Minke!" he greeted him slowly without turning to face him. "So you've come home from exile?"

Raden Mas Minke kept on walking, pretending not to hear. No hands have been held out to help me, perhaps that was what he was thinking then. All doors have been closed to me. Is Goenawan here now to rub salt into my wounds? Whether that was what he was really thinking, I will, of course, never know. But that was what his attitude seemed to indicate he was thinking. Perhaps he even thought that Goenawan was another government agent.

"Where are you staying, Mas?" asked Goenawan without looking at him.

Raden Mas Minke did not answer, he just coughed several times. It looked as if he might have fallen ill while he had been wandering around Betawi.

"You look sick and tired, Mas. Where are you staying?"

Seeing that the man was hesitating, he took Minke's case, which seemed too light to contain anything. When he touched his former friend's hand, he could tell that he had a bad fever. He called a carriage and helped the Modern Pitung up aboard before he had a chance to protest.

Two days later we lost track of him. But as soon as we had ascertained for sure that the man who had helped him was Goenawan, the former head of the Betawi branch of the Sarekat, it was easy to find him again.

So I found out something about my hero, my teacher. This man who believed so much in his own strength now lived under the protection of another. I would not have believed it if the repeat investigation I ordered had not confirmed it. It was almost an impossibility, but that was what had happened.

From four different reports the following picture emerged—that is, after I considered all the material and reconstructed events in my mind. It was very true that Raden Mas Minke was ill. As a former medical student, he must have known what his illness was but he refused to see a doctor. He said that his illness was nothing at all and that he would get better once he had rested.

From what Goenawan told some of his friends, it seemed that the two of them had a certain discussion. It wasn't clear who began the conversation, but Minke told him: "I have come at the wrong time."

"You left us at the wrong time, just when everybody needed your leadership. But you preferred to leave. Wasn't that the reason for our falling out then?"

"I don't think now is the time for an argument," he answered.

"Yes, but we should always evaluate our mistakes, even when they took place a long time ago."

"Of course, but you forget that the Sarekat agreed to my plans to go abroad."

"Because Samadi wanted you out of the way."

So the shooting incident in Bandung remained a secret. Suurhof had never opened his mouth about this either. Perhaps even now he did not know who had shot him. And Minke said nothing about this to Goenawan.

Perhaps he was still not completely sure that Princess Kasiruta was involved in Suurhof's shooting.

"That is an unworthy suspicion," he replied.

"It is no suspicion. The events that followed speak for themselves. He thought that leading the people would be no more difficult from managing his batik concerns. But it turned out that human beings are not pieces of batik. It was lucky he later realized his mistake. And when he realized this, he let the Sarekat fall into the hands of Mas Tjokro. And the result has been nothing but a lot of unproductive noise."

Minke had a personal secret and he would never tell anybody. The pity was that both he and Goenawan thought that the mystery of why the Sarekat had ended up in such a disappointing state and out of their control was hidden in the story that he would not tell.

How pathetic it was. Minke thought that nobody knew his secret, but it was none other than I myself who knew who the killer was and who wounded De Zweep, and who it was who whispered the order to kill into his wife's ear.

It was clear that Minke would not say why he had wanted to leave the Indies then. But I knew the reason. He loved his first child too much. He was prepared to say good-bye to the Sarekat rather than allow its reputation to be sullied because of him. He would take this secret to his grave.

The conversation reached a dead end, and Goenawan did not push him further, especially as Minke was not yet showing any signs of recovering from his illness.

It was Goenawan who explained to him how the Sarekat had developed while he was in exile—not as it had been reported in the press, but the reality. And he listened silently, sometimes shaking his head in disbelief.

"I have not only come back at the wrong time," he commented. "Things have not developed at all as we had hoped."

"It seems they have readied everything for your return, Mas. I know you are in great difficulties."

"Yes, because there are always trials put before us, and I will face these trials and go forward."

"Of course."

"The preparations they have made don't bother me very much."

"Are you serious?"

"Why not? There is only one thing preventing me from acting—the world war."

"Ah, you are drawing too long a bow, Mas. We don't have anything to do with the war."

"All of us bear the burden of this world war. It's a matter for all of us. It will be a block to all our efforts during our lifetime, and it will leave its mark for years to come."

"But the war had nothing to do with your release."

"Who knows what happens in the colonial heavens?"

"And what happens when the war is over?"

"When it is over? My first step will be to sue the government and the bank."

"Mas!"

Raden Mas Minke nodded. He was so thin, yet his mustache was still properly cared for. His eyes shone full of optimism, and his voice was clear and strong just as it had been in earlier times.

"I will hire European lawyers."

"What will you use to pay them?"

"If all they are interested in is money, then there is no point in there being any laws that they have a duty to maintain and defend."

"But they had to work very hard to become lawyers and spend a lot of money."

"But how does that compare with all the efforts of the whole of humankind to finally discover and institute laws in the first place? How much can just one person contribute to humankind's treasury of laws? If lawyers are not angered by the violation of the law, then they should look for jobs as street sweepers instead."

"Yes, that's how you think things should be, Mas. It's not how they actually are."

"We all have to accept reality, yes, that's true. But just to accept reality and do nothing else, that is the attitude of human beings who have lost the ability to develop and grow, because human beings also have the ability to create new realities. And if there are no longer people who want to create new realities, then perhaps the word *progress* should be removed altogether from humankind's vocabulary."

"You are going to fight the government, Mas? Perhaps you have forgotten that you have just been exiled for attacking Governor-General Idenburg?"

"Even if he had not been attacked like that, he could still have exiled me at any time, just to show that he did indeed have the power to do so. Even better. For somebody who considers himself to be chosen by God, his Extraordinary Powers are just another luxury for him to use at any time. In any case, it wasn't me who attacked him in *Medan*."

"Not you? But everybody praised you for having the courage to print that attack."

"It wasn't me. I didn't agree with it at all. I wouldn't have been so reckless, especially when it wasn't at all clear that such recklessness would bring any benefits for the people."

"But it teaches people to have courage."

"Courage to do what? Bravery for the sake of bravery is just as negative as acting arbitrarily for the sake of acting arbitrarily. They are both extravagances, nothing more."

"And when the world war ends, and you take them to court, are you sure you'll win? The lawyers you hire will be more loyal to those in power and with white skins than to a brown-skinned son of a colonized people like us. The government and the bank will be able to pay more than you."

It was said that he laughed when he heard that and answered: "That is just a matter of risk. For some time now people have thought of me as a leader. Now that everybody has watched them inflict injustice and take illegal actions against me and the companies that were under my control, while they all actually belonged to the organization, should I just be silent? Then what kind of leader would I be?"

"But I don't believe you can win, Mas."

"They have always been the victors. So if they emerge victorious in my case too, that is only what everyone expects. But if I win?"

"I can only pray for your victory, Mas."

But the conversation about Minke's plans to sue the government and the bank did not end there.

The unwitnessed conversation between these two people reached me via a convoluted and contorted route and produced big rumblings in many government offices. My office was very busy. And I was the busiest of all. I received order after order instructing me to study all the files dealing with Minke. I carried out the order even though I knew every folio in his file by heart. I read the manuscripts from Ambon again. Nobody knew that I had taken them for myself and that I kept them in my house.

The Bandung State Court reexamined the documentation regarding its orders for the confiscation of the Sarekat companies that were under Raden Mas Minke's direct control. The Betawi police compiled a list of everybody who had ever been close to him and sent out its eyes and ears to see if any of them were preparing to give him any help. The police in Buitenzorg and Bandung did the same thing.

I myself had to visit the banks to carry out my own investigation. None of them would show me Raden Mas Minke's accounts. "As regards this, sir," they said, "we can show them only to Raden Mas Minke himself."

I gave the police the task of finding Meneer Koordat Evertsen, the former executive manager of the publishing side of *Medan.* It turned out he had gone home to Holland and then moved to Surinam, a very wealthy man.

How futile had been the life of De Lange, who had indeed given his life. He had listened too closely to the voice of his European conscience. If he had been able to accept what the colonial authorities had done, then he would still be safe and alive and I would still be a policeman. Even though the government had engaged in deceit, there was no chance it would get caught, because not all cases, let alone cases involving the government, necessarily had to go to court.

The Netherlands police instructed the colonial police in Surinam to investigate Koordat Evertsen. A very intensive investigation and repeated questioning finally produced a confession that he had embezzled from the company because of intimidation from De Zweep and also because there was something in it for himself as well.

Whether Koordat Evertsen confessed or not wasn't important because there was no chance that Minke would ever be able to take his case to court. Moreover, the investigation of Evertsen was conducted merely as a routine checkup. And if the name De Zweep arose, then it would be better for the police to remain silent. And it was no accident that Robert Suurhof had not shown his face for so long. He would be eliminated by Cor Oosterhof. And nobody knew how he lived now since the death of Rientje de Roo because nobody needed to know. And such is the fate of bandits who are no longer of use.

De Zweep! A name that brought forth bad memories. De Zweep had been destroyed when Princess Kasiruta's bullet pierced Robert Suurhof's sternum.

Minke could, however, call on his friends in Europe to expose the government for its crimes. But I had to make sure that such a thing didn't happen. Perhaps he had already sent off one or two letters to them. If that turned out to be true, then Cor Oosterhof would send Robert Suurhof and the remnants of his gang to hell, no matter where they might be today.

If he had not yet contacted his friends in Europe, then we had to make sure he did not do so. Every person who emerged from Goenawan's house was followed just in case they might try to post a letter. And it turned out that nobody tried.

As more reports came in, I found out that Minke had expressed his desire to his friends to send some letters and telegrams. But Goenawan did not understand exactly what Minke wanted from him and so did not give him the money he needed. And the Modern Pitung did not have a single cent to his name. He also planned to meet Thamrin Mohammed Thabrie, but he was too weak to walk that far. He had to postpone all his plans.

That his return from exile was never reported in the press was also the result of the tight rein I kept on the newspapers. He must not become the center of public attention again. He must remain separated from his favorite child, the world of journalism. It was truly an irony that a pioneer of the Native press should get no place in the press at such an important moment in his life as this. The *Oetoesan Hindia*, the Sarekat paper, knew nothing of his arrival in Betawi. Goenawan had severed all links with the Sarekat and so did not inform any of the Sarekat publications.

The leading figures in the Betawi branch of the Sarekat had heard within a week, however. They held a special meeting to discuss what to do. From my desk I was able to make sure that they took no action that would make Minke a public figure again.

A policeman who lived near one of the Betawi branch leaders went to see his neighbor and told him that Minke had been met by ex-

Commissioner Pangemanann in Surabaya and that when they arrived together in Betawi, Minke was taken straight to Police Headquarters. He told his neighbor that he was in the same room as Minke when, in front of Pangemanann and two senior police officers, Minke signed a promise of some kind. He said he didn't know what was in the document. But he was prepared to swear that he heard the police talking after Minke had left and that they had been talking about how Minke had promised to carry out the government's orders to spy on the Sarekat.

These few words were all that was needed. It was very easy to throw such people as these, people who did not know where they were going or what their goals were, into confusion with little reports like these.

The Betawi Branch would take no action concerning Minke.

But Minke himself seemed to be prepared to patiently await the end of the world war. He could be patient because there was no other road he could travel, no other path open to him. Could the others be patient like him?

Among Goenawan's acquaintances was a German doctor named Bernard Meyersohn. He had reported to the police that he had been visited by a Eurasian. But from the very moment that this patient stepped into the surgery, it was clear that he was as healthy as an ox. And indeed, there was nothing wrong with him. As soon as he stood before Dr. Meyersohn he took out a leather whip from his shirt and spoke very coarsely in Dutch: "Do you know what this is?"

"A leather whip."

The doctor was a very simple man. He had come to the Indies for no other reason than to seek a livelihood and find some peace and quiet. He didn't know anything about what was happening in the Indies nor did he have any desire to know. In his simplicity he stared at this patient full of amazement, thinking that he was dealing with a crazy man.

"Are you sure you haven't come to the wrong place?"

"Do you think I am illiterate, Meneer Doctor?"

"Of course not," he answered, observing the whip. "But I have no need of that whip."

"But Meneer does need it. Not as a possession, no. But you do need a beating, I think."

"I am a doctor, not a cow," Meyersohn retorted. "I think you had better leave."

The Eurasian youth hit the doctor very hard on his left cheek. He put the whip away and took out a knife and thrust it at the doctor.

"I am not only a doctor, I am also a German," Meyersohn challenged him.

"That's even better," and the youth quickly lunged forward threatening the doctor, his knife aiming at the doctor's heart. "I think it is better for you if you listen to me rather than make speeches about how brave you are. This knife can rip your heart in two easily. Just listen to me now. In a few hours a Native man will be brought to you as a patient. You must not treat him or give him any medicine. Just tell him that he has dysentery, that's all. Remember? Dysentery. You will be safe and the patient will die. Or indeed, the reverse could happen. The patient could live and the doctor could die. Or both could die, or perhaps both could live. Yes, yes, Meneer Doctor must make the choice as to what is best for you. I think the first option is the best. Understand?"

"That is my business."

The youth's left hand wielded his whip again. One hit to the face and the doctor couldn't see anymore. His hands groped around looking for something to grab hold of. All that he could find was the youth's shoulder. And at that moment, he once more heard him speak: "So Meneer Doctor will not forget this order," and he took the doctor to his chair, wet his handkerchief with water from a bowl in the surgery, and cleaned the doctor's face.

He remained seated in the examination room.

A little while later a horse cart pulled up in front of the surgery. Three men helped into the surgery a sick man who seemed unable to stand by himself any longer. The young Eurasian immediately invited them to go into the examination room.

The doctor examined him and the youth assisted. Then it was the young man who said to Dr. Meyersohn: "Dysentery, isn't it, Doctor? Too far gone, I think? Nothing we can do anymore. The best thing to do is take this poor man home."

The doctor did not answer. And the youth repeated what he had said in Malay to the patient's helpers and ordered them to take him home.

They didn't refuse and they carried the patient outside, put him into the horse cart, and disappeared from sight.

"It's a great pity, Doctor, but you will be closing for the rest of the day," and he stayed there for the next four hours.

It was nine o'clock in the evening. As soon as the youth left, the doctor hurried off to report what had happened to the police. But despite his very sharp memory, he was unable to give the police an adequate description of the youth. Because of the inadequate information the police felt it would be very difficult to track this criminal down. The police did not ask the name of the sick man who had been carried into the surgery. And Bernard Meyersohn never knew the man's name either.

Goenawan took the very ill man home and Raden Mas Minke passed away in his care. . . .

And so that was how my teacher ended his life, leaving behind in this world only the imprints of his footsteps. He had gone in loneliness—he who had been forgotten, forgotten since the moment of his birth. He was a leader forgotten by his followers. Such a thing had never happened in Europe. Perhaps such a thing could only happen and has only ever happened in the Indies, where even bones are rotted by the humidity. But even so, it is better to have been a leader forgotten by your followers than a cheat and a liar who is able to become a leader and gain many followers.

His death made me reflect upon how flimsy and fragile is man's place in this life. I could remember the hands that had fumbled about trying to cut him off from his past and future. And I could hear the voices that were blown onto the wind to make sure he did not arrive at the destination he was seeking. And there was not another person in the world who knew any of this better than I. Here upon my desk I had created magic threads that connected me with him. I could feel every move of his fingers, I could hear his every heartbeat. So I also knew that he did not leave behind a single word when he died.

He had died because of sudden stomach illness. I would firmly hold to the explanation that the youth had given, that he had really been ill with dysentery. Perhaps in the future someone might come forward to give another version, but that will not be of concern to me anymore because this Pangemanann will have left this illusory world. In the end the problem of life is the problem of postponing death, even though wise people prefer to die once rather than over and over again.

Raden Mas Minke had died. He was taken to his final resting place in Karet Cemetery by paid pallbearers. There was only one of his friends who accompanied him—Goenawan. There was nobody else. And there was one admirer who escorted him from afar. That person was Jacques Pangemanann. And when he was lowered into his grave, his admirer also watched from afar. And the admirer felt at ease now, because with Raden Mas Minke's death he need not worry about any problems concerning Robert Suurhof, concerning De Zweep and other such things. Minke had gone to where everybody finally journeys and is journeying now.

14

That there were no reports about his death in the newspapers was enough to make me feel secure. He would remain forgotten.

But had he been forgotten?

More and more people continued in his footsteps and left even more of their own imprints—yes, there were more and more of them. I could see this happening before me. What lay before me on my desk was also a sign of this. It was a book titled *Green Student* by Marco Kartodikromo. Even though I did not like the style, or the way he used the language, nor even the story, I had finished the book.

Answers to my inquiries revealed that Mas Marco had arrived in Java a few months after the death of his teacher. Governor-General Van Limburg Stirum had given verbal orders that no action be taken against him unless it could be proved that he had violated the law. Punishment was no longer to be handed out based on the mere suppositions of prosecutors or judges. It looked as though His Excellency was deliberately forgetting the article Marco had written before he had left to follow Siti Soendari to the Netherlands, an article that had directly challenged the governor-general.

Marco had returned home very quietly. He had once crossed an ocean to be near his love's desire, leaving behind his fame and his activity, the struggle and his devotion to it. Now he returned alone, no doubt to resume his activity and restore his fame, which had begun to fade. It was possible that his struggle and efforts to win Soendari had met with failure.

"This time I will not hold back. I will continue my activity unrestrained until they arrest me and exile me somewhere," he told one of his friends.

He was not arrested, let alone exiled. But he was always prepared to be arrested. His Excellency had his own way of dealing with these rebellious types. He was very careful in what he said and did. He had no interest in using unofficial terrorist gangs to help the government. Neither he nor I knew whether or not this policy would continue for long. Everybody would have to wait to see how things developed.

In the meantime Marco did not appear at public meetings. Neither did he appear in any ketoprak performances. He hid away and wrote and wrote, publishing everything anonymously. But Pangemanann would never forget his style nor his vocabulary nor who his friends were. The tone of his articles was becoming more and more extreme all the time. They were increasingly confrontational and encouraged people to cause trouble.

In these times of increasing social unrest, the government deliberately avoided taking harsh action as it had in the past. I myself had come to the conclusion that this was indeed the official policy of Her Majesty's government in the Netherlands. It was obvious that they were worried that any harsh action could result in even worse unrest.

I was able to get reports on some of what Marco was saying and it seemed that one of the reasons for his return to Java was so that he could make sure that his late teacher, Raden Mas Minke, received the recognition he deserved. But he did not talk anymore about Siti Soendari. And when he arrived in Surabaya from Europe, not having gone ashore at Betawi, he went straight to Solo. He felt no need to go to see Mas Tjokro while he was in Surabaya. But Mas Marco did not carry out his intentions as regards his teacher.

After he received a letter from Europe asking why he had done nothing, he told two of his friends: "At this stage of our struggle we cannot afford to waste energy on sentimentality."

Nobody knew who sent him the letter. He never replied to it. He had angrily burned it. And he did not answer his friends' questions as to who his teacher was. But why didn't he reply to the letter from Europe? Perhaps it was from Siti Soendari, and perhaps too he did not dare do anything that would attract too much attention and result in the government taking action against him.

Come on, Marco, once again you have entered my house of glass. You too are someone who can never be still, just like your teacher. How lucky you are that His Excellency Van Limburg Stirum has forgotten that leaflet on gray-green paper that you once wrote. And perhaps it was not only because he brought a softer policy from the Netherlands. Maybe your behavior, based as it was on such inadequate education, stirred feelings of pity in him.

With such a restless spirit as yours, you would not have been happy for long if you had been able to take Siti Soendari as your wife. After a little while you would be restless again, wanting to do something, to take action, to act. Who knows what else you would have decided to do. If you had really made it to the state of holy matrimony, you would also have come to realize how great was the gap in education between the two of you and you would have suffered all your life.

You were right to decide to return home to the Indies. Without Soendari you could be your whole self again, without other things on your mind. And it was right too that you intended to rehabilitate your teacher's reputation. The situation in the Indies has changed, that's for sure. But there was an easier way for you to carry out your intention, except that you are haunted by the possibility that the government might act against you. If you only knew that His Excellency the governor-general and the Royal Netherlands government were so afraid of the Indies bursting into flames . . . they both had grave doubts about the loyalty of the soldiers of the Royal Netherlands Indies Army and the Indies marines because of the increasing influence of Sneevliet.

The government's assessment was that the most likely place for trouble to start was around Solo, where the Mangkunegaran Legion lived. There were whispering campaigns in the Secretariat calling for the legion not to be allowed new intakes of recruits. Gradually the legion would become a battalion of grandfathers incapable of even carrying a rifle. But you, Marco, you are haunted by the images of the machine gun just at the very moment when you should be taking action, doing something, and striking out, which is what your restlessness demands of you.

If you are able to do this, Marco, to rehabilitate the reputation of your teacher, then you might even end up making clear to the Sarekat something that Raden Mas Minke always wanted to make clear but never dared put down on paper. The Sarekat would receive some guidance as to what stance it should be taking. Perhaps this would have come about, perhaps not.

And if you had studied medicine in your youth and then had gone to interview Goenawan, you would have been amazed. How could a former medical student die of dysentery in a city like Betawi? Nobody would have

known better than Raden Mas Minke himself that he did not have dysentery. He knew what illness he was suffering from. And he would not
have told Goenawan because he would not have wanted to give his family
any wrong ideas. He wanted to go to see a doctor of his own choice. But
the illness worked faster than he had calculated. He died, Marco. And then
you came, yes, you came but you have done nothing for him. . . .

He didn't even come to Betawi to pay homage at the grave. It was I
who did that, alone, as a mark of respect for a man who had set new things
in motion in the Indies. I had gone there as a student and an admirer,
bearing a wreath of flowers. And that was just ten days after he died. And
on the wreath was a black ribbon with white writing as a sign of respect
and veneration: "From somebody you do not know to somebody who is
truly respected and esteemed."

I knew I had wronged him and done ill toward him. And I had no
regret that I had carried out those things I could not avoid carrying out.
He was a leader, someone in the vanguard; he should have been able to
outwit me. In this game of chess he had lost all his men, from pawns to his
king, and now he had even lost himself. All I had lost was my principles.
And what is the price of principles!

Such things as principles are good only for knowing about, not implementing. To know where the sun lies and the reason why it lies there
does not mean you have to try to grab hold of it. In any case Minke should
have known that the pieces I had on the chessboard would never be his.
He should have thrown the chessboard away and challenged me to a fight,
or eliminated me altogether.

Marco still did nothing to carry out his intentions.

The Sarekat Islam was silent. Its headquarters in Surabaya was also
silent. Mas Tjokro, the emperor without a crown, the inheritor of this
kingdom, was also silent. And this silence signaled their return to the embrace of Javanism, the embrace of darkness, as if reason had been thrown
away, as if the Sarekat had sprung forth from cracks in the rocks at the
command of some god, as if there had been no person who had pioneered
it and begun the whole process. Samadi said nothing either. And neither
did Thamrin Mohammed Thabrie, who had preceded Minke in departing
this world.

How different were these peoples of the Indies from Europeans, especially the French. In France everyone who has contributed something
new to humankind receives a respected position in the world and in its
history as a matter of course. In the Indies, among the people of the Indies,
it seems that everyone is afraid he will not have any place in history and
spends all his time trying to control it.

The teacher was a personality whom I admired and respected. After he was separated from his followers for just five years, they have forgotten him.

Modern Pitung, if it turns out there is nobody but me who will remember you, then you will be remembered in history in whatever way you want. One day I will often be mentioning your name. One day. Not now. I pray that God receives and gives you a place in accord with all the good you have done. . . .

I kept to myself my speculation that Marco's return would reactivate the Semarang-Solo-Jogja wing. I had made a promise to myself that I would not lay a hand upon him. I would make him the next object of my studies. I just prayed that my superiors would not issue orders that would destroy my plans.

The situation was becoming more and more tense. There were outbreaks of violence everywhere. A number of the gang leaders who were arrested turned out to be criminals who had shared cells with political prisoners during the Idenburg period. There were signs that in a number of places criminality and politics were becoming intertwined in a close embrace.

The arson attacks on the houses of district officials were no coincidence. The villages along the Semarang-Solo-Jogja axis also showed signs of restlessness. Meanwhile the rajas of Java showed no signs of concern.

This governor-general tended to seek political solutions to such developments but he had not yet found the right path. He hadn't even tried to discuss it with the staff at the Algemeene Secretariat. Van Limburg Stirum remained a mysterious figure. It seemed that his view was that to take administrative action rather than political action would only stir up the situation.

It had been possible to estimate the governor-general's position on these questions, but the news that arrived from Holland shook everybody— the Kingdom of the Netherlands promised to give self-government to the Indies, providing the Indies was able to defend itself and maintain law and order until the world war was finished. Representatives of Indies organizations would be given positions in the new governing councils.

I knew that this promise was the fruit of the hard work and striving of the Indies organizations between 1906 and 1917, while the basis of this proposal was the report I myself had written and which I had later asked my boss to return to me for revision. Or was there some other commission which I knew nothing about that had prepared a similar proposal? I don't know.

It was a very impressive promise. Governor-General Van Limburg

Stirum was very enthusiastic about this and threw off his mantle of mystery. Orders were issued for us to summon representatives from all the important Indies organizations, European and Native. Delegation after delegation arrived at the palace but I was never invited to attend.

These developments truly discouraged me. My new boss did not seem to know I existed or that I received a salary from the Algemeene Secretariat. He never came to see me and never summoned me to his office. The new steps being taken by the home government and the governor-general did not seem to need Pangemanann.

How it hurt to realize that the government had shut its eyes to the services I had rendered all this time. Would my fate be no better than some rag discarded because it was covered in unholy filth?

Couldn't it happen that one day, if the Native organizations gained their self-confidence, they too would establish their own commissions? Then they would hire European lawyers and there could be no doubt that one of these commissions would summon me and examine my hands, my fingers, my thoughts and feelings, and . . . whatever else there was left of me. Where could I run to hide then?

Why did the promise of self-government fill me with such fear and anxiety? Was it because I thought too highly of my own knowledge? Under self-government all the Native organizations would sit in the government councils, would join in the formulating of laws, would oversee the courts and other mechanisms for control. This would certainly be the case if they truly meant self-government. My house of glass would be empty, or perhaps I would end up its new resident. All this time I had been the observer, but if things got out of hand, the situation might be reversed and everyone could end up observing me inside.

But what did they really mean by self-government? As each day passed I tried to worm some more information from them. But to no avail. They kept it a secret or they were as ignorant as I on this question. And I knew for sure that the Native organizations knew no more about what was intended than I. And if it did come about, they would all probably turn upon everything and everybody they had ever disliked. Natives who had grown used to living in a world of illusions, who had surrendered all their reason and emotions to such illusions, could turn into wild beasts whose ferocity knew no bounds. The Indies was not Europe. And how I longed for Europe today, where every individual was respected and valued, and more than that, where everybody had their place in the sun and their rights acknowledged.

Self-government would be a beautiful dream for every Native, no matter whom, because they would have the chance to fulfill their dreams to let loose all the animal passions that they had suppressed because of their fear of the government. I was ready to bet that they did not even know that the promise of self-government stemmed from their own activity during the past years, activity reaching a climax now with the heating up of the Semarang-Solo-Jogjakarta axis.

I could see now that my fate would not be better than yours, my teacher, Raden Mas Minke. And it would have been no better either had you agreed to sign that letter. But you preferred Karet Cemetery to surrendering your self-respect. You were brave and not at all tactical. It should have been you, had you been able to please the governor-general, whom he summoned to discuss all sorts of matters. Yes, that was what politics was like. Today you are a friend, tomorrow an enemy, depending on the needs of the moment. I was the only one who did not turn like the wheel of a cart. I could only be trusted by one kind of power. Only a power as stupid as the Indies buffalo could ever put its trust in such as me.

But it eventuated that the promise of self-government did not result in the unrest along the Semarang-Solo-Jogjakarta axis receding. It was I who was most happy to see this. I used all my influence and connections to whip things up as much as possible. Yes, it is true, I always used to be suppressing those whom the government did not like. But now the government had to understand that the promise of self-government would not satisfy the hotheads of the Sarekat's young generation. The government had to withdraw its promise. It had to. It was permissible for me to use any and every means at my disposal to protect my position, which was now in danger.

Cor Oosterhof was my commander in the field, and he worked without rest. I had given him the authority to find finances from whatever source and with whatever methods he deemed necessary, as long as he was not found out by the authorities. If that did happen, then all links with me would have to be ended, even if it meant silencing him with the point of a dagger or the puncture of a bullet.

The S-S-J axis was becoming more and more active. A young boy, aged just sixteen, short in body, who a few years before had waited on people in the Semarang Tram and Rail Workers' Union office, better equipped than others because he had read some Dutch books and had considerable oratory skills, had now come forward as a prospective agitator of great power. The young lad's name was Semaoen. It was he who reminded people with the most force and the greatest passion that the promise of self-government was nothing but an admission of weakness on the part of both the Indies government and the home government. He explained that the Native organizations therefore should not respond to the Kingdom of the Netherlands' offer.

This young lad, much younger even than my own last-born, had brought a fresh wind to my otherwise dismal thoughts and feelings. It was essential that I ensure that his views be supported. It was essential that the Native organizations not believe in the government's promise. But was Cor Oosterhof capable of carrying out such a political task as this?

In a meeting with him in Betawi, the following conversation took place.

"You know this young boy in Semarang called Semaoen?"

"Of course, Meneer. He is being quite useful to us, yes?"

"It's not for you to be asking me questions. Listen to me. Do you think you can get more people to support him?"

He didn't answer. I knew very well that he had no experience in political work. All he knew was how to wield force. I ordered him to arrange for the whole of the Central Java membership to bring their support behind Semaoen. He just shook his head.

"There is no way we can do that."

I knew that he wouldn't be able to do it.

"You haven't even tried yet."

"Even if you put a pistol to my head, Meneer, I would still have to say that it is impossible."

"But you can keep your mouth shut."

"Of course. You have already taught me what the rules are in this game."

And I knew that there was no way I could use official government channels for this.

I spent over two hours explaining to him what it was that he would have to do. The more I explained the more impressed he became. But the more and more impressed he became, the less he understood. In this kind of work, he was just a snotty-nosed school kid. If he was let loose, he would probably turn out even more stupid than Robert Suurhof.

When I realized that this task was beyond his capabilities, I instructed him instead to continue with his old work, except that he had to intensify it.

"Do whatever you can to convince the young hotheads that the government has lost the capacity to take action against them."

And so more outbreaks of unrest occurred along the S-S-J axis. Semaoen became more and more outspoken, as if the whole world was his and all the people's hearts had united with his. If His Excellency Governor-

General Idenburg had been in power, I think the boy would have ended up spending his youth in exile. It was from the mouth of this young boy that the Natives first heard such new supernatural words as *imperialism, capitalism, nationalism,* and *internationalism.* I never believed myself that this young teenager fully understood the meaning of these, his favorite words.

Thank God it turned out to be unnecessary to organize support for Semaoen. Things developed in such a way that distrust of the government's promise soon became widespread anyway.

Semaoen himself continued to rise, and his call became more and more shrill. My private object of study, Mas Marco Kartodikromo, had long since been left behind. The S-S-J axis, that I referred to in my reports as the S-J axis, also fell under Semaoen's influence, and it was as if the island of Java were split in two along that axis.

His Excellency Governor-General Van Limburg Stirum could not be convinced, even when shown the facts, that the Natives did not believe his promise. Instead, he expressed great admiration for Semaoen. Indeed, it went further than that. Just as it had been with Dr. Snouck Hurgronje, and with the resident of Bojonegoro, and with me also, he wanted to adopt that boy as his own private object of scientific study. Snouck Hurgronje had Achmad Djajadiningrat, de le Croix and van Heutsz had Minke, and I myself had Marco and Siti Soendari. And these were all now out-of-date items. How quickly each generation of Natives sped to new horizons, no longer tied by traditions, each seeming to take off from a different platform, which was in fact the same one—Europe.

It wasn't surprising either that Semaoen never truly understood his own people. He believed too much in the power of European teachings. Unlike Meneer L— and myself, he never fully saw that the peoples of the Indies were not as clear-cut a people as the Europeans. The people here lived in a kind of darkness, enmeshed in the complexities of their world of illusions. Every new thing from Europe that was thrown into that world simply created more chaos and confusion.

So His Excellency Van Limburg Stirum simply nodded when he was told that Semaoen was the adopted child of a European, an expert in Javanese culture.

His Excellency nodded wisely, while Pangemanann's headache got worse and worse as he tried to follow all the new developments. His Excellency never really made it clear what it was that the home government wanted during this time of climaxing restlessness in the Indies. Meanwhile Semaoen was still a puzzle. He was like the sun rising over the eastern horizon, with the moon and stars unobstructed by cloud or overcast, while

Mas Tjokro and Marco faded. They even seemed reluctant to leave behind a shadow. I was neither sun, nor moon, nor star. I was just a man alone, Pangemanann, who could find no way out.

The promise of self-government had become the main topic of public debate. The war in Europe had not ended. The cannons of war vomited forth lead and death onto every field of battle. My second boss had departed for America to become a citizen in that land of liberty. And now the American army itself descended into every field of battle to confront the Germans, who had by this time exhausted their wealth and energy. The Americans arrived on the scene to consolidate the old carve-up of the world, joining in the effort to extinguish the German lust to expand their colonial territories.

While here in Betawi, all the senior colonial officials, including myself, gathered at Tanjung Perak harbor to give an impressive send-off to the Indies delegation departing to the Netherlands to officially accept the promise of self-government directly from the government of the Kingdom of the Netherlands.

I myself could feel how disappointed Mas Tjokro must have been not to be among those invited. There were only two representatives from Native organizations invited. These were Sewoyo, the general secretary of the Boedi Oetomo, and Abdoel Moeis from Sarekat Islam. So these were the only two Native organizations the Government smiled upon. And I knew too that Semaoen and Marco would harden their attitude not only toward the government but also toward Mas Tjokro, the emperor without a crown.

Cannons boomed in salute as the ship departed. The delegation, bedecked in sashes of royal-yellow silk, waved good-bye from the deck. Except for one, they all wore European clothes. The exception was Mas Sewoyo. But he too waved good-bye. And it was that hand too that in less than a month would be held out to accept the Netherlands' promise.

It had been Marco and his friends, then Semaoen and his friends, who had worked so hard to mobilize the S-J axis, but it would be Sewoyo who would receive the reward. But the two of them had no ambitions for that kind of reward; in fact the thought disgusted them. Meanwhile, Tomo buried himself in his medical work at a mission hospital in the small and barren district town of Blitar, and busied himself in an affair with one of his nurses, a Eurasian.

And I myself?

I left Tanjung Perak in a car. When the driver asked where I wanted to go, I didn't answer. I was becoming more and more confused. The political situation had changed. I couldn't keep up with it. There were new developments each day flowing on from earlier developments which had already left me behind. What would become of me? Was it enough to drown all my worries in whiskey?

Suddenly my thoughts turned to my wife and children, who had not sent me a letter for such a very long time.

"Where to, Tuan?" the driver asked once more.

Perhaps I should write to them and send them my photograph.

"To the Marijke Photograph Studio."

"Very well, Tuan."

The car stopped in the retail section in Kotta.

The owner of the shop was a very old European, perhaps already in his seventies. He invited me into the makeup room. I was so shocked to see myself in the mirror. I had never realized and never felt that my cheeks sagged so much. My hair had turned white, even my eyebrows and eyelashes. My eyes were adorned underneath by darkening crescents. The eyes themselves were sunken. There were more and more chicken-claw wrinkles spreading out at their corners. How quickly I had aged. Neither my wife nor my children would recognize me anymore, except to know how I had degenerated. No, I would not have my photo taken.

Once outside the shop, I jumped into the car. How close I was to death, and I had always considered myself to be young, clever, of course, undefeatable, with an impressive personality, and able to manipulate whomever I liked.

I don't know why I began to think of Raden Mas Minke. I ordered the driver to take me to a florist. I asked them to make me up a wreath straightaway, without any ribbon or message. And I ordered my driver to take me to Karet.

Those others had set sail for the Netherlands to accept a promise from the government itself and I—I made my way to a cemetery. I, who had so quickly aged like this, was not considered an appropriate person to participate in this self-government. I, who had done so much for the government. I, who would now reap only the bitter dregs of all this. And how many years did I have left? Yes, how many years? Was not I, somebody recognized as an expert on colonial affairs, qualified to sit in any new government— even if just as an adviser?

You are jealous of Sewoyo, Pangemanann, you are envious, like a little schoolboy envious of another boy's candy.

I entered the cemetery alone. I took no notice of the caretaker, and he himself drew back. I laid the wreath against the northern headstone, because he had been buried a Moslem. I stared at this simple grave—bare brown earth with fat clumps of creeping grass here and there. There was no leafy shade sheltering this grave. No writing or carving on the gravestone to say who was buried there. And there were no signs of the wreath I had laid here that first time.

You sleep peacefully here, teacher! How simple is death. And we will all meet in the peace of the universe of death, whether a king or his slave, whether executioner or victim, whether Rientje de Roo or the most powerful of emperors. How simple was death. De Lange had chosen death. How many more years will it be before I join you, teacher? But I want to achieve something. Something!

My imagination tried to pierce through the mound of dirt down into the grave pit itself. But my imagination was dead, it would not function. Instead, the dried flower petals scattered upon the grass finally registered in my vision. It seemed someone else had sent flowers.

I raised my head to look around and called the caretaker, who was waiting in the distance.

He was waiting to be asked to recite a prayer but I asked him instead: "Has anyone sent flowers to this grave?"

"Yes, Tuan."

"Who was it?"

"People from close by here, Tuan. Jamiatul Khair people, Tuan."

Jamiatul Khair. So there are still those who love him. Jamiatul Khair. What kind of name was that? I seemed to remember it from somewhere.

"You don't want me to read the Yasin Verses, Tuan?"

"Yes, recite them."

He recited a prayer that I could not understand at all. After he had finished he looked at me. No, I would not give you a single cent, just as the government had given me no part at all in its self-government project.

The driver took me wherever I wanted to go. He drove me around Betawi; then when I was ready he took me back to Buitenzorg.

Once again my devoted maid was there to greet me, faithfully copying the old ways of Paulette and the children. Ah, what is the point of telling you about this completely ruined household of mine?

Life did not return to what it had been, because there was a growing emptiness inside me. All that I was ever likely to get as compensation for what I had lost was a pension. A pension! That's it! I could not even see myself in the new government. How miserly was fate with me. I who knew everything about the Native organizations!

And Cor Oosterhof's success along the S-J line in strengthening the position of the young generation of the Sarekat Islam did not change the Indies government's or the Netherlands government's views. So I had begun to lose interest in reading the papers and magazines. My loss of interest in my work was very profound, even though I knew that a degenerating old person like me always associated loss of interest in work with the approach of death. Zest for work was a sign of energy and life. While people are happy at their work, they will want to live; and when people no longer have the desire to work they are in fact shaking hands with death. Cor Oosterhof's enthusiastic reports no longer interested me. Was it true that death was already shaking hands with me? Was it true that I would end up dying before I was sixty? How fast life passes. How fast.

I even left untouched both the press and the official reports about the Indies delegation's activities in the Netherlands. None of it was of any relevance to me anymore.

All that was left for me now was the discipline of recording my thoughts for posterity in these notes.

Ah, you, Pangemanann with the double *n*, you used to laugh at the idea that Minke might have thought of himself as a possible third president of Asia after Sun Yat-sen and Aguinaldo. It turns out that it was you who had unconsciously harbored the dream of such a thing being bestowed upon you by the government. Together with Meneer L— you used to laugh at the Natives, who you thought had been cowed and humiliated by their own illusions. And what was the reality now? Wasn't it true that now in your old age you are being turned mad by your own illusions, just because of the promise of some colonial power?

The Indies delegation's return from the Netherlands maddened me even more. I felt that I had been unjustly pushed aside. I was closer to His Excellency the governor-general than they, so why was it people so far removed from him who were getting his attention now? What was it that I was lacking? Was it just because I was prematurely aging? And anyway, it was my time with the government that had done that to me. Was it right that a person as old as I should be shedding tears of protest, tears I knew would be of no avail at all?

Then when I fell ill again, it turned out that my long absence at the office was hardly noticed at all. It was clear that my skills were no longer needed. My boss had visited me once in the hospital and said he prayed for my recovery. My other colleagues too. How lonely it was when in your old age you realized nobody needed you.

A letter from my son Mark that reported that both my older sons had failed their studies and had joined the British army just added to the pain of my sorrows. What was there left for me to hope for? My children preferred to live in Europe and to be Europeans. I was left here by myself, looked after by a village girl. And I had never even asked my maid who her parents were or where she was born. She stayed with me out of pity

. . . pity . . . pity, not the compassion of love. This was a humiliation for anyone with self-respect . . . self-respect . . . did I have any self-respect left after all the things I had done . . . ?

All I had was a letter from Mark, just a letter, nothing more. And even then it mentioned nothing about his mother, about Paulette, the woman who had been beside me during all the happy times of my youth . . . yes, just a letter. There was no news of Dede. And you, daughter, what has happened with you? Are you married? You have never said. Do you have children yet? You are silent. Perhaps all of you have conspired to throw off your family name, revolted by your Native heritage, a heritage that gave you nothing that you could depend upon.

All that was left to me in this emptiness and loneliness were my memories of the church. If I am ever able to get up from this sickbed, I thought to myself, then on that fine, clear day, I will go to the church, I will make a full confession of all my sins, and I will repent. While I was in my current state I felt that it would be too embarrassing to summon a priest. Using whatever strength I had left, I would clear the clutter that was inside me. Often now my lips pronounced the Paternoster and Ave just as I and my wife used to do together when we prayed with the rosary. I would hold on. Yes, I would hold on.

"Do you know what a rosary is?" I asked my maid when she came to see me once and while she was putting some fruit onto the table.

"What is a rosary, Tuan?"

"Like a necklace, for praying."

"You mean a tasbih."

"Perhaps you call it a tasbih. We call it a rosary. Fetch it from my wardrobe, yes, and bring it here to me."

I gave her the key to my wardrobe. I knew she wouldn't open the drawer where I kept my revolver. I had to trust her. And the next day she arrived with more fruit and my rosary.

As soon as she gave it to me, I kissed the silver cross that hung at its end. And that cross somehow seemed to give some peace within. My whole self surrendered as it had once done in the past. My nerves began to relax. And because of that cross, I gradually began to get my health back. Fifteen days later I was discharged from the hospital. And so once again I was completely dependent on my maid.

My soul was at peace now. I worried about nothing, I hoped for nothing, there was nothing that I desired anymore. The cross had helped me make peace with myself, had neutralized my passions and all their consequences, which had so often filled me with tension and anxiety. And so I had prepared myself to enter eternal peace, that place where all people finally find themselves, of their own will or otherwise.

After resting for a week, I had fully regained my health. Some super-natural power forced me out of my house and back to the office. The welcome back was very cool. I had to accept this as a reality. The labor and thoughts of Pangemanann were truly no longer needed here. Very well, then. God Almighty would do with me as He wished.

I stood at the window in my office staring out at the gardens. An office boy was cleaning up my office, which had been abandoned for these last three months. The head of housekeeping came in with two helpers and took away the pile of newspapers and magazines that I should have been studying.

He said good morning to me, and immediately handed over a pile of the latest editions.

"I see you don't need a drink, Meneer," he began.

"You're not mistaken, Meneer Herschenbrock. Since this illness I have given up drink."

"Congratulations, Meneer," he said, holding out his hand.

I shook hands with him, even though I knew he wasn't truly sincere. He had come to see me hoping that there would be the opportunity to join with me in a drink.

"You can take a drink by yourself, Meneer Herschenbrock."

"I am not so keen either, Meneer."

Alone in this room where De Lange had taken his own life, my thoughts turned more and more to death. Why was I always thinking about death? You are alive, aren't you, Jacques? As a living being, think then about life, not death. Your mind works. Not to use it would be a violation of the laws of life. Come on, revive your enthusiasm for work! Isn't en-thusiasm for work a sign of life, and lack of interest in working a sign of the approach of death? You can live a lot longer yet if you can revive your old enthusiasm for work.

And so I sat down again and began opening the newspapers, the latest editions.

The war in Europe had suddenly come to an end. Germany was de-feated. A great event, there was no doubt about that, a great historical event, but it did not move me in any way. Perhaps my emotions were no longer capable of being moved by anything. Perhaps my heart was now slippery flat, and whatever touched it now would just slide off into nothingness.

And so I turned up at work each day just to turn mechanically the pages of the newspapers. But none of what I read moved me at all. How long would this go on? Until the day, no doubt, when I would receive a letter telling me I would have to leave this office. I had lost all interest in this office upon which the eyes of all the Indies were focused. It had lost all its greatness and awe for me. Power no longer had the same attraction it once had.

The news from the Netherlands was that a parliament would be established in the Indies. And that the Natives would join in governing, because they would help make the laws. Huh! What was the use of a parliament that sat below the government itself? Even if every Native organization ended up with representatives in it. What did I care now anyway!

I was not given any new assignments. His Excellency Governor-General Van Limburg Stirum maintained his policy of using political means only. Good, well, it meant that my work here was indeed at an end. Cor Oorsterhof would continue operations without me, because that was now how he made a living. One day he would be wiped from the face of the earth too, just like those who had gone before him.

Then the reports about the parliament faded away and were replaced by discussion of a *volksraad*, an advisory council of people's representatives. All the papers discussed what its significance was and how it would work and who would sit on it and why it was a good thing for the Indies. It turned out that the royal government of the Netherlands had its own interpretation of what self-government meant. Just a volksraad, a pseudo-parliament.

I laughed to myself. I had put too much store in that promise they made during the war. Now that the war was over they had decided to betray their promise. Why had I allowed myself to daydream about what role I might play in it all?

But more amazing were the developments among the Native organizations. No less than with myself, ambitious dreams were running amok among the leadership of these organizations. All of them were social organizations but now—without waiting for the decisions of their congresses or conferences—they all issued statements declaring themselves to be political organizations in the hope of gaining the honor of being able to send representatives to the volksraad.

It made me want to vomit.

It was then I realized that all these organizations and their leaders were opportunists. The only exception was those active along the Semarang-Jogkarta line. And they would be swallowed up by the ocean of opportunists around them.

So this was the political strategy of Van Limburg Stirum. And it seemed to work. Unrest outside the S-J region receded. The sugar mills calmly got back to work to meet the world demand for sugar that actually had not yet fully recovered. But His Excellency had told a delegation from the Algemeene Landbouw Syndicaat to increase production in all fields because the end of the war would mean increasing demand for the colony's commodities. As if the gods themselves had breathed new life into them, the factories and plantations sprang back into production. The unrest outside the S-J region died down like a fire hosed down with cold water. And it seemed the Indies stood at the gateway to prosperity once again.

The desire to get a seat in the volksraad or one of the provincial councils gave rise to new dreams—to become a public figure, to deliver speeches, to be listened to by fellow Honorable Members, while enjoying drinks paid for with appropriate wages, sometimes even greater than those of a bupati.

From then on I began to see the first signs of an irreconcilable split among the Native organizations. One group wanted to cooperate with the government so that they could get seats in the volksraad, while the others refused to cooperate, saying that such cooperation meant humiliation for the Natives.

I was able to follow all this but it no longer interested me. Opposition fever gave way to politics fever. Van Limburg Stirum's strategy was clearly succeeding.

Then came the finale—the opening of the volksraad on May 20, 1918. The Natives with seats were Mas Sewoyo, Mas Tjokro, and Tjipto, all appointed by the governor-general. Abdoel Moeis, Radjiman, and Abdoel Rivai were chosen by the Natives. Of the seventy or so representatives, only eight were Natives, including two bupatis appointed by the government.

The organizations who missed out did not sit openmouthed in disappointment but competed even more actively to somehow get a seat. And so, without any official pronouncement, political activity and movements gained de facto legality.

And I became even less and less interested, less and less concerned about any of it. To me it was all like drizzling rain falling on my heart, now slippery like a taro leaf, and then sliding off onto the ground to disappear forever. . . .

Then on one fine clear day, while the organization epidemic spread everywhere, and more and more organizations sprang up merrily, and I sat turning over the pages of boring newspapers, my new boss came to see me for the first time.

"Are you well enough to undertake a not very difficult chore, Meneer?" he asked; then he corrected himself. "I shouldn't even say 'not very difficult.' In fact it is a very easy chore."

"I will try, Meneer."

"Excellent, Meneer Pangemanann. We have chosen you, Meneer, because you are the only official here with a French education."

I didn't have the faintest interest and I knew there was no point in knowing why it was important that I had a French education. Everything is in God's safe hands, not those of my superiors.

"Can you go down to Betawi today?"

"Of course, Meneer."

"Very good. The French consul will be waiting for you at ten o'clock."

"Very well, I will leave straightaway."

I had no real desire to find out what it was that I would have to do. For the umpteenth time now a car took me to Betawi. Throughout the journey I had no interest in knowing what was happening. I closed my eyes, I took out the rosary from my pocket, and I began to pray!

The car arrived right on time. I had not been waiting long in the reception room, when I was invited inside to meet the French consul.

"Meneer Pangemanann?" he asked in northern French. I said yes. "I am very happy that you have been able to come today. Your French is very good. Where did you study it?"

I told him all about my education and he nodded happily. He obviously had no colonial experience. His attitude was proper, polite, and he did not at all look at me as a lesser being. I saw in him the Europe I had known long ago. I was humored somewhat. I felt lucky that I had once had the opportunity to live in a European environment that was not colonial.

And even then I was not curious to know what task had brought me here.

"According to the information I have been given by the Algemeene Secretariat, you are an expert in colonial affairs . . ."

My heart began to pound.

". . . especially as concerns matters relating to the Native leaders here."

"Thank you, Monsieur, but I think that is somewhat of an exaggeration."

"Even so, you must know about a man called"—he took out a small notebook from his pocket, leafed through a few pages, and then read out, with both incorrect emphasis and spelling—"called . . . Raden Mas Minke. Forgive me if I haven't pronounced it correctly."

I corrected his pronunciation and he repeated it several times and finished it with a thank you. Meanwhile my heart raced. The name I had not spoken for so long now sounded like a proclamation that some punishment was soon to befall me.

"Are you ill, Monsieur?"

"I am well, Monsieur," I answered, gasping for breath.

The consul seemed unsure and I firmed my resolve. I must have the strength to face whatever might come, because everything that was about to befall me came from God.

He pressed a button and a European woman emerged carrying drinks. She paid her respects to me and then served the drinks. The consul invited me to drink and I drank. It felt cool and it was very refreshing. But I had no interest in asking what it was.

The consul did not speak. He studied my countenance, while I could hear my every heartbeat. I waited for him to speak.

Perhaps this representative of the French Republic would be the bearer of God's punishment upon me. It was in a small church in the south of France that I had married Paulette Marcel, where we promised to go through life together, for better or worse. I had betrayed that promise because of the bottle. As a student I had sworn an oath to be loyal to the Republic. I was still a snot-nosed youth then, but I had made the promise in all sincerity. I had betrayed that oath too and given my allegiance instead to Dutch colonialism in the Indies. I don't want to list all my betrayals here. Betrayal after betrayal—too many betrayals for me ever to redeem myself through anything I do in what remains of my life. And I had not admitted to even a small number of these in confession.

"Are you sure you're not sick?"

"Yes, Monsieur."

"Would you like to listen to some French music before we talk?" Before I could answer he had stood up and started playing a record on his gramophone. "To remind you of France once again, Monsieur," he said again as he sat down across from me. "You probably haven't heard this voice for a long time, have you?"

"May Le Boucq," I said.

I was suddenly startled as I heard myself say that name—Le Boucq. Le Boucq . . . Le Boucq . . . wasn't that the name of the French painter, the veteran from the Aceh War whom Minke called Marais in his books? The former student at Louvain in Belgium? I listened once again to May Le Boucq's voice. And in my mind, I saw a young, sprightly girl Minke had called Maysoroh Marais. From Maysoroh my thoughts wandered to someone called Rono Mellema, to Nyai Ontosoroh alias Madame Sanikem Marais, perhaps now known as Madame Sanikem Le Boucq.

"Do you like her voice, Monsieur?" he asked after the music ended. He went across and turned off the machine and then came back to me.

"Of course, Monsieur, and my children even more than I."

"Then let us begin, Monsieur, yes?"

"Certainly. Let's begin."

"May Le Boucq rendered great service to France during the war that has just ended. It is very possible that the Republic may one day honor her for that. Have you ever met her?"

"I left France twenty-five years ago, Monsieur."

"Yes, of course, you haven't met her. I have been luckier, Monsieur. I have met her. Perhaps you could say I am even a very good friend."

It was possible indeed that this polite French consul was the bearer of God's punishment for me. As we proceeded I began to get an idea of the direction we were heading, toward the place where my sentence would be carried out.

"Are you certain you are not ill, Monsieur?"

"I am well, Monsieur, really," I said, smiling, and I could feel my blood pressure rise, perhaps it was already over 180. My head began to sway and my vision began to go hazy. I felt my throat and discovered that I did not have a temperature. No, I must be strong, I must finish this task. If it was true I was about to receive God's punishment, then I must accept it with dignity, with resignation and trust in God. What meaning would there be to my life if in the little time that remains I lose my dignity altogether?

"Should I call a doctor?"

"No, Monsieur, I am all right, don't worry. Please go on."

Hesitantly he continued: "It's like this, Monsieur. I received a very earnest request from May Le Boucq that I help her mother, Madame Sanikem Le Boucq, find this man, Raden Mas Minke. Madame Le Boucq should be here in about a quarter of an hour."

My vision went black. I gripped hold of the arm rests so that I would not fall off my chair. And once again I told myself that I had to accept all this with dignity, resignation, and trust in God. And so I regained my strength.

"I think I should call a doctor."

"Truly, Monsieur, it is not necessary."

"Is it true that you know a lot about this man she is looking for?"

"I know something of him, Monsieur."

"That is excellent. Madame Le Boucq has been in Betawi for a week now. She has gone to Buitenzorg, Sukabumi, and Bandung looking for Monsieur Minke. She has had no success. She heard that this gentleman had recently returned from exile in Ambon." He stopped speaking, and looked out the window into the main street, and: "Nah, here is Madame Le Boucq now with her pretty daughter."

My vision was clear again. I would now face Sanikem, the spiritual mother of Minke. What a coward I would be if I fainted here now, and what an even greater coward if I postponed finally dealing with this matter.

Monsieur Consul invited me to stand to welcome Madame Le Boucq. And he seemed to give the same respect he gave all people, even myself, who meant nothing to him, let alone to Sanikem.

Sanikem was walking toward the consulate's veranda. Holding her hand was a European girl who looked about seven years old. The little girl seemed friendly and talkative. Sanikem herself looked healthy and full of life.

She must be over forty-five now, I think. Or fifty. Why does she look so young? And her eyes did not show her age at all. She wore a white silk dress decorated with pictures of little flowers, a slim leather belt around her waist, while in her left hand she carried a crocodile-skin bag. Her steps were firm and strong as if she hadn't even reached thirty-five yet.

Her skin was much clearer than that of women who lived all their life in the tropics. Her harsh face was adorned by a smile of infinite beauty. So this was, if what Minke had written was true, the village girl who had been sold by her own father and in her emptiness had then inhaled European civilization and made it her own. This was the Native woman who had been able to maintain her desire for revenge against the colonial government in the Indies and had found many ways to wreak her vengeance.

This was that strong-willed person who had given up nationality, homeland, and village and who had chosen foreign citizenship and had been able to put it to use in no less effective a way than those who had been born citizens. She had chosen freedom for herself. The Law had stolen everything that she had built, but she had not lost anything, especially not her dignity. She had lost her children, yet she held her head high, and knew that life was always a possibility.

And myself?

When the consul introduced me to her and we shook hands, I could feel a rapier of steel thrust into my heart. I was no more than a contemptible animal who deserved nothing but to be kicked and trodden upon. She had striven to build so much and she had done so without leaving behind a single groaning victim.

"Monsieur Pangemanann, I am very pleased to make your acquaintance," she said in very good and fluent French, except that her accent gave her away as being not of French origin. And then little Jeannette Le Boucq chirped away, introducing herself to me as well.

Be strong, be strong, I told myself. And to overcome the feelings of how small I felt, I asked Jeannette: "So you are the little sister of May Le Boucq, the famous singer?"

"Of course I am, Monsieur, I am her sister. And I can sing too, can't I, Mama?" she put the question to her mother.

"You will be able to do whatever you like," answered Madame Sanikem Le Boucq, "and not only sing but warble like a bird."

She leaned up against me, then shrank away, as if she could sense who I really was.

The consul suggested we get down to business, and then Madame Le Boucq told of all her efforts to find Minke, that she had received a telegram from Surabaya informing her that Minke had been released, and that her other adopted child had also searched for him in Betawi and West Java but had not been able to find him.

I listened to her and came to the conclusion that Meneer Darman from the Molukken company in Surabaya as well as Madame Le Boucq herself had visited the house in Buitenzorg. It could have been either while I was at the office or when I was laid up in the hospital. My maid had not told me. I did not blame her for that because the visitors would not have asked for me but for Minke.

"So you must know then where my son is," said Madame.

"Of course, Madame."

She looked so full of joy.

"Could we perhaps visit him today?"

I quickly prayed that the Virgin Mother would protect me and that I would find the strength to go on. I found the strength, and I answered cautiously but resolutely: "Certainly, Madame. The only thing is that Monsieur Minke is dead."

"Dead?!" she cried out, her eyes looking as if they were about to launch out of their sockets. "Dead?!" She went silent all of a sudden. She cried.

The consul bowed his head deeply. He straightened up again, sighed deeply, and observed me.

"Who died, Mama?" asked Jeannette.

I stood and offered my hand in condolence to Madame. She accepted my hand and her eyes glowed, burning up everything they came into contact with. Her countenance seemed to grow harder, more severe, springing from a spirit that had a strength that refused to share itself with pity. I saw no sadness in her, just bitterness, yes, only bitterness.

The consul stood and took his turn in expressing his condolences.

Jeannette hugged her mother around the waist, her face looking up at her mother, and asked: "Who died, Mama? Uncle?"

Madame Le Boucq alias Sanikem alias Nyai Ontosoroh looked down and gazed into her daughter's face, nodding in answer: "Yes, your beloved uncle has died, Jeannette. Your uncle whom we had come here to find."

She sat down again, her lips trembling as she held back tears. Jeannette leaned up against her lap and showered her with unanswered questions.

"Madame," said the consul, "I never guessed it would come to this, Madame, truly I didn't."

"Did he die in Betawi?" Madame asked me.

"Yes, Madame."

"What did the doctor say about his illness?"

Her question made me nervous because I knew that the report about how he died was not in order and that Dr. Meyersohn had examined him but that it was the youth with the whip and the knife who declared it was dysentery.

"It was reported that it was dysentery."

"Who was the doctor who treated him?"

"I don't know that, Madame," I answered, and I was tortured by the realization that once again I had lied. It seemed I was indeed a liar, prepared to lie to a woman who was seeking a loved one. I didn't have the courage to resist.

"Of course you won't know everything, Monsieur," she said in a somewhat cutting voice. "But you must know who was the last doctor to examine him."

"If you need that information, I should be able to find it for you, Madame, certainly."

"Thank you, Monsieur Pangemanann. May I ask you one more thing? Could you take us to the grave?"

"I'd be very happy to, Madame, whenever you like."

"Monsieur Consul," she said, "now that we know how things are, I wonder if you would permit us to visit the grave now."

"If that is what Madame wishes . . . let me arrange transport for you." He stood and left the room. He returned a moment later and said that a taxi would arrive soon.

I managed to make sure that I sat next to the driver in order that I might escape the increasing flood of questions from this woman, who had the ability to see through everything that she studied. I felt that she had begun to be suspicious of me because of my hesitant answer about Minke's illness and the name of the doctor who handled his case. Every educated person would be suspicious about his death, even though at this time a certificate of cause of death from a doctor was not required by law. The fact that Goenawan had gone completely silent since Minke's burial was possibly also because he was afraid that he and his family could become embroiled with the police.

It was only Jeannette who was preoccupied with the scenery along the way, crying out in amazement again and again. Madame Le Boucq remained calm, simply answering her daughter's questions whenever required.

On the other hand I was thrown into more and more disarray. The woman behind me had crossed two oceans to find a loved one. And that person had been destroyed while in my hands. He had been destroyed, but he had finished what he had begun. From that beginning he had multiplied himself into so many other people, spreading like fireflies throughout Java. Perhaps tomorrow or the next day they would spread outside Java too. If he had never started that beginning, then Pangemannn with two *n*s would never have sat in the Algemeene Secretariat, and I also would not have had to handle this little job, a job that could kill me.

My blood pressure did not drop. It was only through the strength of my willpower that I was able to keep going. There was pounding and hissing in my ears, long whistles and the pounding of hammers, just like in a railway workshop. My vision was blurred. I reckoned my blood pressure had gone up at least another ten points. My feet were cold and wet from perspiration.

I tried to remember what Minke had written in his manuscripts. But my memory sometimes disappeared into a kind of nighttime darkness, and then sometimes a flash of lightning would illuminate the dark. But what it illuminated and what remained hidden never came together. It was all a broken jumble.

I had to stand for quite a few moments to clear my vision when I got out of the taxi. The cemetery caretaker greeted us. It was only three days ago that I had been here to place a wreath of flowers on Minke's grave and look! now I was here again.

Jeannette was holding her mother's hand. This little girl, who seemed so clever and capable, loved her mother very much. I walked behind them carrying a wreath that seemed so very heavy. It was only my great respect for him that prevented me from hiring somebody to carry it.

The caretaker followed on behind.

When we arrived at his grave I knelt down, afraid of falling if I continued to stand. When I had placed a wreath here for the first time I had instructed the caretaker to paint the name of Raden Mas Minke on the headstone made from teak. The last time I visited a few days ago I could read his name clearly there. But now it was gone, covered by black tar.

Seeing me kneel, Madame Le Boucq also knelt, Jeannette too. I bowed my head and they bowed their heads also.

I knew that the caretaker didn't really want to come with us but did

so because he was afraid. He thought I was someone important. He didn't
like my coming because I always wore European clothes and now I brought
a woman wearing European clothes and a young child who was completely
European in appearance.

Just as in previous times, a group of people gathered nearby under a
shelter near the fence. They did not like it when people dressed in Christian
clothes entered a Moslem cemetery. There was no reason to be afraid of
them. I always carried a revolver. However many there were, they would
start running at the sound of the first shot.

I called the caretaker.

"Who put tar over the name I ordered you to paint there?" I asked
in Malay.

"Don't know, Tuan. This is the first time I have noticed it. Someone
from the Jamiatul Khair once told me to paint the name there too, but it
was also tarred over. I cleaned it then, now it's happened again."

Madame Le Boucq lifted up her head to listen to the conversation in
Malay. Jeannette looked back and forth at me and the caretaker with quiz-
zical eyes.

"Very well," said Madame in French, "even in your final resting place
you are not allowed any peace."

Those words seemed to be aimed directly at me. But in fact I didn't
know anything at all about this vandalism.

"This is not my doing, Madame," I answered. "In fact, I brought
another wreath of flowers, the second one, just a few days ago."

She observed me with searching eyes.

"It wasn't me, Madame, truly."

"You brought a wreath?"

"Caretaker," I summoned him over in Malay. "You know I sent
wreaths to this grave, don't you, twice, yes?"

"That's true, Tuan," he answered. "The village people here know
too."

"See, Madame, he confirms it."

Sanikem watched me with her searching eyes. And I too focused my
mind's eye on my own soul, just to check if I was still sane at that moment.

"Say a prayer, caretaker!" I ordered him in Malay.

The caretaker quickly squatted down beside the grave and recited a
prayer. Sanikem was still watching me. Jeannette was mesmerized by the
caretaker.

His tormenting prayer seemed as if it would never end. I gazed around
the field before me where there grew all kinds of headstones, from wood,

from river stones, from brick, from bamboo. The whole scene before me was growing with nothing but gravestones, dancing, waving, like hands reaching out groping for something. Aah! the way the woman beside me looked at me. And then the gravestones started trembling and extending themselves. There were some that sprang out so quickly they seemed to want to scratch at me. I closed my eyes and buried my face in my two hands.

You, Pangemanann, you are no different from the dirt on the soles of Sanikem's feet! Her eyes have seen into your brain, your heart, your liver, your kidneys. Just her sideways glance at you has brought you to collapse. You are old now. What else is there left for you to conquer for yourself? Nothing, there is nothing. Everything is against you. Everything, everyone. Even the gravestones growing there before you.

You, Pangemanann, who once received the best education Europe could offer in this century. You are bowing down at the grave of a person far younger than yourself. Was it for his death that you were educated so well? Is this all you will achieve in your lifetime? While Sanikem beside you has built everything she could possibly have built. And all you have done is bring it down. And even then you didn't succeed in bringing it all down.

Madame Le Boucq's hissed whisper in my ear brought me to my senses again: "We will return now, Monsieur Pangemanann," in a French accent that suddenly reminded me of the freshness of Paris at the beginning of autumn. "Jeannette. This is your uncle's grave."

Jeannette did not answer.

They both stood up. Finally I struggled to stand up too. And even then I had to close my eyes to throw off the darkness that attacked me suddenly. I gave the caretaker some money and instructed him in Malay: "Get rid of that tar, get rid of all of it."

I knew I should be in bed under the care of a doctor. But good manners required that I escort Madame back to where she was staying. She did not say a word during the journey. Neither did Jeannette. Let alone me.

The taxi brought us to a guest house, because that was where they were staying. So they would be staying in Betawi for a few more weeks yet.

Also out of good manners, I forced myself to alight from the car. My legs felt heavy, as if they were wrapped in chains. At her request, I sat down. The taxi waited. Jeannette ran into her room. Madame sat across from me, as if she were about to hand down the death sentence on me.

"I believe you had nothing to do with putting that tar on his grave," she said suddenly in Malay, "but everything else was your doing, wasn't it, Tuan?"

I nodded, shuddering.

She calmly stood up from her chair, turned away from me, left me, went into her room, and locked the door from inside.

I disgusted her.

I shouted out to the driver. He came in. I asked him to help me back to the taxi. He drove me back to Buitenzorg. It was a very slow journey, even though I knew the car was traveling at over sixty kilometers an hour. Then he helped me out of the car and into the house.

My maid came out to meet me.

The two of them took me into my room. My maid quickly piled up some pillows so I wouldn't collapse flat on the mattress.

"Driver, summon the doctor at the corner of the street," said my maid as she handed over the fare he asked for.

The driver left, but the doctor didn't arrive. My maid sat beside my bed keeping watch. Ah, what could I ever give her in return?

"Fetch that green bundle in the cabinet."

Without a word she did what I asked and put the bundle down beside me. Inside were Raden Mas Minke's manuscripts that I had taken from the archives of the Algemeene Secretariat.

"Fetch the thick book in my desk drawer," I ordered her again.

She went and brought back what I had asked. This was *House of Glass*, which I wanted to finish with my experiences today.

"Get me pen and ink," I asked again.

She fetched them and handed them to me, protesting: "Tuan is sick, Tuan shouldn't be working today."

I took no notice.

"Tjeu," I said, "you should marry a good man."

She looked at me, amazed that I should say something like that.

"Tuan is sick, don't talk, don't start writing."

I was reminded of Marietje, Minke's maid in Ambon. Minke had given her everything he owned. I would do the same for Tjeu.

"I am writing a letter for you, Tjeu. I am giving you everything I own."

"What are you talking about, Tuan?"

"I am going to Holland. I am giving everything to you."

"Tuan, go to sleep, Tuan."

I wrote out a short letter handing everything over to her, then I gave her the letter, and it made me feel so good to have done that for her. She accepted the letter, but was too amazed to understand what was happening.

"Show the letter to the church later. I want you to go to the church later and tell them I am very ill. Later, when I have finished writing. Get me something to drink!"

She went and I began to write about today. I must be strong. I will not be ready until I finish this. I could feel my mind clear after I drank the cold water my maid brought me. She sat beside me as I wrote far into the night, until sunrise. I concluded with the same words I wrote in a letter to Madame Le Boucq, care of the French Embassy in Betawi:

To Madame Sanikem Le Boucq,

I don't think I need to explain to you about the "everything else." As a wise and farsighted woman, Madame no doubt understands everything. About the facts of what happened, it is all contained in these my notes, House of Glass, *which I now willingly hand over to you. Madame is my judge. I accept whatever sentence you hand down, Madame.*

With this letter, I surrender some manuscripts that are by right yours, the writings of Raden Mas Minke, your beloved son. It is up to Madame now as to what use they should be put to and how to look after them.

Deposuit Potentes de Sede et Exaltavit Humiles.

(He has brought down the mighty from their thrones and raised up the lowly.)

GLOSSARY

Algemeene Landbouw Syndicaat	General Agricultural Syndicate
Algemeene Secretariat	General (State) Secretariat, the offices of the governor-general of the Netherlands Indies
arak	Javanese liquor
assistant resident	For each regency there was a Dutch assistant resident in whose hands power over local affairs ultimately resided.
Betawi	The Malay name for Batavia, the capital of the Dutch East Indies, now Jakarta
Bharatayuddha	A famous Hindu epic, depicting a great war between two families of nobles
Boedi Oetomo	Organization formed in 1908 which drew support from priyayi, officials, and students to promote education and social reform among Natives. This organization collapsed in 1935.
brahman	The priestly Hindu caste; the highest caste

bupati	The title of the Native Javanese official appointed by the Dutch to assist the Dutch assistant resident to administer a region; most bupatis could lay some claim to noble blood.
Culturstelsel (Culture System)	The system of forced cultivation of certain crops enforced by the colonial authorities; under this system, Javanese peasants had to grow export crops such as coffee and sell them to the Dutch authorities at extremely low prices.
dalang	The puppet master who recites the stories and manipulates the puppets at wayang shows
destar	A Javanese form of headdress; a kind of headband
Diponegoro	Prince Diponegoro (1785–1855) led the Javanese in a war against the Dutch (1825–1830, the Java War).
Durna	One of the Kurawa brothers from the Mahabarata epic, told in wayang; a vacillating, deceitful character
Ethical Policy	A liberal concept dating from 1899 that called on the Dutch government to accept greater responsibility for the welfare of Native people. Also associated with policies of reduction of the government's role in the economy and the encouragement of private investment
forum privilegiatum	The right to appear before the White Court
gamelan	Traditional Javanese percussion orchestra
garuda	The mythical magical bird upon whom the gods rode
HBS	The prestigious Dutch-language senior high school
ibu	Literally "mother"; used like Mrs. or Madame

Indische Partij	A political party founded in Bandung in 1911, calling for independence from Dutch rule in the Indies
Indo	A term used to refer to European-Asian Mixed Bloods
Inlander	Dutch word for "Native"; a derogatory term
Insulinde	An association for Indies residents, which became politicized when members of the banned Indische Partij joined it in 1913.
jeng	Short for Ajeng; term of address used among Javanese women contemporaries
kabaya	A Javanese woman's traditional blouse used always in combination with a sarong
kain	Traditional dress worn by Javanese women; a kind of sarong wrapped tightly around the waist and legs
Kartini	Raden Ajeng Kartini (1879–1904), daughter of the Bupati of Jepara, famous for her letters discussing the fate of the Natives, and especially education for girls
keris	Traditional curved-bladed Javanese dagger
KNIL	*Koninklijk Nederlandsch Indisch Leger* (Royal Netherlands Indies Army)
kontrolir (controller)	The junior Dutch administrative officer in charge of a subdistrict, one level below an assistant resident; being close to the grass roots, they often wielded much power on a day-to-day basis.
ksatria	The knightly or warrior caste in Hinduism
kwintal	100 kilograms
kyai	An Islamic teacher or leader
mahjong	A Chinese gambling game
mas	Javanese term of address literally meaning "older brother"; used by a young woman toward a man, it indicates an especially close, respectful affection; it can also be used between men, indicating respectful friendship; by a sister to her older brother; and also by a wife to her husband.

meneer	Dutch for "sir" or "Mr."
mevrouw	Dutch for "madam" or "miss"
Multatuli	Pseudonym of Eduard Douwes Dekker, an outspoken humanist critic of Dutch colonialism and author of the anticolonial novel *Max Havelaar*
ndoro	A term of address used by a lower-class person when speaking to a superior in the feudal class or of similar status
noni	"Miss"; used for Eurasian girls
nyai	"Mistress"; generally a term used to refer to the indigenous mistresses of Europeans in the Dutch East Indies
pendopo	A roofed veranda or reception area often situated at the front of a Javanese dignitary's residence
priyayi	Members of the Javanese aristocracy who often became the salaried administrators of the Dutch
Raad van Indie	Council for the Indies, advisory council to the governor-general, formed of Dutch residents
raden ayu	Title for aristocratic Javanese woman, especially the first wife of a bupati
raden mas	*Raden* and *mas* are titles held by the mass of the middle-ranking members of the Javanese aristocracy; *raden mas* is the highest.
raja	King
ringgit	2½ rupiah
rupiah	Basic unit of currency (100 cents)
santri	Student of Islam; pious Moslem
sarekat	Of Arabic/Islamic derivation, meaning "union" or "association"
Sarekat Dagang Islam (SDI)	Islamic Trade Union

selendang	A sash worn by Javanese women as part of traditional Javanese costume
silat	A Malay form of self-defense
sinyo	Form of address for young Dutch and Eurasian men or Europeanized Native young men, from the Portuguese *senhor*
STOVIA	*Schul Tot Opleiding van Inlandsche Artsen* (School for the Education of Native Doctors); the STOVIA was the only institute of higher learning established by the Dutch colonial authorities during the early twentieth century.
sudra	The lowest Hindu caste; the mass of ordinary people
Sugar Syndicate	The sugar planters' association
tablig	An open Islamic religious consultation
tayub	A semi-erotic folk dance in which the male partner is normally chosen by the professional female dancer from among the audience
tuan	Malay word meaning "master," "sir," or "Mr."
VOC	*Vereenigde Oost Indische Compagnie* (United [Dutch] East India Company), often referred to as "the Company"; the major power in the Indies until 1798 when it was taken over by the Dutch government
volksraad	Advisory council of people's representatives
waisya	The merchant class in Hinduism
warung	Small shop, booth, or stall
wayang	Shadow puppets or the shadow-theaters
wayang orang	Traditional Javanese ballet

wedana   The head of a municipality, one of the
                            lower administrative positions

White Court   Court for Europeans, or non-Europeans
                            with official European status

FOR THE BEST IN PAPERBACKS, LOOK FOR THE

Read each book in the Buru Quartet series, all available from Penguin Books

"The Buru Quartet is one of the twentieth century's great artistic creations."
—*The Washington Post Book World*

☐ THIS EARTH OF MANKIND

Originally recited orally by Indonesian political prisoner Pramoedya Ananta Toer to his fellow cellmates in daily installments, *This Earth of Mankind* introduces Minke, a young student living equally amongst the colonists and colonized of late nineteenth-century Java, who battles against the limitations of his birth.

"Without a doubt the work of a master . . . the sort of novel we automatically love"
—*USA Today*

368 pages   ISBN 0-14-025635-0

☐ CHILD OF ALL NATIONS

The second novel in the Quartet follows Minke's political awakening. Coming to grips with the oppression and injustice of the European regime in his country, Minke, now a writer, struggles to assert his voice and the voices of his people—but he is met at every turn by the corruption of those he trusted and by the tragedies that befall those he loves most.

"A complex and colorful batik of political, intellectual and social life in the Dutch East Indies at the turn of the 20th century."   —*The New York Times Book Review*

352 pages   ISBN 0-14-025633-4

☐ FOOTSTEPS

This third volume of the masterwork continues the adventures of Minke as he and his country move into the twentieth century. Settling in a new town to begin medical school, Minke is determined to leave behind the tragedies of his past, but once again he finds himself caught up in the injustices of colonial exploitation. As he struggles to not only understand his world, but to change it, Minke embarks on a personal odyssey of self-discovery that takes him and the reader through the colorful and turbulent world of the Dutch East Indies, and into the heady dawn of a fledgling nation.

"Here is an author half a world away from us whose art and humanity are both so great that we instantly feel we've known him—and he us—all our lives." —*USA Today*

480 pages   ISBN 0-14-025634-2

☐ HOUSE OF GLASS

Taking on a dramatic new form, the final volume of the Quartet, *House of Glass*, is narrated by Pangemannann, a native policeman assigned to monitor Minke and his followers. It is a book founded, in the words of *The Washington Post*, "on mankind's potential for greatness and shaped by a huge compassion for mankind's weakness."

384 pages   ISBN 0-14-025679-2

FOR THE BEST IN PAPERBACKS, LOOK FOR THE

In every corner of the world, on every subject under the sun, Penguin represents quality and variety—the very best in publishing today.

For complete information about books available from Penguin—including Penguin Classics, Penguin Compass, and Puffins—and how to order them, write to us at the appropriate address below. Please note that for copyright reasons the selection of books varies from country to country.

In the United States: Please write to *Penguin Group (USA), P.O. Box 12289 Dept. B, Newark, New Jersey 07101-5289* or call 1-800-788-6262.

In the United Kingdom: Please write to *Dept. EP, Penguin Books Ltd, Bath Road, Harmondsworth, West Drayton, Middlesex UB7 0DA.*

In Canada: Please write to *Penguin Books Canada Ltd, 10 Alcorn Avenue, Suite 300, Toronto, Ontario M4V 3B2.*

In Australia: Please write to *Penguin Books Australia Ltd, P.O. Box 257, Ringwood, Victoria 3134.*

In New Zealand: Please write to *Penguin Books (NZ) Ltd, Private Bag 102902, North Shore Mail Centre, Auckland 10.*

In India: Please write to *Penguin Books India Pvt Ltd, 11 Panchsheel Shopping Centre, Panchsheel Park, New Delhi 110 017.*

In the Netherlands: Please write to *Penguin Books Netherlands bv, Postbus 3507, NL-1001 AH Amsterdam.*

In Germany: Please write to *Penguin Books Deutschland GmbH, Metzlerstrasse 26, 60594 Frankfurt am Main.*

In Spain: Please write to *Penguin Books S. A., Bravo Murillo 19, 1° B, 28015 Madrid.*

In Italy: Please write to *Penguin Italia s.r.l., Via Benedetto Croce 2, 20094 Corsico, Milano.*

In France: Please write to *Penguin France, Le Carré Wilson, 62 rue Benjamin Baillaud, 31500 Toulouse.*

In Japan: Please write to *Penguin Books Japan Ltd, Kaneko Building, 2-3-25 Koraku, Bunkyo-Ku, Tokyo 112.*

In South Africa: Please write to *Penguin Books South Africa (Pty) Ltd, Private Bag X14, Parkview, 2122 Johannesburg.*